three little birds

Carol E Wyer

Safkhet
Publishing

First published in 2014 by Safkhet Select, Germany
Safkhet Select is an imprint of Safkhet Publishing GbR
www.safkhetpublishing.com

1 3 5 7 9 10 8 6 4 2

ISBN 978-1-908208-31-6

Printed and bound by Lightning Source International

Typeset in 12 pt Crimson and Nueva Std with Adobe InDesign

Find out more about Carol on www.carolewyer.co.uk
and www.facing50withhumour.com
and meet her on Facebook at
www.facebook.com/pages/Carol-E-Wyer/221149241263847

Carol E Wyer   *author*

Kim Maya Sutton   *managing editor and cover artist*

Sally Neuhaus   *cover designer*

Sam Parker   *copy editor*

Walter Richardson   *proofreader*

The colophon of Safkhet is a representation of the ancient Egyptian goddess of wisdom
and knowledge, who is credited with inventing writing.
Safkhet Publishing is named after her because the founders met in Egypt.

Prologue

Charlie was acutely aware of an urgent drumming in her ears. The noise threatened to deafen her. She couldn't move. Even if she had the wherewithal to make an emergency ascent, she was unable to. Her feet were weighted down, rendering her immobile. The bubbles of air that had been floating above her head like silver balloons ceased as she held her breath, transfixed by the sinister grey shape that was now focusing on her. If she weren't so terrified, she might have admired the enormous shark. However, it had fixed its glassy stare on her and was heading towards her, not at speed, but at a teasing, leisurely pace, biding its time before deciding to rip into her flesh. She didn't take in the sparkling white underbelly of the creature or the power of the muscular tail as it effortlessly guided it through the water. All she could see were row upon row of razor-sharp teeth all grinning at her.

Breathe, Charlie, she thought, willing every muscle in her body to relax. Her vice-like grip on her regulator was making her jaw ache. *Remember, stay calm. Don't show your fear.* The voice in her head continued the attempt to placate her in vain as Charlie suddenly and uncontrollably began to shake. The shark picked up its pace. *Why, oh why, did I allow myself to get in this situation?*

Six months earlier...

"Thank you for your company over the last two hours. Join me again tomorrow evening when we'll have some smooth seventies tracks and more groan-inducing gags. In the meantime, snuggle under those bedclothes and enjoy the late show with Sam Sullivan who is coming up next. This is Charlie Blundell signing off." With that, *Dancing Queen* filled the airwaves.

Charlie removed her headset and glanced up at the window separating her from the technician/producer. She could see Mercedes talking to one of the orderlies. Mercedes finished chatting, looked through the glass, and gave Charlie a thumbs-up. The door to the studio opened and Sam bustled in carrying his usual flask of coffee balanced on a Tupperware container of sandwiches and cakes. A large man in his early sixties, he reminded Charlie of Santa Claus. He sported a white fluffy beard and glasses. He presented the late show eight to ten o'clock each evening on City Hospital Radio. He preferred the late show. It got him out of the house every night and meant his wife, Brenda, could watch all the soap operas and period dramas on television in peace. Sam wasn't interested in those. He preferred his music and enjoyed his gig at City Hospital.

"Great show, Charlie," he said as he unpacked his food. "Where do you find those one-liners? I expect half the patients will need their stitches replacing after tonight."

He slipped into the chair now vacated by Charlie, fiddled with the mixing desk and sat back to wait for his cue. He waved at Mercedes who grinned back. She had been joined by Sean, the youngest and keenest member of the team. He was interested in journalism and IT, but could not afford to go to university, so was learning the ropes at City.

"Good evening, you are listening to the late show with me, Sam Sullivan. I have some excellent tracks tonight to help lull you to sleep and if you fancy a late night brain teaser, we'll be doing Sam's Teaser at half past eight. First, let's start with some Simon and Garfunkel and one of my personal favourites, *The Boxer*."

Charlie mouthed, "Bye!" Sam nodded in acknowledgement, now concentrating on a sheet of A4 with his running order and notes scrawled on it. She slipped out of the studio and into the technician's room where Mercedes was shrugging her coat on.

"Hi, Sean. How's it going?"

A thin, pale-faced young man was sitting at the desk, staring at a computer screen.

"Oh good, thanks. I didn't have much to do this afternoon so I hung out here and updated the radio website. I put up photos of the presenters and added a few words about each so anyone listening can put a face to a name."

"That's great. You're really good with the technical stuff."

"Thanks. I enjoy it. I like presenting more. I'm going to try and get Sam to let me read some news stories later."

"Good luck with that. Once he starts talking, you can't interrupt him. He loves that microphone," said Mercedes. "He loves it more than his wife. Come on, Charlie. Let's get going."

Mercedes reversed her wheelchair and manoeuvred it towards the door Charlie held open for her. Charlie accompanied her friend to the car park where she helped her into her adapted vehicle and folded the wheelchair away for her, slipping it into the back of the van. Mercedes was fiercely independent and even though a sporting accident in her late twenties resulted in damage to her spinal cord and the subsequent loss of her lower limbs, Mercedes lived life almost like any other thirty-five-year-old woman. She was married to Ryan, a police officer and the love of her life. They had no children but treated Bentley, their miniature Schnauzer, like a spoilt child.

"You still on for the weekend? I don't want to think of you being on your own New Year's Eve, but I know how difficult it is for you. You sure you'll be up for it?" Mercedes squeezed Charlie's right hand.

"I'll be okay. Gavin is meeting me at the cemetery. I just can't believe it's been five years since we lost her. It only seems a short while ago."

A vision of Amy, her thirteen-year-old daughter, flashed before her eyes. So young, so beautiful yet not destined to live long. She blinked it away.

"Well, if you want me to come along and be with you, give me a call. If not, we'll see you at the house at seven before the others arrive. It'll give us a chance to have a quiet drink before Ryan plays at being Pete Tong, shoves on all his dance CDs and we all end up doing the hokey cokey around our garden. I made him promise not to set you up with another of his work colleagues like at the last party. I'm sorry about Tentacle Trevor. I had no idea Ryan planned that."

Charlie laughed. "It was okay. You've apologised enough. I managed to fend off his advances in the end. Boy, that man had his hands all over the place."

"So, see you Saturday. I'll be thinking of you and if you change your mind ..."

"I'll be okay, I hope. Thanks anyway."

Charlie watched Mercedes drive away. She trundled to her own car and let herself in. The mask she had been wearing began to slip as she pictured Amy—her blonde-haired angel. The pain was still raw inside. Losing Amy had changed her life dramatically. The weeks following her little girl's death had been the worst of her life. Her relationship with husband Gavin took a turn for the worse and a few months later, unable to be together any longer, they divorced. Life became worse for Charlie, who, having lost two people close to her, then also lost her mother to cancer.

City Hospital had saved her from insanity and depression. At City, she could still feel close to both of the people she had loved most as they had spent their last days on wards there. She met Mercedes while on one of her request rounds. Mercedes was recovering from surgery and feeling low. The two of them hit it off and became firm friends. She considered herself lucky to have people like Mercedes in her life. City had given her a sense of purpose. By presenting a light-hearted show, filled with laughter and fun, she could help other sick people. She may not have been able to help those she loved, but she could at least try and help others. She wiped the mascara smudges from under her eyes, started the car and tuned into Sam's show to see if she could guess the answer to his quiz question. Yes, at least she could make some difference.

It was windy when Charlie pulled up to St. Peter's church. St. Peter's, originally built in the thirteenth century, was an ancient Gothic church made of stone with a slate roof and a square tower. It had been welcoming people for centuries. The local community was active here, with a bell ringing club, regular meetings, and services. During daylight hours, it was always open for visitors who needed a few minutes of quiet contemplation. She recalled the day she and Gavin were married there. She could still envisage the faces of their friends and family as she and Gavin had walked back up the aisle, arm in arm, man and wife. She remembered posing for photographs as the ancient bells pealed joyfully. The pathway to the entrance arch was filled with laughing people and strewn with brightly-coloured paper confetti. Outside, on the road, a white horse-drawn carriage had waited to take them to New Hall for the celebratory dinner. The church was the perfect place for such occasions, nestled as it was in a picturesque village that boasted antique shops, local pubs and a sweet village school. Amy attended the school. She had so many friends there. Charlie wondered where they all were now. Amy was christened at St. Peter's too. She didn't cry when the near-sighted vicar dribbled water all over her head and into her mouth. She gurgled and cooed.

The church also held sad memories: the small white coffin sitting in a black horse-drawn glass carriage. The wreaths and flowers lining the path to the church door. An entire village mourning, all dressed in black, wearing sombre expressions. It seemed happiness had travelled full circle and now her baby was here, so she visited most weekends and some days in the week to be with her, or to maintain the grave and ensure fresh flowers were always in the little vase on Amy's plot. It was a peaceful location and the grounds were well-tended. In springtime, bright-yellow daffodils grew throughout. Now, the large pine tree in the corner of the churchyard sported Christmas lights that twinkled even on this grey afternoon.

Charlie stepped out of the car and drifted down the path past the church entrance and into the graveyard behind, clutching a small pink porcelain teddy bear. Gavin was waiting for her by the graveside. He held a posy of freesias. He was enveloped in a large black coat and a striped scarf. She noticed grey streaks in his hair. The tragedy had aged him. He looked tired, but still as handsome as she remembered. The loss had taken its toll on both of them. Gavin held out an arm as she approached and wrapped it around her, holding her to him. They may be divorced, but neither blamed the other. It had just happened. Two people had grown apart. She knew she was mostly to blame. After all, it had been her that had withdrawn from the relationship. Gavin was now remarried to Tessa, a teacher.

They stood in silence, for a while absorbed in memories of their precious child. Neither wished to recall the last weeks of Amy's life, but focussed instead on the happier times. After a while, Gavin knelt and placed the sweet-smelling flowers into the vase in front of the headstone. He stood up again, unable to speak. Charlie bent down and placed the teddy bear on the grave beside the headstone.

"Happy birthday, sweetheart," she whispered, and then sunk her head into her hands as a large sob escaped from her throat.

Gavin held her against him as she continued to cry. When the sobs eased, she looked at him with reddened eyes. He too had tears running down his face.

"If only we could have really celebrated her eighteenth," she began.

"I know," he said, hushing her gently with a soft kiss on her forehead.

They stood again in silence, and then as the wind picked up once more, Gavin clasped her hand and led her out of the churchyard.

"So, how have you been?" asked Gavin as they sat in the pub opposite the church. It had changed hands since the days when they had lived in the village. Neither of them recognised the landlord who served them their drinks.

Charlie looked out of the window that faced the pretty church.

"You know. Keeping busy. I do five days a week at the café and I still do my radio slot every evening and Sunday afternoons at the hospital. I thought I might volunteer to work in the charity shop in town, St Chad's Hospice. All the proceeds go to help the hospice."

She looked at her orange juice and faltered a little before looking up and smiling determinedly. "I'm fine, Gavin. Honestly. I'm just fine. What about you? How are you enjoying life in Devon?"

"It's certainly different," he replied. "I've taken up surfing. Can you believe it? A forty-year-old surfer? I haven't got to the point where I call everyone 'dude' yet, though."

Charlie chuckled. "I can't quite imagine you in a wetsuit or board shorts. I guess the move brought out your rebellious side."

"It made sense to move after, well, you know. We don't need to go over that again. Tessa's family is in Bideford so it'll be convenient when ..." he stopped, flushed, and took a deep breath. "Look, I know this isn't the time or the place and there is no proper way to tell you ..."

Charlie looked into his eyes. She knew what he was going to say. She felt the air whoosh out of her.

"Tessa and I, we're ... expecting a baby. It was completely unplanned and came as a shock but ..." he left the sentence hanging between them.

Charlie squeezed her eyes tightly together, then inhaled.

7

"Congratulations," she said and squeezed his hand. "I mean it. I wish you both much happiness. It's a surprise, that's all. I'm genuinely happy for you both."

They sat for a while longer, but did not know what to say. They had, after all, drifted apart. Amy had been the glue in their marriage and now there seemed nothing but fuzzy affection and sadness.

"The village has changed quite a bit, hasn't it?" said Gavin, after a few moments. "They knocked down the old garage and turned it into a plot for houses and the Spar shop, that's gone too. I wonder what happened to Mrs. Pepper who owned it."

"She moved to Scotland to live with her daughter, by all accounts. I saw Ted, our old neighbour about six months ago. He was visiting a friend in hospital and came by the studio to say hello. He's still got Dolly, his terrier."

"What? Dolly must be about fifteen years old."

"Yes, Dolly loved Amy ..." Charlie stopped herself. She didn't want to wipe Amy out of her heart or mind, but it wasn't helpful to keep reminiscing and reminding Gavin of what they had lost. It was not his fault he was driving that dreadful night. If only she had not caught a rotten cold and had an awful headache. She would have collected Amy from her friend's house. If she had collected her, it might not have happened. She would certainly have chatted longer to Sarah's mum and then they wouldn't have been on the road at that fateful moment.

She looked at Gavin. The pain was still evident. He was thinking the same thoughts; thoughts they had shared for too many years. The angry scar under his left eye from the injury he sustained that night was now faded; it had left its mark. The mark was not as deep as the one left in his soul. He would never forgive himself for the accident. He was overtaking the lorry when it suddenly burst a tyre and veered out, crashing into the side of his car. The guilt ripped them apart as a couple. For the first few months after the accident, they both poured their energy into willing Amy out of her coma and back to life. When she died, Charlie's hurt turned to anger and even she blamed Gavin for a while. They bickered. Then they avoided each other and finally, they separated, each sore, miserable, and tired of fighting.

She took in Gavin's sad eyes. The hurt was palpable. He deserved to live again. He did not warrant the constant guilt.

She patted his hand. "You make sure to let me know when the baby is born and send me photos, please. I want to see photos of it. Do you know what sex the baby will be yet?"

Gavin nodded. "It's a boy."

Charlie was partly relieved. "That's wonderful. You always wanted a little boy. You'll be able to teach him how to be a surf bum!"

Gavin laughed. "Thanks, Charlie. I didn't know how you'd take it and I didn't want to write or phone you about it. I hope you find someone too. I really do. You deserve some happiness again."

They parted after the drink with promises to stay in touch, yet Charlie knew that Gavin had moved on. He had a new life in a new area with a new family. She had moved away from this village and into a city, but her life was still without purpose. It was a good thing she had her friends. At least she wouldn't be wallowing in misery tonight.

"You look gorgeous!" said Ryan, wiping his hands on an apron that bore the words 'Stand Clear—Man Cooking'. He invited her inside and hugged her fiercely. A small coffee and black miniature Schnauzer that had accompanied him to the door was equally effusive and jumped up at her legs, tail wagging furiously, vying for her attention. It wore a blue velvet bow tie.

"Put her down, Ryan. You have to attend to the cooking and Charlie needs a drink!" called Mercedes. Ryan winked at Charlie.

"Yes, boss!" he replied and disappeared again. Mercedes wheeled into the room. Charlie handed over the chilled bottle of Pinot Grigio, then bent down to the small dog.

"Hello Bentley. Don't you look smart in your tie?"

The dog rolled on his back to have his stomach rubbed.

"Ryan's right. You look stunning. You should be in a nightclub surrounded by lustful men, not hanging out with us fuddy-duddies. Fancy a glass of this, or do you want to try some extra-strength beer? Ryan has an enormous crate of it. I can't imagine he'll drink it all."

Ryan reappeared. "I shall. I blame my wife. She drives me to drink." Mercedes grabbed a cushion and threw it in his direction. He ducked and it hit the curtain behind him. He laughed and disappeared again. Bentley raced off to join him.

"I won't ask. I can tell by your face it was just terrible," said Mercedes. She extracted the cork from the bottle and poured a generous glass of wine.

"It's always bad. Every birthday since she died has been dreadful; however, this one was the worst. She'd have been an adult today, and I can't help but wonder what she would have been like. I keep imagining life with her. We'd have been such good friends. We were always such good friends." Charlie stopped before her emotions got the better of her.

"Anyway, it's not about me. This is about the New Year and new beginnings. I bet you are delighted about Ryan's promotion."

"She wants me to wear my new inspector's cap to bed," said Ryan who arrived with a bowl of crisps and some nuts. Bentley followed behind, carrying a chew. He took it to his bed and sat down with it, observing the trio.

Mercedes snorted. "The handcuffs are enough, Ryan," she sniggered and lifted her glass. "To Ryan—a wonderful man—and to his new career as an inspector."

"Cheers!"

"Inspector Ryan Thomson. It has a certain ring to it, doesn't it?" said Ryan, quaffing his wine.

"Oh hang on, that's the doorbell. It'll be Debbie and Alan. I invited them a little earlier than the others. Um, I think they are bringing Alan's mate, Rob. I hope that's okay. He's over from Thailand and they didn't want to leave him on his own. I said he could join us." He scurried off, pursued by an excited Bentley, leaving Mercedes to roll her eyes behind his back.

"Honestly, will he never learn? Sorry, Charlie. Hope this Rob isn't a frightful bore."

It transpired that Rob, sun-tanned from his time abroad, was an amusing and attentive guest who entertained them all with stories of life in Thailand. The evening passed in a haze of laughter and joviality. Ryan and Mercedes were tremendous hosts. After playing several silly games involving passing balloons through various parts of their clothing, drinking too much, dancing to some rather loud eighties music, and avoiding an over-excited Bentley who skidded among them until he tired himself out, they sat everyone down.

"Here we go," said Mercedes, handing a small box to each of the guests.

"What's in it?" asked Charlie, rattling the box.

"Duh! Open it and find out, Miss Marple."

Charlie opened one end and a blue object fell out into her lap. She picked it up and turned it around, looking puzzled.

"It looks like a kazoo."

The others also had kazoos, all varying in colours.

"And why have I got a pink kazoo?" asked Rob. "I should have a blue one. I'm a boy."

"Hand it here. I'll swap with you," said Charlie.

Mercedes laughed at them. Colin was blowing into his green kazoo with force, making his cheeks red.

"It doesn't work. Mine's broken," he complained.

"You stick the large end into your mouth," said Mercedes, causing her friends to snigger. When they had calmed down, she continued. "You're like children. Behave yourselves. It'll only take you a few minutes to learn how to play it."

Debbie was confused. "This is a toy for children," she said. Alan rolled his eyes at her.

"Ah, that's where you're wrong," Ryan replied. "It's used by adults and has a fascinating history. Well, sort of fascinating because no one is quite sure how kazoos came to be used. Maybe the cavemen made kazoos and hummed around the campfires, after all, they didn't have much else to do in the evening."

Rob chuckled. "I could think of something far more interesting to do other than play this."

Alan piped up, "Me too."

"Yes, but that would only take up five minutes," retorted Debbie and they all laughed again.

Mercedes got some order back to proceedings. "As far as I can gather, the kazoo has been around for quite a while in one form or another. All over the world, people used hollow tubes to make sounds. People used all sorts of things, like bamboo, bones, and gourds to vibrate for different sounds," she said. "I read that somewhere in Africa, dried spider-egg sacs were used. I couldn't find any of those so you've been spared that pleasure. They called these sorts of instruments mirlitons and they were around in Europe from at least the sixteen-hundreds or maybe sooner."

Alan stuck his kazoo in his mouth and pretended it was a cigarette. No one paid any attention to him, so he removed it again and listened to Mercedes.

"Around eighteen-forty, Alabama Vest took the idea to a German clockmaker named Thaddeus Von Glegg and they made a kazoo. A traveling salesman, Emil Sorg, saw this object and decided it would be easy to sell. He got together with a metalworker called Michael McIntyre and together they produced the first metal kazoo in nineteen-twelve." She looked around to make sure her friends were still interested.

"At first, it was treated as a real musical instrument. It became part of serious music, then later part of folk music. And today, it is used on some famous songs. Anyway, peeps, enough of the history lesson. We're going to have a few minutes to learn how to play and then we're having a kazoo karaoke party. Ten minutes to master it while Ryan gets the karaoke DVD ready; I nominate Debbie to start. She looks like she could blow a mean tune."

Once Charlie discovered she did not need to blow or hum but needed to vocalize to get sounds out of the kazoo, she had mastered it. It was indeed melodic and bizarrely addictive. Before long, they were all buzzing along to various songs. In between songs, Ryan ensured their glasses remained charged. It was thirsty work playing a kazoo.

All were in exuberant spirits as they counted down to a brand new year and sang *Auld Lang Syne*. Rob ensured Charlie's year started well with a passionate kiss that she rather enjoyed, but felt was fuelled by Ryan's beer rather than any strong attraction for her.

It was almost two in the morning when, having said goodbye to the others, Charlie was sunk into a cushion on the sofa balancing a cup of black coffee on her arm. Bentley was asleep next to her, his bow tie still firmly in place. Ryan had consumed far too many beers, and was slumped in a chair opposite her, wearing his new inspector's cap.

"You're a lovely lady, Charlie," he slurred. He shook his head as if to clear his thoughts. "It's a big shame you haven't found another man. Rob's a fun guy. I think he took a shine to you."

"Actu'lly, he asked me for my phone number," she replied. "I'm not sure though. He's a laugh, but I suspect he's a bit of a lady's man. My tonsils are still tingling after he kissed me."

"He kissed every woman here and almost snogged Colin, which came as a shock to the poor man," said Mercedes.

"Colin should never have worn that floral shirt," sniggered Ryan. "Don't you think you should test the water, so to speak? You should go out with him. It's been five years since you went out with a man."

"I went out with Perry," Charlie protested.

"Nurse Perry Farquharson bats for the other side, my dear, as we all know. You went to a musical together and then out shopping. If I remember correctly, you ended up in MAC where you both got a makeover and Perry insisted on purchasing some lurid yellow nail varnish to match his new cravat. That doesn't count as going out with a man."

Charlie giggled and hiccupped. "Damn hiccups. It always happens when I drink too much. Hang about. You're forgetting Harrison Matthews. I went out with him. Big mistake."

"He was intense, wasn't he?" said Mercedes, rolling her eyes.

"He was definitely weird. He wouldn't leave me alone after we split up. He had real problems letting go."

"He sent flowers to the studio for weeks. It was like a flower shop in there. I didn't like the way he passed by the studio door to stare in through the glass. It was a good thing he left. Something very odd about that guy."

"Yeah, I was beginning to get freaked out by him, but then he left a note saying he was leaving and that was that. There aren't many suitable free men out there. Besides, I'm too old now. I'm going to be forty this year. Yuck! An old maid. Boring and old."

"Rubbish. You're still plenty young enough to live life and find someone again. After all, look at Gavin and Tess. Who'd have thought they'd have a baby? Tess is forty-four!"

"Ryan," warned Mercedes.

"It's all right," replied Charlie. "A baby. I'm sort of pleased for them. No, I'm very pleased for them. It's a bit of a shock, that's all. So much time has gone by and yet I don't seem to have moved on much. I'm such a wimp. I shouldn't be so frightened of change, should I? I'm not complaining, because I love working for the radio and I like my house. I enjoy doing the garden and cooking, but I haven't done anything exciting the last few years. I haven't even been on holiday during that time."

"Gavin gave up his successful career as a lawyer to go and be a surfing and sailing guru in Devon, and then there's Rob who told me all about his exploits in Thailand. Crikey, the man sold a small building business to go and become a photographer! Then, there's me. I have been stuck in my bubble for five years, venturing no further than the Lake District and even then, I came home three days early because it rained and I was lonely."

"I should've gone back into marketing and have a career instead of moping about. Inheriting mum's house and money made me lazy. It all happened at the wrong time. I didn't want to do anything after I lost Amy, then Gavin, and finally Mum. I let too much time drift by. Even now, some days, I tell myself I should get off my backside and find a proper job, but then that stupid voice in my head reminds me I'm too old. I've missed that particular boat. I wouldn't be able to get an interview, let alone pass one."

"You're being too hard on yourself," argued Mercedes. "You do so much good. First off, you have a decent job. You work for Art. He'd be in a right pickle if you didn't bake cakes for the café. They're probably what's keeping the place afloat, because I'm sure the craft items in his shop aren't big sellers. Next, you help oodles of people in hospital. You spend huge amounts of time chatting to them if they have no visitors, you talk to anxious relatives in the hospital coffee shop. You are a positive person and kind. People really like you.

"Your problem is you devote too much of your time to good causes and not enough to yourself. How much money did you raise for that little girl who went to America for a bone marrow transplant operation? What about Tommy Atkinson? You worked tirelessly to get him a guide dog. Not to mention the annual event you organise for the Rainbow Trust. You're far from lazy."

"It seems so little. Besides, I love cooking and my cakes sell well. It's always fun to set up stalls and raise money, so that doesn't seem like any effort. I can't explain the problem 'coz I don't understand it. It's an emptiness. If you look at it from the outside, I'm a part-time worker and volunteer who lives on her own. I've not achieved anything. I'm going to be forty! That seems frighteningly old. And to cap it all, I discovered my first grey hair yesterday. I have no husband, no parents and no children. You, on the other hand, have your family up north. You have Bentley and Ryan who's not only a wonderful man, but is now an important inspector."

"Inspector Clueless!" giggled Mercedes as Ryan began to doze off.

"I heard that," he mumbled.

"Forty," Charlie moaned. "I'm definitely an old woman. I should be doing more with my life, but what?"

Mercedes went over to Ryan and prodded him in the ribs. "Wake up, sleepy. We need your help. I've had an idea."

"Oh no! Not a genuine Mercedes brainwave!" groaned Ryan.

"I know what we'll do. We'll both write out a list of what we want to do, see or achieve this year. It'll be a sort of mini bucket list, no, make that a Carpe Diem list. That's much more positive. I don't think either of us intend to kick the bucket just yet. That'll give us a few objectives for this year. You'll be able to get stuck into projects and tackle goals before you become an ancient has-been and I'll come up with a list of all the things I want to do. Come on, Ryan, fetch some paper. No, first, bring us some more wine. This is going to take some thought."

"Hand it over, Charlie. You've had plenty of time. For goodness sake, it's almost three-thirty in the morning."

"No, I've only managed to think of a couple of things."

"You've spent too much time guzzling wine. That'll do. Hand it over. Now!"

Charlie reluctantly gave up her list. Mercedes put it to one side without reading it and cleared her throat. "Okay, do you trust me?"

Charlie nodded. "Of course, I do. You're my best friend," she slurred. "I love you. I love you too, Ryan. You're my bestest friends and I love you loads."

"We love you too, Charlie, so tonight, we're going to help move your life on."

"Onwards and downwards," giggled Charlie.

"Ryan you're going to be the witness. Charlie, I've not looked at your Carpe Diem list and you haven't seen mine but I want you to promise me something. I want you to do all the things on my list and I'll do yours, as long as they aren't too wild and beyond my physical capabilities. Although, knowing you, I don't need to worry about that."

Charlie smiled enigmatically and then stuck out her tongue.

"Listen up, my friend," continued Mercedes. "I'm pretty brave about most things and I can do a lot of stuff that able-bodied people can do, but there are things I want to do and can't. There are one or two things I physically can't manage, even though I would love to do them. So, my dear, I want you to do them for me. I'll be there with you when you do them, and I'll video them or photograph them, so it's almost like doing them, but I want you to promise you'll do them for me."

Charlie emptied the dregs from her glass. "I'll do anything for you dear, anything," she sang and giggled. "Oops. I am a bit tipsy."

"Ryan, video this so she doesn't back out," said Mercedes.

Ryan tumbled out of his chair and picked up his smartphone. After a few minutes of fumbling, he pointed the phone at them both. "Okay!"

"I'm Mercedes Thomson and this is my best friend Charlie Blundell who has helped me through some pretty low patches in my life and even helped me meet the man of my dreams."

"Who was that, then," said Ryan. "I'll beat him up."

"Shut up, you nincompoop. You know it's you. Charlie was there for me when I needed a friend and she's been my rock ever since."

Charlie tried to protest. Mercedes shushed her with a look. "We have made a New Year's resolution that we intend to keep."

"A New Year's resolution is something that goes in one year and out the other," chuckled Charlie, earning another look from Mercedes.

"Sorry," she mouthed.

"Charlie is going to attempt all the activities and challenges from my list and I'm going to try my hand at those on her list. The lists are going into my desk drawer and only I shall know what is on them both. This is the official agreement." She held up the paper in front of Ryan and swayed a little.

"Keep still, babe. It's out of focus," said Ryan. Charlie sniggered and waved a pen at him.

"Go on, Charlie," he continued. Charlie squinted at the paper, put it on the dining table and scrawled her signature.

Mercedes added her signature, then they raised two glasses to the camera.

"So, are you sure you are going to complete Mercedes's Carpe De, De, Diddlydum list?" asked Ryan, holding on to the wall for support.

Charlie finished her drink in one. "I am. Guide's honour," she mumbled as she curled up on the sofa and fell unconscious.

"How many bottles of beer did I drink?" Ryan surveyed the mess in the kitchen. Bentley scampered over his feet, carrying a sock dragged from a radiator, oblivious to his master's hangover.

"In dog beers you had five," answered an alert and cheerful Mercedes. Bentley dropped his treasure by Ryan's feet and waited for him to play with him. When Ryan ignored him, he trotted back to his bed and proceeded to chew the sock.

"It's not fair. How come you haven't got a rotten head?"

"I drank three buckets of water before I went to bed while you were drooling in the chair. Works every time. I have to get up a lot in the night, but better that than a sore head. Fancy some fried eggs? It's a bit late for breakfast. This is more like a cross between lunch and tea. I think I'll call it lea."

Ryan went grey. "No, I'll pass if you don't mind. Morning, I mean afternoon, Charlie. You look like I feel."

Charlie headed for a chair. "What a night! I ache from zonking on the sofa. I haven't been that drunk for years. I can remember events up to the point when someone tried to shove a balloon down the front of my top and I can recall playing kazoo karaoke but after that, it gets very fuzzy. I can't recollect anything after I said goodbye to the guy from Thailand. Not a darn thing. It's a complete blackout thereafter. Did I do anything stupid?"

Ryan looked at Mercedes who was tucking into a slice of toast with marmite. "No, apart from whipping off your clothes and tearing off down the high street singing *The Streak*, you behaved quite well. Oh, and I expect you might not remember this," she held up Ryan's phone and pressed play.

"Did I really take off my clothes?" asked Charlie before taking the phone from Mercedes and watching the short video.

"Now, that I don't remember," she said having pressed replay twice. "I have no recollection at all of that. Is it for real? Whatever did I write on my list?"

"Aha, that's for me to know and you to find out. I'm only going to divulge the list item by item. You and I have to complete each item before going on to the next one and by the end of them all, you'll be a new, more fulfilled, Charlie. Now, anyone else for eggs?" 19

Charlie did not have to wait long to find out what was on the list. It happened the following afternoon. Mercedes rang her. Charlie muted the film she had been watching and answered the phone.

"I've got to go to London for an appointment with my specialist, so I thought we'd start the list. We're going to lunch."

"That's not much of a challenge, is it? You've not got a surprise where I'm actually cooking the meal or you've arranged for me to be a waitress, have you? I know how you think. You've got a devious mind."

"Devious? Moi? You've got me mixed up with someone else. No, just lunch. I've booked us a table. You can do some shopping if you like and I'll meet you after my appointment. I've arranged it for Friday. Sean said he'll cover your show. You know how he wants to practise presenting. He's been begging to do a few slots."

"Right then. Friday it is."

"I'll be around at nine. That'll give us plenty of time to get there, for me to visit the clinic, and then we'll have lunch."

The journey down was uneventful. Mercedes was quieter than usual. Charlie left her to her thoughts. It wasn't until they were near Watford Gap that Mercedes spoke up.

"I'm sorry. You must think I'm dreadful company," began Mercedes. "I'm actually terrified. I'm seeing a consultant in London."

Charlie gasped. "Are you ill? Is it serious?"

"No, not at all. Quite the opposite. I'm healthy. Ryan and I, well we've been trying to have a baby. We've been trying for over a year. At first, we thought it might not be possible what with me being paralysed and all but I did a load of research on the internet and there are lots of women like me, in similar states of paralysis, who've gone on to have several children." She paused for a moment and concentrated on the traffic in front that was slowing behind a large vehicle. Charlie waited, not wishing to interrupt her friend.

"So, before we made the decision to have kids, I went to my GP and she said it was completely viable for me to have children. So we tried, but nothing happened. Every month it's the same old story. I hope I'm going to be pregnant and then my period starts up like clockwork and I'm horribly disappointed. Sorry, I know this is difficult for you, with what happened to Amy, which is why I've not brought it up before, but it's really getting to me, Charlie. I want to have Ryan's baby so much it hurts. It tears me up and some days I can't think about anything else. It's hard enough being in that bloody wheelchair all the time and making an effort every sodding day, trying to stay positive. It's a drag some days. A real drag and I can be a complete bitch when I'm feeling low. Ryan's been copping it big time recently and it isn't his fault. It's not his fault I'm not able to behave like a normal woman. I get pissed off that I can't do normal things. You've seen me struggling to haul myself off the damn thing to even go to the loo. It's just too much some days. And now, I can't even manage the one thing I want more than anything else in the world: a baby. I'm such a failure."

Mercedes sniffed as angry tears threatened her vision. Charlie was lost for words.

After a few more minutes of listening to sniffing, Charlie asked, "Do you want to pull in at the service station for a while and chat about it?"

Mercedes nodded. They drove the remaining mile in silence, pulled into a space and only then did Mercedes allow the tears to tumble. Charlie put her arm around her and stroked her hair, soothing her as she used to soothe Amy when she was upset. Eventually, a red-eyed Mercedes lifted her face.

"Sorry, Charlie."

"Shh! You have nothing to be sorry for. You've carried this frustration around for too long and it's built up inside you. You need to let it out. Let's get one thing straight, though. You are not a failure. I don't need to tell you how untrue that is. As for having a baby, well, lots of people struggle. We live in a society where it's just assumed you try for a baby and you conceive. There are hundreds of thousands of ordinary couples who struggle. It's probably not associated with being a paraplegic. As you said, there's a plethora of women like you on the internet. The consultant will help you understand what's going on and give you the advice you need."

"I'm so scared he's going to say that there's some complication and I can't have children. Ryan deserves better. He loves children. He'd be such a great father and I feel like I'm such a flipping burden at the best of times. Christ! He's got a wife who's stuck in a wheelchair and is pretty hopeless at some things and now it looks like she can't even give him a child. He shouldn't have married me."

"Now you're being silly. Ryan adores you. He loved you from the moment he met you and he sees way beyond a wheelchair. He'll stick by you whatever the result of tests. If it is bad news, there are other ways of having children. You could even consider adoption."

Mercedes blew her nose noisily into a tissue and nodded once more.

"You're right. I'm letting it get to me again. But Charlie, you understand. You of all people know how hard it is for me some days. I hate being in this wheelchair. I hate what happened to me, I wonder *why me?* And worst of all, I hate myself."

"I also know if anyone is going to succeed and have a baby by hook or by crook, it'll be you. Medical science is wonderful these days and I think you're getting worked up way too soon. You haven't even heard what the consultant has to say. So, put your happy face back on and let's go and find out. Shall I come in with you?"

"I'd rather I saw the consultant alone, if you don't mind. Ryan wanted to come with me, but I want to deal with this myself. I can't explain why. I suppose if it's bad news I need that time and space to digest it, to deal with it before I tell anyone."

"No, I can understand. But if you change your mind, I'll come with you."

Mercedes wiped off the black mascara stains from under her eyes. "Better get going. I don't want to be late," she said without enthusiasm.

"You'll be fine. It won't be bad news. I'm sure it'll be good news."

"I wish I had your optimism."

"I'll lend it to you for today."

"Deal!"

They set off and joined the motorway again. The subject was dropped and conversation became lighter. Charlie concentrated on stories about Art from the café, who having been put on a strict diet by his wife, had taken to hiding food in all sorts of interesting places and scoffing slices of cake at every opportunity when Pat was out of range. The stories of all his antics soon had Mercedes smiling. At Oxford Street, Mercedes swung the van into a space reserved for unloading lorries.

"You can't stop here," said Charlie.

Mercedes grinned. "Bonus of a disabled sticker, a wheelchair and the ability to look like a helpless woman. I can park or stop wherever I like. It's only for a minute. Okay, out you get. I'll meet you at Archipelago restaurant on Cleveland Street at twelve-thirty. Have fun."

"Good luck, Mercedes. You'll be fine. Stay positive."

"Will do. See you later."

Charlie meandered off to the shops where she found little she wanted to purchase. She seemed to have lost her enthusiasm for shopping. She was comfortable in her baggy pullovers and jeans. She did not have many occasions to dress up. Today, she had made an effort and was wearing one of three smart outfits she owned. Even that was a little tight on her. After Gavin and she split up, she had found solace in baking and eating. She had put on quite a few pounds and although she was not too large, she certainly was not the same shapely Charlie she used to be. Many of her clothes from that era no longer fitted. She found it easier to hide her shape under T-shirts and pullovers.

Eventually, worn out by the marauding crowds of shoppers trying to bag bargains in the sales, Charlie flagged down a taxi and requested Archipelago's restaurant. She would be early, but the thought of spending any more time avoiding people was too much to contemplate.

Before long, the taxi pulled into a quiet side street. Charlie paid the driver and went into Archipelago's. It was mesmerizing. It was without doubt one of the most astonishing restaurants she had ever visited. The dining room was stuffed full of artefacts from all over the world, golden Buddhas and palm trees and peacock feathers. To say it was exotic was an understatement.

A waiter took her name and confirmed she and Mercedes were booked in for lunch. He offered to let her go downstairs to the drinks lounge by the kitchen. She agreed, asking if she could be called back up when Mercedes arrived, then descended into a tiny basement room, with a couple of tables and bench-style seating around the perimeter of the room and no windows. It was astonishing. The decor was decadent, a little kitsch and romantic with all kinds of eclectic travel paraphernalia from countries like Africa, India, and

Thailand. She was given a drinks menu—a scroll of parchment that looked like it should have been a nautical treasure map, rolled into a leather scroll holder. From it, after much deliberation, she ordered a strawberry blush, which turned out to be fresh strawberries muddled with vodka, Grand Marnier and topped with ginger ginseng. A few sips later, she already felt better about life. She was alone in the room. It gave her a feeling of adventure, as did the cocktail. So it was a slightly inebriated Charlie who climbed back up the stairs to meet her friend.

"How did you get on?" Charlie asked.

"He confirmed that I'm physically able to conceive. He thinks we're trying too hard and that I'm wound up about it. He seems to think it'll happen if it's meant to happen," Mercedes replied with a smile. "I can't understand it. We've been trying for months and months. Ryan's had tests and he's fine. I guess we'll have to keep trying. I hope Ryan's still got the energy every night now he's been promoted. Enough talk of babies for the moment. I feel like celebrating my good news so let's enjoy ourselves. What do you think of this place?"

"Amazing. I feel like I've been transported to another country."

"That's the intention. Have you seen the menu?"

"I've seen and sampled from the drinks menu. I could drink another three of those bad boys," she said pointing to her now empty glass.

"I thought you were looking jolly relaxed. Bought anything nice?"

"No. It was frantic and I couldn't see anything I fancied. I even got a blister from trying to walk around excited tourists and crazy shoppers. They're mad. They can't help themselves. The second they see the word 'sale' or 'reduction', they herd towards the offering. There were bouncers at every exit to every high street store. I can't imagine how much stuff must get stolen if they need bouncers. Or, maybe they're actually there to protect the staff from crazy shoppers."

A waiter approached with menus, as thoughtfully presented as the drinks parchment. Each menu had been glued into the pages of an old leather-bound book. Charlie read the starter choices and looked up horrified.

"You're kidding. This can't be for real."

Mercedes was watching her friend's face and chuckled. "Ha! I can't afford to send you to a jungle but I could try to give you a similar experience and treat you to some very different food here. I'm ordering and you're eating with me. This is going to be huge fun.

Haven't you ever wondered what it would be like to eat chocolate-covered scorpions or bug salad?"

"No, I can't say I have."

"Now's your opportunity. We're going to have our own jungle bush tucker challenge and I'm taking photos of it. You can start a new scrapbook called Charlie's Carpe Diem list. This'll be the beginning of a new, more adventurous Charlie."

Charlie shook her head in disbelief. "This menu is outrageous," she commented. "What shall we go for?"

"I ordered when I booked us the table and requested some of the dishes they normally serve on the evening à la carte menu. I wanted it to be even more exciting so I've gone for zhug-marinated kangaroo skewer, spicy crocodile bites, Burmese Embrace, and a Serengeti Strut, with a side order of love bug salad and a sprinkle of weaver ants," Mercedes announced. "Don't pull that face. They're mighty nutritious and they're a highly sustainable source of protein. Kangaroo, crocodile, wildebeest, and ostrich are extremely low in fat and cholesterol and therefore provide great alternatives to beef and lamb. All of their ingredients here are organic, free range, and are either farmed or are part of a nationally recognised culling programme; and they use nothing that has been irresponsibly taken from the wild."

"What's Burmese Embrace?"

Mercedes grinned. "Sweet-chilli smoked python Carpaccio, green tea, wasabi crackers, and olive puree," she said, a mischievous grin spreading across her face.

"And Serengeti Strut? Please don't tell me it's giraffe."

"Zebra. Crispy zebra jerky, boerewors, they're a South African sausage, and it comes with carrot and ginger fluid gel and biltong soil. Biltong soil—that's pretty much spices."

"I can't wait," said Charlie flatly, downing her wine in one. The waiter appeared with a couple of businessmen. They were ushered to the table next to the women. Charlie could not help but stare at the gentleman facing her. Dressed in dark blue chinos, crisp shirt, and a jacket that looked like it had come out of a designer boutique, sat a good-looking man in his forties. He thanked the waiter and ordered a bottle of mineral water. He glanced up and caught Charlie staring at him. He smiled at her, nodded politely, and then picked up his menu.

She was reminded of a quote by Hardy Amies who said, "A man should look as if he had bought his clothes with intelligence, put them on with care and then forgotten all about them." This man fitted that bill. He looked masculine and elegant. For a second, she was distracted.

"Earth to Charlie. Grub up," whispered Mercedes, nudging her friend. The waiter deposited an array of dishes in front of them. Charlie ordered another glass of wine. She was going to need it.

"So, Miss Blundell. How do you feel about tackling the bush tucker challenge?" asked Mercedes, pulled her phone out of her bag, and took a photo of Charlie staring at the dishes.

"I think I need some more wine."

"You can do this without wine. People come from all over the place to eat this food. This is a unique restaurant with an incredible menu. Close your eyes and try one of these fried locusts." Mercedes dropped a couple onto Charlie's plate and waited patiently while Charlie pulled faces.

"Come on Charlie. They're not going to harm you."

Charlie pinched her nose, tossed a locust into her mouth and crunched down onto its body, wincing as she did so. After a few seconds, she let go of her nose and opened her eyes.

"I expected it to be hard going, given that its little legs looked all tough and chewy, but there was nothing to them. They're just dry and crunchy," she continued. "If you close your eyes and pretend you don't know what this is," said Charlie, waving the second locust about, "it could be a crisp or a burnt bit of almost anything. Burnt like almost all your food when you cook, for example." Mercedes hooted with laughter.

The mixture of cocktail and wine was going to her head. She attacked the crocodile dish with zeal. It was, after all, a new experience. Mercedes joined her, commenting on each dish and pausing only to take photographs of Charlie eating.

Charlie decided she was enjoying herself. The more she ate and discovered it tasted good, the more she enjoyed it. She caught the man looking over from time to time. He had ordered some sort of bean stew. Not everything on the menu was as adventurous as the dishes Mercedes had chosen.

"This crocodile is really tasty," said Mercedes. She piled some more onto her plate and speared it with her fork.

"A bit like a cross between chicken and fish."

"Only with a plump juicy texture."

Charlie nodded in agreement.

Plates emptied, the women were invited to choose a desert.

"I'm actually too full to try a chocolate locust," said Charlie, wiping her mouth with the napkin.

"I've got that covered. We're going for something called a 'Visit from the Doctor'. It seemed most appropriate given we work in a hospital."

The waiter cleared their plates and announced rather dramatically that both ladies looked dreadfully sick. He claimed they looked at death's door and that he'd call a doctor immediately. His performance attracted the attention of the other patrons in the restaurant, including the men nearby. The man who had nodded at Charlie watched, amused by the drama unfolding. His friend glanced over as well and made some comment. The man smiled and nodded.

Charlie played along and claimed she was indeed feeling terribly hot and unwell. A few minutes later, the waiter re-appeared in a doctor's jacket and with a stethoscope around his neck. He was carrying a large leather chest that he placed on the table between the ladies. He opened the chest to reveal an array of ornate bottles filled with spirits and liqueurs. The doctor explained that they should choose their medicine. Mercedes squealed alarmingly and pointed to a bottle with a python in it.

"That one. We need to take some of that."

The waiter agreed and continued the act, raising the bottle to reveal the python coiled inside it. He explained it was absinthe that had been distilled for twelve years with a year-old python inside the bottle.

"Doesn't absinthe make you go blind?" asked Charlie.

"Who cares? We have to give it a go," replied Mercedes, lifting her phone to capture the bottle.

"Would you like me to take a picture of you both?" asked the well-dressed man. "It seems a shame not to have you all in a photograph."

The women agreed and posed with the waiter and the bottle containing the snake.

He returned the phone and commented, "Hats off for being so adventurous. I'm most impressed."

Mercedes nudged Charlie and said, "Phwoar," under her breath.

Charlie giggled helplessly. The waiter called for a nurse to bring a bowl of boiling water to the table and offered the women a capsule from a small jar, warning them not to ingest it. They were told to throw the capsules into the water, count to three and down their medicine.

"One … two … three! Yeurgh!" Charlie exclaimed.

Mercedes had a coughing fit while managing to simultaneously pull a face of horror. They both burst into fits of giggles. The man, who was paying the bill for his table, looked over and smiled genially at them again. He rose and wished them a good afternoon. Charlie was sorry he had gone. Alcohol and the lunch had made her feel brave. She might have attempted to engage him in chat if he had stayed.

Still sniggering, the women realised that their green capsules had dissolved and released little sponge snakes. The waiter assured them it meant they were now completely cured. They ordered the bill, which arrived in a keepsake box made by a homeless man in South Africa and given to all customers as a reminder of their experience.

"You have passed the first Carpe Diem challenge of the year," declared Mercedes as they left the restaurant and returned to her van. "How do you feel?"

"Like a new woman. I'm sure if I rub my legs together, I'll be able to chirrup," said Charlie, guffawing.

The following week, Sam Sullivan clattered into the radio studio, grinning like a Cheshire cat just as Charlie was packing up from her show. He dropped his bag on the floor, pulled out his plastic boxes containing sandwiches and snacks, and sank into the presenter's chair.

"Have I got a surprise for you," he commented.

"Come on, spit it out."

"Nope. You'll have to listen to my show. I promised Mercedes. My lips are sealed until then."

He slipped on the headphones and began whistling while he unpacked his thermos so she couldn't ask him any questions.

"Mercedes, you horror, what have you done?" she hissed to her friend who feigned innocence. "If you don't tell me, I'll clamp your wheelchair!"

Mercedes wouldn't give in either so it was with some trepidation that Charlie sat in the City Hospital coffee shop listening to Sam's show.

"That was Crosby, Stills and Nash and their classic *Marrakesh Express.* I've never been to Morocco. I've always fancied it though. All those souks, tajines, and mysterious ladies in veils which links me nicely onto my next item. You might know our devious technician, Mercedes Thomson. She works with Charlie on the afternoon show. She's the rich auburn-headed mischief-maker who's often found hanging about the coffee shop scoffing doughnuts and telling jokes. Yes, that one who races patients in wheelchairs up and down the corridors when no one is looking. Well, she has extracted a promise from our delightful Charlie Blundell to take up a number of surprising challenges this year. Our unsuspecting Charlie has no idea what has been chosen for her, but has already been cajoled into eating insects and crocodile, and drinking some disgusting absinthe distilled in a bottle containing a python, yes, the photographs of the event are online on our website. Take a look if you don't believe me. Right now, I can reveal the next challenge live on air.

"Hang on, I just want to cue this background music to *Mission Impossible.* Right, that's it ... remember the original series with Dan

Carter and Cinnamon Carter? Way before Tom Cruise. They don't make them like that, do they? Okay, let's go... Good evening, Charlie. Your mission, should you choose to accept it, is to contact Jasmine from Jasmine's Belly Dance studio in Sutton Coldfield where you have been signed up for belly dancing classes. Now that, I would like to see. Our Charlie sequined up and shimmying. So, Charlie. This tape will self-destruct in five seconds. Good luck."

"And now, another song especially for our belly dancing diva, Groove Armada and *I See you Baby (Shaking that Ass)*."

Charlie flushed. Tina, a matronly woman in her fifties who worked full-time in the coffee shop, was cleaning up after a busy day serving teas, coffees and food. She called out to her, "Do you want to borrow a couple of our tea towels as veils, Charlie?"

"Thanks, Tina. I might just go and tie a couple around Mercedes's neck."

"My cousin Laura did belly dancing, or was it pole dancing, I can't remember? I know she earned a shedload of money from it. She always had new designer gear and swish cars. I asked her one time how she made so much money. She said something about a spearmint rhino. I didn't know what she was on about. Figured that was one of the moves," said Tina, wiping her hands on an apron.

Charlie didn't explain even though she knew Spearmint Rhino was a lap dancing club. She handed over her empty mug of tea, thanked Tina and set off to hunt down Mercedes.

"You promised," said Mercedes, munching on a chocolate brownie while pretending to assist Sean.

"I can't do this. I have two left feet. You've seen me dancing. I need to be drunk to dance and even then, I fall over."

"Well, I can hardly do it, can I? I don't even have two acceptable left feet, two left wheels maybe," Mercedes replied good-naturedly.

"Are you using emotional blackmail?"

Mercedes looked innocently back at her.

"I'll be rubbish. I am renowned for being clumsy. I knock into stationary objects with monotonous regularity. The patients are wary of me when I go about the wards, in case I trip up and land on them. Even you rarely allow me to have a cup or a mug in the studio, on the off-chance I knock it all over the mixing deck. And look at me. These are UGG boots and this is a large baggy sweater. I haven't worn a dress or a skirt in years, let alone some sequined harem outfit. I don't do feminine very well. I'm not petite. I'm five foot eight and in terms of describing my weight, the word solid springs to mind. All I can say is thank goodness you haven't arranged for me to do a Burlesque routine."

Mercedes waved a handkerchief around her face and batted her eyelids in a ridiculous fashion at Charlie, who laughed. Mercedes attempted a shoulder shimmy and made her wheelchair wobble.

"Okay, I'll do it. But only because I promised you I'd do the things on your list. Belly dancing," she mumbled, "I hope it isn't a *waist* of time."

Back home, Charlie nipped next door to visit her neighbour Peggy. She regularly checked on Peggy to ensure she was looking after herself and that nothing had befallen her.

She tapped on the front door. There was a sound of shuffling feet and a clear-eyed elderly lady appeared. She was slight, but there was an energy about her.

"Charlie! Belated Happy New Year! Come in. You're just in time. Bert is going to perform."

Charlie followed Peggy into her sitting room where she was greeted by a loud shrieking.

"Hello Bert. Gosh, what's that you've got?"

"It's a new comb. Bert got it from his friend Jasper in Australia. We're just about to make a little video for Jasper, aren't we, Bert? To say thank you."

A green-blue Indian ringneck parrot, about the size of a cockatiel, sat perched upon a platform on top of a pole. He gripped a plastic comb in his claw and whistled loudly at Charlie.

"He's always pleased to see you."

"Hola," said Bert. He dropped his comb onto the platform and carefully navigated the few small posts that served as stairs. He descended backwards until he reached the bottom post where he perched and whistled again.

"Hola, Bert. Got any new noises for me?"

Bert meowed like a cat, then trilled like a telephone.

"Come on, Bert, let's try a dog for Charlie," said Peggy. "What does a dog say, Bert?"

Bert gave a convincing deep growl and a bark.

"Well done, Bert! That deserves a grape."

Bert paced from one claw to the other, his head turning this way and that, as Charlie removed a small bag of red seedless grapes from a plastic shopping bag and passed a grape to Bert.

"Bert," said Peggy, "Say thank you."

Bert made a kissing noise then took his grape in one claw and proceeded to eat it.

"He's got three thousand friends on Facebook now," said Peggy. "I thought I'd put up a brief video for them and let him show off his new comb. Bert loves the comb almost as much as the mini shopping trolley he got from Santa. He doesn't push it yet, but he enjoys rattling and shaking it, especially when we're watching *Deal or No Deal.* Maybe he thinks Noel Edmunds should do a version of *Supermarket Sweep.* It's an improvement on the noises Bert used to make when we watched Noel's show. Every time someone opened a box and got a blue number, he tutted and then squawked.

"I've been trying to teach him to say 'g'day mate' to Jasper and his Australian fans, but he refuses. Last week, Jasper's owner and I managed to link up on Skype and they talked to each other. Well, made sort of screeching noises. They were both very excited to be able to see each other. Bert kept tapping the screen with his beak. I think he enjoyed it. We'll do it again another time.

"He needs stimulation all the time. It's much quieter for him these days than when we used to live in Lanzarote and had the bar. He was always learning new words and noises there. He loves the television now. Can't get enough of it. Saturday nights are his favourite. So many talent shows and singers. It's like the good old days for him when we held Karaoke nights."

Bert, grape now finished, was making soft kissing noises and bouncing up and down.

Charlie fished for another grape, which he took and consumed greedily.

"He's such a performer," said Charlie, scratching the top of his head. "I came by to see if you needed anything from the shops. I'm going there on my way to a belly dancing class. I need to buy a T-shirt. Thought it would save you a trip."

"How kind. As it happens, I'm out of marmalade. It'll save me a trip. Bert doesn't like marmalade but I enjoy a little on toast for breakfast. I heard on the radio you were going to do belly dancing. How exciting! If I were twenty years younger, I'd join you. I used to be very good at the Jive. I won a few competitions in my youth. We didn't have exotic dances like belly dancing in our day. Dennis, being a Scot, was fond of country dancing. Dashing White Sergeant was his favourite dance. He was most annoyed when he got knee trouble. It stopped him dancing. I bet I could still manage a few steps of it if I tried. Maybe I should broaden my horizons and come with you to your classes," she trilled.

"I'd be glad of the company. I don't quite know what to expect, but I suppose it'll be a laugh. Right then. You've got my mobile number. If you think of anything else you need, give me a ring."

"Thank you, dear. I appreciate that. I'll be able to spend the whole afternoon filming Bert now."

Bert bobbed up and down and launched into various impressions of bells, whistles and noises.

"G'day mate," he said. "G'day mate, g'day mate," he repeated, then gave a low growl.

"Bert, you said it! Aren't you clever? Charlie, it was the grapes. He said it to get grapes. I'll bribe him with some for the video. Thank you very much indeed." She handed a grape to Bert.

"Mmm, mmm," said Bert in a high-pitched voice before demolishing it.

Charlie tickled the top of his beak. He made chirping noises and closed his eyes.

"You are very special, Bert," she said.

"He is. Bert's been the best friend I could have hoped for. He was always engaging, but since Dennis died, Bert's been wonderful company for me. And, thanks to his Facebook page, I have friends from all over the world, too. I'm so glad we brought him back to the UK with us."

Bert made kissing noises, squawked again, and fluffed his feathers.

"I'll get off. See you later, Peggy. Hope he isn't going to be a prima donna for you. Bye Bert."

Bert flew to Peggy's shoulder and accompanied her to the door where he cackled like a witch, then whistled *How Much is That Doggy in the Window* until the door shut.

Jasmine was slight, dark-haired and very beautiful with a flawless complexion and sparkling amber eyes. She wore an emerald-green satin belly dancer outfit and her feet were bare, revealing bright-orange painted toenails. She had the poise and elegance that professional dancers possess. She led Charlie to her vast studio where large mirrors covered three of the walls. Charlie removed her outer garments, hung her coat on the stand in the corner of the room, and scrabbled about in her bag looking for a scrunchie to tie up her mop of unruly wavy champagne blonde hair. While Jasmine searched for the most appropriate music to play, Charlie stared at her reflection. The woman who stared back was dressed in flared black Lycra leggings, a halter top and a T-shirt with the slogan *Keep Calm and Belly Dance* and looked tired and uncomfortable in her outfit.

She sighed. "I hate looking at myself in full-length mirrors. I normally avoid them," she complained, pulling at the bottom of her T-shirt in an attempt to get it to cover her stomach further.

"You need to be able to see how you move, so you know you're performing the moves correctly. It's very good to watch yourself," Jasmine replied. "It's important to have the correct posture. I have two other women joining today so you can form a little group. It'll be more enjoyable that way. You won't be so focused on your reflection."

A tap on the door announced the arrival of one of her fellow students. A large woman in her fifties bowled in. She was clad in a large scarf and a huge duffle coat.

"Brass monkeys weather out there!" she exclaimed, tugging off a noticeable red and white striped woollen hat. Charlie was reminded of the *Where's Wally* character. Catching her look, the woman smiled and twirled the hat about on her hand.

"My mother knitted it. She's eighty-three years old and treats me like a five-year-old. She always knits me stuff for Christmas. She made this too, last year," she pulled off her duffle coat to reveal a brightly-coloured pullover with a large snowman on it. "Hideous, isn't it? Still, it's warm and I was round her house earlier, so I had to show willing and wear it. Poor old soul, she likes to look after me

34

even though I am fifty-four and have three grown-up children of my own. Sorry, how rude of me, I forgot to introduce myself. I'm Susannah."

"Hi, I'm Charlie. I'm also in no position to comment. I've got a pullover with a reindeer on the front and I bought it!"

"If ever you fancy replacing it with a new one, I have a large collection of tasteless, huge pullovers, exceptionally long scarves and a nice array of bobble hats that don't match. You'd be welcome to any of them. Don't suppose I'll need them here, will I Jasmine?"

"No. You won't. I hope you are wearing something comfortable to exercise in, Susannah."

"Oh yes, I went on the belly dancing website you told me about and bought some harem pants. They looked good on the skinny mare wearing them on the website. I look as if someone has inflated my legs. Not a good look on me."

She shrugged off her pullover and spun round showing off her outfit of purple pants and matching crop top. Her stomach hung over the pants. She wobbled it.

"However, I think I'm perfect for belly dancing classes. Can't get a much bigger, wobblier belly than this one. Not so much a muffin top as an entire Madeira cake," she continued and shimmied her shoulders so her ample bosoms bounced dangerously in her purple top.

"I'm really looking forward to this. I read that belly dancing is not only good for fitness but is excellent for women like me, going through the change. I certainly need to feel sexier. My husband, Dave, hasn't seen much action in recent months, what with hot flushes and me feeling off sex. He'll be off with a younger model if I don't sort myself out," she said.

"You'll feel heaps better about yourself in no time," said Jasmine. "I have yet to meet a woman who hasn't enjoyed the classes and hasn't become much more confident about her body. It's wonderful for releasing stress too and for getting fit, of course. He won't be able to keep his hands off you after a few sessions."

"Can't wait. Charlie, what's made you take up belly dancing?" asked Susannah, removing trainers and multi-coloured socks that resembled gloves, covering each toe individually.

"Your mother?" asked Charlie, pointing at the socks.

"Oh no, they're my daughter's. I nicked them from her drawer.

She won't miss them. I couldn't find any of my own that were clean. These keep your feet really toasty warm," she said, wriggling her podgy toes.

"I'm here because of a promise I made while completely sozzled at a New Year's Eve party. My friend has a list of challenges that I have to complete this year. They're really things she would like to do herself but she had a nasty accident a few years ago and is in a wheelchair now. She can't use her legs. She's decided I'm to be her stand-in and I'm going to have a go at her bucket list, or as we call it, Carpe Diem list."

"Wow! That's quite a story. What else are you going to do, apart from this?"

"Not sure. She hasn't told me yet. Knowing her, there will be some outrageous suggestions. This is probably going to be the easiest."

"Hello, I'm not late, am I?" called a woman, peering around the studio door.

"No, not at all, Marcia," replied Jasmine. "Come and meet Susannah and Charlie. Susannah is showing us her new costume."

Susannah twirled again. "And this is my hip belt," she said, pulling a scarf adorned with strings of coins around her stomach. "It's so large it clangs rather than chings. There are more coins on this than there are in the Bank of England's vaults. I needed an extra-extra-large belt. Did you ever see the three hippopotamus dance in *Fantasia?*" asked Susannah. "Well, that's me. I'm like one of those hippos. I hope Jasmine can work miracles. I'll need one if I am going to be a sexy belly dancer."

"Didn't the hippos dance in tutus?" asked the newcomer.

"Yes, but I look in this mirror and all I see is hippo," replied Susannah.

"That's good then because you'll definitely need hips for this activity. And, I have come prepared too," she added, shrugging off a long camel coat to reveal a chubby body dressed in a hacked-off T-shirt, from which spilled a brown belly and under which sat a pair of tracksuit bottoms covered by a neon green scarf.

"Hi both. I'm Marcia, Marcia Black," she said. Her accent belied her Australian roots. She was, at best, five foot tall, rotund, and with large breasts that strained dangerously at her T-shirt. Her eyes twinkled with merriment and she exuded mischief. Her light golden-brown hair was cut in a sharp short bob that framed her round face. She wore several jangling bangles and enormous silver hooped earrings that swung as she moved.

"I guess we make a great pair, Susannah. You're a hippo, whereas me with these dangling earrings and superb physique, I resemble a baby elephant. I'm a little worried about shimmying. I'm not sure I can contain these puppies for too long. I had to strap them down for this class. We won't have to wear nipple tassels, will we, Jasmine?" she asked pointing at her enormous boobs with a grin.

"Goodness me, no," laughed Jasmine.

"Guess that makes me the portly giraffe of the group," said Charlie conscious that she towered above both women. "What a trio. The Wild Bunch!"

Marcia barked out a high-pitched infectious laugh.

"Well, we're off to a good start," snickered Susannah. "This should be called a belly laughing class."

Jasmine assumed a more authoritative air, tossed back her hair and glided into place in front of the women so they were all facing the large mirror.

"We need to start by warming up a little. We can't go straight into dancing or we might do some damage. Right, space out and face the mirror. Stand up as if a string is pulling you up from your head. No slouching. Belly dancing is all about keeping your core well-supported and not stressing your spine. Keep an erect posture—make sure your back is straight and your chest is out."

Marcia stuck her breasts out as far as she could, making the others laugh.

"Not that far, Marcia," said Jasmine, trying not to chuckle. "I can see I am going to have my work cut out with you three. Okay, don't slouch, Charlie. Don't hide your body. You're tall. Be proud of that fact."

She pressed a button on a remote control, which she then placed on the floor in front of her. The sound of modern music filled the small studio. Jasmine attempted to guide her uncoordinated group through a sequence of moves designed to warm their muscles. There were more giggles as Charlie got left and right mixed up, and crashed into Susannah, who puffed and wheezed through the entire routine.

"I'm so sorry," Charlie said when they finally came to the end of the warm-up.

"Hey, it's not a problem," puffed Susannah. "It's not all going to be so exhausting, is it? I might need to have a sit down. I'm not used to all this activity. I'm built for comfort, not speed."

"You'll soon get fitter, but don't overdo it. If you feel too tired, just stop to catch your breath. Charlie, coordination is often difficult at first, but you'll get the hang of it. Could you please remove your T-shirt now so you can see your stomach because we're going to start working it. Don't be shy.

"Right, let's all space out again. Stand up, shoulders back, bend your knees slightly and hold those abdominal muscles in tightly. We're going to try a few simple movements. Copy me. We'll start with some belly rolls. No laughing now. Pull in the top and bottom half of your belly then release them. Release the top first followed by the bottom. Start slowly then increase the speed gradually until it feels natural and easy like your belly is rolling. Very good. That's it."

Susannah pulled a face as she watched her belly rolling. She caught Marcia's eye. Marcia winked and supported her boobs with her hands so she could see her stomach moving.

"Next, we're going to pretend we are Shakira. We're onto the hips. Shimmy the hips as you keep the torso still. Susannah you are jingling like a pro. Hip scarves or belts aren't just to make lots of noise, they help with the pelvic tilt. You need to get one for the next class, Charlie. Okay, start moving the hips from one side to the other slowly and increase the speed gradually. With your knees bent and still ribcage, circle the hips. Move the hips in circles and switch to move them the other way. Now we need to add those arms and hands. Visualise your arms as puppet snakes."

"I look more like a drunken octopus," said Marcia.

"Nonsense," said Jasmine. "Let the arms flow more. There, you've got it. Lift the right arm. Lift the shoulders, the elbow, wrist and the fingers. Now, lower the right arm as you lift the left arm in a similar manner. Lovely. Now you've got some basic moves, I'm going to put on some Arabic music and we'll have a go at a simple shimmy and arm movements."

Jasmine made it look effortless and was so enthusiastic that they soon forgot to be self-conscious and were wiggling hips and arms. Charlie found herself completely involved in the class. It was more effort than expected, but definitely fun.

"And to end this lesson, I'm going to do my party trick and show you how to flutter your bellies. Jasmine raised her arms up high then puffed hard in short breaths through her nose. Her stomach rippled in and out quickly in a fluttering movement.

"Oh wow!" Susannah said. "I may be exhausted but I've got to have a go at that. My Dave will love that movement."

She inhaled and made snorting noises as she tried to let air out.

"You must relax your stomach muscles more. It won't work unless you relax them. Look, I've got a fun exercise to help you with fluttering," said Jasmine. "Get down on your knees and pretend to be pigs. Go on. It works. It isolates the muscles you need to flutter. Don't be shy. Look, I'll join you."

Jasmine took the lead, lowered her body to the floor and made a squealing noise. The women followed suit and dropped to the floor on all fours and began to squeal like pigs. After a while, Marcia started sniggering. Susannah joined her. The women snorted even more. Jasmine joined them and Charlie got caught up in it, too. Hysteria set in.

"Whatever do we look like?" Susannah spluttered. "This little piggy went to market," she said in between laughs.

"This little piggy stayed at home," continued Marcia.

"And this little piggy went wee, wee, wee, all the way home," finished Charlie racing off on all fours with a final squeal and running directly into the path of a pair of men's brogues. She looked up to see a dark-haired, well-dressed man. He was smiling broadly at her. It was the same man who had been eating at Archipelago's.

"Ah! This is a teeny-weeny bit embarrassing," she said. The man continued to grin at her, one eyebrow cocked.

"I'm so sorry, ladies. I appear to have arrived too early. Jasmine, you weren't in your office and I couldn't see anyone in the studio through the window, so I came in hoping to find you. I had no idea that … " he trailed off, lost for words. "Sorry," he said.

He didn't look sorry at all. In fact, thought Charlie, she would rather like to wipe the ridiculous grin off his face.

"I'll leave you to it. Jasmine, I'll wait in your office. Apologies again," he added and swept out of the room before Charlie could clamber to her feet. Susannah collapsed on the floor, guffawing, and Marcia stifled her hysteria by stuffing the end of a sequined scarf in her mouth.

The next morning, Charlie arrived at the Art café early. She kicked the door open with her foot and attempted to manoeuvre around the tables while balancing several Tupperware containers containing cakes.

"Morning, Charlie. I was thinking about you yesterday," said Art, appearing from behind the counter to help her. He took the plastic boxes from her and carried them to the counter.

"I was thinking, maybe you would like to put on a belly dancing performance one afternoon, here in the café, or maybe serve the customers in your outfit!" He waggled large bushy eyebrows at her. She was fairly certain he was joking, but since his large moustache covered his mouth, it was difficult to tell.

"Let me think about that for a moment," said Charlie. "Um... no!" she finished emphatically.

"It was worth asking," chuckled Art.

"What's the soup of the day?" she asked changing the subject.

"Carrot and coriander. I'm doing vegetarian quiches, cottage pies, and apple crumble, too. People love comfort food when it's chilly. Did you get my message about the Death by Chocolate cake?"

"Yep, you sold out. I baked two last night. They are in the bottom boxes. I'll put one out in the display cabinet and leave the other in the larder. You did sell it, didn't you, and not scoff it yourself?"

"I might have had a tiny slice for afternoon tea," he replied, rubbing his stomach. "Okay, down to business. It's Parent and Toddler Group at nine-thirty. Patricia has fired the pots the little ones painted last week, so they can take them home today. You'll need to put out the large tubs of crayons in the Rainbow Room. I've already laid out books and the soft toys."

"I baked two dozen fairy cakes for them. They enjoyed those last week. I put pink and blue icing on the top of them this time."

"Super," said, Art wiping his hands on his apron. "Upstairs in the back room, we have a creative writing group. They arrived first thing, so if you could nip upstairs in an hour with cakes and coffee for seven people that would be much appreciated. I haven't got anyone in the front room. I haven't let it out since last November when we had the upholstery club mending chairs in there. I probably need to advertise it some more."

"Is Patricia working in the craft shop?"

"No, she's halfway through some pottery pieces she wants to paint. She sold three of those fat cow pots last week so she's trying out a line in chubby sheep. A new artist asked us to display some painted mirrors in the shop. They're a little too ornate for my taste but if they sell, we'll get our usual ten percent commission. We'll cover the shop between us. Sales have been slow so I don't think it'll be a problem," he continued, rubbing his moustache thoughtfully.

"Oh yes, I almost forgot. Wendy Patterson kindly donated some more books for our Quiet Room. They're in a cardboard box in the corridor. If you get time, could you arrange them for me, please?"

"Of course. I'll get these cakes out and then do it before it gets too busy."

She unpacked her cakes, cut them into generous-sized portions and displayed them in the cabinet. She was washing her hands when Patricia came bustling through the door dressed in jeans and a large shirt splattered with small globs of clay. She held three small, painted mugs in her hands.

"Not bad at all," she said, waving the mugs. "One or two of the little darlings show talent. Look at this one." She showed Charlie a mug. Someone had painted a rainbow on it and written *Katie* under it.

"That's rather good given the children are only three and four years old."

Charlie looked at the assembled mugs now resting on the counter. She turned one around. It was painted yellow. On the front was a large smiling face with blue eyes and corkscrew hair. *For Mummy* was written in child's writing under the happy face.

"Oh, you would treasure that forever, wouldn't you?" Charlie said, a small lump forming in her throat. "Okay, I'd better get the books unpacked," she continued, hastening away before emotions overtook her. She owned a mug that Amy bought for her. It said *World's Greatest Mum* on it. She never used it, but every now and then, she removed it from the cupboard and washed it with care before replacing it at the front.

There was a regular in the Quiet Room. She sat in her usual seat with a notepad resting on her knee. She smiled at Charlie, then went back to her scribbling. She was a poet and often came into the café to get inspiration and jot down some verse. The café encouraged a variety of artists to visit. Inspired by cafés in France and Prague where great artists, philosophers, and writers gathered in the past to share ideas and enjoy a convivial atmosphere, Art and Patricia sunk all their savings into renovating an old house and transforming it into the Art Café.

There were three separate small rooms at the front of the building: the Quiet Room where writers and readers would enjoy some peace and gather thoughts, the Main Room where customers had access to Wi-Fi and the Rainbow Room.

The Rainbow Room was Patricia's idea. Set up for families, it offered something different to ordinary cafés. Parents could purchase food and drink for themselves, children's meals for their offspring, and also buy a plain pottery plate, cup, or mug. There were special paints for the children to use to decorate their pottery, then Patricia finished it off for them and fired it in her kiln. There was a row of protective plastic aprons hanging in the room for them to use, too. Parents loved the idea and brought their children in to make gifts for relatives. There were also pictures for them to colour with the free pencils that sat in large plastic tubs in the room. There was a soft seating area in one corner where the little ones could enjoy reading a variety of children's books.

Behind the rooms, a restaurant catered for twenty people with a small open kitchen. A corridor with walls covered in artwork, lead from the restaurant to the toilets, and into another room filled with goods created by local artists, ranging from key rings and bookmarks to paintings. Patricia and Art wanted to showcase local talent and give artists a place where their goods might be purchased.

Upstairs, they had two large rooms equipped with tables and chairs that were for hire to anyone who needed a conference room. When they first opened, a Reiki master used one room for classes, but after a while he moved on saying the noise from the café below disturbed concentration. Since then, various groups hired it, but interest was drying up and they were often empty.

Charlie enjoyed working here. She baked her cakes at home rather than risk falling over Art in the cramped kitchen. It meant she was free to serve. Time went by quickly when she was at work, giving her little chance to brood on anything in particular.

The doorbell chimed as a woman entered carrying a squirming toddler.

"Morning Alex. Hello Molly, that's a lovely blue dog you're carrying. What's its name?"

"Doggy," replied the little girl, struggling to remove her coat and race over to the table to grab some coloured pencils.

"A cappuccino for me and a small orange juice for Molly, please," said Alex. "I'll look at the cakes when the others get here."

The doorbell rang again. More mothers with pushchairs came in. It was going to be a busy morning. Charlie beamed at them. She knew most of the mothers and children.

"Hello Lewis. Are you going to paint a picture today?"

The big-eyed boy nodded and let go of his mother's hand to collect crayons. The doorbell chimed once more.

"I'll be with you in a moment," Charlie called to a couple settling themselves in the Main Room. The woman acknowledged her. She was an arresting woman, with piercing blue eyes and the longest hair Charlie had ever seen, golden mahogany-brown in colour and shiny. The woman wore a short skirt, tailored jacket and pale cream silk blouse, but it was her shoes that made Charlie stare at her own scruffy trainers and wish she had more style. The woman was wearing the most glamorous high-heeled black shoes with red soles. Charlie wished she could carry off an outfit like that and look that good. She delivered drinks to the group of mothers, then scurried into the Main Room.

"Morning. Sorry to have kept you. What can I get you?" She asked and dropped her pen in surprise as a pair of twinkling slate-grey eyes looked into her own. The man gave her a knowing smile as she fumbled for her pen, then hesitated for a brief moment before saying, "Suddenly, I have a fancy for a bacon sandwich or maybe a ham one."

Charlie's face turned crimson. It was the same man she had bumped into at the belly dancing class.

Mercedes was finishing a telephone conversation when Charlie ambled in. Charlie wanted to tell her about the man in the café and how she had spent an hour hiding in the Rainbow Room until he left, but Mercedes was too excited to listen.

"I'm in!"

"In what? Trouble? In cognito? In flagrante?"

"No, you daft person. I'm in, are you ready for this? *Nosh for Dosh.*"

Charlie's mouth fell open.

"I adore that show. I watch it religiously. You are going to be one of the contestants? I've always wanted to be on *Nosh for Dosh.*"

"I know. You wrote it on your Carpe Diem list, you ninny. That's why I've had Sean occupied for three days practicing journalistic skills, writing a wonderful character reference for me, and then badgering the show to get me on. They advertised ages ago for contestants so we were worried we'd be too late. Luckily, they had someone drop out at the last minute."

"Sean's been brilliant. Even I didn't know who he was talking about in the email he sent. It was a piece of superb fiction: 'Enigmatic character with a feisty personality who adores nothing better than entertaining and cooking exotic dishes for her friends,'" she read from her computer screen. "He's a good lad. It did the job. That was the producer on the phone. They gave me a quick telephone interview and they love my *sunny disposition.* They're going to come here next month, to film me before they do the scenes at the houses where we entertain three complete strangers for dinner."

"Oh my goodness! That is fantastic. I am so excited for you." Charlie hugged her friend. "Hang on. There is one major flaw in all of this. You can't cook. Ryan always does the cooking at dinner parties. You're the only person I know who can burn water."

"Now then, don't be defeatist. This is your challenge and according to our agreement, I have to complete it. I've got a plan to not merely appear on this show but to win the contest." She touched the side of her nose and gave a wink.

"How? You can't cheat, Mercedes. That wouldn't be ethical."

"Who said anything about cheating? It isn't all about the food. It's about the entire evening and I'll be the hostess that everyone talks about for weeks! No, make that months, afterwards."

"It'll be an incredible experience," said Charlie.

"You've got one of those wistful looks in your eyes. I know why. You'd like to be on the show too, wouldn't you?"

"Of course, I would. I've dreamed of being on it the last three years, impressing guests with my pastries and desserts. You know how much I enjoy cooking."

"And, you are a fabulous cook. We all fight over your brownies when you bring them in. Nil desperandum. You'll be on the show too. You can be like Alfred Hitchcock and make a cameo appearance in the film."

"When they film here, will it be during my radio show?"

"Of course it will, my dear friend. I'll make sure I nip into your studio and bring the cameras with me. I also have another idea of how to smuggle you onto the show without anyone complaining, but that is going to require some careful planning."

Jasmine was ending a session with a group of young women when Charlie arrived for her next class, so she sat in reception listening to the muffled music. Marcia came in carrying a large cloth bag. She snorted like a pig.

"Don't you start that again!" warned Charlie smiling. "I'm not going to make an idiot of myself again today."

"You didn't make an idiot of yourself. Mind you that fella did look rather surprised when you ran into him shouting wee, wee, wee!" She laughed. "I wouldn't worry about it. What are the chances of seeing him again?"

"Funny you should say that. Saw him only the other day at the café where I work."

"Did he recognise you?"

"I'm afraid he did. Made some daft comment about bacon sandwiches. I had to wait until he left before I dared go back out and serve again. Art, my boss, thought it was hilarious and kept suggesting we should get some Peppa Pig books for the Quiet Room or pork scratchings instead of crisps. I've heard every pig-related joke possible."

"It was rather funny, wasn't it?"

Charlie smiled. "I guess so. Have you been practising your fluttering?"

"Oh yes. I've worked hard at it every morning in the bathroom mirror. My cat found the whole thing rather fascinating and sat on the toilet watching me. Weird. By the way, I hope you like this, I made it for you. You didn't have a belt last lesson so I thought you might like this one. I'm into sewing. I make all my own clothes. If you don't like it, don't worry. I won't be offended."

"Thank you," said Charlie as Marcia handed her a tissue-wrapped parcel. Charlie unwrapped the parcel to reveal a turquoise sequined scarf. "It's beautiful. Gosh, really beautiful. Can I pay you for it?"

"Cripes, no. I had nothing to do yesterday afternoon and I happened to have some spare material, and thousands of sequins, so I whipped it up. Thought it would suit you."

There was a lot of excited giggling. The class had finished and the door to the studio was now open. Several young women came rushing out, all talking at once. They were dressed similarly, in baggy black satin harem pants and cropped tops with their names written on them. Each one also wore a veil. One of them wore a large pink sash over the top of her outfit. It read *Wife Number 1*. They didn't notice Charlie or Marcia.

Jasmine followed them out. "Hen party," she said by way of explanation. "They're off to the pub now to show off their new moves and outfits."

"They're braver than me," said Marcia. "It's chilly out there. They'll have some super goosebumps to show off."

"Do you get many hen parties, Jasmine?" asked Charlie.

"More than I used to. This and Bollywood dancing is becoming very popular. Hens today want something different. They still like going abroad or to spa days, but they are trying out all sorts of new activities. I've got a friend who went to Scotland with a group of girls to do some grouse shooting."

"That's different. I sat in front of the television, painting my toenails the night before my wedding. And, I was so excited about the wedding that I couldn't keep anything down, let alone wine. Besides, I wanted to keep a clear head for the big day. The whole hen party thing wasn't important to me. Becoming a bride was what counted for me. It was a bit of a whirlwind romance so I didn't have much time to organize anything big," said Marcia. "Mind you, when I held my divorce party, now that was a proper celebration! Me and a few girls from work all went off to the South of France for a long weekend in a plush villa in Nice and got completely wasted on vintage Dom Pérignon. Dropped a pile of money on the tables at the casino in Monte Carlo, too. Not that Carlton would have missed the money. He was minted. I don't think he missed me either. Last I heard, he'd gone off with a toy boy. Yes, you heard that correctly. He came out, or whatever the expression is, and headed off into the sunset in his GT Porsche with a bloke called Gary who's about twenty years younger than him. It sure explained why he wasn't keen to have children, or sex for that matter, very often.

"I should say at this point that I was a lot slimmer than I am now. I used to turn heads. I was a golden Aussie goddess with no cares in the world and a thirst for adventure. I met him when I was travelling around the world. I took a job as a waitress at a top golf club to earn some money to get me to Europe. I was planning on going to Italy and find my own Italian stud. Plans went awry when he turned up one day for a game of golf. He was such a handsome blighter. He had that posh Brit accent that makes my knees go weak and he was a proper gentleman. He asked if I wanted a drink with him and bought me a glass of champagne. That's the way to a girl's heart, I can tell you. He must've liked my accent or maybe it was because I was talking about touring through Spain, or he was gobsmacked by my outspoken views. Anyways, he didn't go out and play his round of golf. He sat at the bar and chatted to me about Australia and life and all that sort of stuff. I was quite wild in those days. I drove a Harley Davidson motorcycle and I was up for anything. I think that's what he liked best about me. He liked that I was so completely different to him. I think he wanted to shock his family. He'll have shocked them a bit more now, won't he? Anyway, we got hitched after only a few weeks and the marriage lasted ten years," she said and paused. "It was good while it lasted," Marcia added and stared off at a wall for a minute.

Charlie was about to say something when the front door opened again. Susannah came in wearing her red and white woolly hat and coat.

"Girls today," she said with a huff. "They don't care what they look like, do they? Just passed a group of scantily-clad women. Honestly, if my daughter went out like that, I'd tell her off, send her upstairs, and lock her in her bedroom. Even if she is twenty-two years old. They have no idea they look like hookers." She pulled off her coat, caught sight of everyone looking at her own skimpy tight-fitting belly-dancing outfit and burst into peals of laughter. "Oh, what do I sound like? I suppose if I had a body like theirs, I'd want to show it off. Help! I'm turning into a grumpy old woman. Come on Jasmine, sort me out. Make me sexy so I can flaunt my body like that," she continued as she pulled her pants up. "Mind you, I could hardly move after the last class. I discovered muscles I didn't know I had. My stomach ached like mad. It only stopped yesterday."

"Yes, a lot of women say that after the first class. You'll soon see a big difference, Susannah, not only in your shape but your energy levels. I fully expect to see all of you sashaying across to the pub in your outfits in a few weeks' time."

Marcia sniggered. "You're joking. I'm only letting Felix see me dressed like this."

"Is he your new man?" asked Jasmine.

"No, he's my cat. He's a Persian, so that probably explains why he's been enjoying my practice moves at home to Arabic music. There's a new man on the horizon. I'd like him to see me after these classes. It might help seal the deal," said Marcia with a smirk.

"Go Marcia," Susannah said. "Sometimes it's fun to be a little daring. I'm already beginning to feel a little more adventurous. Must be the company."

"Hear, hear!" replied Jasmine. "Now ladies, let's go and belly dance."

The timer gave off a loud ping. Charlie opened the oven door to let the batch of cakes cool. She was tired after a long day at the café, followed by the radio show and then belly dancing. The class was great fun and she had laughed such a lot with the girls, but now she felt drained.

She logged onto her email account and one email caught her immediate attention. It was from Harrison, the man who wouldn't take no for an answer. She opened the message. It began, *Dear Charlotte*. She groaned. No one other than Harrison, or her mother when she was cross with her, ever called her Charlotte. It made her feel uncomfortable. She wasn't used to being called Charlotte, she was Charlie to everyone she knew. Feeling needled she read on:

It has been over two years since you told me we could have no future together. During that time I've tried hard to forget you. As you know, I left City Hospital. I travelled for a while and recently I took up a position in a hospital in Wales.

However, I never forgot those precious times we had. I understand now that you were probably still getting over the loss of your child and your broken marriage. I shouldn't have been so persistent. I hope time has helped you heal.

Maybe we could meet up again sometime?

Love Harrison.

Charlie banged her head against the keyboard three times. No. Not again. She thought Harrison was out of her life. He was definitely not the sort of man she could settle down with. He was clingy and soppy and irksome.

She had first met Harrison at the hospital coffee shop at lunchtime. It had been extremely busy, so almost all the seats were occupied. He'd asked if he could take up the remaining free seat next to hers. He'd seemed reserved and shy. He had only been at the hospital twelve weeks and it was all still new and overwhelming. Charlie had felt sorry for him. Once he had been installed, she'd asked him about his job and chatted to him, much as she did with any of the patients or staff there.

When she had next taken a break at the coffee shop, he'd come to sit next to her again. That time, he'd been keen to talk about his role in the hospital as a diagnostic radiographer. He'd explained, at length, the role of a diagnostic radiographer and how some of them specialised in techniques such as computerised tomography scanning, or magnetic resonance imaging which uses magnetic field and radio frequency waves to produce cross-sectional images of the body. It was all gobbledygook to her; however, Harrison was enthusiastic about his work and so she'd listened politely. He had been working in the X-ray department, but wanted to specialise in angiography and investigate blood vessels. She admired the medical profession and Harrison's desire to be involved in helping cure people.

Harrison was an odd sort. He was a loner who did not seem to bond with his co-workers. He took himself and his job seriously and certainly did not go out with colleagues after work. He was not the confident sort in fact, he nibbled his bottom lip when not talking and looked down when walking the corridors, as if frightened to make eye-contact with anyone. Charlie appeared to be his only friend. So, when he had invited her out for a meal, she had first wanted to refuse, but did not want to bruise his feelings. He'd insisted the meal was purely a thank you for listening to him drone on and making him feel more at home at the hospital. She'd accepted.

She had considered him a friend rather than a date, after all, he was much younger than her and not at all her type, although she wasn't sure what her type was any more. Gavin had just married Tessa and she felt alone and very slightly vulnerable. One thing she had been sure of, she was not attracted to him.

He had taken her to an Italian restaurant in town where he behaved impeccably. He'd surprised her by revealing he could speak Italian and impressed her with his menu and wine choices. He had ensured her glass was topped with wine. He'd spoken with passion about Tuscany, an area he visited as a boy. He had behaved quite unlike the shy man who rarely spoke at work. Here, he'd been in his element and Charlie had found she was warming to him.

They had enjoyed an extravagant meal of cold water prawns and white crab meat served on a bed of mixed leaves, delicious pancakes rolled with goat cheese and wild porcini, served on a bed of rocket with cherry tomatoes and roasted garlic followed by fresh salmon in a light brandy and lobster sauce with prawns and asparagus tips and finished off with fresh strawberries drizzled with Prosecco.

The restaurant lighting had been low and romantic, candles flickering on every table, and soft romantic music playing. They had been the only people there that night and the waiters kept a discreet distance. Fuelled by the best part of two bottles of Gavi di Gavi Marco Bonfante wine, Charlie had regaled Harrison with stories about hospital radio, her life, and her hopes for the future. At the end of the evening, she'd thanked him for the meal and given him a peck on his cheek. He had blushed, then kissed her back on the lips. She had responded to his kiss eagerly, even though a voice in her head warned her to stop being stupid. She had been starved of affection for too long.

She regretted it, of course. She should never have let it get that serious. She should have pulled away, yet an animal urge in her had made it impossible to break from his embraces. The act itself was not particularly memorable. She recalled the clumsy attempts to have sex in his car. She shuddered still at the recollection of the fumbling, murmuring, and the final embarrassing moment when Harrison, far too inexperienced it seemed, had ejaculated way too soon, leaving her frustrated. Harrison had been oblivious to the disappointment and gazed starry-eyed at her. Mercifully, he had not asked if it was good for her. He'd driven her home without asking to come in for coffee, much to her relief.

She had tried to avoid him over the next few days. When she saw his keen face at the studio window smiling at her, she was mortified that she had let emotions get out of hand. She had made vague excuses about how busy she was and how she had no time that week to see him.

The following week, he had blocked the corridor as she raced to get to the studio. He had invited her to the theatre to watch a comedy about doctors. She had been in such a hurry to get to the studio, she'd accepted his offer, without really talking to him. During the play, he had attempted to put his arm around her shoulder. She had wriggled away from it pretending to look for something in her handbag. After the play, she had said she had to rush off to bake her cakes for the next day. He had seemed disappointed that she was leaving him and leant in to kiss her. She'd let him but did not return it with fervour. She had hoped he would sense her reluctance. Thereafter, he had been popping up when she wasn't expecting him: when she had done the rounds to ask patients for requests or outside the studio as she was leaving. Although he was amiable and pleasant, she had developed a niggling feeling about him.

He had invited her to a concert. She had refused, citing work as an excuse. He had looked so deflated that she had felt guilty and agreed to go for a quick coffee with him to make up for it. At the coffee shop, he had stared at her with puppy dog eyes and told her how amazing she was. Charlie shuddered at that memory. She had apologised for leading him on in the car. He had put a finger against her lip when she'd tried to explain and stopped her speaking.

"It's okay," he had said. "I know."

Charlie had thought he understood that it had been a one-night stand and left him, feeling relieved.

However, after that episode, flowers had arrived at the studio on a daily basis. Each bouquet had carried a message

"To Charlie. You are my sunshine. Love Harrison."

"For Charlie. My friend. My rock. With love."

"For the most beautiful girl in the world." She didn't know what to do about it.

"Talk to him," Mercedes had suggested. "Be honest with him. Tell him you don't want a relationship with him."

Charlie had asked him to meet her at a local pub after work. He had arrived carrying a large box of chocolates, a huge smile plastered over his face. He had planted a kiss on her nose.

"I'm so glad you've found time for *us*," he had gabbled, not giving Charlie an opportunity to speak. "I was telling the other radiographers about you today. They can't believe you're my girlfriend," he had continued. "Wine?" he'd asked and, not waiting for a response, headed for the bar leaving Charlie shaking her head in disbelief.

"Harrison, I'm not your girlfriend. We just went out a couple of times," she had hissed at him when he returned with two glasses of wine.

"Of course you're my girlfriend," he'd insisted. "After *that* night. It meant something special, Charlie. You don't make love to strangers."

Charlie had shaken her head. "No, you're wrong. It might have meant something special to you, but me, well, I wasn't thinking straight. I used you. I took your affection and enjoyed it to help me through my misery. I'm so sorry. It wasn't the same for me. I don't want you to think we have anything special. We don't."

She had waited for him to become upset or shout at her or react in a negative way. He had not. He'd merely smiled at her. "I can wait, Charlotte," he'd said.

"Don't you get it? I won't be repeating that episode again with you. It was a mistake. I was drunk and lonely."

"That episode? Charlotte, we made love. That's what people who love each other do. That's why it's called making love."

"For heaven's sake!" she had said, her voice rising. They had been beginning to attract the attention of other people in the pub. "We didn't make love. We had sex. Brief sex. It wasn't even good sex. In your car. Once!" she had hissed, frustrated now. "And, please don't call me Charlotte."

He had looked confused for a moment, then smiled again, annoying Charlie further. He had really not wanted to understand. She had no option.

"Look, I don't want to see you again. Okay? It's over, whatever it was." She had left him sitting alone in the pub, his box of chocolates untouched on the table.

The following day, more flowers had arrived, along with a small, fluffy toy dog. She had given them to the nurses on one of the wards so the patients could enjoy them. Harrison had come by the studio. Mercedes had told him to go away while Charlie had hid in the back office. He had waited by the exit door and when Charlie had emerged, he'd pleaded with her to reconsider and go out with him again. She had refused, so he'd trailed after her along the corridors to her car until she had become angry and told him to leave her alone.

More flowers had arrived. She had felt sorry for him and had not wanted the hospital staff to get wind of it and tease him, so she had taken the flowers home, each day. Then he had visited her at home.

"Charlie, I don't know what I did wrong. Please tell me. I want to make amends," he had sobbed.

Charlie couldn't be cruel so she had invited him in, had made him a cup of tea, and had explained she wasn't ready for a relationship. She'd told him it wasn't his fault, explaining she needed to be alone, that she was still getting over the breakdown of her marriage.

"You are so young and I feel so old."

He had seemed to accept it and left.

For a few weeks afterwards, he had driven past her house every other night on a motorbike and stopped opposite her front door. At first, he had stopped only for a minute or two, then revved the bike and went but then he'd stayed longer, sometimes for an hour. She had known he was there even though he made no contact with her. She had heard the quiet purr of the motorbike engine as it cruised past. She'd peered out of a darkened upstairs window on one occasion and observed him sitting, watching her door.

Then the phone had rung at all hours of the night. When she'd answered, she had been met with silence. On one occasion she had spoken, "Harrison, is that you?" No one had replied. She had unplugged the phone at the socket.

Driving to work one day, she had noticed a motorbike that stayed exactly two cars behind her car. It had trailed her all the way to the hospital. When she had left work, it had been parked in a layby near the hospital. Pretty sure it was Harrison, she had stopped to tell him to quit pestering her. He had been startled when she'd hurtled into the layby, brought the car to a halt beside his bike and leapt out of it, steaming towards him.

"What the hell are you up to? You know where I work. You don't need to follow me about. If you keep this up, I'll report you for harassing me. I'm sick of it. I'm fed up with the stupid flowers and you appearing outside the studio window. I'm sick of you lurking outside the café and if you phone my house once more, I'm going to the police. One of my friends is married to a policeman. I'll get him to arrest you." She had stood hands on hips. Harrison had seemed surprised and hurt.

"Charlotte, sweetheart, I can explain," he had begun.

"Don't call me Charlotte, you cretin! That's not my name. And, for crying out loud, I am NOT your sweetheart. I never have been nor will be. I am not interested in being your sweetheart. Now piss off and leave me alone."

"There's no need to swear at me," he had said, his right eye twitching.

"I haven't even begun to swear properly. Just fuck off, Harrison. I don't want to see you or your poxy bike again."

She had marched back to her car, climbed in, slammed the door, revved the engine and drove off at speed, leaving Harrison sitting on his bike with a strange look on his face.

She had calmed down at home and decided she had been a little harsh on the man. However, he had frightened her, therefore she was right to retaliate. Her outburst would hopefully put off Harrison, who must now surely think she was a deranged foul-mouthed bitch, and not the paragon of virtue that he once believed her to be.

That following night, a motorbike engine had woken her. Then the phone had rung again. She'd answered it. There had been nothing but eerie silence punctuated with one muffled sob. After a poor night's sleep, she had come downstairs to find a note pushed through the letterbox:

Dear Charlotte,

I won't bother you anymore. Be happy.

Love forever.

Harrison X

Harrison was the last person she needed in her life now or ever. She thought about replying to the email, but decided against it. She pressed the delete key with determination. It was best to forget about it. When Harrison heard nothing from her, he would no doubt understand that she was not interested in him. She had more important things to sort out. She had cakes to box up, requests to read, shows to prepare, and a bizarre proposition that she needed to consider.

"Hello dear," said Peggy sotto voce. Charlie was trundling down her driveway lost in her own thoughts and hadn't noticed her neighbour standing outside her own front door.

"Morning Peggy. Is everything okay?"

"Oh yes, thank you. I'm just looking out for the postman. I'm expecting a parcel for Bert. I want to smuggle it in before he sees it. It's for his birthday in a couple of weeks' time. If he sees a box, he'll get excited and want to open it immediately. You must think I'm quite dotty," she added.

"No, I don't. Bert is unique and very clever. Of course you love him. Besides, he's very lovable."

There was tapping at the window followed by barking. Bert was on the window ledge bouncing up and down, trying to attract Charlie's attention. She waved at him. He squawked back.

"Oh drat! He's seen us," said Peggy.

"Look, why don't I take in the parcel? The postman should be here very soon. I'll keep it at my house until you want to collect it for him. That way, you won't have to worry about hiding it from him."

"That would be perfect! Thank you, Charlie. I don't want to spoil the surprise for him. He loves his birthday. I've got him a little hat to wear. You'll come by, won't you?"

"I wouldn't miss it. Last year's was huge fun. He was very entertaining. I especially liked it when he blew out the candle on his cake, then sang happy birthday. Has he got many guests coming?"

"I've invited the Wilkinson children, George, Harry and Oliver and the Mackay girls, Sophie and Elizabeth. I thought that would be enough. I don't want him over-excited. You know how he loves to show off in front of everyone."

At that moment, the postman appeared at the end of the street.

"There he is. I'll nip inside and distract Bert. Thank you again."

"Peggy, what's in the parcel?"

"It's a basketball hoop and ball especially for parrots. I can't wait to see his little face when he opens it!" she replied, eyes twinkling.

"He'll adore it," said Charlie, feeling a sudden burst of affection for the tiny woman in front of her. "Go on, get in before he sees the postman," she whispered as Bert tapped on the window again and began meowing."

Charlie had just managed to balance her Tupperware cake boxes on top of each other and had reached the café when her phone rang. She ran the risk of dropping the cakes so she let it ring and shouldered the door open.

"Morning, Charlie! I'm just making coffee for me and Patricia. Do you want one?"

"That would be lovely, thanks. It's been one of those mornings. I dropped the fruit cake when I removed it from the oven and had to bake another because it fell to pieces. Then Peggy needed me to help her put up net curtains and then she started talking about her son in Canada, so I couldn't get away. I've been running late ever since."

"How old is she?"

"Seventy, I think." She and her husband ran a bar in Lanzarote until they were in their late sixties, then came back here when he got ill. He died shortly after they returned to the UK. She's full of energy though. She washes her net curtains every three months to keep them ultra-white, but the last few times she's been too shaky to climb the stepladder, so I nip around and hang them for her. She's very house-proud. I hope I have her energy when, or if, I ever reach that age. She never stops. Yesterday afternoon, she was in the back garden sweeping leaves up and hauling them about in her dustbin, when I left for the hospital.

"I don't think she's ever been ill. Having Bert around helps. He's her parrot and a very intelligent one, at that. He's been with her a few years now. Bert used to go to the bar with them both. He stayed outside on his perch, near the customers. You can imagine what he picked up from them. It took Peggy two years to get him to stop swearing. He's a wicked mimic. They ran a Karaoke night, every Saturday, so he imitated a few regulars and sings all sorts of song snippets. You should hear him sing *Like a Virgin*. Peggy's always teaching him new tricks, words or songs. Really. I kid you not. Bert even has his own Facebook page where he 'chats' with fans and other parrots from all over the world. Peggy set it up after her husband, Dennis, passed away. It gave her a real sense of purpose and of course, Bert loves the attention too. She can stay in touch with her family in Canada too using Facebook. I really admire these older people who move with the times."

Charlie placed her boxes on the counter, hung up her coat, and set about putting the cakes out.

"Oh, lovely. I fancy a piece of the lemon drizzle cake with my coffee," said Art, putting the cups on a tray.

"No you don't!" said Patricia appearing as if by magic. "You're on a diet. You know what the doctor said about your weight. Maybe Charlie could take you to belly dancing classes with her. You've lost weight, Charlie. I hadn't noticed before. How much have you lost?"

"Not much. I'm just a little firmer than before," she replied, cutting a small slice of lemon cake and placing it onto a plate that she pushed towards Art.

He winked at her, grabbed the slice, and took a large bit before Patricia could stop him. Then he waved a napkin about and pretended to dance. "I'll wear it off, Patty. Look, I can belly jiggle."

His dance was interrupted by the doorbell as a couple of customers arrived.

"I'll get it," said Charlie. "You enjoy the cake."

She forgot to check her phone until much later as she raced to the studio. She didn't recognise the number. Probably a cold caller. She deleted the number and set off to her show.

"Well done, ladies," Jasmine said, applauding them. "You managed the routine perfectly. What an improvement from the last time. No one forgot the moves. And, you look very professional. You look like you've been doing this longer than four weeks."

"If you'd said four weeks ago that I'd be able to belly dance like that, I'd have laughed at you," said Marcia, wiping her brow.

"Same here. I know you told us we'd improve quickly, but didn't believe it would happen so quickly," agreed Susannah. "I love belly dancing. It's funny how remembering the moves to a routine and doing it at the same time as everyone else, can give you such a buzz. I want to do it all again. The music is intoxicating too. Every time I hear a song with a good beat, my hips start moving. I can't help myself. I hope I'm not pushing my trolley down an aisle in say, Asda or somewhere, and they play some music like that. I'll be whooshing off, shaking my booty all over the place, way out of control," she added and demonstrated by thrusting her hips dramatically towards the mirror.

"We've only got one more class and then sadly, that's it," said Jasmine, turning off the stereo.

"It's gone far too quickly," commented Charlie. "I wasn't sure what to expect when I first arrived, but I've thoroughly enjoyed it."

"I'm just going to make a phone call," said Jasmine. "Take your time. I don't have any classes after this. I'll see you on Friday. We'll do the routine a couple of times and then I'll give you a taster of what you can learn if you go on to do any intermediate classes. Thanks very much."

They said goodbye to Jasmine and collected their belongings. Susannah removed her belt scarf and placed it carefully in a large shopping bag from which she extracted a purple and blue hat with large flaps that covered her ears.

"We've improved since the piggy snorting episode, haven't we?" said Marcia with a laugh.

"Oh, don't! I still shudder at that memory."

"I wonder if he ever thinks about that strange woman who, wearing little clothing, ran up to him on all fours squealing," said

Susannah. "I'd have thought that was the stuff of fantasies. Or possibly it's only my husband who has such weird fantasies. He said he'd have liked to have seen it."

"You told your husband?"

"Yes, well," said Susannah, going pink. "We were ... well ... you know ... and it sort of came up."

"Oh my," exclaimed Marcia. "It *was* in the bedroom, wasn't it?" Susannah went redder.

"It was!" shrieked Marcia. "You were playing games in the bedroom and I bet you ended up showing him what happened here in the studio."

Susannah gave her a sheepish look. "Not quite like that, but we experimented and that is all I'm going to say on the matter." She did up her coat, avoiding any further eye contact with the others.

"Susannah, you dark horse. Or, were you a dark pig?"

"No, a naughty schoolgirl who needed a proper spanking, if you must know," replied Susannah with a wicked grin.

"I bet you threw in a few squeals for good measure though," continued Marcia.

"Well, possibly one or two."

"I'm really glad for you," Charlie said. "It's transformed you. And, by the sounds of it, it's transformed Dave."

"Yeah, joking aside, me too," said Marcia. "I thought you were looking a lot happier. It had to be more than just hanging out with us, although we are pretty awesome chicks."

Susannah laughed. "Let's just say, things are getting better. I don't feel I've reached an impasse now and I'm spending every night on my own at home watching the telly while Dave goes out with his mates. Now, better get home. I've got some new moves to show off."

"Night, Susannah. See you on Friday. Are you going straight home, Marcia?"

"Yep, I've got an appointment with a packet of wax strips, a pair of tweezers and an entire tub of body cream. I'm going out with my new man tomorrow and I want to be prepared for any eventuality."

"Hope you have a super time. You can fill us in on all the details next time."

"All of the details?"

"Maybe not all of them."

"Bye Charlie."

Charlie parted company with Marcia and went to her car. It was parked in the small car park adjacent to the studio, next to Jasmine's sparkly new Citroen C1. She threw her bag onto the passenger seat, started the car up, and turned on the radio. Cyndi Lauper was singing about girls having fun. Charlie wondered if she would ever have fun again with a man. It seemed unlikely. For a moment, she pictured the man who had caught her on all fours. Then she shook her head, reprimanded herself for such thoughts and set off, assisting Cyndi with the chorus.

Mercedes had drafted in Sean to help Charlie on her show because the film crew for *Nosh for Dosh* were filming her. They were quite a distraction and several members of staff had already passed by the studio in the hope of being caught on camera. Mercedes was taking the rest of the week off to be on the show and prepare for it.

"Could we have Mercedes sitting there wearing her headphones, please? Yes, if you could wave your pencil at the presenter ... as if you are cueing her in or something. That's it. You're a natural at this, Mercedes. Sorry, what's your name? Sean. Could you keep out of shot? Thank you. Yes, over there would be great, lovey. Watch out for the cable. Trevor, can you shine the light more onto Mercedes? Better, much better."

Charlie wondered how she'd have coped if it had been her. Mercedes seemed to be at ease with it all. She did exactly what the producer wanted and wasn't fazed by the reshooting. They seemed to be dissatisfied with so many of the shots. Mercedes took it all with good grace and kept smiling.

As much as Charlie wanted to be on the show, she wouldn't have enjoyed this part. On the show you only saw each contestant in their natural environment for about five minutes. So far, they had been filming for the best part of an entire day and still did not seem to have what they needed. It wasn't that natural either. The hospital authorities weren't too keen on an entire crew being in the hospital, so they were confined to the studio area and unable to film in the rest of the hospital.

"Mercedes, darling, how about you go outside the studio now to collect a request for the show? I know we're not allowed to go and see the real patients but if, what's your name again? Sean. If Sean could go outside and hand you a piece of paper, you could pretend it was a request. Sean you need to look a bit sorry for yourself. Try and look like you're ill. No not that ill. Fake a limp of something. Davina, slap some white powder on his face, sweets. Make him look poorly. There, that's much better."

"Come on, Sean. This could be your big break. A movie agent could see this and want to sign you up as a zombie in the next blockbuster movie," said Mercedes and wheeled off with the crew and Sean trailing behind her.

Charlie ignored the team as best as she could. "That was *Muskrat Love*, a big hit in nineteen seventy-six for Captain and Tennille. Award yourself two points if you got both of their names right. Here's some more trivia about the song: it is really about two muskrats making love. Is a muskrat just a rat? Anyway, the song wasn't supposed to be taken seriously. In July nineteen seventy-six, First Lady Betty Ford invited the Captain and Tennille to perform at the White House. Our Queen Elizabeth was a guest at that time. They played *Muskrat Love* and the Queen was the only one who didn't applaud when they finished the song. Well, fancy that! One was not amused! Or maybe she didn't understand what it was about either. Darryl 'Captain' Dragon and Toni Tennille were in the news in January this year when, after several decades together, they decided to end their marriage. I wonder if we should expect a new release from them soon, *Farewell my Muskrat Love*.

"You're listening to Charlie Blundell and here's your last trivia question for today: Local lad, Ozzy Osbourne was lead vocalist in the band Black Sabbath, but what is Ozzy's real first name? You can have a bonus point if you know both his first names. No cheating by nipping on Google. Remember, we have nurses watching you. Answers in a minute, but first, just for Spud in ward fourteen, this is *Paranoid* by Black Sabbath. Please don't wave your air guitar about too much, Spud. Enjoy."

She turned off her microphone. Sam came into the studio singing along to the track, "Finished with my woman 'cause she couldn't help me with my mind ... "

"Hi Sam! You're early. Let me guess. New T-shirt? Smart haircut? You're here in case the cameras come in."

"Guilty as charged," replied Sam and slumped down in the chair opposite her. "Actually, it was a good excuse to come in early. We've got the grandkids over and little Rosie is going through one of those difficult phases. I can't stand the noise. It's quieter here. Even with Ozzy yelling," he added.

"Not my first choice but we have to please all the people," said Charlie. "Do you know the answer to the question?"

"John. John Michael Osbourne," responded Sam.

"Correct. You have earned yourself two points. Well done Mister Trivia."

"I confess I cheated. I checked the answer on my phone as I walked into the studio. I knew you'd ask me." He sat back, eyes twinkling. "Where's the star of the T.V. food show?"

"Gone off with one of the walking dead to pretend to collect requests. She should've been just outside the studio. Management won't be pleased if they're mooching about in the corridors. Hang on. Track's ending.

"Hope you enjoyed that, Spud. That was Ozzy Osbourne, or as his mum called him, John Michael Osbourne. Give yourself a pat on the back if you got that right and didn't cheat like Sam the man. Hope you enjoyed the quiz today. Remember it's just for fun. I'll have another quiz for you next week. And now, something to relax us all and get us ready for our evening meal, this is the Commodores and *Easy*."

She turned up the volume on the deck and silenced the microphone.

"Watch out," whispered Sam. "Here come the television crew. Lord above, who's that with them?"

"Sean of the almost dead. He's supposed to be a sick patient. They weren't allowed to use a real one."

"Do they need any other extras? I could go and offer my services."

"Go and see Lesley, the staff nurse at reception. She might lend you a doctor's coat."

"Great idea. I'll go and see what I can do."

Sam pushed back his chair, hauled his large frame from it, and ambled out. Charlie saw Mercedes through the window again. She pulled a face at Charlie. Sean was back in position behind the glass. His face was pasty white. The production team were still filming. Charlie checked the clock. It had seemed such a long afternoon. Thank goodness she wasn't doing *Nosh for Dosh*. She would have found it too tiring. Besides, she was better behind a microphone than in front of a camera.

The four contestants on *Nosh for Dosh* sat around a large round glass table dominated by an enormous heart-shaped floral arrangement.

"So that's how I became a florist," said a large man wearing a sequined waistcoat and bow tie. His hair was slicked back, revealing a shiny forehead. The man, Maurice, was perspiring heavily after spending five hours getting his special meal prepared under the warm lights that were moved frequently about his kitchen to avoid shadows.

He was the first contestant to cook on the show *Nosh for Dosh* and the filming was taking its toll. The team trailed about his florist's shop for an entire day retaking shots and repeating questions until he wanted to scream. It was proving even more stressful since they arrived at his home. He had to put up with them monopolising his house and staging the rooms for viewers to get maximum entertainment. An eagle-eyed member of the team spotted his teddy bear collection hiding in a wardrobe and in spite of his protests, pulled several out, leaving them scattered about his bedroom, where later his guests would go and comment on the evening. He was now very amenable and hoped to score highly by getting his guests drunk on his homemade wine.

"Mercedes, tell us a little about yourself," said Maurice.

"Oh, I'll save that for another day. It's your night, Maurice. The mousse was delicious. Very light indeed. I'm almost tempted to be greedy and ask for seconds, but your next course sounds wonderful too and I want to leave room for it."

"Yes, it was verrey nice," agreed the elegant woman seated opposite Mercedes. We make zees a lot en France, Maurice," she purred. "I don't like to eat too much because of my figure. I 'af to be careful." She smoothed her hands over her flat stomach. When no one commented, she continued. "Ow did you get zees flowers like zees?"

"Claudine, I used florist wire. You can get it heart-shaped so you don't need to bend it into shape. Looks good, doesn't it?"

Claudine nodded in the direction of the camera and opened her mouth to speak again.

"Okay, we'll cut there. Maurice, do you want to go into the kitchen now and prepare the next course? We'll do a piece to camera in the bedroom with Claudine. Patrick has already done a piece up there. We'll ask her what she thought of the meal so far, and so on. You know the routine. Then we'll come down and do the main course."

The crew left the dining room and followed Maurice into the kitchen.

"This is 'arder zan I fort it would be," whispered Claudine. "All ze questions. I shall 'av to try to be carefool. Maurice's wine iz verrey strong and az gone to my 'ed. I cannot be responsible for my comments about 'iz soufflé."

"Claudine, are you ready to go to Maurice's bedroom?"

Claudine pouted, pulled out a small mirror and makeup from her handbag, reapplied some deep red lipstick, then stalked off after the camera in her designer heels. Mercedes smiled conspiratorially at Patrick, the fourth contestant, who was relaxing with his glass of wine. He raised an eyebrow.

"We'll have to watch that one. She's definitely out to win. I hope she isn't going to feed us foie gras and frog's legs when we go to her house," he continued. "Poor Maurice, I have a feeling that Claudine is going to have something to say about the teddy bears on the bed, especially the one wearing the French maid's outfit."

"Happy Birthday to you," sang Peggy, Charlie, and a bunch of children in unison. Bert bounced up and down on Peggy's shoulder in time to the singing.

"Hip, hip, hooray!" shouted the children. Bert whistled.

Bert was wearing a small cone hat. The children, also wearing party hats, were gathered around watching him. He had played peek-a-boo with them, shown them his ring hoop trick and regaled them with a vast array of whistles, calls, and impressions for them.

Peggy cut the cake into pieces for all the children and gave Bert a piece of his own special seed cake.

"It's nice to have the house filled with children and laughter, isn't it?" said Peggy. Bert was blowing kisses to George and making him giggle. "I was thinking the other day that it would be nice to go to Canada and see my grandchildren. I haven't seen them for three years and although I can see them on Skype, it isn't the same as sitting down with them. I wouldn't want to leave Bert, though. It's a shame they can't come over here. Still, why would they want to? They're Canadians. My son is always busy at work and if he gets any free time, he's not likely to want to spend it here, in the UK, in a semi-detached house with me, when he can go to Hawaii, or Argentina, and bask in luxury at a five-star resort. I don't mean to sound bitter. I'm not. I'm glad he's as successful as he is, and he's got such a lovely family. It's just some days, I feel lonely. It wasn't so bad when we lived on Lanzarote. The weather was so much better for one thing, and of course, I had Dennis. I miss him. It seems lonelier here, somehow. Days are darker and shorter. Still, mustn't grumble. Ignore me. I'm being a silly old woman. It's because today's Bert's birthday. It reminds me that yet another year's raced by. Another year without my dear Dennis. And it reminds me that time's too short. Bert's eleven years old now. How time flies. I remember when we first got him."

Charlie patted Peggy's hand. "I know what you mean. And you're not a silly old woman. Look at the smiles on those faces. Those children have had a lovely time. They've watched Bert doing all his tricks. You've given them a super tea and even party bags. How many children can say they've been to a parrot's party? Bert's enjoyed it too. What about Oliver's face when Bert meowed at him? It was a picture."

A small girl with long dark hair and rosy cheeks was tickling Bert's head. He was chirping in delight. The others tucked into the array of cakes, sandwiches, and treats in front of them.

"It was wonderful, wasn't it? He's very good with children. I think it's because they're so gentle with him. He used to be very content with people and all our clients loved him until the day one of them got very drunk and became aggressive. He marched up to Bert while he was dozing on his perch and prodded him with his finger. It frightened Bert witless. He put up with it for a while, but the wretched man kept doing it. Dennis asked him to stop and leave the poor creature alone, but he laughed and stabbed his fat finger right at Bert's eye. Bert went crazy, flapping about and shrieking. Dennis raced over and pulled the man away, but not before Bert bit his finger. It bled such a lot. The man started shouting and said he'd have Bert put down. Luckily, Dennis calmed the man down and the bite was only superficial.

"He came back to the bar a couple of days later. Bert remembered him and got very upset. He flew at the man. Dennis managed to stop him attacking. We asked the man to stay away after that. I never liked him anyway. He was one of those old soaks who spends all afternoon getting drunk and then do stupid things that annoy the other customers. Bert became wary of people after that incident, especially anyone who'd been drinking. I think he could smell the alcohol on their breath. He became aggressive if anyone who'd been drinking approached him, or Dennis, or me. He was suddenly quite protective of us, especially me. We had to keep him close to us at the bar so we could make sure he didn't hurt anyone. Shortly after that, we sold the bar and came here. Bert seemed happier. He prefers quiet, sober people."

As young Oliver let out a whoop, she added, "Although he seems fine with children, even when they are very noisy."

"Does Bert want to play with his new hoop?" asked Sophie. "I can throw the ball for him."

"No, I want to," cried Elizabeth.

"I think he's a little tired of playing now. Bert. What about a song?" said Peggy. "Come on everyone, let's help Bert sing. Do you know *Zip a Dee Do Dah?*"

Charlie observed the scene. She knew how Peggy felt. She felt it too. Once upon a time, she had a family, a life, and a future. Nowadays, she filled up her time with her radio show, gardening, cake baking, and the café. She needed to inject something more into it. She thought about Mercedes's proposition. She decided she would do it. After all, life was short.

Patrick had had enough of the film crew. By the time his guests arrived, he was ready to play up. He was only on the show because one of his staff had dared him. His wife thought it was hilarious. Patrick knew nothing about cookery. Unlike fellow contestants who had asked spouses and partners to hide from the cameras, Patrick was happy to have his wife in the house with him while they filmed. Patrick had taken a dislike to Claudine, decided Maurice was a buffoon, and only had time for Mercedes.

"You could try and take it a little more seriously," hissed his wife as Patrick marched about the bedroom dressed in a smoking jacket, a copy of the *Times* under his arm and a riding crop in his hand.

"No. I'm only doing it for a dare. People want entertainment when they watch this show. They don't give a monkeys about the actual cooking bollocks. I'm going to be a man behaving badly. I feel like being controversial."

"Are you ready, Patrick?" called the producer. "We want to start with you preparing your starter."

"Here goes nothing," said Patrick with a wry smile.

"Oh, please try to behave just a bit," moaned his wife.

"Not a chance," he replied, grinning from ear to ear. "Thank you, love. I'll expect you to run my bath later, as usual," he called as the cameraman and sound engineer filmed him going downstairs.

In the kitchen, he fumbled about looking for his dinner menu. "Now, what am I cooking? Gloria was supposed to buy the ingredients. I wonder where she's put them. Glor!" he yelled. "Where're the tinned baked beans?"

The cameraman guffawed.

"I can't do beans on toast without the beans," he shouted.

Gloria appeared from the bedroom. "Patrick!" she warned.

"She's no fun," said Patrick directly to the camera. "While you lot are here," he added with a wink and picked up his riding crop, giving it a meaningful look. The director clapped his hands together silently. This was pure gold.

Patrick set about preparing his meal, a simple menu of minestrone soup and chicken in red wine. He fooled about throughout the preparation, threw vegetables all over the kitchen top, and decided he had not got the right herbs, so he took out a couple of boxes of ready-made soup and poured them into a large pan.

"And as my French guest, Claudine would say, voilà!" he said, wiping his hands on an apron that bore an image of a scantily clad lady. "No one will be able to tell. Besides, it's very good quality soup. It came in boxes. It's proper posh nosh. I'll add a carrot piece to each bowl. They'll never be able to tell the difference between it and homemade soup."

He then poured a large glass of wine to help him through the next course. He insisted on referring to a recipe book throughout the preparation, making comments about Nigella Lawson sucking chocolate off a spoon.

"She behaves like a dirty tart," he said. "If Gloria licked her finger like that after dipping it in the food, she'd be in trouble. It's bad manners, isn't it? You should wash your hands when you cook, not drool all over them and the kitchen utensils."

He had purchased an enormous chicken for the meal. Since the recipe demanded chicken pieces, he needed to debone his bird, a fact he used to its full advantage as he grimaced and huffed while attempting to attack it with a large knife.

"I don't know," he complained. "It's a lot easier when I go to the pub and Gloria deals with this stuff. This isn't a man's job. Men are on this planet to hunt for food and provide for their women. Women are here to look after us, clean up, and prepare the food," he claimed, draining a glass of Bordeaux. "Glor! Come down here a moment, darling. I need your female skills."

Gloria appeared and with hands on hips tried to guide him through the process of deboning a chicken. Patrick clowned about further and ended up being thrown out of the kitchen by Gloria who not only boned the chicken, but also prepared the sauce. Patrick set the table and read the newspaper while she got on with it. Much later, Gloria let him back into the kitchen and gave him instructions on how to cook the vegetables and chicken.

Patrick finally sorted out the vegetables and made a big song and dance about his desert—ice cream, scooped from a dish and decorated with a fan wafer. He did a little dance with the wafers, decided he better leave the scooping of the ice cream until nearer the time and cried out, "Gloria love, could you run me a bath? I'm pooped. I'd like plenty of bath salts and could you bring me up a glass of champagne too? Lovely. See, ladies, us men are really only cut out for the manly difficult stuff. We should leave the cooking to you."

"Father Abraham and the Smurfs with *The Smurf Song*. Do you remember those lovable little blue people? If you do, then maybe you can answer this question: What colour was Papa Smurfs' hat? While you're thinking about it, here's another couple of facts about the Smurfs that might interest you: The Smurfs were originally called les Schtroumpfs and were invented as a result of a silly conversation over dinner. And how about this? The World Record for People Dressed as Smurfs was set in Swansea, Wales, in two thousand and nine. More than two thousand and five hundred people crammed into a nightclub dressed in blue and white and weren't allowed to have any natural skin showing in order to count toward the record. The previous record had been set just a year earlier, with one thousand, two hundred and fifty-three Smurfs gathered in Castleblayney, Ireland. Can you imagine trying to wash all the blue paint off your skin afterwards?

"Did you know the answer to my Smurf trivia question? It was red. Papa Smurfs' hat was red. Congratulations if you got that correct. How did we get onto Smurfs? Oh, I remember. It all started because Sean brought some jelly Smurf sweets into the studio. Bad for your teeth, but satisfying to chomp. Here we go with an appropriate segue. We're all very professional here on City Hospital Radio? This is The Searchers and *Sweets for my Sweet.*"

Charlie chewed on another sweet and wondered how Mercedes was getting along. It was day three of the contest. They were filming at Claudine's house. Mercedes had been too occupied to phone and fill her in with all the details. She was dying to know what the other contestants were like.

She was also keen to find out what Mercedes had lined up for her. The belly dancing had ended and she was surprised how much she missed the classes, Marcia and Susannah. Susannah had booked a holiday in Morocco with her husband and Marcia had enjoyed a good first date with Mitch, a sports coach she had met on the internet.

"There are so many people in cyberworld," she told Charlie. "I'd never have found another man if I hadn't thought about signing up with an online agency. It's so difficult to find men in the real world. They're all married, in relationships, or there's something wrong with them," she scoffed. "You have to be careful online too. There was one guy who looked really buff. He sent me his photograph and I couldn't work out why he hadn't found a woman. He sent a piccy of him at the beach and he had pecs to make you swoon. He was an Adonis, I kid you not. I agreed to meet him in a bar. It's always wise to meet in a public place. You never know what they'll be like. If they're dangerous, at least you're surrounded by other people.

"We met in Wetherspoons, on the main street. It's usually busy there. I suggested we meet at six-thirty. That's a good time because the pubs have a few early door punters and guys who grab a drink before they go home, but it isn't too crowded. I walked into the bar and looked about for this hunk. I couldn't see him anywhere. I was about to go and sit in a corner and wait for him when an old bloke, about sixty and bald as a coot tapped me on the shoulder and said, 'Marcia?' It was him. He'd sent me a photograph taken forty years earlier. No wonder he was single. I told him he shouldn't do that and he replied, 'Plenty of women do it. Hardly anyone looks like their photo on the dating website. I've met some right dogs and I've been out with women much older than me. So far, you're the only one who looks like her picture.' Then he added, 'Shame! I'd hoped you'd be a bit older. Never mind. I expect you're a goer.' Cheeky bastard. I stormed out."

"Then there was the time a married guy met me. He looked tasty enough. He'd put he was single on his profile, but I spied a wedding ring on his hand. When I quizzed him about his marital status, he said that he had one of those relaxed relationships where he and his wife banged other people. He got most enthusiastic about it saying it was incredible the number of people he and his wife had met online who only wanted a casual sexual relationship. They'd tried swinging, but they preferred this. And get this, his wife was in the same restaurant at another table with a bloke she'd met from the agency. Talk about crazy."

Marcia was right. It was nigh on impossible to find male company if you were over thirty, let alone almost forty years old. Charlie did not want to hang about clubs or bars in the hope she would meet a free agent. However, she did not want to try online dating. The way she felt at the moment, she was too tired and busy for a relationship anyway. Best to stick to her routine.

"This is Charlie with you until six o'clock. I hope you're enjoying the music this evening. We've been asking you to come up with songs about the weather and you've managed some corkers. That's songs with titles or artists to do with the weather. I've got some great tracks for this half hour of uninterrupted music, starting off with The Weather Girls and *It's Raining Men.*"

She sighed. It was never going to rain men in her life.

"Mercedes, 'ow wonderfool. Entrez. Let me show you to the reception room."

Claudine, dressed from head to toe in Yves Saint Laurent, took the handles of Mercedes's wheelchair and propelled her towards the front room. Her crystal-embellished Tulle dress rustled. Mercedes was miffed. She was not helpless. She detested it when people assumed she was. Claudine's heels on her python leather ankle boots clattered on the marble floor as they made their way to an enormous room with rich wooden floors that stretched out into a glass conservatory. At the far end of the conservatory, a table was set with shiny expensive cutlery, plush cotton napkins, and polished crystal glasses. Thick pillar candles on tall black stands completed the effect. Their flames emitted a soft light, enhancing the ambience. To the left of the room, a fire was burning brightly in a magnificent fireplace. Next to it, Patrick sat in a large wingback chair.

"Hi Mercedes," he said, relief on his face. He stood up and gave her a kiss on the cheek. "Come and sit by me."

It was much as Mercedes had expected it to be. Even from the outside, the house was most imposing. It had a mile-long private drive and Mercedes had almost expected a butler to answer the door as she tugged on the rope of the brass bell. She could only imagine the size of the kitchen. She bet it had an AGA.

"Albert," called Claudine. A butler arrived with a tray of glasses filled with champagne. Patrick shot Mercedes a warning look as she stifled a giggle.

Claudine immediately started talking about the house. It had been completely renovated by Claudine's husband, a property developer. "We 'av six barfrooms."

"Plenty of choice then if you suddenly need a barf," mumbled Mercedes. Patrick sniggered. Claudine was too wrapped up in talking to notice. The bell rang.

"I must see oo zis iz," she said regally and left the room.

"Wowee!" said Mercedes when Claudine was out of earshot. "Is she on this show to win a thousand pounds or to show off her house?"

"I think it's the latter. I heard a rumour that they're going to put the house up for sale soon. This is a promotional exercise to ... "

Patrick stopped talking as Maurice shuffled in with Claudine. His eyes were large and his mouth flapped open when he saw the size of the room.

"Oh my! This is astonishing!" he gushed.

Claudine looked pleased at the reaction. "Yes, my husband, ee and iz team renovated zee whole 'ouse. I shall show it to you later but first, you must av some champagne. Albert! Where is zat man? I shall 'af to find 'im!" She wafted off.

"You look—"

"Stupid," said Maurice looking down at his outfit. "I have no idea why I agreed to wear this."

Maurice glanced at his reflection in the huge mirror over the fireplace. "It was the only outfit in the fancy dress shop that had anything remotely to do with France. Normally, I love dressing up, but even I think this looks silly. I'd have liked to have come as Napoléon Bonaparte, but that outfit had been borrowed. Who's Claudine supposed to be?"

"I think she's Coco Chanel or Brigitte Bardot. I can't decide. Either way, it's an excuse to look stunning in designer clothes while the rest of us look like idiots."

"Speak for yourself. I think I look great as Joan of Arc," said Mercedes. "Mind you, this armour breast plate is a bit uncomfortable."

"I hate dressing up," said Patrick.

"Is that why you haven't bothered to?"

"I have bothered. I'm Alain Delon, the famous actor. I even have a hat like he wore in the film *Le Samouraï*. See."

He reached down beside his chair and produced a hat which he plopped onto his head with a smile. "Voilà! Instant fancy dress."

Claudine arrived with the butler who was carrying another tray of champagne-filled glasses. "So sorry to 'av kept you. Dinner will be served in ten minutes," she said. "But first we 'av some traditional French entertainment... "

She clapped her hands and a gentleman with a large moustache wearing a striped pullover appeared at the doorway and began playing the accordion.

"Are you sure it'll work? I don't want to ruin it for you," said Charlie. She was on the phone to her friend.

"You won't. Now, you know what you have to do? Wait outside in your car at two o'clock. By then, the guests will be here and the crew will be actually filming the meal. I'll send you a text when I'm ready for you. Let yourself in the back door. Wait for my cue, press the play button on the sound system on the kitchen top, and then shimmy into the dining room."

"I'm not sure I can remember the moves."

"Of course you can. Those belly dancing lessons have really paid off. You look very exotic when you shake your booty. Come on, you'll be wearing a veil. No one will be any the wiser as to your identity and you can mysteriously disappear after the applause. It'll be great. That way, you're on the show and I get some original entertainment for my guests. Don't forget to shake your money belt thing at Patrick. He'll be mesmerised. He's the hairdresser I told you about. He owns a salon in town. He's definitely not one of those camp stereotypes, in fact when we went to his house, he was quite the opposite. Patrick likes women to be feminine and somewhat subservient. He made his views quite clear. He will love you batting your eyelashes at him.

"Claudine will detest you, so forget about her. She's a complete diva and is determined to win this contest. Luckily, no one enjoyed her endives in cream sauce and her Tarte Tatin was a disaster. I think hiring a man to play French accordion music was a stroke of genius, but the mime artist was definitely over the top. And getting us all to dress as French characters was wacky. The image of Maurice dressed as Marie Antoinette will remain with me for a long time.

"I'm not confident I can win Claudine over with my menu but I'm banking on wowing the two men. I discovered Maurice has a Moroccan boyfriend so it's in the bag as far as he's concerned. You'll be the entertainment that should swing it for me with Patrick. I'm sure he'll give you a perfect ten on his scoreboard. So thanks to you and to my recent cookery lessons, I'm ready to rock. It was very kind of you to ask Fatima to help out."

"She's a smashing lady. When she was in hospital undergoing surgery for gallstones, I spent some time with her. She told me all about her life before she fell in love with a Brit and came to the UK. Her family owned a palatial house, gold crockery and even had servants, you know? Who would have thought it? She once was waited on and now she sweats away in her restaurant kitchen. She's a super cook though," said Charlie.

"She enjoys it. Told me it gives her a sense of purpose and she can keep a beady eye on her husband. Make sure he's not slacking. She keeps those sons of hers on their toes, too. She showed me photographs of her family home, back in Rabat. It's stunning. All white with a green roof. Looks exactly like a small palace. It gave me some fantastic ideas for setting the scene at our house.

"Ryan worked tirelessly last weekend, transforming the dining room into the interior of a desert tent. He hung fabrics and a large Moroccan lamp we borrowed from Fatima. She came over and helped too. It looks magical. She even lent me her silver teapot to make mint tea after the meal."

"I can't wait to see it. So have you got almonds for nibbles and have you put your chick peas for your chick pea soup to soak yet?"

"Almonds for toasting and a large bottle of fizz to accompany them. Check. Chick peas, check."

"Moroccan meatball tajine with lemon and olives," Charlie read from Mercedes's menu card in front of her. "Sounds yummy. For dessert, desert rice pudding with date compote. Lovely and light. Managed to find any orange blossom water for that?"

"Of course. Our local grocery store has everything you could imagine. I'll have to have you around and cook for you when this is over."

"Did I detect a note of enthusiasm?"

"Yes, you did. I've really enjoyed my crash course in cookery with Fatima. It's opened up a new world for me. The meals aren't very difficult to prepare. I'll have to be careful though, Ryan has already started to put on weight since I began cooking dishes for him to try."

"I bet he has. Okay, I'll see you tomorrow. Sleep well and good luck."

It was almost midnight when Charlie turned in. She was nervous about her performance at Mercedes's house, especially as cameras would be on her. She wanted Mercedes to win the coveted one thousand pounds for the best host and meal. She deserved it and if wobbling her belly at strangers helped Mercedes win, then she'd forget her own anxieties and wobble away.

The belly dancing lessons had been such a laugh and she would miss the girls now the lessons were over. They all promised to keep in touch and Jasmine suggested they might like to consider tribal belly dancing classes next.

"Do we get to shout and chant as we dance, then?" Susannah asked.

"No, but you play tiny cymbals on your fingers and dance with other women. I'll let you know when classes start. You could join the end of year Tribal Belly Dancing Float in the annual festival parade if you like it enough."

"I'm delighted with what I've picked up here, Jasmine," replied Susannah. "My husband cancelled his darts at the pub again tonight so he'd be home when I got back," she grinned. "Thanks ever so much. I'm going to go to the gym like you suggested and stay fit. I'm not going to let myself regress to where I was. I can't believe the difference in only four weeks of belly dancing. I actually feel younger."

"Me too," commented Marcia. "I'm going to join the advanced class and then I might even try my hand at pole dancing."

There was no doubt that even Charlie felt more confident than she did before the classes. Jasmine promised they would feel sexier and she certainly felt more womanly. She walked better too. Not as tall and proud as that glamorous woman she saw having coffee with the Piggy man as she now called him, but prouder nonetheless.

Mercedes's idea to swap lists was working well. Charlie wondered what her next challenge was going to be and found herself looking forward to it. The belly dancing classes had been huge fun and she had enjoyed them far more than she thought possible. She hoped Mercedes was enjoying the *Nosh For Dosh* challenge as much.

There was a knock at the door. Mercedes opened it. Maurice stood on her doorstep. "Hello Mercedes," he said, offering her a small box of chocolates. "You look very exotic, my dear."

Mercedes laughed. She was wearing a long pale-grey silk djellaba with exquisite embroidery at the neck. Her red hair was held back with silver clips.

"Thank you. I'm not used to being so elegant. These djellabas are very comfortable to wear. You should get one for yourself, Maurice. They come in all sizes and colours for men and women. We could be trend-setters."

"Mercedes, I think you carry it off far better than I could," he replied. The cameraman sniggered quietly. He loved working on this show.

Mercedes showed Maurice into the lounge where he made appropriate noises about the décor. Brightly-coloured rugs covered the two sofas. Large matching cushions and beaded pouffes completed the Bohemian look. Settling him down with a drink, she wheeled out of the room to greet the second guest.

The format to the show changed little. Each hosting contestant had to greet each guest individually, take them to the lounge or dining room, serve a drink, then greet the next person. It was to give the impression that those invited had arrived separately. In reality, they were all outside in the garage having their makeup checked and being miked up for sound. It was chilly out there and Claudine was muttering about being cold.

"Maybe you should have worn something warmer, my dear," said Patrick, glancing at her thin black short dress."

"'Zis is Chanel," she huffed.

The sound engineer raised his eyebrows at Patrick.

"You're next, Claudine."

Claudine patted her hair and walked off, a fixed false smile plastered on her face.

"That's a nice shirt you're wearing," said the makeup girl to Patrick as she wafted some powder over his face.

"'Zis is Oxfam," he said and winked.

Back in the house, Maurice was admiring Mercedes and Ryan's bedroom. "Isn't this tasteful? Gosh! Mercedes should be an interior designer," he gushed. "Oh what are these," he asked, putting on a pair of maroon framed glasses so he could see more clearly. "Oh, they're awards for races and look at all these rosettes!"

Downstairs, Patrick stared frostily at Claudine and chomped a handful of almonds. Mercedes whisked about the kitchen, ensuring her first course was ready. She managed to navigate around the kitchen in her chair, avoiding the wires and the people invading her home.

"Do you need me to 'elp you carry in zee food? Eet must be difficult for you," asked Claudine, earning herself a frosty look from Maurice.

"No, I'm perfectly able to serve, thanks, Claudine," replied Mercedes, arriving with a tray containing bowls of hot soup on her lap.

"How lovely," said Maurice. "My friend Hassan would love this. The room is perfect. Looks just like the tent I stayed in when I went to the Sahara desert. It was so romantic there. We stayed outside a little town called Zagora. It's near the sand dunes. We sat out in a courtyard and took in the silence. It was warm that night so we sat up late. The sky was so clear you could see gazillions of stars." He took in a deep breath and sighed in contentment. "So beautiful," he continued with another little sigh before changing the subject. "Now then, Mercedes, you know all about us, but we don't know much about you. How did you get into hospital radio?" asked Maurice.

"This is quite a long story. I'll try to condense it for you and before I begin, I'm not into sympathy. I'm perfectly comfortable talking about this and I think it might even have happened for a reason.

"I used to be a jockey. I always loved horses and worked at stables all my young life. I was obsessed with them. I was lucky enough to work for a trainer who saw my potential and I started racing competitively at the age of eighteen. I enrolled at the British Racing School in Newmarket, graduated in 2007, then started training horses for a Sheik.

"They used to call me Little Horse-Whisperer, because I could always get the best out of the horses. I began to race, won a few events, and made a decent name for myself. Anyway, one day, I was out training a highly-strung horse. No one else could handle him as well as me. To cut a long story short, he got spooked and reared. We

83

both tumbled. He landed on me. Luckily, he was fine, but I wasn't.

"Ironic isn't it? I'm called Mercedes like the car brand and now I roll about on wheels. Not as fast as a real Merc though, even though I like to get up speed sometimes." She smiled. "I damaged my spinal cord at lumbar one-two. The doctors decided I'd never be able to walk again. I became a paraplegic. I have to admit it was a very low point in my life. It took several months of therapy to convince me I could carry on with my life in spite of losing the use of my legs. I was at City Hospital to have some follow-up work done on my elbow because it also got damaged in the accident, when I met a radio presenter there called Charlie. She was visiting patients, asking if they wanted any special requests played on the radio. It was after visiting hours and I was having a little weep. She sat beside my bed and talked to me for ages. She visited me every day after that, in fact the entire time I was in hospital.

"After I left hospital, she visited me regularly at home and thanks to her, I pulled myself together. She made me see that my life wasn't over. I decided to behave as normally as possible. I could still do many of the same things I could do before the accident. I bought an adapted van with hand controls. Charlie came with me to choose it. I even have her to thank for finding my husband, Ryan. She invited us both to an evening at her house where he and I gelled. I'd never have met Ryan if it hadn't been for Charlie and I wouldn't have met Charlie if it hadn't been for the accident.

"Anyway, I trained to become a radio technician, got married and am now living happy ever after. It's very rewarding working in a hospital, and humbling too. It puts things into perspective when you see what some people have to go through. Sorry, I really monopolised the conversation there, didn't I?"

Maurice wiped his eyes with the corner of a napkin.

"Maurice," growled Mercedes. "I hope you're not getting maudlin."

"No, no. It's just ... you're so brave."

"Rubbish. There are plenty of people who face far worse than me. It's surprising how you can learn to cope. Anyway, enough of that. Let's finish this wine."

The wine flowed, the conversation grew more animated, and Maurice enchanted them with stories about his time as a teacher in Marrakesh.

"You received a live guinea fowl as a gift from a pupil?"

"Oh yes, they gave me all sorts of gifts. I had to stop them in the end. It was getting awfully difficult. The guinea fowl in particular caused mayhem. I had to take it back to my apartment on the back of my moped. It sat in a box with its head poking out, watching the world go by as I skidded about the streets."

Mercedes spluttered her wine. "Never!" she said.

"It's completely true, my dear. I intended to give it to my flatmate to cook, but by the time I'd got home, I hadn't got the heart to kill the poor creature. We'd formed a bond, you see. I drove it to the nearest park and gave it its freedom. I hope it found a mate there," he added, smiling.

"Was that the most bizarre present you received?" asked Patrick.

"No. I had others. You have to remember that these people lived in all sorts of areas. They didn't have much money, so much of what they gave me, they had grown or cultivated or farmed." He gave Patrick a knowing look. Patrick twigged immediately.

"You mean you were offered cocaine?"

Maurice nodded. "Several times. I refused it, of course. It was then I decided to stop the pupils lavishing gifts on me. I told them the other teachers were getting jealous. It seemed to work, although the following day, I noticed a female teacher headed from her classroom clutching a live wriggling rabbit. I highly suspect one of the pupils had taken my message to heart and decided to spread their generosity."

The meal was devoured. Mercedes cleared the plates away and returned with small glasses for the mint tea and a silver lamp.

"Patrick, would you like to rub my magic lamp and make a wish?"

Patrick laughed, rubbing the lamp with vigour. Mercedes clapped her hands and said, "Magic lamp, silver not blue, please make Patrick's wish come true."

Immediately, Arabian music came from the kitchen. The guests sat in confusion until a belly dancer dressed in a deep-red fringed bra and matching harem pants emerged from the kitchen. A heavy veil hid most of her face, revealing only her large green eyes, made larger by dark eyeliner and black mascara. Her fluid movements were accentuated by the belt around her hips, heavily decorated with coins. Patrick's mouth opened in surprise. Maurice was transfixed by the belt and the hips that swung in his direction in time to the beat of the music. Claudine feigned delight and clapped her hands to accompany the dancing.

Charlie gave it all she had. She pretended she was in the class with the girls and not in front of a live audience. She created seductive movements with her hands, and enchanted with her rhythmical movements. The music transported her back to the studio and all too soon, it was over. The guests applauded. Charlie bowed and backed off to the kitchen again.

"Ah, that's your wish over, Patrick," said Mercedes. "Sorry, you don't get a second one," she said with a wink and poured the mint tea.

At the back door, Charlie grabbed the trainers she'd left on the mat and hastened out before any of the crew could talk to her. She raced over the grass in bare feet, through the open gate and onto the street where she immediately crashed into a man walking down the dimly lit road. Her belt came undone and fell onto the ground with a clatter.

"What on earth?" the man exclaimed.

Charlie took in a sharp breath. It was the Piggy man. He stood with an astonished expression on his face. Charlie drew her veil around her face. "As-Salamu Alaykum," she mumbled, using the only Moroccan expression she had ever heard. Then, grabbing her coin belt from the ground, she hastened to her Golf, leapt in, and drove off at speed.

The phone rang shortly after Charlie returned home. She knew who it would be. She heard excited barking in the background. Bentley and Ryan were back from their exile. They had been banned during the filming. Bentley had attempted to chew the cables and had urinated over the sound engineer's foot.

"Well?" she asked.

There was a pause and then a high-pitched squeal.

"I won! Oh Charlie, I won! I can't thank you enough. It was such a laugh and thanks to your challenge, I met Fatima, I've got a fat, content husband who enjoys my cooking, I now love cooking and we've just won one thousand pounds. Can you hear them?" She rustled the notes. "I think your belly dance clinched it. You should have seen Patrick afterwards. He couldn't speak properly. I think he'll dream of you tonight, or he'll get his wife Gloria to take up belly dancing. Maurice was very sweet. He invited me and Ryan to go and have dinner with him and Hassan next month, when Hassan comes over from Morocco. Even Claudine congratulated me and asked for the recipes. Oh Charlie, what a hoot! I can't tell you how much I enjoyed it. When I read it on your list I felt truly daunted by the prospect. After all, I've never been what you'd call a foodie or a cook. I existed on a diet of chocolate and Pot Noodles until I met Ryan. But now I feel liberated. It isn't difficult to cook and it isn't hard to cook exotic meals. It's been huge fun. Now, you have to take on your next challenge."

"Go on, what is it?"

"You'll find out tomorrow. Sam is going to announce it on his show. Then you must come back home with me and celebrate. I owe you a glass of mint tea at the very least."

"That was Fat Larry's band and a particular favourite of mine *Zoom*. Actually, that's quite an appropriate track for one member of our team. "I have in front of me a pre-challenge for Charlie, just to get her limbered up, so to speak, for the main event. Mercedes wants Charlie to go to Alton Towers with her this weekend to go on *Oblivion*, one of the scariest rides there. She has to perform one extra task that should raise a smile as she plunges down the one hundred and eighty foot drop. I'll tell you more about that later. *Oblivion* was the first vertical drop roller coaster in the UK and the ride can reach a maximum speed of sixty-eight miles per hour. It's the UK's third fastest roller coaster. I'm sure our timid Charlie will enjoy the thrill.

"Mercedes tells me this is just a taster to prepare her for what is to come. Well, we're intrigued, aren't we? Knowing Mercedes, there'll be some excitement and fun ahead. So, here's another track, just for you, Charlie—another appropriate one, *Crazy* by Gnarls Barkley."

Charlie groaned. She hated heights. Mercedes knew she hated heights. She couldn't even go up a ladder without feeling dizzy. There was no way she would be able to go on the wretched roller coaster without throwing up. On cue, her phone rang.

"I have tickets and we'll be going on Saturday. I'll pick you up at seven a.m."

"Mercedes, I can't ..."

"No such word as can't, as you proved to me when I moped about feeling sorry for myself. Come on. It'll be fun. I've always wanted to go on a vertical roller coaster and this one looks humungous fun. You can enjoy it for me. You'll be fine once you're on it. Remember your promise? Trust me?"

Browbeaten, Charlie agreed. If Mercedes could be brave about her injury and still have a normal existence, then Charlie could manage a roller coaster ride, couldn't she? She stood up to leave and bumped into a young nurse as she left the staffroom.

"Just heard the show, Charlie. Good on you. I went to Alton Towers a couple of years ago with my boyfriend. I couldn't get on *Oblivion* or *Air*. I was too petrified. It looked proper scary. I'll be cheering you on. I wonder what Mercedes has lined up for you after the roller coaster."

That was the very same thought going through Charlie's mind and, knowing her friend, she had a feeling it would be something far more challenging than a roller coaster ride.

The queue of youngsters and couples was far longer than she had expected. There was an air of expectation and joking as they teased each other about the ride. Mercedes had ensured they arrived early and now Charlie found herself near the front of the queue. Mercedes was below on the viewing platform.

"It only lasts just over a minute," she told Charlie on the way to the amusement park. "Bet you'll want to do it again."

Charlie wasn't so sure. Dropping down a sharp drop on a roller coaster was about as miserable a challenge as she could anticipate. A group of eighteen to twenty-year-olds were behind her. A tall blond girl dressed in jeans and a smart hooded cream jacket was part of the group. She looked a little like Amy. She had similar cobalt blue eyes and that same spirit of adventure and confidence. The girl caught her glance and smiled back. Yes, she definitely reminded Charlie of an older version of Amy.

They snaked upwards in a straggling line through a large drawn-out helix, crossing buildings and structures. The build up to the ride was clever. Video screens were displayed above them. On each, a sinister man gave the group briefings and hinted at how terrifying the ride was going to be. Amy would now be egging her mum on and giggling. Thoughts of Amy being there prevented her from bolting. It would be difficult to run anyway, sandwiched as she now was in a crowd of excitable people.

Gavin always teased her, saying she was a scaredy-cat. When Amy was ten, they travelled to Paris. It was Gavin who went on the more adventurous rides at Euro Disney with her, laughing crazily as they raced off on the big *Thunder Mountain*, waving at Charlie as they flew high on the *Dumbo* and screaming together in glee on the *Tower of Terror*. Charlie had preferred the more sedate experiences like the gentle *It's a Small World* where they rode on boats through a magical animated world filled with music and colour.

Amy was more like her father, in terms of her character. She was always up for fun or adventure. As a young child, she was fearless, begging Gavin to throw her in the air when she was a toddler, then asking for Charlie to push her higher on the swings in the park.

Amy would have enjoyed this trip. She would certainly have loved this ride and all the build-up to it.

The group of visitors crossed a metal bridge onto an elevated station building where they were put into rows to board the ride cars. Charlie suddenly found herself being pushed towards the front row of the *Oblivion* .

A man in a brown leather jacket and jeans slipped into the seat beside her. A young boy took the position next to him. He looked up at the man and grinned cheekily.

"You okay, Dad? You look a bit white," he chatted.

His father patted him on the head. "I'm fine. Of course, I'm worried you'll scream and I'll have to hold your hand."

The boy laughed and waved his mobile phone at him. "I'm going to take a selfie. You wanna be in it?"

"I'll pass this time," replied the man. "I'm sure your mates at school won't want to see a photo of your old man on a roller coaster. I can't believe you talked me into coming here."

"You said we could do anything I wanted. This is it!"

"I hoped you wanted to go to McDonalds or the zoo."

"Zoo? I'm thirteen! Not five!"

The man turned and glanced at Charlie who was fumbling with her seatbelt which wouldn't buckle up, thanks to her shaking hands. He leant across and snapped it into place.

"Don't worry," whispered the stranger. "Don't tell Toby, but I'm nervous too. I'm only doing this because he begged me to. It's a belated birthday treat."

Charlie sat dumbstruck. This was the Piggy man. Did he recognise her? She held her breath for a minute. The man barely looked at her. Instead, he turned away to talk to his son. Thank heavens. She was unsure if he was telling the truth about being nervous, but was grateful anyway. The man turned back.

"You're not following me by any chance, are you?" he asked quietly so his son could not hear.

"No, I'm not. I could ask you the same question," spluttered Charlie.

"Must be karma then," he answered. "Nice to see you again," he added with a wide smile.

"Happy belated birthday," she called out to Toby.

"Thanks. It was last week, but I was at school and couldn't get a pass out 'cos it was a weekday." He took a photo of the crowd below.

"I see you've dressed more appropriately today," the man whispered. "Pity."

"Be glad I'm dressed. I hate to think what happens to harem pants on roller coasters."

He guffawed.

Toby used his mobile phone to take photographs of himself on the ride. Behind them, a group of teenagers joked as they settled into the seats and waited for the ride to start.

"Don't you puke on me, Gaz."

"As if. But if you want to keep your eyes shut, feel free."

They were soon ready to depart. The sinister voice on a video screen announced some doom-laden message intended to terrify the passengers. Charlie was too nervous to listen to it. Large yellow cage-like belts were automatically lowered, holding the passengers down in their seats and Charlie just had time to check her seatbelt again before the creaking and groaning of steal chains announced they were being lifted upwards.

"Isn't this bril'?" said the young man behind them. "I read about a girl whose seatbelt broke on this ride. Imagine that. That would be well cool. Extra scary!"

"Shut up, Gaz, or I'll twat you," one of the girls said.

"Just sayin'. My bad? Anyone here seen *Final Destination 3*? I just had a premonition that the car would break off and fall over the ... ow!"

"I told you to *shut up*," said the girl. Gaz rubbed his head.

Charlie clutched at her seatbelt to ascertain it was still attached. The cars had almost reached the top and were levelling out. From here, she could see the towers of Alton Towers Hall. *Not too bad, so far,* she thought. Then she remembered the challenge.

"Um, excuse me," she mumbled to the man, "I have to do something silly now. It's for a challenge. I'm not mad or anything."

He looked back at her and waggled his eyebrows in feigned surprise. She didn't care. She was getting used to being caught in stupid situations by him.

"Nothing you do would surprise me," he said and winked.

She unbuttoned the top pocket on her jacket and pulled out a plastic blue kazoo.

"Any requests?" she asked.

92

"*Who's Afraid of the Big Bad Wolf* or what about *If I Could talk to the Animals,*" he replied with a chuckle. She smiled back at him, shook her head in mock irritation, and began playing. She held the kazoo tightly. She did not want to choke on it.

His son looked over at the sound. "Hey, I know that song. It's by the Red Hot Chilli Peppers. It was in the *Beavis and Butthead* movie."

She nodded and continued playing *Love Rollercoaster.* The boy laughed and hummed in time to her playing.

The ride car stopped at the end of the track. Charlie saw nothing but open space under her and ahead of her. They were suspended in midair. The car hung for a few seconds. She was going to fall from the sky. Her eyes widened. She concentrated on the kazoo to prevent the panic from rising any further. She heard the man next to her whistling the tune. Behind her, the teenagers joined in singing the lyrics and as the car plunged into the dark hole of *Oblivion,* Charlie could hear her kazoo parping out the tune and a chorus of voices accompanying it.

"Wow! Awesome," said one of the girls as the cars returned to the platform and the passengers disembarked. "We'll have to try that again, next ride."

"Cool!" said Toby. "Can you play any other songs by the Red Hot Chilli Peppers?"

"Thanks. No, sorry. That's the only one that works well on a kazoo. I mostly do themes to old television shows or *Star Wars.* Kazoos feature on quite a few songs, though. It's a kazoo you can hear in the chorus of *Love Rollercoaster,* too. Kazoos have been used on quite a few famous tracks like Jimi Hendrix's *Crosstown Traffic,* at the end of Dionne Warwick's *This Girl's in Love With You,* and Pink Floyd's *Jug and Blues.* Guess you haven't heard of them though," she added. Toby shook his head.

"No, but I have, and I used to be a huge Pink Floyd fan," said his father, smiling. "And *Jug and Blues* was the last track to feature Syd Barrett as a member of the band," he added wistfully. "Well, well. So you are into music? Me too. I've got a stack of old vinyls I refuse to throw away by bands from that era. Much to Toby's dismay. He believes I'm a stuffy old dinosaur. I have all Pink Floyd's stuff. In fact, as I recall, Pink Floyd did a song about pigs and of course, were famous for using inflatable flying pigs," he continued and grinned at Charlie. She refused to rise to the bait. He shrugged.

"I'm into all sorts of music, especially eighties and seventies stuff."

The man helped her out of her seat while his son meandered ahead, chatting to the teenagers from their ride.

"Thanks," he said. She noticed he was nice-looking. He sported a slight designer stubble. He reminded her a little of Gavin. She liked it when he allowed his perfectly shaven face to grow a little stubble. It made him look sexier. She liked the feel of it as it rubbed her face when they kissed.

"For what?" she asked holding on to the rail. Her legs were being uncooperative.

"For making me feel younger again. It was Toby's idea to come out today and I had my reservations, but I felt twenty years younger on that ride. It was mostly down to you. Maybe I should buy a kazoo."

"Here, take mine. It's magical. When you blow it, you are transformed into a ten-year-old," she said, handing over the toy instrument with a shaking hand.

"Are you okay?"

"Just a little weak-kneed. The ride wasn't my idea, as you might have guessed. I'm not fond of roller coasters. My friend put me up to it. It's a long story, but I am trying out new adventures and challenges on her behalf."

He held out his arm to her. "One good turn deserves another."

She took it, grateful to have his support as they returned to the ride's entrance. They chatted about music and bands they had both seen in concert over the years. She no longer needed his arm, but kept hold of it, comfortable to be with him and enjoying the animated conversation as they discovered a mutual taste in music. She released him with some reluctance.

"Thank you. I feel much better now. One roller coaster ride is enough for me, though. I'll try the teacups next."

"Been a pleasure. I'm Jake, by the way, Jake Meredith," he added.

"Charlie Blundell." She felt a slight flutter in her stomach. There was definitely an attraction there. She wondered if he felt the same.

"We keep meeting under odd circumstances, don't we?" he began, looking deep into her eyes. "So far, I've discovered you've got a spirit of adventure when it comes to food and a head for disgusting drinks. You're also a farmyard animal impersonator, a master kazoo player and an exotic dancer. What else do you get involved in?"

94

"Nothing else extraordinary. You've seen my mad side. The rest of my life is pretty dull."

"Somehow I don't believe that," he said. He looked at her, head cocked onto one side as if he wanted to say something. She had the crazy notion he was going to ask her out.

At that moment, Toby appeared and pulled at Jake's sleeve. "Dad, Abigail's here. She made it, after all." He said, pointing out an elegant young woman dressed in tight grey jeans and a stylish red jacket. Her hair hung like a glossy brown curtain.

"Abigail!" called the boy and raced off towards her. She enveloped him in her arms, then looked over at the man and blew a kiss at him. He waved at her.

"Well, this is where I have to leave you. Are you all right now?"

"Yes, fine, thanks. I hope you and Toby enjoy the rest of the day," she replied somewhat deflated. She recognised the woman. She was the woman who had been in the café with him. The woman with red-soled shoes. He was spoken for. Of course he was. Good-looking single men don't generally materialise like that, only in romance stories.

"Hum into your kazoo if you need a laugh," she added. He smiled, slipped the kazoo into his jacket pocket, and then left her. She headed off to find Mercedes, willing herself to not turn back and look at him one more time. Her legs were still rubbery when she returned to where she had left Mercedes.

"Well done! You're officially no longer a scaredy-cat. So, did you enjoy it?"

"In a way, yes. I almost didn't though. The kazoo helped."

"I thought it would take your mind off the drop, although I think you had other distractions," she said in a knowing tone.

"Funny lady! The kazoo helped me more. He just stopped me from falling over when we got off the ride."

"Of course. He'd be welcome to pick me up any time I fell over. Now, do you fancy a go on *Wobble World* with the tiny tots or would you like to go on this again?"

Charlie was tired when she returned home. It had been a good day. They had explored the rest of the park and enjoyed the other more genteel attractions together. They'd visited the *Haunted Hollow* and had a raucous time at the *Ice Age 4D* experience. She didn't see Jake, Toby or the stunning woman. Alton Towers was vast and it had taken a while to navigate around the park and take it all in.

She felt she had done something important. Although that seemed silly, part of her rejoiced that she had experienced the roller coaster ride. She couldn't quite put her finger on the feeling, but it was akin to feeling braver. She had made a positive step. Riding on the roller coaster playing a kazoo, at her age, had released some inner tension. It had brought out a more youthful side. Amy would have laughed herself senseless if she could have seen her mother at the park. And, of course, Jake had been there. She had enjoyed his attention. She wondered idly if Jake had thrown the plastic kazoo away or kept it. She rather hoped he still had it, then brushed all thoughts of him away. He had an attractive woman in tow and she had no idea how to contact him. Chances of seeing him again were zero, whereas the text she had received from Rob from Thailand left nothing to the imagination:

Hey Charlie. Loved talking to you at the New Year's party. I'll be back in the UK in a few weeks. Fancy picking up where we left off?

He wasn't one to mince words and, as far as she could remember, he had been good company. There would be nothing serious in any relationship with him and it had been a very long time since she had been with a man. The belly dancing lessons, along with her refreshed attitude, had awoken the woman in her. She hesitated, and then, fuelled by the achievement of the day, replied to the text:

Hi Rob. Text me when you get back and we'll meet up. X

Before she could change her mind, she hit the send button. *What the heck*, she thought, it was about time she started enjoying herself again.

There was nothing she wanted to watch on television so she settled down in front of her computer to plan her show for the next day. Her show centred on the principal that light-hearted fun would be a welcome relief for the patients in the hospital. She also believed laughter helped promote healing. On that basis, she spent hours collecting jokes from various online sites and forums, but it was always worth it.

The film *Patch Adams* had given her the idea to try and bring humour into the patients' lives. It was now her mission to make every show as enjoyable as possible. Part of her wondered if Amy had been able to listen to a cheerful voice and lively music, it might have helped her come out of the coma.

She visited the patients on the wards during the week and collected requests from them or their relatives. She often received emails too, requesting songs or asking for good wishes to be sent to people. It was so important to lift people's spirits especially when they were in hospital and worried or frightened about surgery or illness.

She clicked on the hospital website to get her emails and was surprised to see a link called "Charlie's Challenge" to a video on YouTube. She clicked on it and watched a video obviously taken by someone watching the *Oblivion* ride from the ground. It showed the cars groaning up the track from below, revealing the steel girders and structure of the ride. A kazoo was playing *Love Rollercoaster*. The picture switched to show the car sitting at the top of the ride, looking as if it would fall off the structure at any given moment. Next, it showed the people on the ride. Some in the back car had their arms up as if doing a Mexican wave. The kazoo was now being drowned out by loud singing. The camera panned across some of the faces of the teenagers at the back of the car who gave thumbs up, then along the front row where she recognised Jake whistling and herself playing the kazoo, white-faced, but with enthusiasm. The camera then followed the rapid descent of the car as it fell into the black hole of *Oblivion* to a loud chorus of "... baby I wanna ride, yeah ... " The video finished with the car emerging from the tunnel where it twisted and turned on the track accompanied by more whistling and whoops of joy and the unmistakable sound of a kazoo.

Charlie sat in astonishment. Who had taken the video? More importantly, why had it already attracted six hundred views?

The following day, she was greeted effusively by the small team at City Hospital Radio as she walked into the staff meeting.

"See you've created a video star," Sam remarked to Mercedes. "You might have started something with this challenge, Charlie."

"It was supposed to help her gain some confidence and try to inject some excitement into her life. Looks like I might have to alter the goalposts a little now," replied Mercedes.

"Oh no, I know that look. You are clearly up to mischief. How does that husband of yours cope with you? I bet you wind him up all the time."

"No, he always makes me behave. It's his detective skills, you see. I'm powerless once he interrogates me," laughed Mercedes.

"Ah, the lady of the moment. Can I have your autograph please, Charlie? Will you remember us little people when you are a mega important film star or TV presenter?" asked Vernon Toy, another of the presenters, as he came into the room and spied Charlie.

Charlie tapped him over the head with her rolled-up notes. "Idiot. It was a roller coaster ride. That's all."

"Ah! But what next? That's what we want to know. What will you be up to next?"

Sean came into the studio, trailed by a couple of other radio volunteers.

"So, Sean, where did the video come from?" asked Mercedes.

"I thought you'd sent it," replied Sean.

"No, I didn't take it. If I'd taken it, it would have mostly been footage of people's backs from where I was positioned."

"Oh, that's odd. I received a link to the video through the hospital website. There was no email address. It just said 'For the attention of City Hospital Radio'. I thought you sent it to me to upload it onto the site. I put the link up last night and managed to load the actual video from YouTube onto our site this morning. It's attracting a fair amount of attention."

"One thousand hits when I looked," said Vivienne, another technician who also worked part-time on reception at the hospital. "Anyone know why we're here?"

"Meeting," mumbled Sean.

"Twit! I know we're here for a meeting. Any ideas what it is about?"

"No. I thought it was about programme schedules and the like. Maybe they're going to let us have a wide screen telly in the studio with a live link to Sky. I think they've got one like that at Winchester."

"Fat chance. We're on a tight budget here,"

Another presenter wandered in, clutching cups of takeaway coffee, followed by a couple of hospital officials.

"Good afternoon, everyone," said a pale-faced balding man. His hospital nametag, Mr. A. Carnegie was on upside down. Thank you for taking the time to come here for the meeting. I could have emailed you all, given you have other jobs and commitments, but I wanted to talk to you about this face-to-face because I know how special City Hospital Radio is to you all." Charlie felt a familiar sinking feeling in the pit of her stomach. There was bad news. She could tell by the look on Andrew Carnegie's face.

"It's a hard task each year raising the running costs on the radio station. Last year's fundraising events: the dinner dance, the charity stall at the local market, annual grand draw, and charity coach outings brought in one thousand, seven hundred and forty-five pounds. We received support for the service from local businesses, local trust funds, and members of the public who all contributed in their own way, taking the total up to three thousand, two hundred pounds which was barely enough to see us through the year.

I've been in discussions with the board and although we believe that City Hospital Radio is a valuable asset to the community here, and you all work tirelessly and give generously of your free time, we're not going to be able to keep it running unless we find significant funding."

There were gasps all around the studio. Charlie felt ill.

"The equipment is, as you realise, too old and in spite of the efforts of this superb team, and we're all very proud of you, we're not going to be able to maintain it for much longer. On top of that, there are plans to revamp the current studio and use it to house vital medical equipment. The hospital is very tight on space and can't afford to have us taking up valuable room. They say we can erect a structure in the car park of the hospital and use that, but again, that'll cost a large amount to set up and equip. We examined costs for running the radio. I'd like to share them with you to give you an idea of what we are up against. Sarah, can you run down the list of costs, please, for these good people?"

His assistant coughed, then read out, "Ink toner for the printer fifty pounds, six months rental of phone line one hundred pounds, annual subscription to Sky for news bulletins and interviews three hundred pounds, annual internet access and infrastructure six hundred pounds, annual music copyright fees one thousand pounds, annual insurance one thousand, six hundred pounds, and new mixing deck seven thousand, five hundred pounds."

"Thank you, Sarah. In addition to that list, we not only need funds to relocate the studio, and we've had two quotes in for that, but we require funds for upkeep of the system in the hospital. We are behind the times compared to some hospitals. Really we should be offering a more modern Wi-Fi system, but as you know, some wards still have the old bed-head units above the beds and they each cost approximately seventy pounds to replace.

So, it is with a heavy heart that I have to say the prognosis for our little station is not looking too good. If anyone has any ideas of how we can resolve this, or any other fundraising ideas, or a rich relative," he paused but no laughs came. "Please let me know. Sorry to bring you bad news. Let's hope we can turn it around and keep going."

He waited for any comments. Silence hung in the air. Mercedes looked shell-shocked. Sam put an arm around Vivienne who was suddenly tearful. Charlie stood dumbfounded. She couldn't let City Radio go off air. She would fight with every breath left in her to keep it going. The patients needed the station, the community needed it, and she and the team here needed it. She thought about the video hits on the website, took a deep breath and said, "Excuse me, Andrew, I might have an idea to raise some funds."

"Are you sure about this?" asked Andrew Carnegie, after Charlie voiced her idea.

"It's a fabulous idea," said Sam. "Charlie, it's brilliant!"

"I can organise it all," squeaked Mercedes. "I've got some wicked ideas."

"Not too wicked, I hope," smiled Charlie.

"So, the plan is to sponsor Charlie to do outrageous challenges. She'll take someone of the team with her to video the event. Sean will upload the films onto YouTube and onto our website. We'll collect money, as and when she completes each challenge. We'll also turn it into a sort of competition and get the public to choose challenges too. We'll pull one out of a hat each time and Charlie has to complete it. Sounds great. Any ideas for Charlie's first challenge?"

"I know what that should be," said Mercedes. "I've already prepared her for it."

"Okay, what do you suggest?"

"Ta-dah!" said Mercedes, pulling out a leaflet from her pocket.

"Oh no! Mercedes you frightful fiend. You are going to be testing me to my limits," groaned Charlie.

"Throw someone you love off a cliff?" read Andrew. "UK's maddest zip wire. Four hundred and ninety metres long, fifty metres high and reaching speeds of forty miles per hour. Twin parallel wires cross the flooded depths of the old quarry, sheer cliffs rise on either side. Sounds ideal. Sarah, could you please get a press release ready? We'll send you in four weeks' time, Charlie. That'll give us a chance to promote it and get some sponsors. If you could all tell everyone you know, we'll see how this goes. Well done, everyone. Well done, Charlie."

The four weeks went by in a flash. Charlie tried hard not to think too much about the challenge ahead, but it was difficult given everyone in the hospital kept mentioning it. Patricia designed small posters about the challenge. She and Art put them up all over the town and plastered them on the door to the café.

The hospital presenters promoted the event with gusto. Sam spent every afternoon going around all the wards and standing outside the hospital with a bucket, asking people to give generously for the challenge.

"So, if any of you want to issue Charlie with a challenge, write it out on one of our request forms and put it in the large wooden box at reception marked City Radio. You could win the chance to accompany Charlie and have your photo taken with her if she completes the challenge. If Charlie doesn't complete your challenge, we'll treat you and a partner to a slap-up meal at the Zagora restaurant thanks to Fatima. Let your imagination run wild. The wackier, the better. We'll be watching on Saturday to see if Charlie can overcome her fear of heights and slide down the UK's largest zip wire.

Right. Without further ado, let's get onto today's Challenge Charlie track, which is Westlife's *Flying Without Wings*," said Sam, turning up the volume and sitting back in the chair. It creaked. He poured a cup of coffee from his thermos and tore off the end of his corned beef sandwich. He'd be lost without City Hospital Radio. He hoped fervently that Charlie's idea would work. He'd been at the station for ten years. He told everyone he preferred working there to watching soap operas with his wife, but the truth was that he hated being at home. Brenda was always wrapped up with the grandkids, or her book club. She had so many hobbies and friends, whereas all he had was his music, and City. He didn't want to even think about what would happen if it finished. He was sixty-five years old, retired and lonely. City Radio was his life. He drained his cup and put his headphones back on. He hoped Charlie was up to it and silently wished her well.

At the quarry, Mercedes was talking to the girl at the ticket desk while Charlie chewed her fingernails.

"We've been expecting you. Charlie, isn't it? As agreed on the phone, we've arranged for you to do the wire for free. It's for a good cause, isn't it? I've never spent time in hospital but my sister did. I don't know if there was a radio there. She was only in for a day. Are you going with her?" she asked Mercedes.

Mercedes gave her an incredulous look, "I hardly think so. Not in this," she said pointing at her wheelchair. "I'm here to offer moral support and Sean here is here to video the event."

"Oh sorry, I didn't mean to offend. It's just that we have people with disabilities doing the wire. We have all ages here, too. Our youngest was four years old and the oldest ninety-four. There's no excuses," she grinned. "I've done it loads of times."

Mercedes thought for a couple of moments, then replied in a resigned tone, "No, thanks. I'll leave it to Charlie. I don't want to steal her thunder. She's the one sponsored to do the challenge, not me."

There was a queue of people at the quarry waiting to climb the wooden structure and soar over the river below. Sean extracted a video camera from his backpack.

"Hey, that looks professional," joked Charlie.

"Nicked it from my dad. He's had it for ages and doesn't use it. Thought it'd be useful today. Okay, give me a smile and a wave."

Charlie looked into the camera and smiled weakly. She glanced up at the tall structure. Her stomach flipped. Mercedes was in a downbeat mood. Charlie knew why. This was one challenge Mercedes would relish. It had been on her list, after all. Charlie could see the longing in her face. She would love to tackle this activity. She would appreciate the buzz it would give her far more than Charlie and more importantly, it would fulfil that hunger she had to keep proving herself. Charlie was constantly amazed at how Mercedes dealt with her disability. She had her off days, but that was understandable. Charlie knew that Mercedes missed her old life. She had lived a thrilling life up until the accident. Since then, she had succeeded in learning all sorts of skills and ways to have a normal life, but opportunities like this were rare. Charlie decided to give her an excuse to do it.

"Mercedes, I really want to do it, but I can't," Charlie whispered. "I'm getting the shakes badly. I don't think I'm up to it. I feel nauseous." She held onto a wooden railing, looking wide-eyed at Mercedes. "I might be okay if someone comes with me."

Mercedes gave her a quizzical look. Charlie kept up her act. "I can't do this on my own. It's one thing going on a roller coaster, but this is a different matter. I think I'm going to be sick," she turned her head and pretended to gag.

"It'll be okay, Charlie," said Mercedes, taken in by the performance and concerned about her friend. "You heard what the girl at the ticket desk said, I can come down the wire. There are parallel wires, so I could arrange to go down the one parallel to yours. We'll go together," she continued, her face lighting up at the prospect.

"I'd feel safer if you were there with me. Would you? Would you mind?" asked Charlie, still holding onto the rail, thinking she ought to take up acting.

"Of course not. Sean, stay with her while I arrange it."

Charlie pretended to be unsure.

"Come on Charlie, it'll be great. We'll do it in tandem. Nearly forgot. I brought this along for you." She pulled out a plastic pink kazoo. "We've had quite a few emails about you and the kazoo, so we thought we'd continue the theme. You can play something appropriate up there. Have a practice while I organise it. You can entertain Sean with your repertoire of seventies television theme tunes and try to calm down while I'm sorting it with the staff." Charlie saw the excitement in her friend's eyes. Mercedes needed to do this. She would love to experience the adrenaline rush and do something that able-bodied people could do.

Charlie felt a rush of warmth for her friend and grasped Mercedes's hand. "Okay, take your time. We'll wait for you and then we'll go together."

The staff at the quarry were very accommodating and made arrangements to get Mercedes up to the platform. Charlie and Sean moved up the huge structure to the platform above to join her and two young guys in yellow T-shirts. They were helping people into harnesses, attaching them to the zip wire and launching them off high above the flooded quarry.

From the platform, twin parallel wires crossed the flooded depths of the old quarry, sheer cliffs rose on either side. Charlie clung to the wooden surround. She was going dizzy.

"Okay, there?" asked one of the young men.

Charlie nodded.

Mercedes was being fitted with her harness.

"Come on Charlie, it's show time," she said in her best Jim Carrey voice. "Wave at the camera."

The young men ensured that both women were securely fastened.

"Here you go, Mercedes," said Sean as he fitted a headband around her hair. It held a small camera. "I'll film you from above and that camera will record as you both go down the wires. Have fun."

"If you could just step forward," said the young man to Charlie. They waited to hear that the people ahead had landed. There was a crackle from the walkie-talkie and a disembodied voice announced the way was clear.

Charlie couldn't think. It was so high. She felt slightly faint. She heard a noise. Mercedes was being launched down her wire. Charlie had no choice, she let herself fall forward too. She fell above treetops and hurtled down towards the water. Mercedes spun to face her and opened her arms out wide. Charlie felt free. She was flying. It was exhilarating. Mercedes continued to face her and waved her arms like an orchestra conductor. Charlie pushed the pink kazoo she had been clutching in her hand, into her mouth, and blasted out *Come Fly With Me*. She had little time to take in the scenery, the trees, the ducks, and other wild birds on the water below. It was all a blur. The air whistled past her ears. She felt euphoric. In no time at all, she began slowing down as she approached the landing site. She saw Mercedes being caught by the staff members on the other side of the river. Slowing further, Charlie arrived gracefully on terra firma where she was unhitched from her wire. She weaved her way to Mercedes, now back in her wheelchair.

"Oh my! That was seriously the best thing I have done in years," said Mercedes. "Can I do it again?"

There were no houselights on in the street when Charlie was dropped off back at her house. The euphoria she experienced had stayed with her the entire trip home. Mercedes had gone down the zip wire for a second time, this time with Sean. All three high on adrenaline, the drive back had been filled with laughs and songs. They had stopped at a pub on the way home and celebrated their success with a drink. They had phoned Sam to tell him Charlie had completed the challenge. He had been almost as excited about it as they were.

"I'll pass it on to the others," he'd said after cheering. "Sean, are you going to upload the video tonight?"

"Might be the morning now. I'm going to be pretty bushed by the time I get in. I'll make sure it's up before Charlie goes on air tomorrow afternoon."

"Catch you all tomorrow. Sleep well. And Charlie ... a few challenges came in for you today. How do you feel about wing walking?"

"You are kidding me?"

"Yep. Yes, I am. There is no wing walking challenge. There are a couple of other things though to make your eyes water. Speak to you tomorrow."

Charlie let herself in and waved goodbye to her friends. She suddenly felt deflated. It was just her again. Silence closed in on her. She snapped on the television for company and went to the kitchen to get a glass of water. It was clear and starry outside so she navigated by the light streaming into the kitchen window.

As the tap ran, she looked outside into her back garden. Her brain suddenly sharpened up. There was a movement in her garden under the large apple tree. She froze. There. She saw it again. She focused as hard as she could. She couldn't see anyone. It was her imagination. She was tired. There was no one out there. She took her water and went back into the lounge to settle in front of a late night game show. Outside, a figure dressed in black unfurled from the base of the apple tree and hurried away over her garden fence.

The Art café was almost full when she arrived the following morning. Sundays, it was open from ten o'clock until four o'clock. Charlie didn't normally drop by when she wasn't working there, but she woke up feeling discombobulated and didn't fancy a morning in by herself. The thrill of her achievement the day before was waning and she wanted some company.

"Hi Charlie," shouted Art from behind the counter. "You forgotten what day of the week it is?"

"Ha! You're so funny, Art," she replied, scooping a menu from the counter to read. "You should be a comedian."

"Leave the jokes to Charlie," said Patricia, bustling up to the counter, pad in hand. She kissed Charlie on the cheeks. "Well done. I'm so proud of you. That took guts to go down the wire. Have you found out how much money you raised yet?"

"No, it's still coming in. Vivienne is in charge of counting it up. I hope to get some idea later today. I get another challenge then, too. I came in for a quick bite to eat before the show."

"I recommend my sticky toffee pudding with custard. It's scrummy."

"Sorry, I can't eat that. It'll put inches on me and since the belly dancing I've managed to keep the weight down. I'll have a slice of carrot cake instead and a Peppermint tea, too, please when you've got time. Thanks. Patricia, do you need a hand?"

"No, I've got it covered. It'll die down soon. You go and sit down."

A couple vacated the window seats in the Quiet Room so Charlie settled down there with her notes for the afternoon show. Her phone vibrated. She pulled it out of her pocket and read the message:

I'm back on Wednesday. Fancy meeting up? Rob

With all the excitement of the challenges she'd forgotten about him.

How about after my radio show on Friday? I'll meet you at the hospital. X

You're on. See you at the main entrance at eight.

Patricia arrived with her tea and cake. "Someone looks happy," she commented. "I've just arranged my first date in years," replied

Charlie. "I feel all giddy now."

"That's terrific news," said Patricia. "Is it the guy that came in here yesterday, asking about you?"

"Er, no. Rob's not back in the UK yet. What did this guy look like?"

"Tall, good-looking. About forty years old. Stubble on face. Reminded me of that chap Matthew Fox from *Lost*."

"That's Jake. He's not a contender."

"He saw the poster about you in the window and asked what you were up to this time. He nearly spluttered coffee over his suit when I told him."

"He thinks I'm bonkers. Was he with a woman?"

"No. He was with a young boy. They spent some time in the shop looking at all the goods, then bought a beautiful anthracite necklace that Lucy, the young designer from Uttoxeter made. It was the first piece of jewellery I've sold of hers. She'll be so pleased when she finds out."

"I suppose they were buying it for Abigail."

"Who's Abigail?"

"Not sure. She's a stunner. She's either his girlfriend or wife. I don't think she's Toby's mum. She's far too young. Toby likes her though, judging by the hug he gave her at Alton Towers."

"Oh, never mind."

"I don't mind."

"Of course you don't," said Patricia with a knowing smile. "Better get on. Let us know about the next challenge and we'll do some more posters."

"I don't mind. I've got a date with Rob. I don't mind at all."

A couple of teenage girls, one slightly shorter than the other, both with shoulder-length curly black hair and dark eyes were hanging about the corridor near the studio. Charlie smiled at them.

"That's Charlie," said one, nudging the other. "Hi Charlie, we've brought some money for you. Our Nan is in the Florence Nightingale ward. She's been here for two weeks. She loves listening to the shows. You read out a request for her last week–Gladys Powell."

Charlie nodded. She remembered Gladys. She spoke non-stop about her twin granddaughters. Charlie remembered their names.

"You're Naomi and Iona," she said. The girls looked pleased.

"She told us all about you doing the belly dancing and the roller coaster ride."

"We saw you on YouTube," said the smaller of the two. "That was really funny."

"Nan asked us to say something about the challenges at school and we did. Mister Ingram, our head teacher made an announcement at school assembly. It's not much, but we hope it helps keep the radio station going. Nan has converted us all. We listen online at home. You're all good, but you're our favourite presenter."

The girl handed over a large plastic sweet tin. It was labelled *Charlie's Challenge*. Charlie removed the lid and gasped. It was full of five pound notes, pound coins and even a few ten pound notes. "This all came from schoolchildren?" she asked.

The girls nodded in unison. "And some of the teachers and parents," said the taller one.

"There's two hundred and eighty-two pounds," announced the smaller one.

"You must come into the studio and meet everyone so they can thank you."

They all tumbled into the studio where Sean was leaning back in his chair staring at a computer screen. "Afternoon, Charlie. Hi Ladies!" he continued, raising a hand of acknowledgement to the girls.

"Sean, this is Naomi and Iona. They're Gladys Powell's granddaughters. They've raised a lot of money for us. I thought they might like to meet some of the team."

"Sure. Look, George Hardman is on air for the next twenty minutes. Why don't the girls go in and say hello to him. They can even say hello to their grandma on air. That'll surprise her."

Naomi went pink. Iona giggled.

"Do you want to be on the radio and say hello to George?"

Naomi nodded. Iona giggled some more. George was the youngest of the presenters. At only eighteen, he was putting in a few hours a week at City Radio in preparation for a career in radio. He had an easy manner. Many a nurse had fallen for his winning smile.

"Sean, let George know after the next record and I'll take the girls in to meet him."

While the girls were chatting to George and telling the audience how they raised money for the radio, Sean had a chance to talk to Charlie.

"I uploaded the video to YouTube before I came in today. Take a look."

He clicked onto the site and pulled up the video. Charlie watched the events of the day before as seen through the eyes of the camera. The video only lasted a minute and fifty seconds, but it captured it perfectly. Mercedes's camera worked perfectly and Charlie relived the afternoon as she saw herself whizz down the zip wire and then play the pink plastic kazoo. She looked as cool as a cucumber and even managed to smile at the end of the trip while waving her kazoo at the camera. This wasn't the Charlie who sat at home watching old films in her tatty jeans. This wasn't the same woman who hated almost everything about herself. This Charlie radiated confidence and fun. She stared at the images again.

"That looks so professional," she mumbled. "I can't believe it's me. I look different."

"You knock yourself too much. That's how we see you, Charlie," Sean said, winked, and went back to the desk ready to cue in the news.

The girls left the studio, excited at having met George. "We're going to visit Nan now," said Naomi. "She'll be stoked that we mentioned her. See you again."

Charlie sat in the back room waiting for Mercedes to arrive and her slot to begin. Vivienne came in carrying an accounts book.

"Total so far, five hundred and sixty pounds, twenty pence," she said.

"Is that including the contribution made by the local school?" asked Charlie nodding at the jar Vivienne held in her other hand.

Vivienne nodded. "Yes. It's not a bad start."

"Somehow I expected it to capture people's imagination. I'd hoped for more than that. Guess I'm being greedy. People don't have lots of disposable income."

"It's very difficult to make people comprehend the importance of the radio station, Charlie. If you were raising money to help a small sick child or for a hospice, that would have greater appeal. The problem is that many people don't understand how a radio station can help people unless they've been in hospital and seen for themselves. It's particularly difficult when we're just one little station broadcasting to a small audience in an ocean of radio stations. Nowadays, there's so much choice for people, especially with internet radio. You did incredibly well to raise this amount. It took six months on the charity stall in the market to get a similar amount last year. Don't be deflated."

In spite of her words, Charlie felt depressed. Somewhat naïvely, she had hoped that her challenge idea would capture the town's imagination and she would be able to save the radio station by only doing a few challenges. She couldn't let it knock her though. She still had a show to present.

"Knock, knock," said Mercedes banging on the door. "Wazzup?"

"I didn't raise as much money as I wanted."

"Pfft! Is that it? That was only one challenge. Ah, my poor unsuspecting guinea pig. Wait until Sam's show. I have much more planned for you," said Mercedes giving her best evil laugh.

"Today's Sunny Sunday joke comes from eleven-year-old Tom Baker on Nicholas Ward. Thank you Tom. Tom's joke is: *Doctor Doctor: I'm addicted to Twitter. Sorry, I don't follow you.* Boom, boom! That made us all laugh in the studio. I hope you've enjoyed the show and you'll join me tomorrow night for more jokes."

Charlie shut off the microphone and picked up her handbag.

"Don't go just yet," said Sam. "I want to see your face when I read out the next challenge. Sit down opposite me and we'll do it live."

Charlie moved opposite Sam and let him prepare for the show. He cued his first song.

"You enjoying it then?" he asked.

"I suppose, in a funny way, I am. It's quite exciting not to know what I'll be doing next. It's certainly kept me busy. I haven't had time to drip about the house being miserable."

"Somehow I can't see you as miserable. Now me ... I can do miserable with bells on," he chuckled. "Ever since I retired, I've been a right old grumpy guts. Brenda says it's my age. I think it's because life's turned out to be quite different to what I expected. I thought when I retired, we'd have more time together and enjoy getting to know each other again. I thought we might go hiking at weekends or go on some big adventure and hire a campervan to tour Europe, or buy a motorbike and head off up to Scotland on it. Oh, I don't know what I expected. I didn't bank on her having other interests and friends, or the grandkids always being at ours. They're great kids but ... well, she never wants to be away from them. In fact, she sees more of them than she did of our own kids. She's always busy. She never seems to have time for us. Life doesn't always go in the direction you hoped, does it? Still, I don't need to tell you that. Oops, here we go. The track's almost up."

"Good afternoon people. It's Sam the man here again. I've managed to keep the lovely Charlie Blundell behind for a few minutes so we can chat to her about the next challenge. In front of me is the secret envelope with Charlie's next challenge. We discovered several audacious challenges dropped into our box last week and this one was selected at random from them."

He pressed a button and immediately the music from the film *Jaws* played. Charlie shook her head in dismay.

"The clue's in the music, folks. Diving with sharks is popular with many backpackers and gap year students and often, they go diving in cages to see these creatures. Not for our Charlie. There'll be no cages involved. We're challenging Charlie to have a close up encounter with ten foot sand sharks. We've arranged for you to be sent to South Africa to dive with the toothy monsters."

Charlie's mouth dropped open.

"Oops, sorry, I don't mean South Africa. I mean Chester Sea World. Oh people, if you could only see Charlie now. She looks like she's going to thump me. I think I'd better play the next song. I was going to play *Shooting Shark* by Blue Oyster Cult, but I couldn't find it so here instead is *Hold the Line* by Toto."

Mercedes was sitting in the technician's room wearing a diving mask and a snorkel when Charlie marched back in.

"Very funny, Mercedes! Whose idea was this? Diving in a tank of giant sharks."

"I think it was Ernest Peters in Esther Ward. He's only in for a few days for minor surgery and said he rather liked the idea of you in a wetsuit. He's a cool guy, especially for eighty," said Sean while Mercedes removed the steamed-up mask and snorkel. "He used to be a diver for the navy, years ago. I'm sure he'll give you some tips and pointers."

"I'm guessing there's a bit more to this than just rolling up and ogling a couple of sharks."

"You guessed right. We've enrolled you on a PADI diving course. You'll be doing the learning bit online, followed by five confined dives at a local swimming pool. I'll give you details of when and where. The two open dives sadly, won't be taking place in Barbados, but at Dosthill Quarry in Tamworth," continued Sean in a matter-of-fact voice. "If you manage the online course part without any problems, and fit in your dives on these dates we've provisionally chosen for you, you should easily be ready to go to Chester in four weeks. Once more that'll give us time to raise interest in the challenge and some funds. Mister Peters will be chuffed you're doing his challenge. You're okay with this, aren't you?"

"I'm not sure yet. I'm more worried about squeezing into a wetsuit than swimming with sharks at the moment."

"Hey, who doesn't look good in neoprene?" Mercedes chipped in, placing the snorkel and mask on the table. "The mask's for you. It comes with love from a well-wisher."

"Who? Who knew I was going diving?"

"Dunno. Someone in the know must have leaked it out. Sam knew. Art and Patricia know. Maybe they blabbed. Or, maybe Mister Peters told his family. Anyhow, you have some equipment to play with and an online course to study, so off you go, little mermaid. We'll get on and do the hard part, raising funds, getting sponsorship and trying to find an insurance company willing to insure you." Mercedes handed the mask and snorkel to Charlie.

"Oh, before you go, you might want to watch this to help you."

She rummaged in a plastic bag, pulled out a DVD and passed it to Charlie.

"*Finding Nemo*. Hilarious. You're just hilarious!"

Charlie sat in her car, hands trembling. She could not tell her friends. It was irrational. She was behaving like a child. She had already overcome her fear of heights. This was bigger, but she could overcome this.

"Charlie Blundell you are a big baby. Get a grip," she said out loud. It did not help. Her mobile rang, interrupting her thoughts.

"Hello?"

"Hi, Charlie. It's Susannah. Susannah from the belly dancing classes, in case you know other Susannahs."

"Hi! How are you?"

"Very good thanks. I have been listening to the radio shows online. Heard all about your latest challenge. I might have an idea to help raise money for the station."

"What is it?"

"Did you see the film *Calendar Girls*?"

"Yes, but there is no way on this planet I'm taking my clothes off for a calendar. Not even for charity."

"Hell, no! I thought you could do a Challenge Charlie calendar with photos of all the challenges you have taken up. January could be you eating that gruesome locust. February, a photo of you with us belly dancing girls. March, you on the roller coaster. April, you and

Mercedes zip lining. There's a very good picture of you both on the hospital radio website. What do you think?"

"Hey, that's a good idea. I'll tell the team about it tomorrow. Thanks Susannah. So, how are you getting on at the gym?"

"Pretty good. I've lost another eight pounds and Dave says I'll soon have no belly left to dance with. I feel much better. I was scared I'd get diabetes like my mum, but since the classes I feel much healthier. I've changed our diet at home too. Less crap. We both eat homemade soups and casseroles now. I'm really glad I took up belly dancing. I'm not so moody and I have loads more energy, as Dave discovered," she gave a low suggestive laugh. "What about you?"

"I don't have much time to exercise but I'm still feeling the benefits of the classes. I do some of the moves at home in front of the mirror each evening. Worrying about these challenges has helped keep the weight off." Charlie wavered remembering what her next mission was going to be.

"You okay, you sound a little less perky than usual? Your voice sounds odd."

"I … er … I'm struggling with this next challenge. Promise you won't laugh if I tell you something?"

"Of course I won't laugh. Not unless it's hilarious, then I might not be able to help myself."

"I suffer from selachophobia."

"Isn't that a wheat allergy?"

"No," said Charlie, laughing in spite of her anxiety. "It's a fear and I mean total fear of sharks. I have no idea why I suffer from it. It started when I was a child. I remember checking the bath for sharks. I wouldn't take baths because they scared me and one holiday with parents I ran screaming from the hotel pool yelling 'Shark!' because I thought I saw one when I looked in. You're not smirking, are you?"

"No, not yet."

"When Gavin and I got married, he took me to the Bahamas for our honeymoon. It was beautiful there. Gavin wanted to go snorkelling, but when we went out on the boat, I couldn't get into the water. I pretended I was feeling queasy. He took me a second time and I really tried. I stood on the side of the boat. Gavin jumped in and held out his arms to me. He called me. I geared up, took a deep breath, jumped in, peered down, spotted the bottom way below, and began freaking out. That sounds melodramatic, I know, but for me, an extreme attack of panic is quite discrete. I don't scream and carry on. My body stiffens and my face twists into one of those expressions that could easily be mistaken for erotic pleasure. Luckily, Gavin recognised the subtle differences between my trauma face and my pleasure face and got me back onto the boat where I sobbed for a while.

I explained my phobia to him and he understood. I've never had to worry about it, until now. I was about to tell the team that I can't do this challenge, when you phoned. I hate letting them down. They are so excited about it and have organised it all, even down to the PADI course. I hate myself. This isn't something I'll get over by having someone hold my hand, either. I've been hyperventilating in the car thinking about it."

"I've an idea of how I may be able to help. Don't tell your colleagues you can't do the dive just yet. Do you get any time in between finishing at the café and starting your shift at the hospital?"

"Yes, I have about three hours free. I finish at one. Why?"

"I'll meet you at the café at one on Wednesday. Don't think about the dive or sharks until then. Promise me? Go home and have a relaxing bath and a glass of wine. Or, on second thoughts, take a relaxing shower and have a couple of glasses of wine!"

"I'll do that. I'll think nice thoughts, practise my shimmying and wait for Wednesday. Don't forget to bring your magic wand."

"I'll bring my magic wand and an invisibility cloak so the sharks won't be able to see you."

Business was brisk at the café the following Wednesday. Patricia had a steady flow of people visiting the craft shop; Charlie noticed several leaving with packages.

"Things seem to be picking up, Art," she remarked as she waited to collect an order from him.

"It's Patricia. She's discovered new inspiration. It's down to those animal pots. They're selling well and she seems to have attracted new customers. She worked late last night painting one batch. She got up early too, to finish a new one."

"It's really good to see the place so busy. I'll have to go and check out the pots before they all sell out."

Charlie served her customers and nipped out to the craft shop. There was a large poster on the door to the room. It was a photo of her sailing down the zip wire with a request under it for sponsors.

Patricia was wrapping a purchase for a customer, a middle-aged woman wearing a dark red cape and matching hat.

"Hello Charlie. I heard about the latest challenge," said the woman. "My neighbour, Marjory, is in City Hospital at the moment. She's not too well. I visited her yesterday evening. All she could talk about was you diving with sharks. Her son lives in South Africa and he did one of those cage dives off Cape Town. Scared him witless, apparently. The sharks got frantic about the food and kept bashing into the cage. There was one really large one that kept knocking into the bars. It actually bent them. Her son said he thought he was going to get eaten. Luckily, they raised his cage and got him out before that happened. Marjory went on and on about how brave he was."

Charlie gripped the countertop and willed herself to smile. Her heart rate accelerated.

"That's ten pounds, please, then Mrs Higham," said Patricia. The woman fished about in her handbag, extracted her purse, and pulled out the correct amount.

"I bought her one of Patricia's new range as a present," she continued, pointing at a display. On the table was a group of pencil pots with comical faces. They stood on their fins. Each had large open mouths revealing sharp teeth. They were sharks. In front of them was a sign: 'Buy a friendly shark. All proceeds go to Charlie's Challenge.'

"Aren't they fun? Well, good luck, dear. I hope the sharks in Chester aren't as bad-tempered as those South African ones."

She left the room and disappeared down the corridor. Patricia put the money into the till and recorded the sale in a notebook on a page headed 'Charlie'.

"We wanted to help the radio station. We know how much it means to you and everyone there," explained Patricia. "Mercedes told us about the new challenge last Sunday morning when she dropped by with Ryan. She swore us to secrecy, because you hadn't been told. I'd just sold the last of my chubby sheep pots and when she told me, I had one of those Eureka moments. I came up with the idea of these new pots."

Charlie managed to let go of the counter and embrace her friend. Now wasn't the time to explain her irrational fear. She fervently hoped that Susannah was going to be able to assist. Although Charlie couldn't imagine what she could do to stop the panic that was beginning to build up.

"You are one of the kindest people I know. Thank you for doing this. You should keep some of the money for yourselves, though."

"No, I wouldn't dream of it. We're fine. Besides, since you became a minor celebrity, we've had loads more people coming to the café. I'll have to get you to sign photographs and leave them here."

The doorbell chimed and Charlie scurried off to serve. She felt awful. How could she let so many people down?

Susannah came in at exactly one o'clock.

"Gosh, I almost didn't recognise you," said Charlie. "You've changed so much. You're slimmer, obviously, but you've changed in other ways. You seem so composed and happy."

"I've got my mojo back, Charlie. I feel younger than I've done in years and Dave, well, he can hardly keep up with me if you know what I mean," she chuckled. "He asked if he could have a night off, last night." She winked. "Right. Are you ready?"

"Yes, I'll just fetch my coat and bag. Where're we going?"

"To someone who has the power to sort out your *little problem*," she whispered. "He's helped me such a lot. I would never have come to belly dancing classes if he hadn't given me enough confidence to join. I've been seeing him for just over a year. He can perform miracles."

They drove to a leafy street in Birmingham and parked outside a smart Victorian house.

"Here we are. Alastair's expecting you. You're on your own now. He's a lovely man. I'll come back and get you in an hour."

Charlie left Susannah in her car and walked up the path to the front door. She rang the doorbell and was met by an effusive medium-sized black Labrador carrying a soft toy in its mouth. It wagged its tail and broad backside so enthusiastically, Charlie thought it would fall over itself. It dominated the doorstep until a thin man in his fifties with a balding head and kind green eyes appeared.

"You must be Charlie. Hi, I'm Alastair. Come in. Don't mind Nero. He's very friendly and doesn't bite."

The Labrador continued to wag his tail in delight. He dropped the toy, sat down and gazed at her with large amber eyes.

"No, Nero, she hasn't come to play with you. Come on. Bring your fluffy with you. He's taken to you, Charlie. He doesn't often give up his fluffy to strangers."

Alastair helped her off with her coat and hung it on one of the coat pegs by the door, then led the way to a large sitting room. Nero trotted behind, toy in mouth, and headed to a large beanbag next to Alastair's desk, where he flopped down and draped his head over one end to observe.

"Welcome to my office. Susannah told me you have a phobia you need to get rid of. She didn't fill me in completely, so if you don't mind, could we have a quick chat about it before we begin? Take a seat."

Charlie sunk into a large winged cream chair and glanced about the room. It was light and uncluttered. The walls were painted in a subtle grey. A modern bookcase stood against one wall. It was jam-packed with books. Her chair was adjacent to a stylish fireplace that housed a cream log-burning stove standing on a black marble slab. Above the fireplace was an enormous mirror that added depth to the room and reflected a calming painting of blue skies. Alastair lowered himself lightly into the chair opposite her. Behind him was an expensive looking desk, as uncluttered as the room, empty apart from a laptop that was folded up neatly next to a notepad and pens.

On the wall next to the desk hung a photograph taken underwater on which were written the words:

'Fear is only as deep as the mind allows.'

"So, Susannah said you have a morbid fear of sharks," he began in a gentle voice.

"Er, yes. It's silly really," she said. "I've been terrified of sharks for years. I can swim although I haven't swum since ..." She gulped.

He looked directly at her. "No, it's not silly, Charlie. Many people have fears and phobias. They grow out of all proportion and then take over that person. You've made the most important step by coming here and speaking to me. Tell me, have you ever been to a hypnotherapist before?"

"No, my uncle Ernie was hypnotised once though, on stage at a working men's club. He kept clucking like a chicken. My Aunt Maude told everyone about it and said his chicken impression was so realistic, she thought he was going to lay an egg."

Alastair smiled. "Fortunately for you, I don't work like that. Could you imagine the scandal if I transformed patients into chickens? Mind you, I'd be okay for omelettes for a while."

Charlie laughed, relaxing a little. Nero looked up at the sound, then snuggled down with his fluffy toy.

"Is there any reason you want to get over this fear? Or, have you merely decided you don't want it anymore?"

"I need to get over it. I am supposed to be doing a dive with sharks for charity and I don't want to back out of it. I would let down far too many people. I'm not sure I can even take the diving course that's been arranged. I might be okay at a swimming pool but an open dive ... It's a stupid fear. It's bizarre. If it were spiders that would make sense, but sharks? I shouldn't be bothered by sharks. It's not like they're going to suddenly come swimming into the supermarket while I'm shopping, or leap out of my plughole when I'm washing up my breakfast bowl."

"I agree, that's not likely. The fact you're here is the first step to conquering your fear. You need to understand what fear is and how to control it. Fears arise in the unconscious part of our minds. You need to be able to use the conscious part of your mind to control it, that's all. Hypnotherapy works by bypassing our conscious minds and focuses on retraining our unconscious. It won't take many sessions to fix the problem. Then you'll be able to swim with sharks, pat them on their heads, and tickle their tummies or whatever you want to do."

"I hope you can help. I'm so embarrassed about it. It's not something I tell people. I can't even remember how it all began. It just happened. One day, when I was very young, I became scared witless about them."

"I'm going to just talk to you about fear and how to cope when you feel frightened. If you'd like to just relax in the chair, we'll get going."

"What, no swinging pendulum, or a watch on the end of a chain?"

"No, I don't require gimmicky accessories. I'm going to use a special technique called the Rewind Technique. Just sit back in the chair and if it helps, close your eyes, then breathe in and out. Imagine waves of relaxation running down your body from your scalp downwards, washing out stress. Let the waves run in time with your breathing, first washing down over your head, then your neck, then your torso, then arms, and finally your legs. Feel the muscles in your body relaxing as the waves of relaxation wash over them and breathe in and out ..."

The chair was extremely comfortable. Alastair's mellifluous voice drifted over her, calming her nerves. She became aware of the sound of her own breath as she breathed rhythmically in time to his voice. The more she concentrated on his voice, the slower her heart rate became and the more she felt herself drift into a relaxed state. She closed her eyes for a moment and listened.

"There's a part of you which is separate from the conscious. That part knows how to produce dreams at night. It knows how to relax you deeply, and it knows how to grow your hair, digest your food and blink ... all beyond your conscious awareness. It knows more than you do about many things that happen in your body and your mind. It's that part of you I am going to talk to."

Charlie thought Alastair's voice sounded a little deeper and slower as she continued to listen.

"When you go into hypnosis ... you just start to feel a little dreamy ... sometimes you start to focus on sensations in the body ... like comfort and warmth in your hands ... or you begin to notice your breathing ... and the way it ... slows ... a ... little ... and often your eyelids start to feel a little heavier ... like they're feeling sleepy ... and sometimes images flit into your mind ... of pleasant places ...

121

like the way the sky looks so blue on a summer's day at the beach ... or the birds sing in the woods sometimes ... and when you ... drift into hypnosis ... you pay less attention to the room around you ... as you really just start to forget about all that ... and ... drift inwards ... "

Alastair stopped for a moment. Charlie's breathing was inaudible, her face was relaxed and her eyelids fluttered from time to time. He needed to bring her anxiety to the surface and then guide her to a safe place.

"Charlie I want you to imagine somewhere where you feel safe and at ease. Have you got a safe place?"

Charlie smiled.

"Now, I want you to imagine you are there. You're feeling at ease just like you do now. There's a TV set and a video player with a remote control in there with you. Now, you're floating to one side of the picture, out of body. You can see yourself sitting comfortably in there. You're watching yourself watching the screen, but you can't see the picture. There's a film playing of the first time you became frightened of sharks. The film's going to start at that point and will play all the way through, but you are safe. The film will end when the event is over."

Charlie's face tensed. Her brow furrowed. Alastair watched as Charlie wrestled with her emotions. She calmed again.

"Charlie, keep listening to me. You're going to float back into the body that's watching the film. You're at the end of the film, at a safe point. Pick up the control. Use it to rewind the film quickly to the point where it began. Now, I want you to use your control and watch the same film while pressing the fast forward button. Go quickly through it with your finger on the fast forward button. The film will race past."

Charlie's face changed again and her head turned from side to side as she wrestled with her inner demons.

"Well done. Remember, you are completely safe in this nice safe room. You are very relaxed. You're feeling calm. Next, you're going to rewind the film, only this time you'll do it more slowly."

Alastair repeated the exercise several times with Charlie, suggesting she changed the speed of the control until he thought she was showing less emotion at the scenes.

"So, Charlie, when you put on the wetsuit and go diving, you will feel confident. You will feel calm. When you dive with the sharks, you will be confident and relaxed."

He paused, then in the same gentle tone said, "You know how when people are at that point where they are about to wake up after having been asleep, and bit by bit they start to become more aware of their surroundings again, and of their body resting there ... you are going to feel that way. It's almost time to come back into the room and wake up. You'll notice you are becoming more aware of my voice again. You'll feel refreshed and alert. It's almost time to come out of your sleep, Charlie."

Alastair brought Charlie back to full awareness. Nero raised his head and watched them both.

"Oh goodness. I feel quite a bit better. That was incredible."

"I think you should come along for another session after you do your first dive in the swimming pool, then another before you do an open dive, and of course one follow-up appointment before the big dive. Would you like a cup of tea now?"

"Thank you, I'd love one. You didn't ask me to tell you what was on the television screen," she said.

"I don't need to know. You needed to discover where it all began, because now you can deal with it. That's what matters."

There was a knock at the door and a woman dressed in a long shirt and leggings came in. Nero's tail thumped against the floor.

"Hi, I'm Julia, Alastair's wife. I brought tea and biscuits, but if you'd rather have coffee?"

"No, tea's lovely. Thank you."

"Don't let Nero convince you he's hard done to. He gets his own special biscuit every night before bed and plenty to eat during the day, don't you, you greedy boy? Stay. No begging. You are far too podgy to eat biscuits."

Nero's eyebrows knotted in disagreement, but he remained on his bed, tail thumping.

They chatted for a while about Alastair's interest in hypnotherapy and further techniques Charlie could use to help relax herself. It transpired that Julia was one of his first patients.

"I think he hypnotised me to marry him," she laughed. "I'm sure I didn't fancy him when I first met him."

"Of course you did. You knew you fancied me once you looked deep, deep into my eyes," Alastair joked.

Charlie checked her watch and excused herself.

"Thank you very much, but I need to get going. I've got to get to the studio."

Susannah was waiting for her.

"Think it worked?" she asked as soon as Charlie climbed in.

"I'm not one hundred percent sure, but I feel a lot better about going diving and taking my PADI licence. It's amazing, isn't it, how one small incident years ago that you can't recall, can be a trigger for a phobia or fear that can traumatise you for years after?"

"Tell me. So you discovered what caused you to be scared of sharks?"

"Yes, and now I should be able to handle it better. Well, let's hope so."

Friday arrived before she knew it. Her head was too occupied with diving information, the radio show, and work at the café to give much thought to anything else. However, Friday afternoon, she hadn't a clue what to wear or how to go about preparing for a date.

She looked at her bed covered with discarded clothes, the floor that was now a carpet of footwear, and scurried to the kitchen to talk to her friend.

"Mercedes, help!" she cried. "I've no idea what to wear. I should never have agreed to meet Rob."

"Don't be daft. You're out of practice, that's all. You're far too used to dressing for work, then slobbing about at home. Have you got sexy underwear?"

"I've got a matching black set of semi-sexy underwear. You're not going to suggest I saunter out in only my knickers and a coat?"

"Now there's a thought. Sexy would be better, but semi-sexy should do. Where are you meeting him?"

"It was going to be at work, but parking is darn near impossible there, so I texted him and suggested the pub near the hospital to start with."

"Good, that gives me time to give you a makeover before you leave the studio. I'll bring my magic bag of tricks so don't bother doing your makeup. I'll do it at the studio while you're on air. You can play a couple of tracks back to back and I'll fix your face and hair. Now, what to wear? For a meeting in a pub, with thoughts of going off for a meal and hopefully passionate sex, I suggest you squeeze into your tight black French Connection trousers. Team them up with your best Zara boots, and the silvery top I bought you last year for your birthday. You'll ignite his fire as soon as he lays eyes on you. Don't worry. We'll sort it all out at the studio. I'll see you later. Now, go and run a bath and don't forget to shave all your bits. You might strike lucky!"

"Have you got a manual? I think I've forgotten how to do that too."

"No one forgets how to have sex, Charlie. Not even you!"

True to her word, Mercedes ensured Charlie looked fresh, attractive, and sexy. Her hair was loose around her face in gentle waves created by a pair of tongs and much cursing. Her eyes looked large and clear, enhanced by eyeliner and lengthening mascara. In her outfit, she looked lean and toned. She mentally thanked the belly dancing lessons for giving her poise. Show over, she headed off as the last track played. Sam was already at the desk thumbing through a newspaper for items to talk about. She twirled for Mercedes.

"Sexy and feminine with a hint of glamour. You'll pass," said Mercedes. "Good luck. Hope you have a fabulous time. Don't forget to fill me in with all the details. And, I mean all. Here, take this lipstick in case you need to touch it up."

She handed Charlie the bright pink fuchsia lipstick she had slicked onto her lips.

Charlie hurried off to The Tradesman's pub to meet up with Rob. Her stomach was filled with gentle butterflies. It had been a long time since she had been out with another man. She could not recall the events of the New Year's Eve party, but she remembered the kiss he had planted on her lips.

She parked her car, checked her reflection in the rear view mirror, took a deep breath, willed herself to be calm, and headed towards the pub entrance. The inside was packed with customers. There were no free tables. She searched for Rob and spotted him. He was propped up on a stool beside the bar dressed in white cotton trousers, a white shirt, and a pale pink satin jacket. She grimaced at his attire. It was more suitable for Thailand than a pub in Birmingham. He noticed her and waved her over. She hesitated for a second, wondering if she should continue before joining him.

"Charlie, very glad you're here. He dropped down from the stool to kiss her. She didn't remember him being so short. In her heels, she towered above him. He made a clumsy attempt to kiss her. She had to stoop. He missed her mouth completely, and her cheek, and ended up slobbering slightly on her neck. Then he took her hand and pressed his lips to the back of it.

"Wonderful to see you. What would you like to drink?"

"I'll have a small glass of wine, please. I'm a light-weight with drink. Besides, I brought the car."

"I seem to recall you were knocking them back at that party," he said with a crooked smile as he attempted to get the barman's attention. "We can always leave your car here, if necessary."

Charlie nodded. She was being stuffy. She needed to loosen up. She did not want Rob to think she was a boring old biddy.

"Good idea. We can enjoy a few drinks that way. So, what are the plans this evening?"

"I thought we'd stay here. There's Karaoke later. That could be a laugh. I do a mean Meatloaf impression. The beer's good and they have beer-battered fish with homemade chips and mushy peas," he continued, pointing at a chalkboard showing the specials of the day.

"Heaven! I love fish and chips. And bangers. Three years of Thai food and I'm desperate for some British grub. There's only so much green curry you can eat. And beer. I miss the beer."

He waved his empty pint glass at the barman. "Another glass of this excellent beverage," he shouted. "And a large glass of wine for the lady," he added, winking at Charlie. "Talking of food, you look delicious, Charlie. Very tasty."

The barman poured the drinks while Rob continued to mumble on about food he liked. At last, the barman handed over the drinks.

"Can we order food here? Well, when I mean here, I know we can order food in the pub, I meant here, at the bar?" asked Rob. He then laughed loudly. He sounded like a donkey braying.

Charlie wondered if Rob had been waiting at the pub long. He seemed tipsy. His voice was very slightly slurred. Maybe he was nervous.

"I'll get you a couple of menus. When you're ready, go to the area over there by the sign that says 'food orders' and give Georgia, the girl wearing the black apron, your order."

"Thank you, my good man," Rob replied, bowed at him, then winked at Charlie. Charlie cringed.

"Do you want to find somewhere more private to sit?" he asked.

"There's a table near the door. The couple sitting there are just leaving. We could grab that."

"Splendid. Allow me to carry your drink, dear lady," he said, fumbling for the glasses. He misjudged and knocked hers flying to the ground where it shattered.

"Oops! Silly me. How clumsy. I guess I must still be suffering from jet lag. Let me get you another."

People stared at them. Charlie reddened. She shuffled over to the table where she lowered her head and wondered if she should do a runner.

"Here we are, Charlie," boomed Rob before she could drum up courage to race off. "I got some nuts too, to help soak up the alcohol. Not that we want to soak up too much," he laughed and slurped his pint.

The man now attempting to sit opposite her was surely not the same man she remembered from Mercedes's party? Was this the man who kissed her with such passion?

"So, what have you been up to since the party?" he asked, wiping foam from his upper lip with the back of his hand, then sliding it down his trousers, leaving a smeary mess.

"Oh, work, radio. Not too much. My life isn't as exciting as yours."

"It's probably more exciting," he said, downing a quarter of his pint in one gulp.

"I hardly think so. Photography in Thailand trumps working in a café in the UK."

He looked away for a moment.

"So, have you taken any more photos of elephants? You told me about the orphan elephants you visited. The ones that played football. Sounded wonderful."

"No," he said flatly. "Not taken much recently. Lost my enthusiasm. Things change. I'm not bothered about elephants anymore. I'd rather watch the Villa play football. The players have better ball control. Well, some days they do," he said and smiled at his own wit. Charlie was stumped. What could she talk about?

Rob managed to focus on the conversation again. "So, how's your friend in the wheelchair ... Mazda and her fella, what's his name?"

"Mercedes. Mercedes and Ryan."

"I knew it was a car brand. Mercedes. That's an odd name for a girl."

"The car was actually commissioned by Emil Jellinek, an Austrian entrepreneur and one of Mercedes Benz's best customers. He named the car after his daughter, Mercedes. So, it really is a girl's name," she said. Rob looked vacantly at her. She gave herself another mental telling-off. He didn't require a lecture on car manufacturers. "They're fine. Ryan's enjoying his new job."

"Salesman!" said Rob.

"Policeman. Actually he's an inspector. He's really enjoying it. Mercedes still does voluntary work at the hospital radio with me. She did a zip wire challenge with me a while ago. It was amazing. She has no fear."

"What's a zip wire?"

Charlie explained.

"That sounds ... entertaining," he replied. He took another swig of his beer and sat in silence, staring at the nuts on the table. Charlie didn't know what to say next.

"I went on a roller coaster, too. I had to play a kazoo."

Rob sniggered. "Sounds childish. Why did you have to play a kazoo?"

"It was the challenge. A bit of fun …" her sentence hung between them.

"I'm back home in the UK, you know?" he mumbled after a while.

"What, for good?"

"Yeah. She booted me out. My job there didn't pay much, so I couldn't stay even if I wanted to. Besides, I didn't like it much. I only took up photography because there wasn't anything else there for me. It was different for her. She taught little kids in a local school and did healing. Healing! What's that all about?" he snorted. "I've come back home. Hope to get a job here."

He stared at his glass, a forlorn look on his face.

"I didn't know you were in a relationship. I thought you lived in Thailand alone."

Rob laughed without humour. "No. I'd never have gone to Thailand on my own. I now officially hate Thailand. I only went because of her. *Her* being my girlfriend, lover, partner, whatever. Scarlett. That's her name. She's, how shall I put it? Alternative. She's into yoga and crystals and all that razzmatazz. She always wanted to go to the East and especially Thailand." He stopped for a moment.

"I had a bit of a bad time before we went. I struggled with my business. In truth, it was going to the wall. Ha! That's a good joke, isn't it? Wall? I was in the building trade? Get it?" he laughed a hollow laugh and drained his glass.

Charlie nodded dumbly.

"Scarlett saw it as the chance to take off and do something exciting. She said it would be romantic. She talked of nothing else for months until she wore me down and I gave in. I didn't have anything to lose. Or, so I thought. She said we could start a whole new adventure together. It wasn't an adventure. It was hot, sweaty, difficult and miserable. It was an adventure for her. She met someone else over there and dumped me. Three years. I gave up everything for her. Three years." His eyes took on a faraway look. "Still, I'm back now and you and me, we can have some fun, right? Another drink?" he asked and stood up, faltered, then staggered in the direction of the bar. Charlie groaned. She could try and phone Mercedes. They could concoct a reason for her leaving early.

"Charlie?"

She looked up. "Oh, hi!"

It was Jake.

"I thought I'd say hello. Don't want to interrupt your evening with …"

"Oh, that's Rob. He's just someone I barely know," she replied quickly. "You're not interrupting at all. In fact, I was thinking of having an early night and going home."

They could hear Rob talking in a loud voice to the barman. "What's the difference between a new wife and a new dog? After a year, the dog is still excited to see you." He exploded into fits of bitter laughter.

"Yes, well … thought I'd say hello. Heard you were taking on another challenge. I bought one of those little pottery sharks from the café and the owner told me about it. Hope it goes well. I have to say that you are very adventurous. I'm full of admiration for what you've been doing."

"I'm only doing it for the radio station. To be honest, I'm petrified about the next challenge. Give me a roller coaster and a kazoo anytime over diving with sharks."

He smiled a warm smile.

"I'm sure you'll be fine. You could always try playing them a lullaby on a kazoo."

Charlie laughed. "Great idea. I'll try that."

He appeared to be on his own. He smelled of warm citrus aftershave. He seemed pleased to see her. His eyes never left her face. She wondered what it would be like to kiss him.

"Seriously, you'll enjoy it. I went diving years ago in the Cayman Islands and saw a nurse shark. They look fierce, but they won't hurt you. They're just fish."

Charlie was grateful for his interest, but didn't want to talk about the shark challenge. She still wasn't sure how she'd cope.

"So, have you still got the magic kazoo?"

"Oh yes. I tried it out only the other day. I can now manage to play the theme tune to *The Simpsons!* I keep it in my bedside drawer. I look at it every morning to remind me of you and the fact that I'm not really old."

She felt a slight tingling sensation. Jake was flirting with her. She could see it in his eyes and in that smile.

"You alone?" she asked.

"I was supposed to meet Abigail, but she broke off half an hour ago. Her husband phoned her and asked her to go out with some of his clients."

Charlie was delighted. Abigail was not his girlfriend.

"I thought Abigail might be your wife," she said with a light laugh.

"Crumbs no. Heaven forbid. She isn't my type. Far too bossy. No, I'm not married, nor do I have a girlfriend," he added.

Charlie tried to read his body language. He was displaying a definite interest in her.

Rob broke the spell. Charlie couldn't believe how drunk he was.

"Hello, hello, who's this bloke, then?" he said as he approached the table. "Is he bothering you, Charlie? You're not pestering my lady, are you? Because, if you are, matey, I'll have to sort you out." He put down his pint and jabbed his forefinger into Jake's shoulder.

Jake bristled, but kept his temper. "We're friends," he hissed. "So, back off." He turned away from Rob who wobbled unsteadily behind him. "Well, good luck again," he continued, moving his attention back to Charlie. "Night, Charlie. Lovely to see you."

"Wanker," muttered Rob. "That's it. Run off, you prick."

Jake turned back. "Did you say something?" He asked, his eyes narrowing.

"No. You must be hearing things, old boy," Rob replied with a sneer, putting emphasis on the word 'old'. He was so busy trying to outstare Jake, he misjudged where to put the glass of wine and for the second time that night knocked it over, only this time, it went all over Charlie's top. She yelped and shot out of her chair, upturning her handbag.

"Oopsie daisy!" boomed Rob, trying to wipe her front with the sleeve of his jacket.

"Don't worry. I'll sort it." She pushed him away, stuffed her purse and phone back into her handbag, then raced off to the toilets to wash off the mess before it stained her blouse.

It took several minutes to remove the stain and dry her top under the hand dryer. When she came back out, Rob was nowhere to be seen. Neither was Jake. She asked the barman if he had seen them.

"They both went outside. The bloke in the white trousers was in a right state. He's been here since six o'clock and I reckon he drank at least five pints and four shots. I wasn't going to serve him any more drinks. He was pissed enough. Wouldn't be surprised if that other bloke didn't lay one on him. White trousers got very abusive after you left. Started shouting and carrying on. I'm glad they cleared off."

She thanked the barman and left, fuming that Rob had deserted her. What an idiot! She ought to feel sorry for him. His life was in a mess, but he did not deserve her sympathy. Fancy leaving her like that. And, as for Jake. He might have waited to see if she was all right instead of merely squaring up to Rob like some testosterone-fuelled juvenile.

The car park was empty. Clearly neither of them bothered about her. That was it. She was off men for good. She'd managed for the last few years without them and could manage for many more.

She stomped over to her car and opened the door, threw her handbag in and was about to join it when she saw movement on the edge of the car park. It was a man. She peered at the figure. He seemed to be writhing under the lamppost that lit the car park. Clutching her mobile in case she needed to phone for help, she took a few steps closer to the figure. She gasped. He was naked and trussed up against the lamppost. His head was bowed as he tried to escape his bounds.

She moved closer to see if the man was injured. He made some guttural noises and sobbed. It was Rob. She hastened towards him, but it was only after she was close enough to free him that she could make out writing on his bare chest. In bright pink fuchsia lipstick were the words, "I'm a prick".

Charlie was furious with Jake. How dare he humiliate Rob in such a way! He didn't have any right to do that. Okay, so Rob was a prat and had behaved badly, however, there was no need to thump him, strip him naked, then tie and gag him with pieces of cloth torn from his pink jacket. He could have been discovered by anyone leaving the pub. It could have been incredibly humiliating for him. As it was, it was bad enough. She would tell Jake what an A-hole he was when she next saw him. Luckily for him, Rob was so drunk he couldn't remember exactly what happened and didn't want to press charges.

His clothes had been dumped in a pile nearby. At least she wouldn't have him sitting naked in her car. Trying to dress him was almost impossible. She remembered how Amy had wriggled as a small child. Getting her gloves or socks on had always been difficult. She got Rob to put on his own underwear and after some more persuasion stuck a leg into his dirty white trousers. He clung to her shoulder and wobbled several times. She was aware that anyone could arrive at any time and see them, so she was not too kind in dressing him. She shoved his trousers over his scrawny backside and latched them at the top, then forced his arms into his shirt. She abandoned the idea of shoes and socks. He could get into the car without them.

They drove around for a while. She opened the car window to let out the stench of alcohol. Finally, she found a twenty-four hours McDonalds drive-through. She ordered coffee. They sat in her car while he drank it and sobered a little. He remembered arguing with Jake. Jake told him he was a muppet for getting drunk and ruining his date with her. Next thing, he remembered being hit. He touched his eye. It was already closing up and would be deep purple by morning.

When he was finally coherent enough to remember where he was staying, she drove him to his digs. He was silent throughout the journey, slumped in the seat. She doubted he would contact her again. It was just as well. She did not want to see him again. Her life was perfectly okay without the likes of Rob and Jake.

For the moment, she would concentrate on her challenges. They might be mad and frightening, but at least they gave her something to focus on. She practised her breathing techniques until she felt calmer. The next time she saw Jake, she was going to tell him exactly what to do with that kazoo.

"You're joking," spluttered Mercedes. "No way!" She nudged Ryan with her elbow and pointed at the phone in her hand. They were both sitting on the sofa. Bentley was snuggled between them, head on Mercedes's knee. Ryan was trying to watch a detective series on the television. "I'll tell Ryan, but I won't tell anyone else. Promise. Well, well. Who'd have thought it? Maybe that Jake fellow fancies you."

"Even if he did, I wouldn't go out with a Neanderthal like that. He didn't know Rob. He just got all puffed up, probably because Rob called him a prick, and then smacked seven bells out of him. That's barbaric."

"Yeah, you're right. If Ryan hit someone who came onto me, I'd think that was a bit OTT, too. As for stripping him and leaving him outside tied up ..."

Ryan muted the television and tried to listen in.

"That's got his attention. He's just muted Morse."

"I'll let you get back to it. I'm over my rant now. Needed to talk to someone about it. Thanks for listening to me. I might just have a shower, then watch one of the films I recorded. You're a good friend."

"You're a good friend, too. Go grab a glass of wine and chill. You can come over here if you prefer. You'd be more than welcome. It's not that late."

"No, I wouldn't dream of interrupting your romantic night in with the two inspectors. I'll see you at the radio station. Have a good evening."

"See you Sunday afternoon, then. You did say Rob was wearing a pink jacket, didn't you? And white trousers?"

"You're not laughing, are you?"

"No, I'm not laughing. Well, just sniggering a bit. You have to admit, it's quite funny in a way. At least you didn't get stuck with him all night. He might have tried out the Karaoke machine and made it a whole lot worse."

Charlie laughed. "Yes, he claimed he did Meatloaf impressions. I don't think I could have stood him singing *Bat Out Of Hell*."

"From what you told me, he'd have been better off singing that other Meatloaf hit, *Life Is a Lemon and I Want My Money Back*. I think you had a narrow escape there. Okay, my lovely, I'd better go. Morse is about to solve the murder. Ryan thinks he knows who the murderer is. We'll see if he's as good as Morse. Sleep well."

"Charlie's date," she explained once she ended the call. "With Rob. The guy was blind drunk. He chucked wine all over her and when she came back from the toilet, he'd vanished. He was outside in the car park tied to a lamppost butt-naked. Charlie says a guy she knows, called Jake, took offence at Rob's language and thumped him. Then he stripped Rob while he was unconscious, and tied him up. He also scrawled a message over his chest in Charlie's pink lipstick. She's pissed off about that. It was the new lipstick I gave her. She doesn't have much luck, does she?"

Ryan kissed Mercedes's forehead. "It'll happen for her. She just hasn't met the right guy yet. I could fix her up with Pete. He and his wife have just separated. He's a good-looking guy."

"He's called Pervy Pete. And, he's called Pervy for a good reason. You keep out of it. Your track record of finding boyfriends for Charlie isn't great. Stick to solving crimes. You're good at that."

She squeezed his hand. He turned up the volume on the set again. Mercedes wasn't paying much attention now to the drama. She felt sorry for Charlie. Charlie didn't deserve to be all alone. She had too much love and kindness to give. Playing Cupid wasn't going to help Charlie. Fate needed to play its part. She quietly asked the universe to find someone nice for Charlie. After all, the universe and Charlie had given her Ryan.

Back at her house, Charlie found it difficult to settle back into her usual routine. She stood in front of the bathroom mirror, dragging damp cotton wool across her eyes and scrubbing her face free of all makeup. Her cheeks were red. What a waste of time it had all been. So much for a new relationship.

Her annoyance was now directed at herself for being so silly as to think she could attract a man at her age. She wasn't anything special to look at and she wasn't extraordinary. She was an ordinary woman whose marriage had failed and who had lost the most precious thing in her life. She picked up the photograph of Amy she kept by her beside. Her heart still ached when she looked at it. She could hear

Amy's laughter when she closed her eyes.

She kissed the photograph and headed for her computer. She could go onto Facebook and see if anyone she knew was up and online. She didn't go on it too often, but she liked to play some of the games there and Candy Crush was her favourite. She noticed Susannah had been online and posted a photo of her and Dave on holiday in Marrakesh. Susannah was wearing a Fez. Charlie cheered up at the sight of them.

A couple of the nurses from the hospital were online commenting on the television show *The Voice*. Most people seemed to have logged off.

An alert went off to say she had mail. She checked and groaned. It was an email from Harrison:

Dearest Charlotte,

Have you thought about me at all? I'd really like to meet up again. I have changed.

Love Harrison

This was ridiculous. How stupid was Harrison? Could he really think for one minute she would want to see him? She was sick of men. She typed a response:

Harrison,

Firstly, I really don't know why you would miss me. We had nothing in common. I have not thought about you at all and I don't want to see you again. I don't want a relationship of any description with you. Please don't try to contact me again. I am blocking you from my email contacts.

Lastly, my name is Charlie.

She pressed send, then wondered if she had been a little too hard. Blast him! He was a pain. She didn't want him thinking there was a remote possibility that they would meet up. She blocked his name from her email, turned off the computer, and poured a glass of wine. She would watch something amusing and distracting before bed. That should sort out her mood.

Charlie curled up in her chair, feet tucked under her, glass of wine in her hand, and watched Sacha Baron Cohen. Before long, she felt the tension shift and began to enjoy *Borat*. She was enjoying it so much, she did not hear a car drive slowly past her house and pull into a parking spot on the road nearby. She also did not hear the creak of her back gate as a man in a leather jacket came into her back garden and sat under the tree.

"I've sold out of shark pots again!" shouted Patricia from the back room. "I can't make them fast enough. Who'd have thought people would want to put utensils and pens into open-mouthed sharks?"

"They're rather nice-looking sharks," said Art. "They're not exactly like the toothy monsters of the deep, are they? If they looked like the real thing, people wouldn't want them. You've managed to make them look enigmatic. They're quite cute."

"Thanks Art," said Patricia, returning to the kitchen. "You're cute too. I've made one hundred and fifty pounds for Charlie already. I hope it helps."

"Of course it will. Every little helps. If everyone did something like this, they'd make lots of money and the station would be able to stay on air. It's nice to do something for Charlie. She's always generous to others."

"Yes. She's a good soul. She's no idea that she is liked so much. I've never known anyone who can appear to be so confident and do so much for others, have so little confidence in themselves. She's been on her own too long. She really should get out more. I was glad she did those belly dancing classes, but since then, she seems to have retreated back into her house and shell.

"I wonder how her date with that man from Thailand went. She seemed quite excited about it. I haven't seen her like that before. I hope something comes of it. I'd really like to see her dating regularly. Mercedes was saying the same thing, only the other day. She's worried that Charlie's given up on herself. Since she heard about Gavin and his new baby, she's become more work-driven. It's such a good thing Mercedes got her occupied with these challenges. She hopes it'll help make her see there's more to life than the radio station and maybe get her meeting people, more specifically, men. Mercedes has also arranged for a really dishy diving instructor to look after her when she does her pool dives. Just in case this thing with the other guy from Thailand doesn't work out.

Mercedes told me she went round to see her a couple of weeks ago at her house and Charlie's got photos of Amy on display in almost every room. She's kept Amy's old toys, too. It's so sad. There're a group of teddy bears and toys arranged on a bed in the spare room as if they're waiting for Amy to return. Mercedes said it made her want to cry. She's determined to help Charlie find a new man in her life and move on."

The conversation was interrupted by a well-dressed man, their sole client, who had been sitting in the Quiet Room for an hour.

"Could I have another coffee please?" he called.

"Certainly, sir. Do you want anything with that? We've got some very tasty cakes. I can highly recommend the chocolate one."

The man shook his head. "No, thanks. I'm watching my weight."

"Yeah, me too," said Art, patting his large stomach and smiling. "Not as much as I should be though."

Patricia went to her studio to throw some pots. Art made the coffee. The man continued typing on his laptop. When Art returned with the coffee, the man barely acknowledged him.

Art returned to the counter and was soon occupied serving some new customers. He didn't pay much attention to the man who sat for another half an hour, typing on his laptop. He didn't observe the man looking up each time the doorbell rang. Eventually, the man came up to the counter, paid for his coffee, then went to the toilet. On his return, he carefully and quickly removed the poster of Charlie zip-lining. He folded it and slipped it into his laptop bag before leaving the café unnoticed.

It was dark outside, but lights burned brightly inside the indoor swimming pool. Charlie emerged from the ladies' changing rooms. It had taken her ages to psyche herself up for this. Gathering courage to put on the wetsuit had been task enough. Coming out to the swimming pool area had taken longer. She had run through her breathing techniques several times before she could face the voluminous pool.

Her instructor, Liam, was already in situ in the water talking to a couple in their late twenties. Charlie groaned. Looking at them, she was not only scared, but she also felt ancient as she picked her way to the steps leading into the shallow end. Liam exuded youth and vitality. Even from this distance she could see he was only in his twenties too. He had dark blond hair, longer than was the fashion for young men. It suited his tanned face. His wetsuit was hanging undone at his waist, revealing a superb six-pack. Charlie was too busy concentrating on squashing her fear to fully take in his muscular torso; however, she knew he was what Mercedes would call 'well buff'. He noticed her hovering by the waterside and motioned for her to join them. The pool was deserted apart from the four of them. Tanks and diving equipment were lined up along the side of the pool. She placed her own mask and snorkel on the side of the pool and stood on the steps. She closed her eyes, swallowed hard and thought about her safe place. There were no sharks here. It was only a swimming pool. It was filled with chlorine. There were no fish of any description, only people. She checked the water. The lights reflected in it. There was nothing untoward there. She heard the others laughing. Liam was recounting an amusing story about a fellow diver peeing on jellyfish stings. She looked over at him. He smiled back. His teeth were impossibly white. A few more breaths and she climbed down the steps. The water was warm. She waded over to the small group.

"You made it! Hope that wetsuit wasn't too tricky to get into. Most people struggle at first, especially with the zip at the back. It's something you get used to after a few attempts. I managed to fall over in the changing rooms at a dive shop when I bought my first suit. It wasn't a pretty sight. I was trying to get my left leg into the suit, lost my balance, and fell through the curtain into the room. Can you imagine it? Legs tangled up in a rubber suit, wearing nothing but a pair of M&S pants?" He laughed. Charlie thought he looked more Calvin Klein than M&S. "Anyway, enough stories about rubber suits. Charlie, this is Felicity and Craig. They're both doing the PADI course so they can go diving in Barbados when they go on honeymoon."

"How wonderful! Congratulations. Are you getting married soon?"

"In six weeks," replied Felicity, hanging onto her fiancé's arm. "We thought we'd get our licences here, then we can do our open dives over there in the warm seas, rather than a quarry or in the freezing cold seas here."

Liam laughed, "Hey! You'd be surprised at the stuff you can find in a quarry. We've got perch, tyres, old cars, and shopping trolleys. You'll not see anything quite as exotic as that in Barbados. Guess it'll just be you and me at Dozzi then, Charlie. Dosthill," he corrected himself when he saw her puzzled expression. "Dosthill Quarry, the UK's original national dive site and one of the prettiest inland dive sites in the UK with resident sturgeon, carp, and a sunken Parcel Force van to explore."

Felicity giggled. "I think I'd rather take my chances in Barbados."

"I'll be surprised if you find any time at all to go diving," Liam joked and laughed. Craig joined him. "I like your thinking, mate," he said, earning a stern look from Felicity.

"Righty-ho chaps! You've read all about diving, you've taken some tests and passed them and now, you're going to get familiar with some of the equipment. I brought fins along for you, but we won't bother with those yet. First off, we're going to learn how to put on the mask correctly. You need to be able to spit and wipe for this part."

Liam talked them through setting up equipment for a dive. He punctuated each task with an amusing story related to it. Charlie found him pleasantly distracting. He showed them all how to set up their tanks and attach them to the buoyancy diving jackets. The tank was heavy, but Liam supported most of its weight as they buckled up Charlie's buoyancy diving jacket. Once on, he was thorough in checking all her buckles. She was acutely aware of his hands firmly pulling the straps. She moved up the pool to stand in water that was chest height. The tank was less heavy now. However, the second she put the regulator into her mouth to move into deeper water and to descend into the pool she found she couldn't breathe. She gripped the mouthpiece so tightly between her teeth she thought she'd chew through it. Terrified, she tried to clamber over to the side of the pool. The tank made her clumsy and slow. She clung to the side of the pool with both hands. Liam quickly joined her. She saw concern in his eyes. She spat out the regulator and gulped for breath.

"Look, you don't have to do this," said Liam as she struggled to catch her breath. Her heart was battering against her ribs. "If you want to sit on the side and watch, go ahead. I'll help you remove your jacket. I'm not going to force you to do this."

"No, I'm being silly. Give me a minute," she replied. She shut her eyes and thought about her safe place. She breathed in. She made an effort to relax all her muscles.

"I'm okay. Let's do it."

Liam squeezed her hand. "If you change your mind, let me know. You won't be the first to give up at this stage."

She waded back with Liam to join the others and, following his lead, let air out of her jacket to descend the few feet to the bottom of the pool where they all sat. Liam gave her the okay sign. She returned it.

A film began to play in her mind. She saw two small figures in an inflatable dinghy. She turned the film off. She didn't want to watch it now. She needed to concentrate. She forced herself to focus on Liam. He was showing them how to recover a mask in the event it accidentally came off. He did it effortlessly and then pointed at Craig. Craig removed his mask, blinked a few times, then calmly placed it back over his face, pressed his palm against the top of the mask, tilted his head back, blew hard until the water came out and repositioned the mask. He gave the okay sign to Liam. Felicity was next. She too managed to clear her mask and refit it. Charlie was dreading her turn. Liam pointed at her and instructed her to remove the mask. She breathed in and pulled the mask from her face. Almost instantly, she became blind. It was blurry. The water stung her eyes. A familiar sensation of panic rose in her throat. Her mind raced back to the film. Two children in a dinghy. The sea is calm. Suddenly, the dinghy rises and falls sharply. An oar falls into the sea and floats away. The dinghy is rocked again by a force in the water. Something nudges the side. One child screams and falls against the opposite side, gripping the rubber tightly. Water splashes into the face of the other child. The child sputters, then screams.

She forced the image from her mind. She needed to retrieve her mask. She wrestled with it, attempting to locate the front, struggling to slip the strong elastic over her head and finally, forced it over her eyes and nose. She tilted her head backwards, pressed the mask against her forehead to release it a little below her nose, and snorted air to dispel the water. The glass cleared slightly. She repeated the procedure. The mask cleared completely. She checked the strap. It was fixing the mask tightly to her face. She was in a safe place. Liam gave her the okay sign. She gave it back. She breathed again. *Safe* she told herself. *Safe.*

Charlie stopped off at her neighbour's house on her way home. Peggy came to the front door, a large towel draped over her right arm and a plastic spray bottle in her left.

"Shower time," she explained.

Bert was standing on the lounge doorframe. He swooped down and landed on her shoulder with a loud squawk. He then tried to kiss her.

"Mmm mmm," he said.

"No, I don't have any grapes, Bert. I've only come to see if you and Peggy would like a cake. I'm baking a batch tonight for the café."

"Mmm mmm," he repeated, his head bobbing up and down. Seeing there were no grapes, he flew back to the doorframe where he watched them both.

"That's very thoughtful of you, dear," said Peggy. "Are you making any fruit cakes? I think we'd enjoy one of those. You must let me pay you for it though."

"Absolutely not. I won't accept payment at all. Well, you can let me give Bert a shower. That'd be payment enough."

"Done," said Peggy, passing the towel to Charlie. "Drape that over your arm. You'll get jolly wet doing this."

"Not a problem. I still have damp hair from my diving lesson."

"Oh yes, I forgot to ask. How was it?"

"It was better than I expected. I managed to get my mask off and back on again without too much difficulty. I'm doing the pool lessons with a couple of lovebirds who want to go diving on their honeymoon. I get to team up with Liam, the instructor, every time we do something. He's very nice."

"Nice?" asked Peggy, raising her eyebrows.

"Pleasant. Professional. No ... he's not my type. He's too young anyway."

"Don't discount younger men, my dear. There was a programme on television about ladies in their late seventies and eighties, who are with young men of thirty-nine or forty. You're never too old, it seems."

Charlie pulled a face. "Whatever do they have in common? I can hardly manage to think of things to say to Sean at work, and he's only twenty years younger than me."

"They said they were in love, but I don't know. Seemed peculiar to me. Fancy having sex with someone who is younger than your own son, when all you really want is a cocoa, watch *Countdown,* and an early night!"

Charlie spluttered at Peggy's comment.

"Come on, Bert. It's time for your shower. Go see Charlie. Charlie, spray some water into the air so he knows it's time."

Charlie squirted a mist of water into the air. Bert paced along the doorframe.

"Shower time. Show Charlie how clever you are."

Bert descended onto Charlie's arm and allowed her to puff water at his feathers. He held his wings up so she could get to all the feathers.

"Upside down, Bert," said Peggy. Bert hung upside down so Charlie could spray under his wings. He then flew back to the doorframe, shook his head and sneezed.

"Bless you!" said Peggy. "Again, Bert."

Bert flew to his bowl on his perch, grabbed some seeds, then returned to Charlie's arm, moving about for her to spray him. Once more, he hung upside down and then flew off to the doorframe. He cocked his head to one side.

"Say, *thank you, Charlie,*" said Peggy as she took the towel and bottle from Charlie.

Bert cocked his head from side to side.

"Thank you," he repeated.

"Good boy. Now you look handsome for Sunny."

"Sunny?"

"His newest fan. She's a young cockatiel, only three years old. She's the most wonderful colour yellow. She lives in a large house in Norfolk with a male cockatiel called Sky who's almost seventeen. He's very entertaining. He can sing *If You're Happy and You Know it,* among other songs. Sunny doesn't sing and seems to screech at every opportunity. Most female cockatiels are like that. They hiss too. Her owner, Marigold, hoped Sunny and Sky would get along together, but it hasn't happened. Sky doesn't seem to like Sunny. The owner thinks it's because he's jealous. Sky's even taken to furiously pecking his perch when Sunny is near. Apart from that, he ignores her. Poor Sunny is feeling lonely.

Last week, Marigold was on Facebook watching the video of Bert with his comb and Sunny began making 'wheep' noises, as female cockatiels do. She came and sat beside the computer and stared at Bert. When Marigold replayed the video, Sunny made the same noises, so we suspect she might be in love with Bert.

We're going to use Skype tonight and see if the birds hit it off. It's like a blind date. What do you think, Bert? Do you think you'll like Sunny? Say *Hello Sunny.*"

Bert, fluffed his feathers. "Hello, hello. Shut up fool!" he said in a deep voice.

"Now Bert. This isn't the time for B.A. Baracus. He's been watching the *A Team* with me. I bought a box set on DVD. We've been watching them all week. He normally prefers comedies though, don't you Bert? We've got all of the *Fawlty Towers* episodes and he's partial to a little *Allo Allo.* He loves Officer Crabtree. Officer Crabtree, Bert. What does Officer Crabtree say?"

"Good moaning," said Bert on cue. He then thrilled loudly like a telephone, cackled like a madman, and launched into a variety of other noises.

"Thanks for letting me give him a shower. Hope Sunny is impressed with his efforts. I'll bring the cake around in the morning."

"Good moaning," called Bert and cackled again.

"I'm sure he understands everything," said Charlie.

"Oh yes dear, he does," replied Peggy. "See you tomorrow. Gosh! Wait. I almost forgot. This was outside your house. It was in front of the door. I saw it when I was weeding. I brought it in because it looked like rain and I didn't want it to get wet."

Peggy pointed out a small cardboard box in the entrance. It had been hand-delivered.

"Thanks, Peggy. See you tomorrow."

Back inside her own house, she retrieved her scissors from the kitchen drawer and slid them down the tape holding the box together. Inside she discovered something plastic with a label attached to it. She read it. *Inflatable Perfect Man. Measures approximately fifty centimetres by nineteen centimetres by eleven centimetres when inflated.* She shook the plastic out to check. It was indeed an inflatable man in a white shirt, black trousers, carrying a bunch of roses and a red heart.

She shook her head in disbelief. What a strange present. It was no doubt a joke gift from Mercedes. She would get to the bottom of it the next day when she saw her friend. Right now, she needed to bake some cakes.

147

"Kiki Dee and Elton John there with that classic *Don't go bacon my heart. I couldn't if I fried,* or something like that. Righty-ho, it's time for joke of the week. Golly, it comes around quickly, doesn't it? Our winner this week is Geoff Milligan in ward twelve for this little gem:

'My son's been asking me for a pet spider for his birthday, so I went to our local pet shop and they were seventy pounds. Too expensive, I thought. I can get one cheaper off the web.'

Geoff thank you very much. You made Mercedes laugh the most on the Mercedes-ommeta that measures how funny a joke is. In case you want to know how funny that was, here's Mercedes."

Charlie cued in Mercedes's laughter. It rang out merrily, making her smile at the sound.

"So, if you want to be the winner of joke of the week next week and win a giant packet of Minstrel chocolates thanks to the generosity of the hospital shop, then post yours in the City Hospital Radio box at reception, or hand it to one of the presenters when they do their request rounds. Congratulations Geoff. Don't eat them all at once.

Onto our children's television theme tune feature now. Each week, we hunt out and compile a list of tunes to bring back memories of television shows you might have watched as a child. We asked around the studio and discovered Mercedes humming along to *The Magic Roundabout,* George knew all the lyrics to *Spongebob Squarepants* and Sam asked if we could play the theme tune to *Muffin the Mule.* Here's a few for you. Can you remember the names of the shows?"

Charlie started the tracks up and pressed the button to talk to Mercedes.

"So, you didn't send me the inflatable man?"

"Not me. That's a weird thing to do, isn't it, and I'm not weird," said Mercedes. "Only a bit weird. Could have been Rob. He's weird. Or that Jake. He's weird too. Or Susannah ... "

"Yeah. Guess so. I should keep it. It's the closest I'll get to a man."

"What about Liam?"

"What about him?"

"Isn't he divine?"

"Liam's very nice and looked after me. He's also *very* young. He

148

would have no idea who *Roobarb and Custard* were. He'd probably even struggle recognising *Scooby Doo*. My guess is he was brought up on a diet of *Pokémon*. Consequently, he's too young for me. He definitely won't appreciate my back catalogue of *Dallas* DVDs. So, have you been playing matchmaker?"

"I thought it was worth a go. He's got the best six-pack I've ever seen. Does it matter if he's a little younger than you? Think of the fun you could have with him!"

"I'd feel dirty and not in a good way. I'm at least twenty years older than him. That would make me a cougar. How old do you have to be to be a cougar? It's forty, isn't it? What do you call a woman older than a cougar who dates younger men?"

"Smilodon, I think," scoffed Mercedes.

"Smilodon?"

"Sabre-toothed tiger. That's pretty old. 'Bout the same age as you." Charlie wagged her finger at Mercedes. "Funny lady."

"You better stick to your inflatable man. At least he'll sit quietly beside you while you watch old movies together and won't complain about your wrinkles or your grey hairs."

"I get the point. However, Liam is not my type."

"Well, what is your type?"

Charlie closed her eyes and imagined Jake holding her arm. Jake? No. He was now Jake the jerk. No one else came to mind. "I don't know, Mercedes. I think I'm beyond help."

"No one is beyond help. Not even a hopeless case like you."

Charlie stuck out her tongue.

"Now who's being childish? Are you sure Liam's the one who's too young?"

Charlie shook her head and signalling she was going back on air, disconnected.

"On the sixth of August, two thousand and two, at the Blue Planet Aquarium, Ellesmere Port, Cheshire, thirty-year-old Robert Bennett had his hand bitten while diving, by a captive three metre (that's ten foot in old money) sand tiger shark. I hope they've got proper safety measures in place for Charlie at Chester. Sounds quite dangerous," Art remarked, reading from the iPad.

"Shh!" warned Patricia as the door opened. She removed the iPad and headed towards the craft shop. "Morning Charlie. How did your diving lesson go?"

"Yeah good, thanks, Patricia. Art, the cakes are still in my car. I couldn't get a parking spot near the café today. There are cars everywhere."

"That'll be thanks to the event going on upstairs. Some top journalist's giving a talk about writing and he's got about twenty-five people up there listening to him," said Art. "And, he wants a word with you during the coffee break. Something about doing a piece on your challenges. Should get you some publicity. I said you'd be happy to talk to him. That's okay with you, isn't it?"

"Of course it is. Twenty-five. That's the most we've had here."

"I know. It's great. None of them have been here before. I'm hoping they'll become regulars. I offered coffee and tea to them, but they're happy with water and soft drinks for now. They'll come down at ten-thirty for a break, cakes and coffee. I'm hoping they'll stay for some lunch after the event," he said, rubbing his hands together. "Right, I'll get Patricia to look after the café and come and give you a hand with those cakes. I'll need them for all these hungry people."

It was ten-thirty on the dot when Charlie heard scraping of chairs and thudding of feet above. The budding writers were descending. Patricia joined Charlie and was prepared, notebook in hand, ready to guide the customers towards free tables.

The new customers soon flooded into the room in small groups, where they spread out and examined menus. Patricia began taking orders. Charlie was about to take an order for a table of middle-aged women who were discussing the pros and cons of self-publishing when Art called her over to the counter.

"The journalist is waiting upstairs for you. Go have your interview. We're on top of it here. Could you take up his coffee and this piece of lemon cake?"

"Sure," she replied. She removed her apron, picked up the coffee and cake from the counter and went upstairs to join the journalist. She knocked at the door and went in.

"Hi, I'm Charlie. Art said you would like to interview me about the hospital radio station." A man dressed in jeans and a white shirt was standing with his back to her, looking out of the window at the street below. He turned to face her, a large grin on his face.

"Hello Charlie. How are you? All ready to face the sharks?" asked Jake.

"You," she gasped. "You're the journalist who wants to interview me?"

"That's me," he replied. "That cake looks delicious. Is this one of your famous cakes I heard about this morning from your boss? He spent ten minutes telling me what an ace cake maker you are. You are indeed a lady of many talents."

Charlie hung onto the plate and cup. Jake cleared his throat. "I thought yours would make a great little story. You see, I recently started working for the *Birmingham Gazette*. I'm a last minute replacement on this though," he added, pointing at the empty spaces around the table. "The journalist who should have been here is sick, so I stepped in. I'm not sure I've given them the right advice, but I did my best." He paused and ran his hands through his hair. Charlie was surprised to note that such a simple gesture was sexy. She erased those thoughts immediately. She was not going to be suckered in by this man. He continued, "My editor wants me to focus on *good news* stories taking place in the area. I thought about you straight away. I guess it was the kazoo that did it for me." He paused again, his smile widening. "Your story is perfect. Lovely lady does crazy challenges to keep a little-known hospital radio going. I wanted to hear more about it from you. It'll get you some coverage and probably bring in some more funds for the station." He leant against the table, gauging her reaction. She wasn't sure if his eyes were mocking her or not, but she was getting angry. She slammed the cup and plate onto the table in front of him. Coffee slopped out onto the saucer.

"Well, you've got a right cheek," she began.

"What do you mean?" he said, noting the two fiery spots on her cheeks. "I thought you'd be pleased. I wanted to help you promote your challenges ... "

"Oh did you? How very magnanimous of you," she retorted, hands on hips.

"Hospital radio stations aren't ordinarily high on people's radars," he said raising his voice to match hers. "At least, if you get some press coverage, you'll highlight the cause. The way you're going about it, it'll be futile. You'll not make enough money to save City Hospital Radio," he continued. "People are bombarded by good causes. There are so many out there. You need to stand apart from those. People need to engage with you and what you are trying to do. It'll all be a waste of time and effort and that would be such a shame.

I can make a difference. I can show how important the role of City Hospital Radio is to the community. I can even follow you on your remaining challenges. People love reading about fun news items and wacky stuff. Your story covers both of those angles. How many women would play a kazoo while haring down a zip wire for charity? There certainly aren't many who would dive with sharks. You even have the support of the local community. Look at all the shark pots downstairs. They're selling, purely because of you. With the right wording we could really grab their attention. Isn't that what you want?"

Charlie clenched her fists. She knew he was right, but she was not going to be asking this particular journalist for any assistance.

"What do you know about hospital radio and people's radars? What makes you think I can't do this on my own? As you said, the shark pots are selling. And, who are you to decide to help me? You barely know me. I don't need any help thank you. I can manage perfectly well without your sort of help. I suppose you thought you were *helping* me with Rob, the man in the pub?"

Jake looked down at his feet. "Well, yes. I guess that wasn't my finest moment, but he really annoyed me and he was behaving really badly, like a proper ... "

She glared at him. "Prick?"

"Erm. Yes, a prick. You shouldn't be hanging around losers like that," he continued, again running his hands through his dark hair. "You've got much more about you. You don't need idiots like that."

"Oh really? Suddenly you're an expert on who I should see. It's none of your business, mister nosey journalist. I don't need either your opinion or your advice. You've got a nerve waltzing in here, trying to impress me, pretending to offer help when you're probably waiting for me to make a fool of myself again. I wouldn't be surprised to read a column all about the daft woman who scurries about on her knees, making pig noises."

Jake raised an eyebrow. "Well ..." he said, attempting to lighten the mood.

"See! I knew it. I don't trust you at all, especially after what you did to Rob."

"But he deserved it," Jake protested.

"No," she said firmly. "He didn't deserve it. You went too far and I am not interested in your proposition. Goodbye."

Charlie turned smartly on her heels and walked off. She marched downstairs, past Art and the people in the café.

"Charlie?" called Art.

"I'm going home. See you tomorrow," she shouted and left.

Charlie drove straight home. She flung open the back door and headed for the kitchen. She crashed and banged about in her cupboards looking for her teabags. Who the bloody hell was this man to try and interfere in her life? He knew nothing about her. He had seen her on only a few occasions. They had shared a few minutes together at Alton Towers, discussing music and suddenly he felt he could bash up men he didn't approve of, decry her efforts at helping the radio station and arrogantly decide to play some sort of avenging hero.

She found some teabags at last and dropped one in a mug. She turned on the kettle and stood, fuming. At that moment, there was a loud shriek, followed by fluttering. Bert landed on her kitchen top.

He growled loudly. She screamed. Bert unperturbed cocked his head.

"Christ Bert! What the heck are you doing here?"

Bert bobbed up and down. "Hello, hello. Good moaning. Mmm mmm."

"You idiot. You scared me half to death. How did you get in?"

She looked about the kitchen and discovered the window was ajar.

"Oh no! I must have left it open last night after I baked the cakes. I remember opening it because it got too hot in here. Anyone could have broken in."

Bert made kissing noises and murmurings.

"Come on. I've got some grapes in the fridge and then you're going back to Peggy. She'll be worried sick about you."

She opened her fridge, pulled out a container of grapes and gave two to Bert. He took them in his claws and flew to the top of her kitchen door. She phoned Peggy.

Peggy picked up immediately. "Oh Charlie," she began.

"Don't worry. I've got him. He got into my house through an open window. He's perfectly alright. Frightened me to death when he landed on my kitchen top, but he's fine. Do you want to come around and fetch him?"

"I'm on my way. Naughty Bert."

Peggy arrived a few minutes later. Bert flew straight to her and kissed her. "Love Peggy," he said.

"I've never known Bert fly off like that," said Peggy as she sat drinking tea with Charlie. "He always stays indoors and only comes into the garden when I'm there. He only ever stays near me. I thought I'd lost him."

"How did it happen?"

"It was just after you left this morning. I heard you leave. I was getting breakfast for us and saw your car go."

"I left earlier than normal to get some more flour and cake stuff from the supermarket before I went to the café. I ran out last night."

"Bert was looking out of the window and making all sorts of strange noises, so I peeped out too and saw a man standing in your flowerbed and staring through your front window. I wasn't sure if it was a burglar. He noticed me and signalled to me. He seemed nice enough. Didn't look like a burglar at all, so I opened the front door and spoke to him across our fence. He asked if you were in. I told him I thought you'd gone out. He explained he was a journalist."

Charlie felt the tension rise again. That man was too much. Fancy tracking her down at her home. Nosey parker, journalist.

"Anyway, I said I didn't know when you'd be home and it'd be best to find you at the hospital later today. He nodded, thanked me, and went. I decided to pull some weeds while I was out there. Then, when I came back inside, Bert had gone. I didn't notice him fly off. I called and called him." Peggy pulled a tissue out of the sleeve of her cardigan and wiped her eyes. "Oh Charlie, I thought he'd gone forever. I went up and down the road, shouting his name. I took seed cake and asked all the other neighbours if they'd seen him. Someone phoned the local pet shop in case he got handed in. I was beside myself. Thank goodness you came home early and found him. I was going mad with worry. I don't know what I'd do without him." Bert sat on her shoulder, cooing.

"You frightened me, Bert," said Peggy rubbing his beak. "I'm so glad you didn't go far. Who's a lovely boy? Bert's a lovely boy."

"Bert's a lovely boy," repeated Bert.

"Did Jake, the man you saw, say anything else?" asked Charlie

"Only that I needn't tell you I'd seen him. He wanted it to be a surprise for you. Oh dear, have I ruined the surprise now? What a silly old lady I am. I got so worked up about Bert. I shouldn't have said anything."

"Not at all. I've already seen him. He came to the café. It wasn't much of a surprise. I told him I wasn't interested in his silly interview."

"That's a shame. He seemed such a nice young man. I got the impression he was quite keen to see you and not just to interview you. Oh well. There are plenty more fish in the sea."

"Yes, and there are some large sharks, too," said Charlie and shivered.

"It's been done too many times," said Mercedes. "I think it's a good idea, but I don't think it'll wow the public. Calendars need to have more appeal. The Woman's Institute started that craze for subtle nude calendars. I've seen firemen charity calendars and even Greggs, the bakers, produced one with some great photographs of naked ladies with Chelsea buns placed strategically covering their anatomy. Unless you want to strip off, along with some of the doctors and nurses here, I don't think a calendar would work. That's my thought on the subject, for what it's worth."

"You're right. We'll abandon the idea of a Challenge Charlie calendar. Any further ideas?"

"Not at the moment. The shark dive is pulling in money. Sean dressed up as a large furry shark at the weekend and collected money from hospital visitors. Patricia's pots have been popular and we can't do much more at the moment. We'd have to go for really wild ideas if we wanted to raise the profile to an entirely new level, like send you volcano boarding."

"Volcano boarding?"

"Yes, snowboarding is old school these days. The most extreme way to slide a slope is at Cerro Negro in Nicaragua. It's a live volcano, which erupted as recently as nineteen ninety-nine, and has become a hotspot for extreme boarders, who can reach speeds of up to eighty kilometres per hour as they course down the volcano. You get to hike up, have a boarding session and finish off with mojitos."

"The only bit that appeals is drinking mojitos."

"You have no spirit of adventure."

"I do. I'm not prepared to do anything completely barmy."

"Fair enough. I'm a prime example of what can happen if you try to live in the fast lane," replied Mercedes.

"Oh Mercedes. I didn't mean you were mad."

"I know you didn't. No one has been a better friend than you, throughout all of this. I get these mad desires. I get consumed with the idea that I want to do something exciting. Look at all the paraplegic athletes there are. They're all fulfilling their needs. They're inspirational. I could take up a sport. There's wheelchair basketball and wheelchair hockey. There's so much. I've been checking it out. Ryan says it's frustration that's making me aim high and I should start with more sensible achievements, then build up. Do you know there was a paraplegic woman in Whistler, Canada, who actually bungee-jumped in her wheelchair? I watched the video. It's incredible. There's an organisation called 9lives adventures that helps people like me experience extreme activities such as skydiving. It's abroad though. I thought about starting with something easy like rock climbing. Apparently you only really need to have strong shoulders. I'm thinking about going to the gym and work out. I fancy having a go at rock climbing."

"Are you sure you really want to do all these wild activities? It's not just a protest because you can't have what you really want?" asked Charlie gently. "I'm sure Ryan would walk over hot coals for you, and hold your hand while you climb Mount Everest, but he'd be inconsolable if anything were to happen to you while you were experiencing one of your big adventures. You have to consider him too now, Mercedes."

Mercedes shrugged. "You're right, as usual. Ignore me. I'm having one of my off days. Put it down to my period."

"Oh. So no joy again?"

"No. I think I might try another specialist. I'm sure this one has missed something. We go at it like rabbits almost every day. Ryan thinks he's going to wear it out!"

Charlie laughed. "Poor man."

"He should count himself lucky. How many men get it offered on a plate every day? Better get going. I have to go to town and get some provisions. I might see if I can get the van up to eighty miles per hour on the dual carriageway. That can be today's excitement," she said, looking downhearted.

Charlie did not know what more to say. Mercedes would recover. She always bounced back. Nothing would keep her down for long. Yet, Charlie could see that her friend was becoming more and more frustrated about being unable to conceive. Maybe she should mention adoption again. It might be their only option. If Mercedes did not settle down soon, heaven knows what she would take up to fill the emptiness inside her.

The day of the open water dive arrived. Charlie had spent the afternoon before at Alastair's, undergoing another session of hypnotherapy. He went through the relaxing techniques with her and was sure she would be able to do the dive.

As she stood beside Liam at Dosthill quarry, she was happy about not feeling too frightened. Liam had bustled about her and made sure she was comfortable in her suit. He made plenty of jokes and went through what they could expect to see in the quarry. It seemed strange to be alone with him. Felicity and Craig were not doing their open water dive with them.

The quarry was surrounded by leafy trees. Charlie was pleasantly surprised to see that there were changing room facilities, a dive shop, and even a catering van. Liam promised to treat her to a bacon sandwich after the dive.

She stood at one of the platforms with Liam. They studied the map of the quarry so she knew what to expect. Liam, mindful that his student was a nervous diver, took his time with her and explained all the sights below.

"We've got a caravan, a boat, a couple of cars, and a barge down here. I don't expect you to discover them all, but it's good fun looking out for them. As for fish, well we have some. We've got jack pike, giant pike, golden carp, and giant perch. They're completely harmless."

Charlie felt a shiver run down her spine. Liam noticed the concerned look on her face.

"They're perhaps the shyest fish in the whole of the UK. Besides, the vis isn't too great down there today, to say the least. Hence the torch," he added, pointing it out to her. "You'll be lucky to see me next to you, let alone trembling fish hiding in the weeds. Focus on me, enjoy the experience, and complete your PADI licence. After all, this is a training dive site, not the Caribbean, and training is what we're here to do. Ready to go, buddy?" He gave her arm a friendly squeeze.

"Yes, I'm all yours. Let's do this."

"Hope you don't mind cold water. It's chilly in there. That's why we're wrapped up in these dry suits today rather than the wet ones you're used to. They're thicker and should help keep some of the cold out. Come on, let's waddle over and join the ducks."

Liam took her out towards the platform. As they prepared for the dive, a couple of male divers wandered over to them, carrying equipment.

"Hi. Not seen you before. First time here?" asked the older of the two, looking over at Charlie.

"Yes. I'm not sure what to expect."

"It's a nice site. We're all very friendly here. You'll want to come back for more. We're here to get in some interval diving before we go away again to Egypt. Boys' week away. We go every year. Leave the women at home and go off to check out fish."

"The water's a lot warmer over there," said the other, peering into the quarry. "We don't often come along in the week. We normally only dive here at weekends. It can get fairly busy then. Today's dead by comparison. Hardly any cars in the car park. Looks like there's only a few of us here. Better get prepared, I suppose. Your first time here?"

Charlie nodded. All of a sudden, she was unsure about the dive. She had a ridiculous idea that there would be sharks in the water. She began to tremble. The older of the two men noticed.

"Hey, don't worry. It's perfectly safe down there. Besides, you're with one of the best instructors. He'll make sure nothing happens. You'll love it. Concentrate on finding the treasure down there."

"Treasure?"

"Well, old cars, caravans and the like. See how many treasures you can find. Concentrating on that will concentrate your mind. It's a wonderful experience. Trust me. I've been doing it for years and only ever had good times. Relax and have fun."

"Thank you," Charlie said.

"Have a good one, guys." Liam smiled at them and turned to Charlie, "Ready?"

"I think so."

"I can wait if you need me to. Even if I have to sit in this tight suit all afternoon."

"I'll be fine in a couple of minutes. Need to prepare," said Charlie.

She shut her eyes and thought about her last session with Alastair. She had come away relaxed. She knew if she could control her breathing and focus on the safe place in her mind, she would manage it. She thought about Amy. Amy would be cheering her on. Amy wanted to swim with dolphins. Charlie regretted that she never had that chance. She would do this. She would see the fish and the old broken bits of sunken treasure for her. It might not be dolphins, but it would do.

"I'm ready," she said with more confidence than she felt.

"That's my girl," Liam replied.

He and Charlie checked their tanks, jackets and masks, then entered the water via the platform that jutted out into the quarry. The cold took Charlie's breath away. She paused, then as instructed, deflated her buoyancy control device little by little, and descended into the murky depths. She used the drop line to make her way down. The sound of bubbles escaping from her regulator was soothing. Her breath became more regular. Liam checked she was okay. They swam away from the line, Liam leading. The sensation of floating was very calming, although she continued to grip her regulator tightly between her teeth. Soon, Charlie could make out the shape of a van ahead of her. Liam shone his torch on it. It was abandoned. Charlie had little idea of time as she concentrated on her breathing and on Liam. They floated above the old abandoned van. Liam shone his torch into various weeds to try and spot fish, but they avoided the light. The further Charlie and Liam swam, the worse the visibility. Charlie's mind became fully occupied with managing her buoyancy and staying close to Liam who continued to check on her, and shone his torch onto every submerged structure he could find. At the edge of the quarry, hiding in the green weeds was one solitary fish. It was quite large. Liam hovered over it, but it merely stared at them. Charlie felt euphoric. She wasn't frightened.

It was soon time for Charlie to make a controlled emergency ascent. They had discussed how to do it and following Liam's signal, she removed her regulator and kicked off towards the surface at speed, exhaling as she had been taught, allowing air to escape her lungs and not build up and cause problems. It was the final enormous release for all the pent-up emotion she had been clinging to for so long. At the surface, she burst out laughing. Liam popped up beside her, pulled out his regulator, and removed his mask.

"Congratulations," he said. "That was one terrific ascent. You went off like a cannonball."

They clambered out of the quarry and helped each other remove their tanks and jackets. Charlie pulled down the top part of her suit and dried herself off with the large towel Liam handed to her. The flimsy swimming costume she wore underneath the suit was wet and she shivered with cold. However, the relief at having completed the diving certificate was so great that she hugged Liam tightly. He returned the hug with enthusiasm. Deciding that the air in the tank had gone to her head, she pushed away before her embrace could be misconstrued.

"Thank you, Liam. You're a fabulous instructor. I couldn't have done it without you. Now, what about that bacon butty? My treat. To celebrate."

After drying off, the two of them sat in his car eating bacon sandwiches, enjoying a warm cup of coffee, and telling jokes.

"So, this man is stranded on a desert island, all alone for ten years. One day, he sees a speck in the horizon. He thinks to himself, *it's not a ship*. The speck gets a little closer and he thinks, *it's not a boat*. The speck gets even closer and he thinks, *it's not a raft*. Then, out of the surf comes this gorgeous blonde woman, wearing a wet suit and scuba gear. She comes up to the man and she asks, "How long has it been since you've had a cigarette?"

"Ten years," he replies.

She reaches over, unzips this waterproof pocket on her left sleeve and pulls out a pack of fresh cigarettes. He takes one, lights it, takes a long drag and says, "Man, oh man! Is that good."

Then she asks, "How long has it been since you had a drink of whisky?"

"Ten years," he says sadly.

She reaches over, unzips the waterproof pocket on her right sleeve, pulls out a flask and gives it to him. He takes a long swig and says, "Wow, that's fantastic!"

Then she starts unzipping the long zipper that runs down the front of her wet suit and she says to him, "And how long has it been since you had some REAL fun?"

And the man cries out, "My God! Don't tell me you've got a set of golf clubs in there, too."

Charlie groaned.

"Hey! That's my best joke. You wouldn't want to hear my bad ones," said Liam. "Is that the time? Crumbs. Sorry. I've got to do a

162

dive session at a private house for a group of wealthy people who've got an indoor swimming pool. They're going to some private island on holiday in a couple of months. I wonder if they'd like a private dive guide to accompany them. Okay, better hand you your certificate and pass. You'll need them to go on that shark dive. Want to hear a joke about sharks?"

"I'll pass on that, if you don't mind. You can be happy in the knowledge you ended on a high with that last one. Thanks again."

"You're welcome. Hope you enjoy your shark dive."

Charlie clambered out of Liam's car and ambled back to her own, stopping to drop off the empty cardboard cups in the dustbin. Liam tooted his horn and drove off. She waved at him. The other two divers had not yet surfaced. The lake was empty apart from a man taking photographs near the platform. She got into her car and left. It was only as she drove down the road that she imagined the man had looked vaguely familiar. She dismissed the thought, looked down at her new diving certificate on the passenger seat and punched the air. She felt quite confident she could dive with sharks now.

"*December 1963*, open brackets *Oh, What a Night*, closed brackets, from Frankie Valli and the Four Seasons. What a fabulous song! I've read glowing reviews about the show *The Jersey Boys* that follows the success and breakup of this successful group. I would love to see it. If any of you have seen it, let us know what you thought. Maybe you've even seen Frankie Valli in concert, do let us know. Which is your favourite Four Seasons song? Could it be one of their earlier hits or this one also from nineteen seventy-five?"

Charlie cued in *Who Loves You* and tipped her head against the headrest on her chair. She was feeling exhausted.

"Oy, Missus. Wake up!" yelled Mercedes through her headset. "You can't go to sleep on the job. These people don't want to hear you snoring."

"You come and take over. I'm bushed," replied Charlie.

"In all seriousness, you do look a little peaky. You're not feeling ill, are you? I bet you've been overdoing it."

"Had a busy shift at the café this morning and then I dropped Peggy off at her monthly widows and widowers club. She's getting a lift home with someone called Gordon."

"Oh I see. Did she say much about him?"

"He's a new member and she thought she'd better protect him from all the other ladies. She's invited him home for afternoon tea."

"Hope Gordon likes parrots and doesn't wear a toupee. Does Bert still land on people's heads and then laugh hysterically?"

"Yes. He still does that. He hasn't done it to me recently. He sits on my shoulders and keeps blowing me kisses or growling."

"I should go and see him and Peggy again soon. They're such a scream. Last time I went around, Bert became besotted with my wheelchair. He sat behind me on one of the handles. I taught him to make noises like a car. By the end of the afternoon, he could say 'vroom, vroom'. Okay, you'd better get back to it. Only another ten minutes to go, then you can clock off."

Charlie muted the intercom and prepared to talk to the listeners. No matter how tired she felt, she would not let them down. She had a final request in front of her. It was for a young mother who was due to have an operation the following day.

"So, this is my final track for today. It's especially for Lisa, who's nil by mouth tonight. It comes with much love from your husband Tom and your daughter Emily. Emily says she loves and misses you very much and she's cleaned her room for when you come home so you won't have to do any housework. Lisa, for you, chosen by Emily, it's *Three Little Birds* by Bob Marley."

Her eyes filled. She stared at the ceiling, waiting until she could be sure the tears would not fall. Some days were harder than others. She had met both Lisa and Emily. She envied their precious relationship. What made it harder was that she used to sing *Three Little Birds* to Amy whenever she woke because of a nightmare, or was afraid. Amy often crept into her parent's bed and snuggled up against Charlie who stroked her hair and sang softly to her. Amy knew all the lyrics to the song. They fed the birds in their garden and Amy was convinced the same three little birds from the song visited. Charlie still hung fat balls for the birds.

When she was eight years old, Gavin and Charlie took Amy to Tenerife for a summer holiday. They spent a lot of time on the beach and visiting the island's attractions. One day, they visited the Loro Parque, a wonderland filled with all varieties of parrots. They watched a parrot show where clever birds performed tricks much like Bert, and snuggled up to their keepers, murmuring affectionate noises when they were rewarded. Amy was captivated by their antics. They rode bicycles, sang, did calculations, and flew freely around the room enjoying every minute of their show and the attention from the audience. After the show, they walked through Katandra Treetops, a huge walk-in aviary where dozens of parrots and other birds flew around freely and occasionally landed on the trio. Amy was ecstatic. They walked on swinging bridges high among the treetops and got up close and personal with cheeky Lorikeets, Galahs, Palm Cockatoos, Cockatiels and some brazen Victoria Crowned Pigeons who attempted to steal from Charlie's open bag. Amy had her photo taken holding a beautiful yellow parakeet. She had simply adored the parrots.

"One day, when I'm a big girl, I'm going to live with the parrots on a special island like this with palm trees and love them and play with them and teach them tricks," she declared that night in bed, clutching a blue toy parrot purchased from the souvenir shop. From that day onwards, she believed the three little birds in the song were parrots and they would make everything all right. Charlie had kept the blue toy parrot. It was called Loro and it sat on her bed, near the bedside cabinet where Amy's photograph stood. Her thoughts were interrupted by Mercedes.

"I don't know who you've impressed with your dulcet tones, but an email arrived from the New Alexandra Theatre in Birmingham. You've been allocated two front row tickets for *The Jersey Boys* on December the ninth. They're from an anonymous purchaser. You lucky lady."

Charlie was dumbstruck. "I can't accept these," she said.

"Why not? They'll only go to waste if you don't use them. You could do with a good night out. Besides, it's months away. That'll give you plenty of time to think of someone to accompany you. What about Liam?"

"Will you stop going on about Liam. He's too young to remember Frankie Valli. I'll think about the tickets. I'd really like to see the show."

"There's also an email here from the *Birmingham Gazette* asking to do a piece on your challenges. You okay to do an interview tomorrow?"

"Only if it's not with that jumped-up Jake Meredith."

"Doesn't say who they're sending. Shall I email them back stating *anyone but jumped-up Jake Meredith?*"

Charlie chuckled. "No, I'll do the interview, but if it's Mister Meredith, I shan't be responsible for my replies or actions. What time do they want to do it and where?"

"Says tomorrow afternoon between one and two, here at the hospital. Also, can you wear your wetsuit for the photographs?"

"No, I damn well can't!" Charlie spluttered. She heard muted laughter. "You're winding me up again, aren't you?"

"Only a little. I'll tell them one o'clock and you'll be in flippers and swimwear."

Charlie finished her show, chatted to her friends, and left for home. There was a red Honda CRV parked outside Peggy's house. It seemed Peggy had succeeded in inviting Gordon home, not only for afternoon tea, but for dinner and the evening.

Inside her own house, she turned on the radio and prepared some food. There was no doubt that life was lonely once she got back within her four walls. She was more used to being alone than when she first split up from Gavin, but she still felt some days that it was an empty existence. She longed to have someone to talk to. She missed sharing her life with a companion.

She poured a glass of wine and turned on the computer. There had to be more to life than hanging about on social networking sites. She pulled up her Facebook page and checked to see who was online. Most of her friends were not. They were no doubt cooking meals for their families or watching television with their spouses. She had a new friend request from Liam. She accepted it and clicked onto his wall to leave a message. She was distracted by the photographs on the page. His header was a picture of parrot fish taken in tropical waters. She admired the clarity of the sea and the vibrant colours of the fish. They did look like parrots with their curved beaks. They were fascinating. She picked up her glass of wine. A few months ago, she would not have been able to even look at photographs taken underwater. She had made huge strides. She raised the glass to her bravery.

She left a message thanking him for his patience and jokes, and clicked on some more of his photographs. Some were taken at Dosthill. There were various pictures of Liam with clients posing for the camera, several taken underwater of the rusty old van at the bottom of the quarry and then one taken abroad of a large shark. Charlie's blood ran cold. She clicked off the page. It was too late. Her mind was drifting back to that day. The film she hated playing in her head clicked on automatically and began to roll ...

Two children, a boy and a young girl are in a small rubber dinghy. They are laughing and paddling the dinghy out to sea. The girl can see her mother sitting on the beach with another lady. The children are paddling close to another dinghy. Her father is in the other boat. He is smiling at her.

"Okay, Charlie?" he calls. She nods even though she is finding paddling a bit difficult in the sea. The current is making it heavy-going. She is determined to stick at it. She wants to prove to the boy in front that she is not a silly little girl. She wants him to think she is almost as grown up as him. She begged her father to go out to sea with them. He only agreed because she pleaded non-stop. That is why he is in the other dinghy.

"You're only eight. The sea can be very rough and dangerous," he said.

167

"Robin's allowed to canoe," she replied stubbornly. "He goes out all the time."

"Robin has lived by the sea all his life. He's a strong swimmer. And, he's three years older than you."

Charlie crossed her arms and stared at her father. "I can swim too."

"Let her go," her mother chimed in. "This is Sussex, not the Gold Coast in Australia. She's hardly likely to get chewed to pieces by sharks or drown in huge waves. Go with them, then you'll be near them in case the tide turns, or it gets too much for her."

"It won't," said Charlie, defiantly.

Now she is sitting in the dinghy with Robin. Robin is her father's godson and thinks she is a silly little girl. But she is not. She's going to show him that she's just as good as he.

"Better watch out for sharks, Charlie," says Robin. He turns and smirks at her. She gives him a cold look.

"There aren't any sharks here. It's not Australia," she retorts.

"Oh, there are sharks alright. Great big ones with huge teeth. They'll rip your legs and arms off in one bite. Blood will pour out and other sharks will come and eat you too. Be careful you don't fall in. You won't last a minute. They smell fear," he added.

Charlie looks into the sea. There are no sharks here. This is England. She stops paddling. Is that dark shape in the water veering towards them? She looks at her father. He is talking to Robin's father. If there was a shark, her father would see it. Robin is just being stupid. Boys can be so stupid sometimes. There is a knock against the dinghy. It rocks dramatically. Robin calls out to the men. "Hey, something hit the boat."

"Probably a small wave or some debris," replies his father unconcerned. The men continue paddling.

There's another knock against the dinghy. This one is stronger than the first. Charlie wants to shriek, but she is afraid Robin will laugh at her. He's probably doing something with his paddle to make the dinghy rock. He has tried to tease her several times this holiday. He put a large plastic spider on her pillow and made her scream when she went to bed. She is not going to let him scare her again.

The men are pulling away in their dinghy, oblivious to the fact that the children have stopped paddling.

"Stop messing about," hisses Robin.

"I'm not," says Charlie. "It's you."

"It's not me!" he replies.

There is a swish of a fin and another knock. Suddenly, the dinghy rises and falls sharply. An oar falls into the sea and floats away. The dinghy is rocked again by a force in the water. Something nudges the side. Robin screams and falls against the opposite side, gripping the rubber tightly. Water splashes into Charlie's face. She coughs.

Before she can catch her breath, a large shark lands in the dinghy where it thrashes about. Charlie can see its teeth. There are hundreds of them, all pointed and white. It's going to tear her legs off. She shrieks loudly. In the confusion, Robin falls into the sea, leaving Charlie with the thrashing shark in the dinghy. She screams, but no sound escapes her mouth. There are shouts and calls. Charlie can only focus on the dark soulless eyes of the shark. It is staring at her. The dinghy is going to capsize. She's going to fall into the water with the shark and it's going to bite her. It's going to rip her arms off and its razor-sharp teeth are going to shred her flesh. She finds her voice, shrieks again, flails, and tumbles into the salty water. All she can think of is being eaten by the shark. Her arms windmill in helpless attempts to get as far away from the dinghy and shark as possible. The current is too strong for her. She is not as good a swimmer as she thinks. The shark will smell her fear. It's nearby. It's going to rip the skin from her body. She feels pulling on her arms and screams. She takes in lungfuls of water. She can't breathe. It's getting confusing. Her head is going muzzy. She knows she's dying. She feels intense tugging at her arms and legs. It's the shark. It's eating her. She can't feel it tearing at her. Her legs and arms have no feeling. She can't think anymore. She's too scared to understand what is happening. She loses consciousness.

She wakes. Her father is hovering over her. She is on the sand. She coughs up salty water and is sick. She sees she still has legs and arms. Robin is being hugged by his mother. He doesn't look so grown up now. He's crying.

"It's okay, Charlie. It's okay," says her father. "It's all over."

But it wasn't over for her. A few days later, Charlie saw a newspaper in the local shop with her photograph on the front page. It was headline news for a while. It was the only shark to be seen off

169

British waters. It was a three foot long starry smooth-hound shark. It escaped when the dinghy capsized, but not before her father had seen it. She and Robin had been fortunate to have no injuries. Well, no physical injuries. Robin got over the event and even managed to brag about it at school. Charlie, however, refused to talk about it. Her mind locked away the incident and protected her from the memory. Now it was released. She had to face her fear.

She picked up her wine glass. Her hand trembled. Wine spilt onto her table. Charlie watched the blood-red stain spread out in front of her and wondered if she really was up to the challenge.

"I don't believe it," said Mercedes.

"It's true. Gordon's car was still parked outside when I left today and just as I was getting into my Golf, the front door opened and revealed Gordon, dressed in little more than a pink dressing gown. He collected the milk from Peggy's doorstep and waved at me!"

"Well, I never ... Who would have thought Peggy would get involved with another man? How long has it been since they started seeing each other?"

"Ten days."

"So, she didn't put out on the first date then?" said Mercedes with a giggle.

"Don't be wicked. I'm not sure if they have sex and I don't want to know."

"Don't be such a prude. Of course they're having sex. You don't stop having sex because you're old ... or in a wheelchair," she added. "Only nuns and presenters who seem to be scared of having any relationship abstain from sex," she added.

Charlie snorted. "I'm not scared of having a relationship. I can't seem to find anyone to have one with, that's all."

"I handed you Liam on a plate."

"I told you he was too young for me."

"You idiot. He was a total beefcake and he had the hots for you."

"No, he didn't. He might have had the hots for someone though. He put a message up on his Facebook page the other day ranting about the ratbag who broke into his car, slashed his diving suits and ruined his diving equipment hidden in the boot. They left a note, too. He put up a photo of it. It said, *this should stop you flirting with other people's girlfriends.* Poor Liam. He says he's no idea who the lunatic is and why he's left the note. He thinks someone has got him mixed up with another diving instructor. I feel sorry for him. He was always so nice to me."

"See, you had an opportunity and you blew it. He was obviously a total stud. That's horrible though about the break in. Diving equipment is pricey."

"So were the repairs to his car. He's very miffed about the whole affair. I didn't think he was a flirt though. He was genuinely kind especially when ... " Charlie stopped herself but too late.

"Go on," urged Mercedes. "When what? You're hiding something."

"No. It's nothing," said Charlie, attempting to avoid Mercedes' intense gaze.

"Tell me immediately, or I vill set zee dog on you!" she said.

"It's nothing."

"I'm not going to let this drop, Charlie. I can tell by your face it's not nothing. Do you want me to shine a light on you and torture you, or are you going to tell your best friend what happened?"

Charlie took a deep breath. "I was a bit frightened about doing the open dive and he managed to take my mind off it. He had the right manner and coaxed me down. That's all."

Mercedes stared at her friend. "There's something else. I can tell. Spill the beans. You don't keep stuff from me. We trust each other."

Mercedes was right. Over the last few years, they had become very close. Mercedes knew all about her life with Gavin and Amy and had done so much to help her find her way again.

"You'll laugh when I tell you. I had a bad experience with a shark when I was very young and I'm a bit scared of sharks. In fact, I'm pretty terrified of them. I also hate swimming or water."

"Oh my goodness! Why didn't you tell me about this? I'd never have put you up for the challenge. Oh Lord! I've been making jokes, too, about sharks. What happened? Did you get bitten by one?"

Charlie explained the incident in the dinghy. It was the first time she had voiced the events from her childhood. Mercedes sat in silence. When Charlie finished, she drew up to her and patted her on the hand.

"You should've told me. I would've understood. We'll pull the challenge. It's no big deal. I can come up with something else. You should've confided in me. I wouldn't have laughed."

"No, don't pull the challenge. If I've learned one thing from you, it's to face up to seemingly unsurmountable challenges. You're the bravest person in the world. Not only have you overcome your physical problems, but also the mental ones that accompanied your injuries. I can remember the frightened woman who'd given up on life. The one who blubbed in hospital with good reason. The one whose life had been destroyed. She picked herself up and not only learned to lead a normal life again, but stayed amazingly cheerful and became very funny. You laugh at everything and never let what happened to you get you down. If you can deal with all the shit that was thrown your way, I can get over some daft incident that happened years ago."

Mercedes looked down. "Some days, I'm not brave or funny. I've been such a cow recently. I keep wanting to cry and scream at the same time. I threw a saucepan across the kitchen the other day for no good reason other than I felt like it. I scared Bentley and then I felt horrible. I get fed up always having to make an effort. Everything is difficult and some days, it can be frustrating, but as you know, life is short. Sometimes, much shorter than you'd like, so we should grab every opportunity. There are days when I loathe this wheelchair with every fibre of my being, but it's been thanks to you, Ryan, my family, friends, and dear little Bentley that I've come to terms with it all. This is who I am. For whatever reason, I ended up like this and I can cope. When it gets hard, I think of all the people in my life. I'm blessed to know them and I have lots to look forward to. So do you. I don't want you to do something that will petrify you or harm you, but if you can overcome this, you'll feel fantastic. I do every time I achieve something. However, if you want to change your mind, tell me and we'll scrap the challenge. I'll understand."

Charlie held her friend's hand tightly. "I'll do the challenge. I'll let the journalist come along and interview me and we'll save the radio station. It's not for me. It's for everyone who enjoys working there and for all of those who feel better for listening while they're in hospital. If it hadn't been for that station, we'd never have met. I owe it."

"Enough of this sloppy stuff. Shall I break open the wine?"

Charlie giggled. "Tea's fine. I don't want to get too blotto. I need a clear head for this dive tomorrow."

Mercedes manoeuvred her chair so she could fetch the milk from the fridge. Bentley was asleep, tired from playing ball in the park. His legs suddenly shot out and he made whimpering noises.

"Oh bless him," said Mercedes. "He's having a little doggy dream. I wonder what he dreams about. Maybe he's chasing his ball, or a cat."

"Or you in your chair. No wonder he's pooped. I've never seen a small dog run so fast trying to keep up with its owner."

"It gives us both a workout," replied Mercedes, looking down at Bentley. "Got to live up to my name. I'm thinking of getting a Mercedes AMG 63 badge for my wheelchair." She laughed. "Isn't he adorable?"

Bentley snuffled and turned over in his bed where he continued to snore gently.

"So, do you think Gordon's a goer or do you think he has a large supply of Viagra?"

"Mercedes! I don't even want to imagine that scenario," Charlie replied, a smile playing on her face in spite of her comment.

"Yeah, right," scoffed Mercedes, pouring the tea. "You know, you should consider joining a convent."

Charlie arrived in plenty of time for her dive. It was taking place after the aquarium shut to the general public and only the divers and friends would be allowed in. Mercedes had arranged for her to meet Heather Lock, the journalist from the *Birmingham Gazette*, for an interview, ahead of the dive.

They waited by the entrance to the aquarium. Charlie spent the time trying to stop her hands from shaking. Mercedes was accompanying her. She was attempting to do a wheelie in her chair to take Charlie's mind off the event. Charlie had barely spoken all trip, in spite of Mercedes best efforts.

"What time is it?" asked Charlie.

"This is the fifth time you've asked me," said Mercedes, giving up on her wheelie. "It's a minute later than the last time you asked me. Hang on, there's a car pulling into the car park, right now. I bet that's her. I'll go off and powder my nose inside while she conducts the interview. I also need to phone Sean. Good luck. Hope she's nice."

Charlie read the notice by the entrance for the twentieth time. She still had no idea what it said. "Breathe," she told herself.

A man strode towards her from the car park. He carried a notepad. Charlie groaned.

"Before you say a word, I didn't plan this. I didn't even know I was going to do this story until a few hours ago. Heather had to go off last minute to interview a politician who's suspected of having an affair, and I was called in. I didn't want to come and I knew it would annoy you, but they had no one else. Besides, I figured if I didn't come, no one else would write about it and then you wouldn't get the publicity you need. And deserve," he added.

Charlie glared at Jake. "Okay. I'll speak to you, but let's keep this professional."

"Of course," replied Jake. "I had no intention of doing otherwise. You okay?"

"I'm fine," she said.

"You look pretty nervous. I can't blame you. I'd be nervous," he said, checking his pockets for a pen. "Ah, here it is. Shall we start, Miss Blundell?" He grinned at her. She felt a flicker of warmth in her stomach. *Traitor*. She ignored her body's responses, adopting an icy attitude instead.

"So, let's go through the whole Charlie's Challenges idea. I know the reasons behind the challenges. Maybe you could tell me how it all started."

Charlie gave him all the facts, aware that he kept looking into her eyes while still managing to take notes. She reminded herself that he was a cad and, gritting her teeth, answered his questions. The interview was soon over.

"One last thing, I received some background information for this interview," he said, put his pad into his jacket pocket, and ran his hand through his hair. "Was your maiden name Asquith by any chance?"

"Yes, it was," said Charlie wary of this line of questioning.

"Ah," he said and nodded knowingly. "Then, that's perfect."

"Why? What are you up to?"

"Nothing untoward. It's just that Heather was Googling about sharks and discovered some old news items. One was about a small girl called Charlotte Asquith who almost drowned when a shark leapt into a dinghy. For some unfathomable reason, I put two and two together."

Charlie froze. There was a cough beside her.

"Hi. I'm Mercedes. I'm the reason Charlie is here. You must be Heather. Funny, I had you down as a blonde in a tight black skirt."

Jake laughed. "Yes, I'm Heather, but you can call me by my nickname, Jake, and I'm afraid I my legs let me down as far as skirts go. Hairy knees."

"I hear waxing can fix that," Mercedes responded with an ever-widening smile. "We've met before, haven't we?"

"You were gorging on ants and trying to make yourselves go blind by drinking absinthe, as I recall."

"I thought I recognised you. You were at Alton Towers, too. You were wearing that very same leather jacket and sat next to my friend on the roller coaster ride. In fact, now I come to think about it, I think I've even noticed you in my local post office. Now, I must tell you, I'm sorry, but I'm a married woman. As gorgeous as you are, I have promised to stand by my man."

Jake laughed. "I was visiting an ex-colleague from by-gone days. It was his suggestion that we dined at Archipelago's. He's been before.

I wasn't as adventurous as you two ladies with my food, or drink," he added. "Recently, I moved into a new house to be closer to my son's school. I guess it's in your neighbourhood if you've seen me about. I'm heartbroken that you won't consider me as potential sugar daddy material, but I quite understand." He waggled his eyebrows at Mercedes.

Charlie interrupted their conversation. "You know about the shark episode?"

Jake turned back to her. "Yes, but I haven't said anything to anyone. I expect it was traumatic for you. But, surely you can see it gives this story a whole new angle. It should make it more front page than back. I hope you don't mind if I include it."

"Do you?" asked Mercedes.

"I don't know. Do I want people to know I'm scared witless when I see sharks? That I tremble, shake, can't breathe, and almost wet myself with fear?"

"You won't feel that way after today. You're about to prove that anyone can face a fear, no matter how big it is and get over it?" Jake explained. "You're an example for others."

"Exactly my thoughts, too," said Mercedes, looking up at Jake, a smile on her face.

"Okay. I s'pose so. I don't know. I just want to get this over with." Charlie shook her head to try and get some coherent thoughts in place. "Do it. I can't think about it at the moment. I've got to go to a meeting and get ready. I need to prepare myself."

"Of course you do. Go ahead. You'll be fine. Honestly, you will. I'll watch, if I may. There's a terrific wall-to-ceiling glass window. We can see everything from there. So we can both be with you, in a sense. Is that alright with you, Charlie?"

Mercedes was making strange faces and nodding like mad.

"Whatever," mumbled Charlie.

Charlie left Mercedes talking to Jake in animated tones. She was too worked up to even argue with him or tell him what a jerk he was. Mercedes seemed to have taken a shine to him in spite of everything she knew about him. She had no time to consider Jake, or the story he wanted to run. She was met and ushered into a room. It was time to dive with the monsters.

There were several people in the briefing room. Charlie was surprised at the number. Were they all mad? Young and old were sitting in the room, listening to the briefing, some looking wary and others with excited expressions plastered over their eager faces. She was drawn to the woman and young girl seated next to her. The girl was little more than twelve. Her mother was petite with dark hair. She smiled the entire time and occasionally patted her daughter's hand with affection. Charlie barely heard the safety briefing. She was only aware that sharks got fed every few days and that this was not one of those days. She had been chosen to go in the first team of four with the young girl, her mother and a man who seemed confident. He talked non-stop about a group of Barracuda he had eye-balled during a dive. They were told to go backstage to get kitted up.

"Hi, I'm Mandi. This is my daughter, Melissa."

The girl acknowledged her. She was bright-eyed with excitement.

"Nerve-wracking, isn't it? I don't know why Melissa isn't more scared. I'm so proud of her. She's only thirteen. She only became PADI certified this year. I wish I'd been more adventurous when I was her age. The most exciting thing I used to do was go roller-skating or hang upside down on the climbing frame in the park. Kids today. So different."

Charlie nodded dumbly. Melissa was busy putting on her suit. Mandi squeezed into her suit, too, chatting all the while. Charlie was grateful. It helped to focus on something other than her nerves.

"So, I guess you've not done this before?"

"No. It's a challenge. I'm doing it for charity."

"Good on you. I hope you raise lots of money. At least it's not as tiring as running a marathon, eh?"

They were requested to leave their fins off. Only the safety divers wore fins. Instead, they were weighted to ensure that they stayed down in the water. Three safety divers, equipped with spears, dropped into the tank ahead of the divers.

"I hope we don't need those chaps," whispered Mandi. "Still, better they're there. I wouldn't go in alone."

They made their way to the tank. The man was first to go in. He descended quickly and was followed closely by Mandi.

"If she doesn't come in by herself, throw her in!" Mandi told the instructor, nodding in the direction of her daughter. She needed no encouragement and having given Charlie a big smile, Melissa donned her regulator and jumped in right behind her mother.

Charlie's heart thumped wildly in her chest. She gave herself no time to think and following Melissa, she jumped in, sinking immediately down into the huge tank. She landed at the bottom.

Charlie was acutely aware of an urgent drumming in her ears. The noise threatened to deafen her. She couldn't move. Even if she had the wherewithal to make an emergency ascent, she was unable to. Her feet were weighted down, rendering her immobile. The bubbles of air that had been floating above her head like silver balloons ceased as she held her breath, transfixed by the sinister grey shape that was now focusing on her. If she weren't so terrified, she might have admired the enormous shark. However, it had fixed its glassy stare on her and was heading towards her, not at speed, but at a teasing, leisurely pace, biding its time before deciding to rip into her flesh. She didn't take in the sparkling white underbelly of the creature or the power of the muscular tail as it effortlessly guided it through the water. All she could see were row upon row of razor sharp teeth all grinning at her.

Breathe, Charlie, she thought, willing every muscle in her body to relax. Her vice-like grip on her regulator was making her jaw ache. *Remember, stay calm. Don't show it fear.* The voice in her head continued to attempt to placate her in vain as Charlie suddenly and uncontrollably began to shake. The shark picked up its pace. *Why, oh why, did I allow myself to get in this situation?*

More sharks appeared. They arrived from nowhere. They circled the group. Charlie saw teeth. Hundreds and hundreds of teeth. Her mind screamed silently at her to escape from the tank, then she noticed Melissa. The girl appeared transfixed by the beauty of the creatures. She was admiring them, trying to attract her mother's attention to share the experience with her. The sharks swam above them. The duo was unperturbed. As if a magic hand had pressed an invisible button and summoned them, so the sharks lost interest in the divers. They drifted off into the water in search of more interesting sights. Other fish came into view. Charlie felt a serenity she had not experienced before. She was aware of her breathing. It was no longer ragged. It came in calm intakes and lengthy exhalations: the result making her feel more relaxed than she had in years. She noticed the flashes of colours on the smaller fish as light reflected from them and marvelled at how nature could succeed in painting the small creatures with such rich hues.

The sharks continued to swim overhead. They seemed completely at ease with the intruders in their world. They did not advance on the group. They were no longer threatening. Their ever-present grins no longer terrifying. In fact, they seemed no more frightening than the other curious fish that darted about. They were not going to attack. Charlie knew it. She could sense it. This underwater world was harmonious and more intriguing that Charlie could ever have imagined

There were all varieties of sharks including the exotic angel and guitar sharks to the larger nurse sharks, lemon sharks and odd looking zebra sharks. They all possessed a grace and even the reef sharks and large nurse sharks no longer frightened Charlie. It was as if she had swallowed a magic pill. She felt at peace here in this enchanting place. A stingray drifted against Charlie's arm and she felt its velvet skin for a brief moment as it flowed gracefully over her.

Mandi and Melissa sat together on the floor of the tank, searching for something. Charlie joined them. She saw what they were hoping to find. It would make a fantastic memento for the young girl. She lifted the trophy from the floor. It was a white shark's tooth. She handed it to Melissa. As she did so, a large sand tiger shark hovered overhead as if watching, and then, with a powerful flick of its tail, swam away.

Too soon they were summoned to the surface. A reluctant Charlie joined the others as they left the tank, one by one, aided by the divers. Charlie's feeling of awe had been replaced by one of joy. She would have happily returned to the tank and sat for another hour observing this new wonderland. She was not the only one to feel that way. Melissa exited with a squeal and hugged her mother tightly.

"That was the best thing, ever!" she exclaimed.

Her enthusiasm was infectious and soon all four were hugging, then talking at once about what they had seen. They scurried off to change and share their experiences with those who had accompanied them and watched from the other side of the glass.

Back at the entrance hall, Charlie discovered Mercedes in conversation with a man holding a microphone. A television camera was set up and manned. They noticed her as she came in. Mercedes backed away. The man lifted his microphone.

"And so, this is Charlie Blundell. The lady who was once attacked by a shark, lived to tell the tale, and has now overcome a lifelong fear to take up a challenge to save a hospital radio station," said the man.

Charlie recognised him. He was one of the local BBC evening news presenters.

"How do you feel now, Charlie?"

"Relieved. Relieved and ecstatic. That is an incredible experience."

"Was it difficult to face your fears?"

"It was. I have to thank Alastair for helping me and of course, I've had the support of my dear friend Mercedes who has overcome far more than an irrational fear of sharks."

"Well, I'm sure you've inspired many to tackle challenges and fears, Charlie. Thank you for taking time to talk to us and good luck with the next challenge. I'm sure it'll be a breeze after this one."

They turned off the microphone and chatted for a few minutes about the radio station, then the small crew left to cover another story.

"How did you manage to get the cameras here?"

"I didn't. Jake sorted it out. He phoned a friend on the way here, told them it would make a great story for tonight's news and arranged it for you. That man is perfect," she purred. "I think he's smitten by you, you jammy cow. Why else would he get the television involved?"

"Because he is an arse. An arse who attacked a friend, tried to spy on me, dragged up my past, and is trying to prove he's a big man by impressing me with his contacts. He's one of those blokes who thinks he needs to prove something. So, where is the big shot? He might have fooled you, but I know he's up to no good."

"He had to leave. He said something about his son and went. Not before he watched you go into the tank though. He wanted to congratulate you. I think you're being harsh on him."

Charlie was surprised that she felt some disappointment that he had departed. However, he was lucky because now, she felt strong enough to tear a strip off him for his past actions. It was a shame he was not there to face the new Charlie.

"Drop it. I don't want to sour my elated mood. Let's go celebrate. I think we deserve a bottle of champagne. We are staying the night here, aren't we?"

"I booked us into a hotel."

"Fantastic! Come on, best friend. Let's go paint Chester red!"

"Yes, then when you're drunk, I can tell you what your next challenge is going to be."

"Does it involve sharks?"

"No."

"A kazoo?"

"Maybe."

"Jake?"

"Oh you guessed it. You're going to learn to be a knife thrower and Jake will be your subject."

"Seriously?"

"Nah! But if you can convince him to do it, we'll go for it next time."

"Forget Jake. Let's party."

It was a green-faced Charlie who arrived back home the following afternoon. Peggy banged on the front door as soon as she had sat down.

"Charlie, I saw you on television. Bert recognised you and barked at you. You were wonderful."

"Come in, Peggy."

"Sorry, dear. I can't stay. I have a date. I'm going to the theatre with Gordon." Peggy's cheeks were rosy. She looked years younger.

"So, you and Gordon. Is it serious, Peggy?"

"I'm afraid it is. At our age, you can't afford to hang about. He's a lovely man and Bert thinks he's super too. He kissed him today and sat on his arm like he used to with Dennis, chirping affectionately. I have a feeling Gordon might even pop the question tonight. He's booked a table at a very smart restaurant before the performance. He's been whistling all day."

"All day?"

"Yes, he's more or less moved in with me. It made sense. No point in heating two properties and his is awfully large. He prefers living in our street. He says it's much friendlier here. He hardly speaks to his neighbours. Mind you, they always seem to be abroad."

"You really like him, don't you?"

"I do, Charlie. I didn't think for one minute I'd want to be with another man after Dennis passed on, but Gordon makes me feel so alive, and he's so funny. I laugh and laugh when he's about. I know it all seems a bit rushed, but when it's right, it's right."

"Peggy, you go and enjoy yourself. And if Gordon puts a ring on your finger tonight, I want to see it first thing tomorrow morning."

She pulled the little lady into her arms in a warm embrace. She felt so fragile. Life was precious. She was so pleased for Peggy.

"I must go back. Gordon was playing ball with Bert and I bet the little devil's propelled balls all over the lounge."

"Gordon or Bert?"

Peggy laughed. "Bert. If ever they decide to hold parrot Olympics, he'd make a champion ball thrower. They end up everywhere. He has a superb aim. He managed to hit Gordon on the nose with one plastic ball. I'm sure he did it on purpose."

"Have fun tonight."

"Thank you. I hope you raised lots of money. You looked so composed on television. I'm proud to know you."

Shutting the door behind her, Charlie thought about how much she had changed in such a short while. She had Mercedes to thank for taking her out of her comfort zone. She picked up her mobile and gave her friend a ring:

"Just checking on you."

There were muffled noises and cursing.

"You okay?"

"I'm fine. Dropped my blasted ball of wool. It's rolled off and Bentley has grabbed it."

"Wool?"

"That funny stuff that comes from sheep. You can get it in all different colours."

"Ha-di-ha. What are you doing with wool?"

"It's one of your daft challenges from your list. I've nearly finished it. I'll show you when I next see you. You really were the dullest person on the planet coming up with this. Why ever would you want to knit a onesie?"

Charlie snorted loudly. "I didn't write that. Surely, I didn't put that on my list? I can't knit or sew."

"I'm afraid you did and worse still, I've spent weeks knitting one. I'm just sewing up the last of the squares on it. I'll bring it in tomorrow and you can model it for me."

"Like heck I will."

"If I can waste my precious hours knitting the wretched thing, thanks to you, then you can try it on. You can wear it during the show. I insist. If you don't, I'll make Ryan wear it and come around to your house posing in it. He'll sit on your doorstep so everyone can see him. You wouldn't do that to him, would you? Poor Inspector Onesie!"

Charlie could not hold the phone for laughing. "I give in. I'll wear it. But only in the studio where no one can see me."

"Deal. Can you get in early tomorrow? An hour before the show?"

"Yes. Why?"

"I need your help with something. See you then. Bentley! Come back here with that yarn!"

"Go get Bentley. I'll see you tomorrow."

When she walked into the Art café the following morning, Charlie was treated to a round of applause, led by Patricia and Art. She felt like a celebrity. Throughout the morning, people congratulated her on her dive and commented on the television interview. The feature had included some footage of her sitting calmly with Mandi and Melissa, discovering the shark's tooth on the floor and handing it over to Melissa, while a large shark swam above them. She had done it. She had no more fears to face. Mercedes had been right. She was not the same woman. Basking in the limelight, she decided that nothing would stand in her way now. She would tackle any challenge thrown at her, save the station, and then make some important decisions about her life. She had been hiding away too long.

The doorbell clanged, announcing the arrival of customers. She looked up to see a red-faced Jake. She prepared to battle with him.

He marched up to her and from behind his back, pulled out a bunch of flowers. "These are for you. To say congratulations. I watched you go into the tank, but I had to leave. I had to collect Toby from the hospital. His mother was too busy."

"Is he alright?"

"Thanks, he's fine. He hurt his ankle during a cricket match. The school feared it was broken and whipped him off to hospital, but it transpired it was only sprained. I dropped him off back at school last night. He didn't want to miss tuck night!"

He noted the confused expression on her face. "That's when they are allowed to buy sweets and chocolate from the school sweet shop and scoff them in their bedroom," he explained, raising his eyebrows. Charlie smiled at the thought.

He changed the topic. "So, these are for you. They are to ask forgiveness for forcing you to share your story. I'm sure reliving it was horrific, but it was such an opportunity for you. The television crew were far more interested in filming you when I told them about your past history. I hope you didn't mind."

For an instant, Charlie forgot she was furious with Jake. He didn't seem like the sort to be aggressive. All she could see was a nice man who was undeniably charming and handsome. She gazed at the mixed bouquet of flowers.

"These are beautiful. What are these blue flowers? I've not seen them before."

"They're from my garden. I put them in the bouquet. They're borage, also known as starflowers. I have a couple of borage plants. You can eat the leaves. Traditionally, borage was used in cooking and for medicinal purposes. Nowadays, they're mostly used commercially for their oil. I like the look of them. I sometimes use a few leaves for decoration on my food. I added them to your flowers, because they represent courage."

He managed to look bashful. His face searched hers for approval and found it.

"Thank you. I'm genuinely touched. So, you're a gardener?"

"Not really. I have a small plot for vegetables and herbs. I enjoy cooking, so I like to have fresh herbs."

"Do you want a coffee?" She had asked the question before she had thought about it.

"I'd love to, but I have a meeting with Abigail."

"Thank you for the flowers. You shouldn't have."

"I should. I still owe you an apology for that incident with the fellow in the white trousers."

"I think you owe him the apology," she replied tartly.

"Well, I wouldn't go that far," began Jake.

Charlie felt her blood beginning to boil. Who was this man? One minute he was kind and generous and the next, he was stand-offish and arrogant.

His phone rang before she could say any more.

"Must take that. Well done, Charlie. Oh, I almost forgot to tell you. The newspaper are going to run a lengthier feature on you and have assigned me to cover the story. I'll be going with you when you take your next challenge. Mercedes said that would be fine. See you soon."

He left with a smile on his face, chatting into his mobile, oblivious to the fuming woman he had left behind.

"What beautiful flowers," said Patricia. "Are they from an admirer?"

"No, they're from a dickhead," answered Charlie, dropping them unceremoniously into a large vase. "One who needs to be taught a firm lesson."

187

She found herself receiving more pats on the back as she walked down the corridors at the hospital. Staff she did not know called out to her. It was all a little surreal.

Vivienne was the first to leap out at her. "Charlie, you were amazing. I've collected over two thousand pounds thanks to your dive and the publicity surrounding it. Money has been coming in all morning. It's looking promising for the radio station now. Just need a few more thousand and we'll be home and dry. The website has been getting hundreds of hits. Sean has posted your television interview there."

Charlie was thrilled. She drifted into the studio to discover Sean holding a large multi-coloured onesie against himself while Mercedes took photographs.

"Hi Charlie. What d'ya think?" she said.

"Wow! How long did this take you?"

"I started it at the beginning of the year. I knitted each square section and then sewed them all together."

"It looks like Joseph's coat of many colours. Or in this case, onesie of many colours. It's incredible." Charlie burst into her version of a song from the musical *Joseph's Technicolour Dreamcoat*, "I wore my onesie, with golden lining. Bright colours shining, wonderful and new."

Mercedes looked proud of her achievement.

"I must have been very drunk to have written *knit a onesie* on my list."

"Drunk indeed. So, now you have to do your bit because you actually wrote *knit a onesie for a charity fashion show and get a friend to model it.*"

Charlie looked horrified.

"You kid?"

"Never. I can prove it if you like. I have the document at home. Since we swapped challenges, I got to knit the onesie and you're the friend I'd like to model it. Boy, were you drunk that night! Still, knitting has been extremely therapeutic. I think it was the concentration required to knit, not to mention the motion of those needles. I did some every night while Ryan was out. It's actually enjoyable after a while and dare I say it? Addictive. It also has the same effect as drinking several mugs of cocoa. I've been sleeping better at nights. You ought to try it. I knitted Bentley a little woollen jacket based on this pattern. He wore it to the park last weekend when it was chilly and was admired by quite a few dog walkers. I was approached by a woman who wanted me to make one for her pooch. I might start my own line of doggie onesies. They'd be brilliant for cold weather.

Anyway, back to the present. We've got a photographer lined up and you're going to parade in that," said Mercedes gleefully. "You won't be alone. I wanted to bring Bentley to model his jacket, but I wasn't allowed, so I rustled up a few nurses to join you. We're doing an impromptu event for some of the patients in the coffee shop. I managed to get the local boutique to offer up some designer clothes. The nurses are going to wear those. It's good advertising for the boutique. It only took one long phone call yesterday. Of course, you'll be the real star of the show. So, Miss Blundell, squeeze your sexy bottom into your designer outfit and prepare to strut your stuff. Your audience awaits in the coffee shop."

Sure enough, the coffee shop was set up for the event with chairs arranged either side of a makeshift catwalk. Four nurses were gathered in the kitchen area, clad in various outfits, while the owner from the boutique adjusted the garments to fit them. The first nurse, wearing a short blue skirt, boots, and a long shirt belted at the waist, sashayed out to cheers. Music pumped out of the speaker in the coffee shop.

"This is madness!" Charlie whispered.

"It's just a bit of fun. The audience loves it. They've got vouchers to use in the boutique all this week. They get twenty-five percent off all the clothing. It helps build a relationship with the community," Mercedes replied. "Get into that wonderful outfit. You're going on last."

Charlie removed her jeans and T-shirt and wriggled into the woollen garment. "Are you sure I wrote this down on my list?"

"'Fraid so."

The first nurse returned as a second, wearing a peacock blue cocktail dress and carrying a jacket draped over her shoulder in professional model style, left the room swinging her hips in time to the music. Minutes dragged as Charlie stood dressed in the outrageous onesie. Somebody using a microphone was describing each outfit to the audience. Tina from the kitchen passed Charlie a biscuit. "Here, take your mind off it. I think you've got a lot of guts to do all of these challenges. I'd never have the nerve."

Charlie thanked her and nibbled on the chocolate biscuit. She was going to look a prize fool. However, did that matter? The last nurse returned to the kitchen and joined the other three who were now dressed again in uniforms. It was time for Charlie to go out.

"All for one and onesie for all!" Mercedes yelled as Charlie left the room. Charlie was aware of wolf whistles as she attempted to swagger down the catwalk, conscious of the itching wool.

"Here, modelled by our lovely, adventurous Charlie, is a one-off *designer* creation." Someone cheered. Charlie thought it sounded like Mercedes.

"Give us another twirl, Charlie. Beautiful. Imagine snuggling down in front of the television in this deliciously warm little number. Easy to put on, comfortable to wear, it can be yours if you bid the right amount. All proceeds will go to the Save City Hospital Radio Charity, so can I start the bidding at ten pounds?" Charlie was forced to stand looking goofy as the crowd bid for her outfit.

"Thirty-five ... do I have forty? Forty to the lady in the front row ..."

Charlie turned around to show off the outfit. Mercedes had wheeled in and was now at the front of the room. Charlie wagged her finger at her.

"Charlie you can't bid for the item," said the auctioneer with a laugh. The crowd chuckled. Out of the corner of her eye, she saw Jake. He was leaning against a wall, notepad in hand and smiling at her. She wished he was wearing the onesie. That would wipe the smile off his smug face. She ignored him and kept beaming at the crowd, turning this way and that so they could all see it.

"We'll also throw in a signed photo of the lady herself and one of her kazoos that she used on her earlier challenges. Thank you, madam. Thank you, sir. "

The bidding continued at a pace. Mercedes was rocking lightly in her chair in excitement. Charlie lost track of who was bidding.

"One hundred and fifteen pounds ... going once ... going twice ... sold! Sold for one hundred and fifteen pounds to the gentleman at the back of the room. Sorry, but Charlie does not come with the outfit, sir. We'll get it to you as soon as she's removed it. Ladies and gentlemen, thank you for your time and your generosity." The auctioneer walked in front of Charlie to shake her hand, obscuring her view of the audience. A camera light flashed.

The crowd applauded. Charlie looked about, spotted Mercedes and a few others from the studio, but Jake had vanished. Had he bought the outfit? He had been the only person at the back of the room. Why would he want it? He certainly could not give it to Abigail as a gift. The crowd began to disperse. Charlie raced to the kitchen, removed the onesie, and pulled on her jeans. Tina was preparing some food and the nurses had dispersed.

"That was great. Fancy someone paying that amount of money for a onesie. You can buy them in the supermarket for a few quid. Someone's a fan," she added.

"Or bonkers," replied Charlie.

She walked back into the room in time to see the gentleman who had acted as auctioneer putting on his coat.

"I've got the onesie. Are you giving it to the man who bought it?"

"He said to leave it at reception and he'd send someone to collect it later. He had to rush off. Did you want to thank him?" said the man.

Charlie really wanted to tell Jake to clear off and stop trying to be nice. "Yes. It was good of him to buy it. I expect he only bought it to help the hospital."

"Oh no. He bought it for himself. He said he was a good friend of yours." The man winked in a knowing manner. "He told me that in confidence, of course. He said he'd be able to think of you every time he wore it. It would almost be like having you there with him. How sweet. Have you been with him for long?"

"No time at all," spluttered Charlie "So, I really must thank you for encouraging everyone here to bid so much money."

"Not at all. My wife spent quite some time here last year. She enjoyed the radio shows. Kept her mind off the pain and so on. Well, see you again."

Charlie headed back to the studio. It was almost time for her show. Jake was bothering her. She could not fathom what he wanted. One minute he acted normal, but the next, he was quite odd. Men were becoming a complete mystery to her.

That night, Charlie was curled up in her chair, dozing in front of a reality television show and dreaming of Jake dressed in the knitted onesie sitting beside a log fire. He made the garment look very attractive. He ran his hand through his hair and gazed at her, indicating she should get in the onesie with him. There was plenty of room for two. It stretched as she climbed in with him, then held them together like a tight blanket. Logs crackled on the fire. A wine bottle stood uncorked next to two glasses by the fire. Charlie wrapped her arms around his warm body and smelt his citrus aftershave as she nuzzled his neck. The doorbell woke her from her slumber.

She stumbled to the door. Peggy stood on the step. She waved her veiny hand at Charlie. A small diamond and sapphire ring sparkled in the light from the doorway.

"Oh Peggy! He did ask you!"

"He most definitely did. He went down on one knee at the restaurant. It was a brave thing to do. Especially with his arthritis. He got stuck by my chair. A waiter had to help pull him back up. It was hilarious."

"Come in. We'll celebrate."

"I can't. We're going down the club to announce our engagement and then we have to plan the wedding. We're going to have a civil ceremony in the city and a week away somewhere romantic for our honeymoon. I went to Bognor Regis in a bed and breakfast with Dennis. We didn't have much money for a honeymoon. This time, Gordon is booking us a cruise to the Caribbean."

"Oh goodness! That's incredible. You'll love it."

"I'm sure we shall. However, I have one big problem. Actually, it's a little problem. It's a chatty, lovable problem."

"Bert?"

"The very one. I hate to ask but … "

"Of course I can. I love Bert. You can tell me what to do and I'll look after him. It's only for a week and he seems quite happy to be around me."

"That's such a weight off my mind. You are so good to me. And to Bert. He'll be very pleased to be with you. I wouldn't trust him with anyone else. I'll make sure he has all his toys and his perch and so on. Do you want to have a trial night with him to see if you're sure?"

"I'll definitely have him, but maybe I'll have a trial night as well, in case there's anything I'm unsure about. We'll sort out one and he can come and have a sleepover at my house. That way, it won't be so strange for him. In fact, we should arrange a couple of sleepovers before his proper holiday with me."

"You know, you're just like a daughter to me? I'm so glad you live next door."

"Don't embarrass me."

Peggy's eyes filled with tears. "I'd better go before I do something silly and start crying. I'll talk to you again about Bert and the wedding. I'd really like it if you could come and be one of the witnesses."

"I'd be honoured to. Thank you."

"That's settled then. I'd better go and get Gordon. I left him examining a box of 'Just For Men' hair dye. I told him he didn't need it, but he seems to think he does. He brought it from his bathroom. I think the sell-by was about five years ago. I ought to make sure he hasn't tried it out. I don't want to marry someone who looks like Gomez from the *Adams Family*, do I?" Peggy tittered and with a merry wave scurried back up the path to her house.

Charlie went back to her chair with thoughts of Peggy and her new beau. Life was full of surprises. Her phone vibrated with a message:

Baby Oliver born eleven o'clock. Eight pounds two ounces. Mother and baby doing well. X

So, Gavin was a father again. She sent a message of congratulations. Yes indeed. Life certainly was full of surprises.

"The challenges haven't been pouring in as thick and fast and we hoped," announced Mister Carnegie. Mercedes, Charlie, Sean and Vivienne were all cramped in his office with him. "Thanks to the publicity from the newspaper and the television interview, we've got a quarter of the money we need to build the new studio. We're still a long way off our target and we need to widen our net. Most people associated with the hospital have given money and so we need to try and get it from businesses and members of the community who may not have heard of us. I don't know if we'll reach the target yet in spite of all the marvellous ideas. I hope so. Sorry to put a dampener on the Challenge Charlie idea, but I thought it important to be honest."

"Some of these challenges that people have suggested are ridiculous. Even I would balk at them," Mercedes said.

"What have you got?" asked Mister Carnegie.

"Running with bulls in Spain, wingsuit flying, complete an Ironman Triathlon, swim the Channel, and shave your head."

"I suppose I could shave my head," began Charlie.

"Absolutely not," interrupted Mercedes. "It would take forever to grow back your beautiful hair. I can't let you do that."

"There was one that came in this morning," said Vivienne. "It was in the box when I opened it. "Zorbing."

"What the heck is zorbing?" asked Mister Carnegie.

"It's when you climb into a giant see-through inflatable ball and roll down a hill or onto water," replied Sean. "It's like being in a human washing machine. I had a mate who did it. Crazy, but quite good fun. He screamed a lot on the way down and ended falling out of the ball upside down and confused."

All eyes turned to Charlie. "Zorbing? Where do I need to go?"

"My friend went to the site near the M25. I remember he posted some photos on Facebook. The zorbing venue is located in some picturesque woodland at the top of Salmons Lane. There's a great viewing area so your friends can watch. I think there's one nearer at Nottingham, too."

Andrew Carnegie tapped at his computer and found the website for the event. "It looks quite interesting. Wait a minute. This looks even more exciting. What about this?" He read the description from the website, "Adrenaline junkies will love our Harness Zorbing which involves two people superman-diving into the ball, getting strapped in face to face and zorbing down hills at speeds building up to thirty-five kilometres per hour. Watch as your fellow zorbonaut laughs and screams their way down the run, and the sky and grass blend into one blur of exhilaration. Nothing can quite describe the sensation of hurtling down a steep hill in a ball, but that's what makes zorbing so unique!"

Charlie put her hands behind her head. "Sign me up. I'm doing that."

"I'm not going to be able to do it with you," said Mercedes.

"I suppose I could," offered Sean.

"That's very kind of you, Sean, however, I know exactly who's going to do the challenge with me. Book it, Mercedes."

The following Saturday, Charlie followed her satnav's instructions to Southwell and parked her car beside Jake's.

"Hello Charlie. Not seen you since the catwalk. Glad to see you're not wearing the onesie today," he chuckled. "Still, you managed to make it look glam."

She gave him a cool stare. "Thanks. Although, I wonder what type of man would buy a onesie for himself."

"Well, it was for charity. I expect whoever it was bought it to help the cause, not to wear to work."

She nodded. That was the response she expected. He was not likely to admit he bought it so he could think of her whenever he wore it.

"So, zorbing," he continued. "That's a real craze these days. I see you've chosen another brave challenge."

"It's not that brave."

"Well, I don't think I fancy being harnessed into a large ball and chucked down a hillside. I'd be sick."

"Really?"

"Yep. I reckon so. What made you decide to do this challenge? You weren't frightened by a guinea pig as a child, were you?" He looked at her, expecting her to laugh. "Sorry, that was feeble. I was only trying to lighten the mood in case you were feeling nervous."

"I'm fine, thanks."

They climbed up the hill side by side. Jake chatted.

"I meant to tell you. I unearthed some information that might interest you," he continued, oblivious to the determined look on Charlie's face. "It's all about a shark god. In Fijian legends, the fierce sea-monster Dakuwaqa was the guardian of the reef entrance of the islands. He was fearless, headstrong, and jealous. He frequently changed himself into the form of a shark and travelled around the islands, fighting all the other reef guardians.

Another shark god told him about the great strength of the gods guarding Kadavu island. So, Dakuwaqa, being the ferocious warrior that he was, sped off towards Kadavu to battle it out with these gods and, on nearing the reef, found a giant octopus guarding the passage.

The octopus had four of its tentacles securely gripping the coral and the other four were held aloft. Dakuwaqa charged the octopus, but soon discovered he was being squeezed to death by the octopus's four free tentacles. He begged for mercy and told the octopus that if his life was spared, he would never harm any people from Kadavu wherever they may be in any part of Fiji waters. The octopus released him and Dakuwaqa kept his promise, and the people of Kadavu have no fear of sharks when out fishing or swimming. Even today, when local fishermen go out for a night's fishing, they reverently pour a bowl of yaqona, a plant that is made into a drink, into the sea for Dakuwaqa. So if ever you want to go swimming with sharks again, you need to go to Fiji."

Charlie was in truth interested in his story and impressed that he had taken time out to read about it and tell her, but she was also cross that Jake had the ability to turn on his charm at will. She highly suspected that in a few moments, the other side to his personality would emerge.

They walked through a wooded area and emerged into a clearing. In front of them was an enormous net. They climbed up the slope to one side of it and towards the top. Jake had gone quiet. Charlie noticed a frown on his brow.

"Something up?" she asked, although she was not too bothered if there was.

"I was glad to see there was a net. I read about a Russian man, aged twenty-seven, who was killed zorbing in Russia. It was tragic. His inflatable ball fell off a snowy cliff and he broke his neck and spine."

He looked thoughtful. Charlie was shocked.

"That's dreadful," she said, shaking her head.

"It was really sad." He was silent for a moment and paused to examine the slope. "Denis Burakov. That was his name. He was married with two young daughters. His companion Vladimir Shcherbov, was hospitalised with concussion and multiple lacerations to the head and body, but miraculously survived. The report makes for grim reading. I'm glad there's a large safety net here. The slope isn't as steep as some and I don't think you'll bounce too much. And, I see they've erected safety barriers to prevent the ball from going off course. It seems safe. If only there'd been some safety measures for Denis. Some of these companies want closing down." He moved off back up the slope. Charlie was surprised at how much he seemed to be concerned for her safety.

"Sorry," he mumbled. "I didn't mean to scare you. It's just that the accident was so needless and could have been prevented. You'll be fine here."

Charlie agreed. They continued up the slope along a track strewn with wood chippings. It was a warm morning and birds were singing above them in the canopies of the trees. They passed a couple of picnic areas Jake pointed out.

"Could have brought the smoked salmon and champagne celebration breakfast."

Charlie nodded. She was perplexed. He took her silence for anxiety and maintained the silence, plodding up the slope and making mental notes for his article. They approached two more wooden safety rails running either side of what was undoubtedly the run for the zorb. There was a viewing area above the run where a couple of people were observing the team's preparations for the experience. A large zorb was being placed at the top of the run. Looking back down, Charlie noticed more people making the ascent. They climbed the steep slope in pairs. Charlie could make out small red-jacketed figures standing by the net. They were no doubt staff members. Two young athletic-looking men also wearing red jackets appeared from behind the zorb to greet them.

"Hi!" they chorused. "You must be Charlie and Jake."

"Yes, that's us," said Charlie.

"You're first up today. No need to hang about. We're all ready for you, so jump in, and have a ball!"

One of the men opened up an entrance hole into the ball, big enough for a person to clamber through. Charlie launched herself onto the floor of the zorb. It was extremely bouncy. She could not get a grip and tumbled backwards, landing in a seat.

"That was lucky," she said brightly. "I might have been ages trying to get into this."

"Make yourself comfortable," said the pleasant young man who was holding the ball 'door' open. "Settle back into the seat and I'll strap you in." Charlie wriggled into position. She was facing forwards, looking directly at another harness opposite her. The man leaned forward through the hole and attached the strap buckle around her waist. She felt like she was on a roller coaster again, but this time she had no vision. She could only see the plastic interior of the ball. She watched as the young man strapped down Charlie's feet.

"Don't want them lashing out and harming your husband."

Charlie was about to protest, but the young man smiled pleasantly. She let it drop.

"Comfortable?"

"As much as you can be, strapped tightly inside a huge inflatable ball," Charlie said with a nervous laugh.

"It's good fun. Wait and see. Okay, Jake. It's your turn. In you go."

"No, I'm not going in. I'm here to write about the experience for the newspaper."

"You can't write about it if you're not here to see what it's like," called Charlie smoothly, a smile playing across her face. "How will you know what I went through? You can't see my face or hear what I say, unless you're beside me," she continued. "Come on, Jake. You only live once."

"She's right, mate," said one of the men. "Go on. It's only a ball. Hop in. It's as safe as safe can be. Hope you didn't eat too much breakfast though."

He eased Jake through the hole with a firm push. Jake bounced, landed on his back staring at the top of the ball, and then scrambled about until he flopped into the seat opposite hers. "Charlie, I'm not that convinced about this," he mumbled as the young man secured his harnesses and closed up the gap in the zorb. His face had turned pale.

"You'll be fine. You'll enjoy it."

"No, I don't think so. I think I'd rather wait outside. I can't seem to shake the story of the Russian tragedy from my mind."

"Are you ready, guys?"

"Er ... " began Jake.

"Yes," shouted Charlie.

The men pushed the ball off the platform. Charlie and Jake were rotated upside down. The ball then set off on its own momentum. It bounced and shook and rolled them over and over and over.

"Argh!" yelled Jake as they bounced down the hill.

Charlie tried not to scream as she was propelled upside down and back upright, then upside down again. It was all a blur. Her stomach somersaulted and she was aware of the taste of regurgitated orange juice she had consumed for breakfast.

Over and over they went, tossed about wildly, straining against the harnesses. They bounced and bounced, then swirled around helplessly in the ball. Charlie could not see the expression on Jake's face. He was a blur. She became completely confused. Was she upside down or the right way up? She was thrown about like a rag doll and grateful that she was strapped in. Jake moaned loudly as if in pain.

Suddenly, the ball halted. It had landed in the strong net, been restrained, and was caught by the staff. They rolled it so Jake and Charlie were seated upright again. Jake's hair was at all angles. He was white-faced.

"Did you enjoy that, folks?" asked a girl, sticking her head through the hole in the ball.

"Huge fun," said Charlie although she was not too convinced she could walk out of the ball. She felt very dizzy.

"I thought it was the end of the world and I was going to die," said Jake as the girl undid his harness.

"Oh, so you did enjoy it then," said the girl with a grin.

It took much effort from the staff to remove Jake from his seat and pull him out of the hole. He was queasy. They sat him on the grass by the side of the run.

After a few minutes, he smiled weakly at Charlie. "You okay?" he asked.

She had not expected such a chivalrous response. She had anticipated a rant from him and some macho aggression.

"I'm fine. Bit wobbly though."

"I've never felt so weak," he declared. "I've clearly shown my true colours. You now know that I am a wussy. Toby was right when he teased me on the roller coaster. I wasn't keen at all. It was only because you played the kazoo and were obviously even more scared than me, that I held it together. That was horrible. Being thrown about upside down. Totally helpless. Feeling sick. Awful!" He paused for a moment and looked over at her. "Would I do it again? Yes. If you were there opposite me, I would."

He reached for her hand and squeezed it. "You're quite something, Charlie Blundell."

Charlie was flabbergasted. She had just tormented this man and he was not angry with her. More confused than ever, Charlie pushed herself to her feet.

"I set you up, you know," she admitted. "I wanted to pay you back for what you did to Rob."

"What is it with you and this Rob character? I thought he was an idiot. Why are you so angry with me? This seems a harsh punishment for my actions."

"You think so?"

"Yes, I do," he retorted, now annoyed with Charlie. "You made me go through that dreadful ordeal because of what I did to Rob?"

"I did. And you deserve worse."

Jake shook his head in disbelief. "You are quite ... mad."

"I'm mad? You're ... you're a testosterone-fuelled bully!"

Jake looked at her in disbelief. "You've got to be kidding. You clearly don't know me."

"No, I don't and I don't think I want to. Let's keep this a purely professional relationship. You can question me, but stay away from my friends and my house. If you decide you can't write about my experiences any more, I completely understand."

"What about the radio station? If I refuse to complete this assignment and keep you in the public eye, you'll not get the money you need."

Jake got off the ground and was testing out his legs. He suddenly wobbled over to a patch of grass where he vomited. He wiped his mouth with the back of his sleeve, then looked disgusted for having done so.

"Hope you're satisfied, Ms Blundell. You've certainly got your revenge."

Charlie placed her hands on her hips and willed herself to not feel sorry for him. She was going to give him a catty reply when he leant over and was sick again. She decided he had endured enough. She walked back down the slope and left him. He could find his way home without her.

"No matter what you do,
I'll still be there for you."

The poem, such as it was, came in an envelope marked with her name. It had been delivered by hand. She read it again. It was unsigned and had been typed in decorative font.

Jake was definitely some sort of Jekyll and Hyde character. No wonder his wife had left him. She tore up the poem and dropped it in the bin in the kitchen without giving him another thought.

She browsed through the brochures she had picked up at the travel agency. There was a whole world to explore. She had wasted enough time. She fancied a trip somewhere exotic. She had a list on the table in front of her. It was her new bucket list. So far she had added:

Ride on a gondola in Venice
Try a Bollywood class
Have a champagne lunch on the London Eye
Visit every capital city in Europe
Take a ride in a hot air balloon

It seemed that there was so much she should try and so much she could still accomplish. Mercedes would be more impressed with these choices than those she had written at the beginning of the year. This new Charlie was ready to tackle life. She blew a kiss at a photograph of Amy on the wall.

She had even considered studying for an Open University degree in marketing. However, there were other degrees she could also tackle. She was overwhelmed by the choices. A career in media seemed plausible, even night classes offered new exciting subjects for her to attempt. Charlie sat back and wondered why she had not thought about this before now.

Her phone rang.

"Hello?"

This was the third time it had rung.

She hated cold callers. They were a complete nuisance.

"If you are not one of those stupid machines that randomly selects numbers, bugger off. I'm not buying anything, I don't have a PPI and I've never felt tempted to buy a timeshare."

The phone went dead. Obviously not a machine, she decided.

The phone rang again several minutes later. She snatched it up.

"If you ring me once more, I'll come round there and shove your phone up your ... "

"Please don't finish that sentence," said a quiet male voice. "I called to say that the last piece I wrote about you zorbing will be in tomorrow's edition of the *Birmingham Gazette*. I hope you like it and you get further donations to your worthy cause."

"Oh, Jake, it's you. Sorry."

"No need to apologise. I spoke to the editor, but they have no other staff free to write about you so you're stuck with me. Mercedes told me where to meet you for your next challenge. I'll be there. I'll maintain a healthy distance though, in case you feel you want to carry out your threat about the phone."

So he was sticking by her no matter what she said or did to him. He was quite nutty. She picked up the phone and dialled Mercedes to find out what her next challenge was to be.

"You timed that right. I was about to phone you. This is a corker of a challenge. I've been sent an invite by a flying school. They saw you on television. They're willing to take you up in an aerobatic plane and let you perform some stunts with their pilot. How mega cool is that? I would kill to do this challenge."

Charlie was surprised at her response. She punched the air with her fists. She was genuinely excited. This was not the same woman who balked at riding a roller coaster.

Someone had replaced that woman with this new, improved version.

"It'll be the best challenge yet," Mercedes said when Charlie had finished making whooping noises. "Are you doing one of those stupid victory dances?" she asked.

"How did you know?"

"I just know, that's all."

"When am I going up?"

"At the moment you're booked in for a flight in three weeks, weather permitting. If it looks no good, you'll get a call and they'll reschedule the flight. Chocks away!"

Charlie checked out the flying school's website in order to learn more about the company and their aerobatic stunt plane, the Cap 10. It was going to be an outstanding challenge and an opportunity to raise lots of money. She reflected on how far she had come. She may be a middle-aged woman, but her confidence had reached new heights. Yet, a small voice inside her spoke up and reminded her that her body was not twenty years old, even if her mind had decided it might like to be. Once the stunt challenge was over, what would she be prepared to do next? There was a limit to how many wacky activities she could attempt. If it were not for trying to save the radio station, she wondered if she would tackle these wild challenges at all.

Charlie remained in a confident mood throughout the following week. She ordered a book about flying to help prepare her for the challenge and began to learn the phonetic alphabet. It would be quite an adventure. On Wednesday, Art and Patricia popped out to the Cash and Carry store, leaving her in charge. The café had been busy, but was now enjoying a quiet spell. Her show for that afternoon was prepared and she was looking forward to a night in after it, with a film, a pizza, and a bottle of wine. The café doorbell jangled. Toby came in, followed by a reluctant Jake.

"It was his idea," Jake said before she could open her mouth. "Toby wanted to come here. He likes the chocolate cake and he wanted to get his mum a present for her birthday from the craft shop."

"Hi Charlie," shouted Toby. "How's it going?"

Charlie decided to be polite for Toby's sake. After all, he was unaware of his father's actions.

"It's all good, thanks, Toby. What about you?"

"Oh you know? Not much. School … homework … the usual. Dad's been watching me play hockey for the school A team. We won three-nil and I scored two of the goals, so he's brought me out to celebrate."

"Congratulations. Are going back to school this afternoon?"

"No. I'm at St. Edmund's near Birmingham. It's a boarding school. I stay there most days. On some Saturdays and Wednesdays though, we get to miss lessons for away matches. If parents want to, after the match, they can take the kids out for the afternoon and evening. I'm staying with dad tonight, so I'll go back to school in the morning. It's the end of term next week. We're packing up for the summer holidays so I'm not missing much. Dad said it'd be okay to miss school tonight."

Charlie looked at Jake who kept his head down. Fancy sending your child away to school, she thought. Jake must have read her mind.

"I'd have liked him to go to the local school, but his mother wanted the best for him," he mumbled.

"I like it at St. Edmunds. We get to do all sorts of sports, and adventure activities. We do shooting and golf. I play trumpet in the school band too," replied Toby.

"You could've done sports or music at the local school too," said Jake.

"Yeah, but I'm going to be a barrister like mum, and I need a good education for that. I'm not going to be able to study Latin at the local comp, am I?" he added, giving his father an exasperated look.

"The way you argue, you'll make a terrific lawyer. You didn't get that skill from public school. You'd have been fine at the school in town. Local comprehensive school didn't hurt me," began his father.

Toby harrumphed and pulled out his mobile phone.

"What can I get you both?" interrupted Charlie, noticing the atmosphere was becoming charged.

"I'd like a large slice of chocolate cake, please and a coke," Toby said. "And my dad wants to ask you out."

Jake's neck turned red. His mouth flapped open.

"Toby!" he spluttered.

"Well, you do. Why else do you keep coming in here every other day, hoping to see her? You've been playing songs on that blue kazoo ever since she gave it to you. I heard you playing the theme tune to *Rocky* last time I stayed with you. All the radios in your house are tuned to City Hospital Radio, even the car radio. You've got enough of those shark pots back home to start up an entire pottery shop. And, you spend hours writing articles about her. It's obvious you like her. You should tell her. It's true what Mum says. Some days, you need a sharp kick up the … "

"Toby," growled his father. "That's enough. "You're embarrassing Charlie."

Toby looked at Charlie. "I'm not, am I?"

Charlie coughed. "Err. A little. I think it'd be better if you let your father do the asking out."

"Well, he's too shy to ask. Mum says he lacks confidence as far as women are concerned. That's what she said word for word. He's always been the same. If she hadn't asked him out, they'd never have got together. She had to ask him out three times before he got the message," Toby continued, oblivious to his father's discomfort. "Mum says he's a lovely man, but he needs prodding sometimes. He's what she calls a dreamer."

Jake raked his hand through his hair, an anguished look on his face. Charlie almost felt sorry for him.

"Enough of what Fiona, ah, your mum thinks. Enough. Okay? This isn't the place."

"Just helping. Mum says you should always speak up for yourself."

"Right, well, thank you, Toby. I'll get your order and a coffee for you, Jake?"

Jake nodded.

She heard angry whispers as she cut the cake. She concentrated on preparing the drinks. She experienced a warm glow in the pit of her stomach. Jake wanted to go on a date with her? Then she remembered why she was annoyed with him and the feeling departed.

She returned with the drinks and cake. Toby was playing a game on his mobile phone and ignoring his father. Jake tried to avoid her gaze and fiddled with the menu.

"Ask her," muttered Toby as he continued thumbing his phone, propelling round cartoon birds at some pigs sitting on buildings.

Jake coughed and squirmed in his chair.

"As my son has so charmingly interfered and put me on the spot, would you be interested in going out with me for a meal, or drink this weekend?"

Charlie looked into his eyes. She noted the creases around the edges of his eyes and the warmth in them. His chin was covered in a light stubble again. He seemed unsure of himself, not the big shot journalist she had spoken to a few days earlier. He was dressed in dark brown chinos with a smart Tommy Hilfiger shirt. His beaten leather jacket hung on the back of the chair. His dark hair was cropped and bore the slightest trace of grey. He oozed masculinity. Masculinity, with a touch of vulnerability. She looked at him, thought for a moment, sucked on the end of her pencil and replied, "No, not a chance."

Toby looked up in astonishment. "What? I thought you were ideal. He's been all, you know, starry-eyed since he met you."

"Starry-eyed! I don't think so. He can be the tough guy when he wants and I recently found out he has a strange taste in knitted items of clothing. Thank you, but no thank you," she continued, turning when she heard the doorbell ring. "Excuse me. I have other customers to serve."

She dealt with the other customers. Toby came up to the counter some time later.

"Dad's gone outside. I think he's upset. Can I get a necklace from the shop please for my mum? She really liked the one we bought Abigail. She's having a birthday bash. I'm allowed to invite some friends from school to stay over for it. There's going to be a Robbie Williams impersonator. Pity she couldn't get the real Robbie to come."

Charlie looked at the enthusiastic child in front of her. He was a bright lad and very polite. He clearly took after his mother with his large blue eyes and blonde hair. His nose was sprinkled with a few freckles. She supposed his confidence came from the school environment he was in. She had read that children at private schools were more gregarious. Amy would certainly never have spoken out in front of her parents like Toby just had, and yet, he had done so with no malice. He had acted like he was Jake's older brother.

"Do you know which one you'd like?"

"Yes, there's a green one I saw last time I came. I think she'll like that. Dad's given me the money for it. I ran out of pocket money. Spent it all in the tuck shop." He gave a mischievous grin that made Charlie chuckle.

"I tell you what, you fetch the necklace and I'll wrap it for you. Save you doing it. I'll put in one of our handmade bags."

"Oh thanks. That'd be great. So, why don't you like my dad?"

Charlie was caught out. "I do like your dad. He's very nice. I don't want to go out with him. I don't think we'd get on."

"He can be really good fun sometimes. I don't think he's a tough guy like you said. Although, he did shout at Simon for letting me go on his quad bike. He got jolly aggressive then. Mum said it was because he was worried about me hurting myself. He's not been out with anyone since mum and he spilt up. That was ages ago, when I was little, about eight years old. It was before I went to boarding school. Mum said he's turning into a hermit. There's a crab called a hermit, you know? It hides in its own shell. That's like Dad. He doesn't go out much. He likes it when I come around and visit. We go out together to the cinema or bowling. You're the first person who's made him smile in ages. He was singing in the car coming here. He doesn't usually sing. Mum's boyfriend Simon sings sometimes when he's drunk. He sings really badly. He's a senior partner at a law firm.

He's got a villa in Mallorca. That's an island near Spain. We go on holiday there every summer. We went last year. Simon let me go out on his Sunseeker yacht with him. It's wicked and very fast. Very cool. It's moored in Puerto Portals. All the millionaires keep their yachts there. Oops, mum's present," he said, suddenly remembering why he was there.

He disappeared into the craft shop and re-emerged seconds later, necklace swinging in his hand. He handed it to Charlie who wrapped it in tissue paper and dropped it into a pale green bag. Toby played with his phone as she did so.

"Thank you," he said as he took the bag and his change. He looked at the present and up at Charlie who smiled again. "Pity you don't fancy dad. You're very pretty. He was going to play Super Mario Galaxy 2 with me. I hope he's not going to be all mardy now. I much prefer it when he's happy. You could come round and play with us if you like. It's a great game and we're getting Chinese takeaway."

Charlie hesitated. Toby looked hopeful; his blue eyes reminded her of Amy's. He stood waiting for a response, eager and assured. It would be cruel to turn him down. She was torn. "Go on," he said. "Pleeeeease," he wheedled and smiled sweetly.

"You'll make a superb lawyer. You'll convince the jury your client is not guilty every time with that smile. Go on. I'll come round, but only because you asked. Don't expect me to fall for your dad or anything. It'll be after my radio show. I finish at six. "

Toby grinned. "He'll be much happier now."

"What's your address?"

"Give me your phone number and I'll text it to you. Then you won't lose it," said Toby, scrolling for his contact list.

Charlie gave him her number and heard a beep as the text was sent.

"See you later. About half past six. Bye!"

Charlie checked her phone. Jake lived in a street quite close to Mercedes and Ryan. She was still unsure as to how she had been manipulated into going around to Jake's for dinner. Toby was definitely going to make a good lawyer.

She didn't tell Mercedes about the invitation. Mercedes would read too much into it and insist she made more effort with her appearance. As it was, she fully intended turning up in her clothes from the studio. If he was put off by jeans and a sweatshirt, then that was too bad. She guessed the other women in his life wore nothing but designer clothes. Abigail did—she still did not understand where Abigail fitted in—and Fiona would for certain.

Show over, she slipped away before she could get caught by anyone and drove to Jake's house. It was a pleasant detached house with a small front garden. The door was fronted by two small bay leaf trees in large blue pots. The garden was neat and had been recently weeded. The path was bordered by lavender plants. As she brushed past them, they emitted a perfume that she always associated with summer.

She rang the doorbell and was greeted almost immediately by Toby, clutching a games console.

"Hi Charlie! Glad you could come. Dad's having a meltdown in the kitchen. I told him takeaway was fine, but he wanted to impress you with one of his cordon bleu meals." Jake appeared behind him and placed a hand over his son's mouth in jest.

"He's joking," he said.

There were muffled noises from under his hand as Toby protested. "Come inside, Toby. I think you need to go and get Charlie a drink. We agreed you'd be the drinks waiter."

Toby pulled away from his father's hand.

"We didn't agree on that at all. Oops, sorry. Manners. Come in, Charlie."

Charlie entered the hallway. It was spacious. The carpet was new. The walls had been painted in cream and a couple of sunset prints hung on them. A small wooden table stood to one side. On the table was a jar for keys and a photograph of Toby and Jake, arms around each other. They were smirking. It had been taken recently.

"Come inside and sit down," encouraged Toby. "Do you like Mario? Maybe you'd prefer something else? We've got loads of games."

She found herself in the lounge. It contained a light blue sofa, a chair, a simple desk, and a filing cabinet. A plasma screen television dominated one wall. On the floor, in front of it, were various games and DVDs scattered about. "It normally looks tidier than this, but when Toby's here, it gets well-used," Jake explained. "It's my office, too, but it's what we call the boy's room. Go ahead and sit on the sofa."

Toby threw himself into the chair.

"So, what would you like?" Jake asked.

"Wine. A small glass though, please."

"White or red?"

"White. Thanks."

Jake went off to the kitchen. Toby looked up at her. "You still doing challenges for the radio?" he asked.

Charlie nodded. "I'm going to be flying in an aerobatic stunt plane in a couple of weeks."

Toby put down his console. "Really? That's lush. I'm going to learn to fly. I'd like my own aeroplane one day. I'd get a small one, like a Piper Arrow and go off at weekends. Hugh's parents have a jet. They can't fly it themselves. They hire a pilot to take them away. Hugh said I can go with them all, one year."

"You've got some wonderful ambitions," said Charlie.

"Mum says there's no point in letting the grass grow under your feet. She can fly. She learned to fly a helicopter. She doesn't do it now. She's not got any time. She's got lots of clients and cases to deal with. She even works when she's on holiday. It cheeses off Simon, but she says it has to be dealt with."

"This Fiona you're talking about?" asked Jake wandering back in, carrying a glass of wine, a bottle of beer, and a bottle of coke. He handed out the drinks.

"Workaholic," he explained to Charlie. "Loves it though. I don't know where she gets all her energy."

"Vitamin pills and a macrobiotic diet," replied Toby in a matter of fact tone. "Chelsea prepares her food in the morning. Mum takes some of it to the office and eats it there."

"Chelsea's her home help and cook," said Jake.

"Chelsea's a good cook. She makes a wicked cottage pie, but Dad's pie is much better."

"Nah, I'm only average. Just had a lot of practice," continued Jake. "I hope you like goats' cheese. I've done a starter of warm goats' cheese on toast with some onion chutney followed by boeuf bourguignon. I've gone all French tonight. Only because I had the ingredients and it's easy to prepare. It's nothing special."

"Sounds great," said Charlie, realising that she was, in fact, rather hungry.

"Shall we eat now or do you want a pre-dinner match on the console?" asked Toby.

"We'll eat, Toby. We've got time to play afterwards," said his father. "Would you excuse me while I go and prepare the starter? I won't be long. Toby will look after you. He's got verbal diarrhoea so just tell him to stop talking if he's asking too many questions." He winked at Toby, picked up his beer, and left.

"Is it difficult to be a radio presenter? Do you have to take exams?"

"It's not hard. Yes, you need to do a course, but I only work in hospital radio and that's a lot simpler than major radio stations. It's a similar principal, but there's a lot more to do and far more equipment in the professional studios."

"Do you want to work in a bigger studio?"

"I don't think so. I'm quite happy at the hospital. It's more of a hobby than a job."

"Is the café your real job?"

"I guess so. I enjoy the baking side of it most."

"You made the chocolate cake?"

Charlie nodded.

"It's lush. Even dad admitted it was the best he'd had. You're good at it. You could have a cake shop."

"That would be fun," said Charlie, thinking it was indeed a nice idea. "I could make cupcakes and sell them. That's a good idea."

Toby fiddled with his bottle, picking at the label. "Mum says it's a good idea to know what you want to do and then choose a career path. Some days I think I'd like to be a lawyer, then other days I want to be a pilot. Hugh wants to be a grime music artist like Dizzee Rascal or Tinie Tempah, that would be dench."

"Dench?"

"Cool. It means cool, except cool isn't cool anymore. Hugh's really into that sort of music. He plays it in the bedder. That's where we sleep. I share with Hugh and Thomas. Don't tell Dad about the music. I don't think he'd approve of it. It's a bit, you know?"

Charlie made a motion of sealing her lips with an invisible zip. Toby grinned.

"You don't have to decide what you want to do yet, you know. You've got plenty of time to decide. I wanted to be a vet when I was your age. I changed my mind completely and did an office job which was great, but I left it and now I'm doing something quite different."

"What sort of office job?" asked Toby, swigging his coke from the bottle and staring at her intently.

"I was in marketing. I worked on campaigns to help companies sell their products. It was interesting," she replied.

"Mum's got an office in London. It's on the top floor. She can see the London Eye from there. She's got another in Birmingham too. I've been to both of them. Abigail has an office, too. Hers is smaller than my mum's and busy all the time."

Charlie could not help herself. "Abigail?"

"Abigail's my mum's sister. She's my aunt."

Jake came through. "Dinner is served," he announced and bowed.

"Funny, Dad." Toby stretched and stood up. "Can I have a beer?"

"No," said Jake firmly.

"Simon lets me."

Jake's face went dark for a moment. "No. You know the rules here. No beer. You're too young. This way please," he continued, ignoring Toby's pleading looks.

Charlie was ushered into the kitchen. Modern cream kitchen units, cooker, and double sink filled one end of the room. A breakfast bar with a black marble top divided the kitchen from the dining area. A black glass table had been set for three. Someone had thoughtfully displayed a vase of flowers as a centrepiece. She noticed an array of cookery books on a cream dresser along with a black telephone, a notepad, and a pot of pens. It was one of the shark pots from the café.

Jake served the starter. Toby took up the conversation where it had been left off.

"Abigail's an agent. Isn't she, Dad?"

Jake, who was chewing, nodded.

"Not a detective agent. That would be brilliant. I'd love to have an aunt who was a detective. Abigail helps people who write books. She finds them publishers. Dad's written a book. Abigail's going to find a publisher for it and then he'll become famous."

Jake choked on his toast. "Toby, I think you're jumping the gun. It's early days. It will probably get rejected."

Charlie sampled her food. It was superb. The chutney made the perfect accompaniment to the cheese.

"Is this chutney homemade?" she asked, savouring the combined flavours of the goats' cheese and the chutney.

"Yes. I'm a bit of an old housewife sometimes. I should join the Women's Institute except they'd probably throw me out for singing *Jerusalem* off-key. I was bored last year and didn't have much work on, so I bottled some jams and chutneys. You like it?"

"It's excellent," she said. "I'm impressed. I suspect the Women's Institute would throw you out because you're a man. You could try dressing up."

Toby piped up, "Like Mrs Doubtfire," and sniggered.

Jake pursed his lips and gave a good impression of the character, "Carpe dentum. Seize the teeth."

Charlie could not help but laugh.

"So you've written a book. What's it about?"

Jake looked down at his plate. "It's a sort of cookbook," he mumbled.

"Sort of?"

"Yes, a sort of love story with recipes," Jake added, but was reluctant to elaborate.

"Oh!" Charlie couldn't think of anything else to say on the subject. She was astonished.

"Dad's always been good at cooking. He used to be a chef, didn't you, Dad?"

"I'm sure Charlie doesn't want to hear about all that. Let's talk about your new challenge, Charlie. Flying. Now that's exciting."

They did not revisit the subject of Jake's career before he took up journalism. Toby maintained centre stage and talked about school, his teachers, and his friends. Plates were emptied and taken to the kitchen. They all moved off to the boy's room where Toby dragged out a variety of video games for them to play. He finally settled on a bowling game to give them all a sporting chance.

"I want *Call of Duty—Ghosts* but Dad won't let me get it," he stated as he lined up his virtual bowl and made a strike. He cheered.

"Sorry son, but I don't like those violent shooter type games. They're not healthy for you."

"Hugh says he plays it. He's got all the latest games including *Titanfall*."

"What Hugh does or plays is for his parents to decide. Both your mother and I agree on this matter. No violent games. You may be thirteen going on twenty, but you're still only just thirteen. You can get those games when you're a little older. There are plenty of good games that don't have so much violence in them. You know I'm right. You didn't even enjoy Laser Quest when you went to Hugh's party. You're only trying to keep up with your mates. We both know you'd rather beat your old dad at a racing car game or bowling."

He ruffled Jake's hair. Jake acknowledged him with a grin.

"Your turn, Charlie."

Charlie felt more relaxed than she had for a while. Jake's house was friendly and comfortable. She was enjoying the company. Toby acted far older than his years and was trying hard to show his father off in a good light. Jake had impressed her, not only with his cooking, but his easy manner. He treated Toby like an equal and together, they made her feel very much at home.

"Strike!" she shouted as she too knocked down all her virtual pins.

Toby high-fived her. Jake groaned. "I am being trounced by you two. It's bad enough being beaten by Toby on a regular basis, but you too? I feel such a failure."

Toby and Charlie battled it out with Toby winning the game. "It was inevitable," he said as they turned off the game. "I get stacks of practice at this."

Charlie decided it was time to depart. It was with some reluctance that she started to make her excuses.

She was interrupted by Toby who exclaimed, "I have to go upstairs and do some prep. I forgot I had some maths questions to do for tomorrow. Mister Nailer is not the best teacher to make angry. He puts you in detention if you do something wrong. Hugh was chewing gum in class last week and he had to do five detentions. That's harsh. See you later."

He beetled off, leaving the adults staring at each other.

"Make that thirteen going on thirty," said Jake. "I think my son has just made a strategic withdrawal so we can be alone. He certainly hasn't brought any maths books home with him that I know about. Fancy another drink?"

Charlie was amused. "It would be a shame to race off after his plans. Thanks, I'll have one last glass of wine. I hope I'm not over the limit." They walked back to the kitchen where Jake filled two glasses.

"You can stay here tonight," said Jake, passing Charlie the glass of wine. Seeing the horrified look on her face, he clarified his statement, "There's a spare room upstairs with an en suite. It's in the loft so you won't even have to put up with being on the same landing as us."

"That's very kind of you, but I'd better go home. I don't want to send out any wrong messages to Toby."

"Okay, I understand. Kids, eh? I take it you haven't got any."

Charlie sipped the wine. "I did have. I had a little girl. She was the same age as Toby when she was seriously injured in a car accident. She didn't pull through. I willed her to recover, but she didn't."

Jake's face changed. He stretched out a hand and placed it on top of hers. "I'm so sorry, Charlie. That's dreadful. I can't imagine what you've been through. When Toby went to live with his mum, it tore me apart. I hated the fact she sent him to boarding school. I could've looked after him and been there for him. I can only guess what it's been like for you. I'm truly sorry."

His tenderness touched her. This was a man who had a deep caring nature. From what she had seen tonight, he relished being a father. It was unfair that he'd been denied the chance to be the father he wanted to be. Life was like that. Unfair.

Changing the subject, Charlie asked, "Are you going to tell me more about your book?"

"There's not much to tell. You'll laugh when I tell you. It's a romantic story supported by recipes. It's about a man, passionate about cooking who attempts to woo a woman with his recipes."

"You surprise me. I hadn't got you down as the romantic type."

"I think I told you once before, you've got me wrong. Fiona got me wrong, too. She thought I'd be more adventurous than I am. She spent years trying to encourage me to get involved in more masculine pursuits. It didn't work. I don't even like football. I enjoy writing, cookery, and the simplicity of nature. She got bored in the end. Simon, her new man is much more ambitious than I ever was.

Journalism was only a means to an end. Fiona forced me to go into that, too. She complained that I had a degree in English and yet preferred to spend my days cooking at the local restaurant. She thought I had more talent than that and was underusing my potential. She badgered one of her clients in the industry and they took me on. I turned freelance and covered stories from over the country and abroad on occasions. I became disillusioned with it all. I asked for more local assignments and began to write good news stories. The world has so many problems that sometimes it's good to read about positive stuff.

Writing articles for magazines and newspapers paid bills. Mind you, as Fiona became a main player in law, we weren't short of funds. I only do it today because I'm not likely to be employed for my chef skills. I've not cooked commercially for years. Even now, I'd rather write a novel, cook a meal for friends, or work in my vegetable plot than write some article about the local council charging for emptying recycle dustbins. At least the good news stories are more interesting. The problem is that most people enjoy sensationalistic news or rubbish about so-called celebrities. I'm gradually losing heart, if I'm honest. Simon, on the other hand, is a go-getting fireball. He never stops. He and Fiona suit each other. They both work incredibly hard. I wish they had more time for Toby. I fear he's going to be a carbon copy of his mother and burn out by the time he's forty. I'm going to take him on a walking holiday in Derbyshire this summer. See if I can get him to appreciate the simpler things in life. He's surrounded by wealth at home. I thought we'd do some camping and rough it. Have a go at some outdoor cooking. Maybe do some bird watching and even fishing."

Charlie was flabbergasted. This was not the Jake she thought she knew.

"I'm rubbish at some of stuff that dads are expected to be good at. Going on the roller coaster was as adventurous as I'd been in a long while. That was until you cajoled me into that flaming zorb thing. Toby was astounded when I told him I'd been zorbing. He texted all his friends at school and bragged about it."

"You went diving. I remember you telling me about the nurse sharks."

"Actually, I made that up," he said, looking bashful. "You looked so anxious. I thought it would help you relax. The only sharks I've seen were at the aquarium." He paused. "I'm glad I went zorbing with you. I felt pretty horrible afterwards when you left me throwing up, but now I'm glad. It was an experience I won't forget."

The wine was making her bold. She needed clarification. "Is that why you sent me the poem?"

"What poem?"

"The bizarre one I found on my doormat in a hand-delivered envelope. It was two lines long. And went something like: 'It doesn't matter what you do. I'll always be there for you.'"

Jake looked puzzled. "I hardly think so. I didn't send it. It's not very good, is it? It's hardly a Shakespearean sonnet. Besides, I don't even know where you live."

"Of course you do!" exclaimed Charlie. "You came to my house the morning you gave that talk at the café. My neighbour spoke to you. She thought you were a burglar, but you told her you were a journalist."

"Charlie, I can assure you that I did not come to your house or speak to your neighbour. Honestly. I've no idea where you live."

Charlie was not convinced. She harrumphed.

"I have absolutely no idea what you are talking about. I did not write or send a poem, if you can call two lines a poem, and I did not speak to your neighbour. Do you think I'm some sort of lunatic? Do you think I'm so sad and lonely that I'd write a drippy thing like that? One minute you're accusing me of being aggressive, the next, some sad sop!"

"Don't play the injured party here. You have got an aggressive streak. Look what you did to Rob."

Jake sighed. "Charlie, you keep going on about this. What is it I'm supposed to have done to Rob that is so bad it warrants your anger?"

"One, you hit him. Two, you stripped him naked. Three, you tied him up to a streetlamp and left him almost unconscious after writing a cruel message on his chest in my new lipstick."

"I did? No, actually I did not. Hit him? Never. Why would I hit him? I don't like violence. I detest it in fact. I've seen some horrible things during my travels as a journalist that I prefer to forget. I won't even let my son play a violent video game or watch a film with a modicum of violence in it. It's not the way to deal with things. As for stripping him and tying him up, there's no way I'd have done that. What sort of sicko would do that?"

Charlie was flabbergasted. "So tell me, what happened?"

"After you went to the toilets to clean your blouse, Rob got nasty. He insisted it was my fault that you'd gone off. I explained you'd be back, but he was so drunk I don't think he understood. I suggested we go outside because he was shouting too much. He didn't want to go and started lashing out. Another guy came to my aid and helped me walk him outside. Between us, we got him into the car park. There, I told him that I thought he was an idiot for being so drunk. I suggested he sit down on the steps at the pub for a few minutes, take in some air, and go back and apologise to you. I told him if I'd been on a date with you, I wouldn't have been so stupid as to blow it by getting wasted. The last I saw of him, he was sitting with his head in his hands, looking sorry for himself. I left him there. He was fine when I last saw him. I cannot enlighten you any further as to what happened to him. I assumed he would wander back in after a few moments. I came back home and watched television."

"It wasn't you?"

"Charlie, look at me. Do I look like the sort of man who would go ballistic and attack another? I'm more the sort to roll over in a battle. Words have always been my weapon of preference. If Rob said I attacked him, then I'm afraid he's lying."

Jake looked directly at Charlie. He was telling the truth. From what she had seen and heard tonight, she knew in her heart, he could not have performed such a heinous act.

"I can't prove my innocence with regards to Rob, but I can with your neighbour. Look, take me to her. She'll tell you I'm not the man she saw."

"If it wasn't you?" Charlie stared at the ceiling. Her head buzzed. The realisation of what had happened and who it was that had attacked Rob, finally hit her.

"The man who helped you remove Rob from the pub. What did he look like?"

"Tall, young. Going a bit bald. Looked geeky. I didn't pay too much attention to him. Rob was trying to deck me at the time. The bloke grabbed Rob's arm and led him outside. I took the other arm."

Charlie shook her head. "I'm so, so sorry. I've made a dreadful mistake. It wasn't you. He set you up. It was Harrison. Harrison's back and he's behind all of this."

"Is he dangerous?"

"I don't think so. He's just weird. He was hung up on me at one point. Sounds like his fascination might have grown into an obsession if he attacked Rob because he was out with me. I wonder how he knew. I hope he hasn't been following me."

Charlie told Jake about Harrison. Jake said nothing until she had finished.

"I'm guessing you didn't buy the onesie at the auction either," she added.

Jake snorted.

"No, of course you didn't. You didn't see another man at the back of the room, did you?"

Jake thought for a while. "Now you mention it, there was a bloke. He was old though and had a moustache and grey hair. Can't imagine he'd have bought it. He didn't look like the same man in the pub."

Charlie rubbed her face and sighed.

"Jake, I can't apologise enough. I was convinced you were to blame for Rob. I feel dreadful about it. I'd better go now. It's getting late. I should be going."

Jake took her hand again. "No, don't go. I have a horrible feeling if you leave now, we'll never recapture this moment. We've reached some understanding. We've crossed that bridge finally. I've been hoping ever since I saw you at Jasmine's that I'd be able to spend some time with you. Well, more than that. I have made my feelings quite clear. I'd love to see you again. Stay here tonight. No strings. We'll just enjoy what's left of the evening and this bottle of wine. Besides, Toby went through a lot of trouble to get you here."

She smiled. His face was earnest. Now she no longer doubted him, the attraction that had lurked inside her came to the forefront. She leaned in, drawn by his eyes. He stroked her hair from her face. She could feel his warm breath. She brushed her lips against his. It felt natural and exciting at the same time. They kissed. He was gentle and tentative in his response. Warmth flooded her body.

"I'll stay the night, but I'd better take the spare room ... this time," she said.

Breakfast at Jake's was a cheerful affair. Jake played his kazoo loudly as he prepared scrambled eggs for everyone. Toby, delighted that his father seemed to have a new girlfriend, insisted on finding out as much as possible about Charlie. He questioned her about films she had seen, music she liked, television she watched, books she read until she felt exhausted. Jake put an end to the inquisition by insisting Toby get ready for school.

"I don't want your housemaster telling me off again. Even if it is the last week of term, I'll get a black mark if I make you late for chapel."

"I really enjoyed myself last night," said Charlie, finishing her orange juice.

"So did I. It was," he hesitated, searching for an appropriate word, "Special. Very special. Like you."

She moved swiftly across the kitchen floor. "You're pretty special yourself," she responded, moving into his arms.

"I'll phone you later," said Jake after a passionate embrace.

"I'll be waiting. I'll let you decide where we go on Saturday. It's a shame Toby can't join us. Still, his mum would be upset if he weren't at her birthday party."

"We'll have time over the holidays to take him out. Together," he added.

"Better go. Busy day. I'll talk to you later, you wonderful man."

He kissed her again.

Charlie shouted goodbye to Toby who was still upstairs, kissed Jake once more, and left, oblivious to the motorbike that was parked several spaces behind her car or the man in leathers who was standing by a postbox. She needed to get back home because Bert was coming around for the day and his sleepover. There was a good supply of grapes and her sofa and chairs were draped in covers. Peggy assured her Bert was very good and kept mess to the area surrounding his perch, but Charlie was taking no chances.

Peggy came to the back door that led directly into the kitchen, Bert on her bent forearm and Gordon behind, laden down with Bert's overnight equipment. Gordon was short, barely an inch taller

221

than Peggy, and slim built. He looked younger than his seventy-five years. He had maintained a full head of thick silver hair. His face bore little trace of lines and his periwinkle blue eyes were full of life and energy. His demeanour matched Peggy's perfectly.

"Just put the stand there, Gordon, next to the shelves by the radio. That's super."

"Where shall I put his food, my love?"

Peggy flushed. "On the top."

Gordon did as asked, then scratched Bert's head with affection. Bert made kissing noises. Gordon put an arm around Peggy. "No fretting. He'll be fine here. It's bright and cheerful. Home from home. In fact, it's very like your home. Don't worry."

"I'm not worried. It feels odd. I'm not used to leaving him anywhere."

"He couldn't be with anyone better," Gordon assured her and winked at Charlie. Charlie decided they made the perfect couple.

"Off you go, Bert. Say hello to Charlie," said Peggy, shaking her arm gently.

Bert flew straight to Charlie shoulder. "Hola," he said. "Good moaning. Grrr!"

"Very good, Bert. You'll make an excellent watchdog."

Bert flew about the kitchen, then into the lounge to check it out. He flew to the window ledge and back onto the door connecting the lounge and the kitchen. He whistled. He then flew about some more, and finally settled back on his perch where he marched up and down, head bobbing. Peggy explained his routine. Charlie had arranged to spend the morning and some of the afternoon with Bert, then would leave him to his own devices while she presented her radio show. He would most likely doze while she was out. She would leave out a few toys and treats and turn on the radio quietly for him so he did not feel lonely.

Peggy and Gordon left them to it. "Be good, Bert. Be good for Charlie," said Peggy. Bert cocked his head to one side and whistled.

The moment they went, Bert burst into song, "How much is the doggie in the window," he sang, then cackled.

Charlie sang with him. She played ball with him and encouraged him to score a few goals with his hoop. After a while, he was content to watch her potter about the house and sat on his perch, making a variety of noises and whistling.

Charlie caught up with some baking, gave Bert some grapes, and thought a great deal about Jake. He was incredible. She squirmed in pleasure as she recalled the evening before. Toby had returned to the room and announced he was going to bed. She and Jake had sat talking for ages, then the inevitable happened. They were drawn together by an invisible magnetic pull. It seemed so natural. Although she was aching with desire, she pulled back from him. "It doesn't seem appropriate to carry on here."

"No, you're right. We should go upstairs," he said, kissing her neck and making her knees go weak.

"I can't, Jake. Not with Toby in bed. It's not right. Yet. I'd hate him to hear us."

Jake nudged up her neck and under her ear. Then pulled himself away.

"I agree. I think you know how much I like you," he laughed. "The evidence speaks for itself." He continued as he adjusted his trousers. She giggled and kissed him.

"I feel really mean now. I'll make up for it. Promise. Tomorrow. Well, tonight now."

"That sounds like an invitation I won't want to pass on."

"It's a date. Could you come to my house?"

"Certainly."

"Oh hang on. Blast! I forgot, I can't do tonight. I can definitely do the next day. Make it after the show. About eight o'clock. I'll leave you my address. Now, I'd better tear myself away before my resolve weakens and I throw myself into your arms again."

"I suppose so," he replied with reluctance. "I'll fetch us more wine. That'll give me a chance to calm down."

When he returned, he wrapped his arms around her and they lay on the sofa together. He asked her about Amy, and Charlie found herself speaking about her daughter without sobbing. He shared his own past. He spoke about how he had always had a dream to be a chef thanks to his mother who had taught him to cook. He opened up about his relationship with Fiona, who mesmerised him and emasculated him in equal measures. It was a doomed relationship. He was never going to be able to match the energy and drive that Fiona possessed nor indeed reach her lofty ideals. After numerous attempts to make it work, their marriage had died a natural death leaving him worn out and off course. His career as a journalist had taken him to some war zones where he had learned to hate suffering and the evil that humanity could inflict on others with passion and now, well, now he wanted to spend time with a son who was rapidly growing up and would soon no longer need him.

They laughed about the circumstances leading up to the evening and recapped on how they had met. Jake revealed he had fancied her from the beginning when he saw her in the restaurant, not dreaming he would see her again.

"I couldn't believe my luck when you ran into my feet, squealing."

"Oh please, no! That was my worst moment. What were you doing at Jasmine's? I could never work out why you were there."

"I was following up a piece for the *Gazette*. Jasmine was part of a troupe of dancers performing in Birmingham at the Rep. I interviewed her. That was the piece that got me the permanent job at the *Birmingham Gazette*. I can't tell you how glad I am I made that decision. I took the job because it meant I could be nearer to Toby's school and see him at weekends if he fancied time away from school. I never imagined it would lead me to you." He stroked her face. "Fate, karma, call it what you will, I was obviously destined to meet you."

Charlie felt herself falling for him. Somehow, he completed her. He was sensitive, kind, and honest. She would never doubt him again.

They parted company in the early hours of the morning. They slept in separate rooms. Charlie did not sleep much. She wriggled about in delight for the few hours before sunrise. At last, life was looking much brighter.

Having been active all day, Bert decided it was time to nap. He sat quietly on his perch and before long, he had put his head under his wings. He was fast asleep. She tiptoed out of the kitchen, pulling the door to. It would soon be time for her to go to City Hospital. She could not wait to tell Mercedes about her new beau.

As she climbed the stairs to get changed for the hospital, she heard a soft knock at the door. Thinking it was Peggy coming to check on Bert, she opened it fully, a smile on her face. The smile disappeared in an instant.

"Harrison," she gasped.

Harrison stuck his foot in the door so she could not shut it, and forced his way in, grabbing her firmly by the arm and shoving her into the lounge.

"Hello Charlotte," he hissed after pushing her onto the sofa. "How nice to see you again."

"What do you want?" she asked angrily. Her arm hurt and she rubbed it tenderly.

"That's no way to speak to your boyfriend, Charlotte."

"You're not—" she began. Harrison shushed her.

"Don't, Charlotte. Don't make me angry. Don't make me any angrier than I am. I'm at breaking point. Do you want to know why?" He strode about the room, checking the window to make sure no one had seen him going into the house.

"I'm going to tell you exactly why I'm at breaking point. I've given you everything you could want or need and you've shamed me. You've abused my love and treated me badly."

"I don't want to make you angry," said Charlie, the seriousness of her situation dawning on her. Harrison had changed. His face looked drawn. He smelt sour as if he had forgotten to wash for a couple of days. Worse still, he was intimidating.

"Poor, little Charlotte," he said in silky tones. "All alone in the world and sad after her husband left her. Poor 'I'm not ready for a relationship' Charlotte. Poor confused Charlotte. Well boo, bloody hoo! You're a fraud, Charlotte. A tease. A liar. A slut!"

Charlotte began to tremble. Harrison's tone was menacing. She could smell drink on his breath as he leant towards her and hissed the last word.

"So, let's look at the facts, shall we? Once upon a time, a nice innocent young man asked a lady out. She fooled him into thinking she was interested in him. She invited him to join her for coffee. She led him on. She took advantage of his good nature, making him believe she liked him. She waited until he was smitten by her and seduced him. Then, she dropped him like a hot coal. You know the story, don't you? You know it because that lady was you. You gave me the come on and made me love you. You used all your female guile and like an idiot, I fell for it. Then, when I thought you and I were a perfect item, you told me you didn't want to go out with me. You came up with some cock and bull story that I was too young for you and you didn't feel it was appropriate. I wasn't too young to make love to, was I? However, I listened to you. I thought I understood your bizarre reasoning. I was young, yes. I was young, but I would change for you. I would be the perfect boyfriend. I would do anything for you. I tried to explain. I tried so hard to convince you." He rubbed his neck. Spittle had landed on his chin. His eyes rolled.

"But you were cruel and refused to accept my gifts, or my love. You'd had what you wanted from me. I licked my wounds and tried to make you see sense. Finally, I thought I'd made a breakthrough with you. You opened the door and listened to me. You held me while I cried on your shoulder. You understood and it was all going to be okay. But no, you told someone at work that I was *stalking* you and I got fired! Yes, I was fired. Don't look surprised."

"Harrison, I didn't. Really I didn't."

"Well someone did. You must have told someone at the hospital and they blabbed to the authorities. I was summoned in front of some wanker who tried to talk down to me. They wanted to book me in to see a therapist and get me some counselling! Cheeky gits. I didn't need any counselling. I told them what they could do with their advice, therapists, and counselling. I lost my job, my hopes, and my future thanks to you. Well, you and that other stupid cow who complained about me at university. They had to drag that up too. Could I get another job? No! I couldn't. I had to go back home to my dad with my tail between my legs. I didn't tell him I'd been fired. I told him I was on study leave. Silly old fool believed me.

But, do you know what? I forgave you, Charlotte. I knew you were different. You were different to all the other women I'd met. You were frightened and alone. You'd been through so much pain. Your husband had deserted you and you'd lost your little girl. I understood the loneliness and confusion. I've been through that, too. I went through it when my mother died and left me with my bad-tempered father," he spat.

He paused, consumed by memories. Charlie wondered if she could escape. She slid to the edge of the sofa. He noticed her subtle movement and redirected his thoughts.

"Don't even think about it, Charlotte. Where were we? Oh yes. I was explaining why I forgave you. You see, you'd proved you loved me that night in my car. You can't deny what happened. It was beautiful. Magical. You were my first love. I understood that deep down, you loved me. You only needed time to sort out your emotions and heal. I gave you the time. I stayed away.

When I thought you'd be ready to start living again, I sent you a lovely email. You sent a rubbish one back. But I didn't harbour a grudge. I guessed you were just feeling low. After all, you're facing middle age now and must be beginning to feel insecure. I know about that. My mother went through a phase at your age. She cried a lot of the time. She used to get emotional and shout at me. It's a female thing. I decided you needed someone to care for you. It was time for me to prove I was strong and mature, just like you wanted and needed. I helped you, Charlotte. I was an unseen hand that helped you in your quest to get funds for the radio station."

Charlie shivered.

"I'm the one person you can trust," he continued. His eyes darted around the room. Charlie recognised the signs. Harrison had mental health issues. She was not sure how to deal with it. She decided silence was best.

"Who do you think sent the video of you on the roller coaster to the studio?"

"You," she whispered.

"Correct. It was me. I watched you. You had no idea I was in the crowd filming you. You didn't see me. You've not noticed me the last few months. I've been around. I've seen you come home to an empty house, bake cakes, and watch films on your own. I've listened to you on the radio. I decided to give you a boost. You like working on the radio so much, I decided to help the station when I discovered it needed funding. I even bribed those kids behind you to sing along with that ridiculous kazoo. I overheard you planning with that friend of yours in the wheelchair. You were jabbering away about it in the coffee shop at the hospital, oblivious to the old guy sat behind you. That old guy was me. Ha! Bet that's surprised you. You even kindly let me know which song you'd be playing—*Love Rollercoaster*. Very amusing. I figured if people saw an entertaining video of you, they'd be more likely to send in money to save the radio station. A video of a woman going down a roller coaster wouldn't be much fun, but one where it seems everyone is enjoying the woman playing her silly kazoo, now that would be entertaining. I was right. It worked, didn't it? It got thousands of hits."

Not wanting to annoy him, Charlie nodded in agreement.

"Yes, it was me. Clever old Harrison." He stopped again. He stared at her with wild eyes. "You weren't grateful though, Charlotte. You betrayed me. You met up with a man in a bar near here, even though you should have waited for me. He wasn't worth it, was he? What an absolute loser." He chuckled. "I bet he didn't see you again after that night. No, of course he didn't. He was a waster. He was a weasel. He blubbed like a little baby when I tied him up. He begged me not to thump him again. He deserved to be splattered across the car park, but I didn't do that to him, even though I wanted to—cretin that he was. I gave him a couple of punches to make him see sense. He whimpered and curled up into a little ball. Do you want to be with a man like that? Well, do you?"

"No," said Charlie, wishing the torment would end. She was now late for her radio show. Soon, Mercedes would phone to ask where she was. They would worry that she was not there. They might drive round and save her from this lunatic.

"So, after that episode, I sent you an amusing gift. I thought it would be funny. You like jokes, don't you? You read them out to patients on the wards. You enjoy a laugh. I sent you the perfect inflatable man to keep you company until you came to your senses. He was more of a man than the fool at the pub and more of a man than that kid who took you diving."

Charlie breathed in sharply. "That was you, too? You slashed Liam's diving suits and damaged his car, didn't you?"

"He asked for it. I saw you. You couldn't resist him, could you? It must have been difficult. He was always giving you the come on. He thinks he's some sort of hunk with his perfect body, his perfect teeth and his perfect bloody hair," he spat, rubbing a hand over his slightly balding head.

"He was always showing off his body like some sort of human peacock. Preening himself in front of you. You fell for it. You threw yourself at him at the quarry. You rubbed yourself all over him like a bitch on heat. You tart. It was disgusting. Don't deny it. I observed you both at Dosthill quarry. You sat in his car together after the dive. I was pretending to take wildlife photographs around the quarry.

You didn't notice me. I zoomed my lens in on you both to make sure you weren't doing to him what you did to me. It was a good thing you weren't. He wanted you to. I could tell. Dirty little sod. I bet he was dying to go diving with you again."

Harrison rubbed his eyes. "He won't be trying it on too soon with any other ladies. I fixed him," he growled. Harrison began to pace about the room. In between words, he grumbled incoherently.

"You told me I was too young and then you tried to seduce him. He was much younger than me. You hypocrite!" he snarled. "Still, I forgave you. He led you on. I forgave you again and tried to help you and your stupid radio station. I was at the hospital coffee shop as usual, when I found out about the charity clothes show. Yes, I hung out there most days. It reminded me of when we first met. Tina had no idea it was me," he chuckled. "She thought I was some old bloke. I took my dad's clothes. They're too large and hang on me, but with a fake beard and wig, no one recognised me. Not even you." He stopped, waiting for her response. When she gave none, he resumed his angry rant.

"I was horrified you were prepared to let a complete stranger buy clothes you'd been wearing. It was opportune I was there. I couldn't have anyone else buy something my girlfriend had just removed from her naked body. But it was meant to be, wasn't it? I was supposed to buy it. It was almost like receiving a gift from you." He smiled. "That garment still smells of you. I've held it in bed every night since I bought it. It helps me remember you and how you made me feel." He stopped, lost in thought. Charlie made a decision. This had to end.

"Harrison, I think you need medical help," she stuttered. In one swift movement, Harrison strode towards her and slapped her hard across her face. She was stunned. Her hand flew up to her face to protect it, but too late. He hit her hard again.

"I've managed perfectly well without your advice, Charlotte, or help from anyone," he said in an icy tone. "I don't need help. What is it with you people? First my mother, then my father, then the hospital authorities, and now you?" He paced about the room, muttering. Charlie was about to make another attempt to run when he spun around.

"There was a time when I would've done anything for you. Surely you can see that, now. Who else would be thoughtful enough to send you a brand new mask and snorkel for your dive? I didn't want you to have to use one that someone else had used. Think of all of those germs? That's thoughtful, isn't it? Who would have sent tickets for a show you were desperate to see? I thought we could go together. I thought we could share a perfect weekend away. Yet, all the time, I was trying to help you and I was making all this effort, you were busy behaving like a slut," he spat, his face wrinkled in disgust. He licked his dry lips, recovered and continued. Charlie sat in fear.

"My, how you've tested my patience, Charlotte. I was prepared to let it all go and then what did you go and do?"

Charlie winced. Her stomach sank.

"You spent the night at that journalist's house. The entire night," he said with menace in his voice. "If the upstairs light hadn't gone on when it did and if I hadn't watched you undress and go to bed alone, I'd have come in and killed you both. This can't go on. You have to be dealt with." He stopped to lick his lips again. His eye twitched and he rubbed it.

"I've come to a decision. You're coming with me where I can keep an eye on you. That way, you'll not be able to parade about flirting or misbehaving. I'm taking you with me to Wales. I inherited a cottage in the hills a few months ago. My father died, you see. He lived there in isolation. He didn't like people much. Preferred to hide away from the public. After my mother died, he took off there with me in tow. It's in the middle of nowhere. We'll be able to have plenty of time for each other. You'll learn to behave and respect me. You'll see how much I've matured and we'll be deliriously happy."

Charlie hugged her knees. "It won't work, Harrison," she ventured. "People here will try to find me. I have friends who'll want to know what's happened to me." *And Jake,* she thought. *He'll want to know where I am.*

Harrison guessed her thoughts and sniggered. "Oh poor deluded Charlotte. I'm afraid I've been one step ahead of you. Your friends won't come looking for you." He collapsed into Charlie's chair and casually draped one leg over the other. Leaning forward, he smoothed her hair off her face. She recoiled. He smiled. His smile reminded her of the sharks. His teeth were small, sharp, and pointed.

"No one will look for you. I hacked into your computer while you were out a few weeks ago. I was almost caught by the old bat next door, but I got away with it. Gave her some story about being a journalist. I got into your email account. You should have chosen a better password than Amy and her date of birth. It didn't take me long to work that out." He tutted. Charlie let out a stifled sob.

"Today, I sent an email from your account to City Hospital Radio saying you'd been offered a trip of a lifetime by a dear friend and although it was rude to go without saying goodbye, you just had to seize this golden opportunity. I explained you'd enjoyed doing the challenges so much that you'd developed a new lust for life. When this exciting new venture presented itself, you couldn't refuse. The challenges had made you see that life was for living. I said it was all very last minute, but you were catching a flight later today and you'd be in contact in a few weeks. By then, they'll have forgotten about you and certainly won't be able to track you down. It's only manned by volunteers. You've not broken a contract. They'll soon forget you, especially when the radio goes off air due to lack of funds. With you gone, they're not likely to raise the money, are they?"

Charlie shook her head in disbelief.

Harrison continued, pleased with the response. "I sent one to the Art café, too, and," he paused for effect, "I sent one to that journalist. *It might have meant something special to you, but me, well, I wasn't thinking straight. I used you. I took your affection and enjoyed it to help me through my misery. I'm so sorry. It wasn't the same for me. I don't want you to think we have anything special. We don't,"* he said in a girly voice. "I also told him that you won't be repeating that episode again with him. It was a mistake. *I was drunk and lonely.* Does that sound familiar? It should do. It's what you told me. You ripped me apart, Charlotte."

"I'm sorry," whispered Charlie.

"Of course you are. I know you are. We can resolve this, Charlotte. You and I. We'll have plenty of time to fix it," he replied. His demeanour changed. He was suddenly happier.

"We'll leave together later after Mrs Nosey next door has gone to bed. We'll take your car. I came here by taxi. I'm so clever. I haven't left anything to link your disappearance to me. Your journalist friend won't be bothering us. I doubt he'll be interested in finding you. He's not got the same tenacity as me. Patience pays off in the end, you know. His ego will be deflated. He'll be upset that you thought he was not for you. I bet he's not used to women telling him that. He'll be torn up over the fact that he was used."

He sat back in the chair, played a drumroll on his knees with his hands and chuckled. "I can imagine his face when he reads the email. He'll be gutted. Still, he'll get over it. Men who look like him always find new girlfriends. They have it all. It's easy for them. Women chuck themselves at them. It's not like that for all of us. Some of us have to try much harder."

Tears spilled into Charlie's eyes. She refused to give Harrison the satisfaction of seeing them. She blinked them away, raised her head, and confronted him.

"It won't work. You can kidnap me or do whatever you plan, but I'll spend all my life rejecting you and attempting ways to escape from you." She gulped. Harrison was giving her a steely look.

"I don't love you. I'll never love you," she repeated, heart quickening at her bravery. "I love Jake." There, she had said it, and she knew it was true. She may not have known him a long time, but she felt it was right. He was the man for her. They were soul mates.

Harrison's eye twitched again. "Rubbish. You'll forget him. He doesn't worship you like I do. I've got a whole room in my house dedicated to you. I've got photographs of you all over the wall and some small mementos of our time together: the menu from the Italian restaurant, the ticket stubs to the comedy show we saw. I've even recorded some of your radio shows and play them when you're not on air." His tongue flickered out again. "I need some water. I have to take my pills. He rummaged in his trouser pocket and pulled out a small brown pot." He rattled it.

"Kitchen?"

Charlie indicated the door. She was not going to run around after this nutter. She would try to get away while he went to the kitchen. If she could run quickly enough, she could get to the front door and scream. That should alert the neighbours. Harrison second-guessed her again.

"Oh no, you don't. It's going to be different from now on. I'm the boss. Come on, you're coming with me."

He seized her arm and dragged her off the sofa. He was much stronger than she anticipated and although she struggled, he held on to her, pinching her arm tightly. He grabbed a handful of her hair and hauled her up. She whimpered.

"If you just behave, everything will be fine," he whispered into her ear.

She kicked out. He lost his grip. She wriggled away, squirming from under him. He lunged at her legs. She kicked at his face. He grabbed her ankles and hauled her backwards along the carpet. She could not cry out. The friction from the carpet burned her arms. She attempted to kick him once more, landing a blow between his legs which made him double up. She struggled to her knees and scrambled to the door. She was almost within reach of the door handle when he launched himself at her and rugby-tackled her to the ground, landing heavily on top of her. There was a cracking sound and pain seared up her arm. She let out a sharp scream. Her wrist was on fire. Oblivious, he pulled her to her feet, ignoring her pleas, herded her back into the lounge and pushed her towards the kitchen.

He opened the door with a snarl and shoved Charlie ahead of him, grabbing her hair again. Tears rolled down her face. From one corner came a growling, followed by barking.

Charlie called out, "Bert! Help!" There was a flurry of feathers and claws as something propelled towards Harrison. It dived at Harrison's face. He yelped in pain and raised his hands to bat it away. Bert flew at him again, pecking at his face and eyes. Harrison shrieked and covered his eyes. Charlie seized the moment to race for the front door. She heard Bert screeching in anger. She stumbled into the hallway and pulled at the doorknob with her good hand. The door opened. She ran outside. Darkness was falling and she almost didn't see the man blocking her path.

"Charlie, is everything okay? Charlie, speak to me, sweetie."

It was Jake. She flung herself into his chest and sobbed, "I didn't send the email. Harrison—"

She pointed back at the house. Jake took in the tears, her injured wrist, and her bruised face.

"Wait here," he whispered. He raced into the house. She could hear anguished screams. She held her broken wrist and wept.

Peggy tickled Bert's beak. He made soft, appreciative responses. "What a brave boy," she murmured.

Jake was on Charlie's sofa, one arm curled around her shoulders. Gordon had made everyone a cup of sweet tea, and was now sitting on the arm of Peggy's chair, listening to the story of what had happened.

"You were very courageous to rush inside, Jake," said Peggy. "That man could've been dangerous and hurt you."

"I didn't think about that. I was furious at what he'd done to Charlie. I heard angry screams from the kitchen and expected him to be on the rampage. I intended confronting him and trying to reason with him. Fortunately, Bert had taken care of him. Harrison was holding his bleeding nose and moaning loudly when I found him hiding under the kitchen table. Bert was throwing plastic balls at him. He's very intelligent, isn't he? He whistled when he saw me and said 'G'day mate,' then he hurled a ball at Harrison's face, and cackled like a witch."

"Bert's my hero," said Charlie. "And you, of course," she continued, giving Jake's arm a squeeze.

"That's a nasty bruise he left on your face, my dear," said Peggy. "And how's your wrist feeling?"

"It's bearable, thanks, Peggy. The pain killers have helped. It'll heal. I think it'll take poor Harrison longer to recover from his ordeal with Bert."

"I'm sure the hospital will look after him and more importantly, evaluate him. He needs to be in care. He'll recover in time. You have to feel sorry for the man," said Jake.

"See, that's what I like about you. You're very caring," said Charlie. "I was so upset when Harrison told me he'd sent that email to you. You must have thought I was a right bitch."

"Not at all. I was puzzled because firstly, it made no sense, given the events of the night before, and even though it was signed *love Charlie* I had a feeling it wasn't genuine. Call it intuition. Then, Mercedes phoned me. She said you hadn't turned up for the show and had sent a ridiculous email stating you were going away on an adventure. She was concerned. She knew it was completely out of character to behave like that. You're far too close to her to tell her such news in an email. She wondered if I'd seen you, or heard from you. I mentioned the incident with Rob and we came to the same conclusion, so I shot around. She phoned Ryan immediately after speaking to me. That's why the police arrived so quickly. Harrison should have guessed your friends would be suspicious. I'm surprised he thought he could get away with that. Surely he knew you better than that."

"He didn't know me at all. He was in love with a fantasy. Turns out he'd been warned before at his previous employment because he kept annoying a young nurse. He followed her about the hospital and repeatedly asked her out. He'd also been reported at university for hanging about girl's residences late at night. Mercedes admitted that she told someone in HR about him pestering me. The manager did some digging around and discovered the complaints about him. Based on that information, they confronted him and he went wild. They didn't actually fire him. He stormed off. He disappeared shortly after that, moved in with his sick father. His father passed away recently. I guess that was the final straw. It tipped him over the edge. He was so desperate for someone to love, he didn't think sane thoughts."

"I'm very happy that you've found someone normal to care for you, dear," said Peggy as Jake stroked her hair tenderly. "That makes two of us with happy endings."

Bert thrilled.

"Sorry, Bert. I mean three of us. I meant to tell you. Bert and Sunny are in love. They enjoyed their Skype call so much, Sunny is going to come and visit him at home. If they get on as well when they meet up, we're going to invite her to live with us when we get back from our honeymoon. Her owner is thrilled that Sunny has found a new boyfriend. Sunny will be a welcome addition and she'll keep Bert on his toes."

Bert whistled and shook his feathers, then said, "Mmm mmm."

Mercedes put down the phone. "The challenge is off," she announced.

"It's off?" repeated Charlie.

"Yes, that idiot Harrison really lost the plot. Fancy breaking into the hangar and smashing the stunt aeroplane with a hammer. The company has insurance for the aircraft, but it'll take a few months to repair it. Good thing they captured it all on CCTV. It showed Harrison bashing away at the aircraft. The police are going to charge him. I expect he'll get off; after all, he clearly has issues. His lawyer will plead some sort of mental breakdown in his defence. They discovered the hammer at his house. He'd left it in a pannier on his motorbike along with a can of petrol. They think he might have considered setting fire to the hangar. What a nutcase! I'm so glad he didn't manage to kidnap you and hide you away to be his love maiden, or whatever his ridiculous plan was. He was always odd, but I'd never have guessed he was going to completely fold like that."

"It was quite possibly one of the most terrifying moments of my life. He was out of control and I didn't know how to respond to him. I hope he gets some treatment."

"He'll get plenty. Don't concern yourself over him."

"Have we any other challenges we can attempt?"

"There are a few, but that was the best one. Besides, you're very limited now you have a wrist in plaster. The hospital authorities aren't keen for you to do anything outrageous, especially given what has happened. They're trying to dumb it all down. After all, Harrison was a hospital employee and the situation with him should've been dealt with differently. We also seem to have reached an impasse as far as collecting new money is concerned. Seems most people who live locally have already given generously."

Charlie bit her lip. This was disappointing news.

"I could still shave my head," she began.

Mercedes gave her a look that silenced her.

"There must be something I can do that doesn't involve using my hands, but is still appealing to the public."

"Charlie, I think we're going to have to admit defeat," said

Vivienne. "You've done so much and we raised significant funding thanks to you. If it'd been merely for the upkeep of the old radio, we'd have succeeded. It's only because we need to build a new studio that we're short of funds. We'll keep on with our efforts and I'm sure we'll be able to raise enough over the next year or two to start building."

"That's too far away. I wanted to be able for us all to stay on and have a new studio to move to at the end of the year," said Charlie.

"Look, you've given us a fantastic start. Be happy you've done that. We're all resigned to going off air for a while. Hopefully, in a couple of years, we'll be able to start afresh."

Charlie looked away. She had failed. Stupid Harrison had put an end to the fundraising for City Hospital Radio.

"On a brighter matter, have you decided what you're wearing to your birthday party next month, or do you and I have to go out and do some serious shopping?" asked Mercedes.

"I've ordered a new dress online and I'm rather excited about it. Hopefully, the plaster will be off by then or it'll ruin the look. Thank you so much for organising this party for me. I was trying to ignore the fact I'm going to be the big four-oh but now, I'm looking forward to it, thanks to you. I can't believe you've booked Swinfen Hall for it. That's so upmarket. You are without a doubt, the best friend in the world."

"I know. You're very lucky." She chuckled. "It's not every day you have a big birthday, a lovely friend, and a new man to celebrate it with. Gosh! Is that the time? I have to go. Got an appointment. See you later."

Mercedes disappeared and Vivienne went off to man the reception desk. Charlie felt she had let everyone down. There must be another way she could raise enough money for the new studio. At the moment, however, she had no new ideas as to how she could accomplish that.

The month passed without any further hope on the challenge front. Mercedes revealed the challenges remaining on her own Carpe Diem list, but they were way too expensive to fund or too ambitious for Charlie to complete with her broken wrist. They included driving in a Segway rally, white water rafting, ice climbing, coasteering and flying on a trapeze at a circus.

Since the excitement and publicity surrounding the shark dive, interest in Charlie's challenges and support for the radio station had waned. People had donated towards the cause and, or, had too many other demands on their resources. It was summertime, with holidays to be enjoyed and outings planned for families. Many businesses were short-staffed as people took their annual holidays, so trying to organise press coverage or an event itself was proving impossible.

The team gathered to take a decision on the fate of City Hospital Radio. Andrew Carnegie agreed that the amount raised had been remarkable and he would keep it safe for the station's future. They would stay on air for a few more months until the hospital requisitioned the studio, then they would have to abandon the station. The mood in the room was downbeat. They were defeated.

Jake invited her to join him and Toby on their outward bound adventure in the Peak District. First, they were going to set up camp in a picturesque village beside the River Manifold called Ilam. Toby was fascinated by the history of the village, once cut off by the Plague and had borrowed a copy of the play *The Roses of Eyam* by Don Taylor from his English teacher for Charlie to read. From there, they intended venturing further into the Peak District and walk the Kinder Scout, a moorland plateau and nature reserve. En route, they were going to meet instructors from Peak Pursuits activities and have a go at gyhll scrambling. Toby had been delighted to discover this involved scrambling up waterfalls.

She was thrilled to be invited, but decided it would be better to let the boys have time together.

"Okay," said Jake after she refused his request. "I think Toby would love to have you along too, but I can understand why you'd rather not join us."

"It's not that I wouldn't enjoy being with you both, it's that Toby's at a vulnerable age. He'll get much more out of the week if you two spend proper quality time together. He might even open up more to you because you're away from the usual home environment. I'm sure he feels a bit overwhelmed by Fiona at times and says he wants to be a barrister just to please her. Give him time out. He'll have fun doing dad and son stuff."

"Pity I'm not much good at it," he said.

"You're much better than you think. I don't know many thirteen-year-old boys who'd even agree to go away with their fathers. Let alone spend a week in a tent. You'll be just what he needs."

Charlie assumed correctly, because as soon as they returned from their trip, Toby decided he no longer wanted to be a lawyer or work in an office.

"I want to go travelling, when I finish school. I'm going to explore. I might even be a game keeper. What do you think, Dad?"

Jake ruffled his hair. "You can be whatever you want."

Toby stayed with his father for half of the summer holiday. Jake and Charlie ensured his days were filled with as many enjoyable trips, sights to see, and days out as possible. All too soon, it was time for him to return to his mother and go abroad with her and Simon. He trundled down the stairs carrying his heavy backpack.

"Do I have to go to Majorca?"

"Of course you do. Your mum will be looking forward to having you home."

Toby harrumphed. "Now then, Toby. You know she loves you. She would be very upset if you didn't go. Besides, I thought you really liked doing all that cool stuff with Simon, you know, the boat, trips out to beaches, that sort of thing."

"It's okay. Mum spends most of the time sunbathing though and Simon's alright, but he doesn't talk to me like you do. He calls me Sonny and he always pats me on the head, like I'm some sort of dog, or something." He looked forlorn.

"Come on, Toby. This isn't like you. We've spent holidays together before and you've never been reluctant to go back home to your mum."

"It's different now. You're much happier and you do all sorts of fun things. I had a blast going karting with you, and climbing that indoor climbing wall. Pity Charlie couldn't do it because of her wrist.

I liked everything we did; going to Cadbury's World and visiting the Thinktank in Birmingham with Charlie. There's been so much to do. Majorca's boring. We never go anywhere. I get to swim in the pool and ride my bike, but it's not as much fun as being here with you both."

Jake put an arm around his son, marvelling at how tall he had suddenly become. He seemed to have sprouted in four weeks. It was not going to be long before he would find going out with his father a drag. He was growing up fast.

"Look, you'll enjoy it once you get there. When you come back, I'll still be here, with Charlie, and you can come around any time you want."

"Dad," he said quietly.

"Yes."

"Could you ask mum if I can become a weekly boarder and not full-time? A lot of the other boys do that. They spend weekends at home and only come back to school on Monday mornings. There's only really me, Hugh, and Thomas who stay at school all the time in my year. I asked her before, but she said it would be impractical. Can I come and spend weekends here with you both?"

Jake felt a lump in his throat. "Of course you can. Go away with your mum and Simon, have a great time, and if that's still what you want to do when you come home, I'll talk to her and arrange it."

The look on his son's face was reward enough, but inside he felt the happiest he had for a very long time. He gave his son a man hug, but found the boy clung to him more than usual.

"Thanks Dad. You're the best. I'll send you a text from Majorca and don't forget to give Charlie her birthday card from me."

A car horn hooted outside the house. Fiona had sent Simon around to collect Toby. He waved from the front seat of his silver Audi TT convertible.

"I won't forget. Take care, mate. See you in a few weeks."

Toby climbed into the car. Simon patted him on the head. Toby threw his father a look of exasperation and shrugged. Simon sounded the horn, waved at Jake and pulled off the front drive with speed. Jake shook his head in dismay, then remembered his conversation with his son and went back inside, humming.

Jake collected Charlie at seven o'clock. She had spent the afternoon being pampered at a beauty salon, having treated herself to a body massage and a facial. She also had her hair done.

"Spectacular," said Jake when he saw her. Her new scarlet red dress was eye-catching. It fitted over her curves, adding a sexual allure to her figure. It suited her colouring and her ash-blonde wavy hair that framed her face, making her look much younger than forty.

"You might want to take a peek at your birthday present before we go out." He passed a small box to her. "Happy birthday, Charlie." He kissed her. Both were reluctant to part.

"Better open it or we'll probably not make it to the party," he said with a small smile.

"I'm game. Fancy being late?"

"More than anything. However, I promised Mercedes that I'd make sure you got there bang on seven-thirty, so open your present, and don't worry about the frustrated old guy standing beside you."

She thanked him, ripped open the gold wrapping paper, and lifted the lid on a velvet box. Inside was a pair of diamond drop earrings.

She gasped. "These are too much. Oh Jake, you shouldn't have."

"I thought they'd set off your new dress beautifully."

"They're fantastic. I love them. They're so glamorous."

"And suit you."

"I don't know how to thank you."

"You don't?" scoffed Jake. "I'll remind you how later tonight, if you're sober."

She hugged him and they kissed again.

"Right, birthday girl, let's get you to your party."

Swinfen Hall car park was full when they arrived. There was, however, one place left vacant in front of the magnificent building. A large hand-written sign marked the space: *Reserved for Ms Charlie Blundell VIP*.

Jake opened the passenger door for her and together they went into the hotel. Mercedes had booked a function room for the event. It was enormous. Tables and chairs for groups of ten were set up around the room. To one side, a buffet had been set out. Helium-filled balloons bearing the number forty rose from tables. *Happy Birthday* confetti was scattered around the centre of each table. There was a long bar, currently swamped by people ordering drinks, and a dance floor. A DJ was playing music at a low volume and disco lights flickered colours across the floor. The room was buzzing. As Charlie entered, the noise abated.

Someone shouted, "She's here."

Silence fell over the hall, then a voice began, "Happy birthday to you … " others picked it up and the entire room sang in unison. Cheers rang out.

"I am completely overwhelmed," said Charlie.

"Save the speeches for later," yelled Mercedes. "It's party-time!"

The DJ was asked to begin the party in earnest. Dance music filled the room. Charlie was surrounded by friends wishing her a happy birthday. There were over one hundred people. All her colleagues from City Hospital Radio had turned up, as had several of the nurses she knew and Tina from the coffee shop. Peggy and Gordon were also there, sitting together with others that Charlie recognised as ex-patients from the hospital.

"Bert wanted to come, too, but we bribed him to stay at home by leaving him some new crackers to eat," Peggy explained.

"I look forward to having him stay again in a few weeks' time. Guess we'll be partying again when you get married."

"Of course we shall. It won't be as big an event as this, but it'll be a good enough shindig."

In one corner stood Susannah with her husband Dave, an amiable man who wore a permanent smile on his face and seemed determined to keep his hand on Susannah's backside. They were in conversation with Marcia who had brought along her new boyfriend, Mitch, a beefy rugby player and coach from Cardiff. Jasmine was also there, dancing with an athletic man who was later introduced as her husband, Robin, an ex-ice skating champion who now judged ice-skating competitions all over the world. Art, Patricia, and several of her favourite customers who frequented the café had also turned up to celebrate her birthday. Art started on the buffet ahead of the others while Patricia was occupied talking. He waved at Charlie, gave her a thumbs-up for the food, piled his plate high with vol-au-vents, and went to hide in another room to scoff them. Charlie was dragged onto the dance floor by a group of female patients she had befriended at the hospital, including Fatima who'd helped tutor Mercedes for the *Nosh for Dosh* challenge. She wanted Charlie to show off her belly dancing moves. Charlie refused, but Susannah took up the challenge much to the delight of Fatima's sons.

A couple of hours later, the buffet was demolished, the birthday cake had been cut and distributed, but the drinks continued to flow. The atmosphere was most convivial. The dance floor was full to brimming, with some people dancing beside the tables, and Marcia dancing on top of one.

The Time Warp finished. Mercedes picked up the microphone.

"Ladies and gentlemen, thank you all for coming tonight. If you wouldn't mind returning to your chairs for a moment, I'd like to seize this opportunity to say a few words."

The guests drifted back to the seats they had taken when eating the buffet.

When everyone was seated, Mercedes continued, "As you know, we're here because it's Charlie's birthday. An important milestone of a birthday."

She paused for a second. "However, we're here for another reason, one you may not know. At the beginning of the year, Charlie and I wrote out a few bucket list challenges. Not so much bucket list as carpe diem challenges. Neither of us are getting younger and it seemed fitting to try and do things that were rewarding. Charlie was, well, to not put too fine a point on it, drunk. Actually, she was completely wasted." There were laughs from the crowd.

"Given the state she was in and because I'd also consumed more than my fair share of alcohol, I decided we should swap lists. I still don't know why I came up with that idea."

"Because you're a minx!" yelled one of the nurses.

Mercedes nodded. "That'll be why."

She continued, "So, as a consequence, Charlie got to do all my exciting challenges, sampled bush tucker cuisine, rode a roller coaster while playing a kazoo and went zip-lining, and I got to do Charlie's choices. That meant I had to learn to cook and knit!" She yawned in an exaggerated fashion and earned some more laughter.

"No, to be serious for a moment, they weren't dull challenges. Let me explain. Charlie's choices weren't centred around herself. Mine were. I wanted to have a go at adrenaline-filled experiences and out-of-the-ordinary activities. Charlie's involved doing something for others. She decided she would learn to knit. Not just knit. She wanted to knit a garment that would appear in a charity fashion show. I have to admit here, that I was the person who determined that the garment would be a onesie," she added and smirked.

"As we know, Charlie's an ace cake-maker and loves cooking. She wanted to be a contestant on the television show *Nosh for Dosh*. It says on her list, and I have it here: Be selected for T.V. show *Nosh For Dosh* and win the prize. Actually, what it says is: 'Be selected for T.V. show *Nosh For Dosh* and win the prize, then share all the money with my friends. Buy everyone lottery tickets with the prize money. Let's all have a shot at winning.'" Mercedes halted as a buzz went around the room.

"So, Ryan and I took the prize money to the local shop and bought everyone in this room five lucky dip lottery tickets. They're in envelopes under all the chairs. If you'd like to feel under your chair now, there should be an envelope stuck to it. Pull it off and you'll find a lottery ticket inside it." People rummaged about under their seats and removed the envelopes. A couple of people stood up, turned over their chairs, and tugged at the envelopes secured by thick pieces of sellotape.

"Blame Ryan for those," shouted Mercedes, laughing. "He didn't want any to fall down and spoil the surprise so he taped some up with extra sticky stuff. I think it's crime scene tape." There were guffaws and chuckles.

"I would just like to add that the local newsagent is extremely grateful for your business and gave me a free chocolate bar to keep me quiet, while he attempted to churn out all these tickets. I think he had a lie-down after he'd finished. Even his machine went slow towards the end!"

"Don't forget to check your tickets later. They're for tonight's draw. Okay, just to sum up. I think Charlie had some fun experiences by doing my list and thanks to some of them, she managed to raise almost five thousand pounds for City Hospital Radio which is a heck of an achievement. See, she even managed to turn my list into one that helped other people. She's a wonderful woman. I know you all agree with me. I'd like to thank her for being such a good friend to us all. I'd also like to thank her on a personal level. Thanks to her list, I can now cook and I enjoy it."

"I enjoy it more," shouted Ryan.

"I've taken up knitting professionally and have started a new business selling knitwear for dogs, called Ruffwear, so if you want a new coat, or onesie, for your woofer, then contact me. Sorry, I had to get the plug in," she added.

"The challenges also taught me to relax more. Knitting is incredibly therapeutic and lowers blood pressure, heart rate and so on. Who'd have thought it? Well, that has had other benefits. Ones I couldn't have imagined possible." She looked over at Charlie who clamped her hand to her mouth. Mercedes gave an imperceptible nod.

"I'm going to return the list to her. There's one last item on it that I think she needs to do herself, so Charlie, thank you again and happy birthday."

The crowd applauded. They gave three cheers.

"Speech, Charlie!" yelled Art. Charlie stood up, walked to the front and took the microphone from Mercedes.

"I'm not very good at speeches," she began. "So I'll keep this brief and promise I won't tell you any jokes. I am completely overwhelmed by the whole evening. Thank you all for being here and sharing my birthday with me. I am so fortunate to know you all. A huge thank you to Mercedes and Ryan for organising this event. I don't know where I would have been without you guys. That's all from me. Thank you again and enjoy the rest of the evening." There was more applause, then the music started up again. The DJ played *Lady in Red*. Jake took her hand and guided her to the dance floor where they glided together lost in their own private world. She nuzzled into his neck. He held her gently. People around them dematerialised as they swung in rhythmical harmony. Charlie had never felt happier. Jake pulled back and looked into her eyes.

"I love you, Charlie Blundell," he whispered.

"I love you too, Jake Meredith," she replied.

"Come on," he said, taking her again by the hand.

He eased them through the dancing crowd and outside. It was warm and stars shone out from a midnight-blue sky.

"Whenever I look at the stars, I'm reminded how small and insignificant we all are," Charlie said.

"In the great scheme of things, I suppose we are microscopic and unimportant, but it's the here and now that's important. And some people are far more significant in our lives than others. I hope you'll decide to play a major part in my life, Charlie Blundell."

Mercedes interrupted them. Ryan accompanied her, carrying a bottle of champagne and four glasses.

"Well?" said Charlie grasping her friend's hands in hers. "Am I right in assuming that you and Ryan are going to be parents?"

Mercedes nodded, eyes shining with excitement. Ryan handed the glasses to Jake and opened the bottle.

"I thought so. It wasn't just what you said tonight. You've been positively glowing for a fortnight. I had a feeling that might be the reason."

"See, good friends can work on some telepathic level. I wanted to tell you, but I didn't dare until it was confirmed. You're the first to know. Apart from my beloved inspector, naturally."

"Oh Mercedes. I can't tell you how thrilled I am for you."

"The consultant was right. I was too worked up. I needed to unwind and stop thinking about getting pregnant. You know me. I want things now and I get frustrated when I can't do them or have them. Your challenges were just what I needed. I forgot about my disability and learned to enjoy therapeutic hobbies. I refocused and it happened," she said, rubbing her still flat stomach.

"I'll soon have a proper challenge on my hands and won't yearn to do daft, extraordinary activities to test myself. Having a child and bringing it up will be enough, for now."

Ryan filled the glasses. "To Charlie," said Mercedes.

"No, to you both and to the new life. It's going to be the luckiest child in the world to have you two as its parents."

"This is for you. You have no idea how long it took me and how patient Patricia had to be with me."

Mercedes handed Charlie a wrapped present. Puzzled, Charlie opened it. It was a small piece of pottery painted in blues, greens, and yellows. It was of three parrots sitting together on a branch. Charlie gasped.

"Oh my! Oh Mercedes! However did you manage to make this? It's spectacular!"

"I have to say it was the most difficult challenge you gave me. I've spent an eternity with Patricia trying to get it right. We had so many failed attempts. If it had been one parrot, you'd have received it several months ago, but three. That tried my patience. I kept having accidents with them and broke them or got one wrong. In the end, I made three separate ones, then together, we stuck them onto one branch. They're pretty robust. Three solid, chunky parrots who look very pleased with life. Patricia was incredible. She has the patience of a saint. She helped me paint them, too, because by then, I was petrified I'd break them once more. And she glazed them for me."

Tears rolled down Charlie's face. "This means so much. You know how much, don't you?" she stammered.

"Of course I do, Charlie. That's why I refused to give up. They're not the best porcelain parrots in the world, but they've been made with love. Just as much love as you'd have poured into them. I know why you wanted to do this. If you still want to do it yourself, I'm sure Patricia will help you."

"No, these are perfect. I love you, Mercedes. You are the kindest, sweetest ... "

"Stop right there. I don't do mush. You know how grateful I am to you. This is nothing by comparison. Now, wipe your eyes. You look like a Goth."

Charlie smiled and rubbed at the mascara under her eyes. They raised their glasses again. An emergency exit door to the hotel crashed open. They turned around in surprise.

Susannah came rushing out into the night, breathless, "Thank goodness you're here. We thought you'd left," he said.

"Is everything okay?"

Susannah caught her breath. "It's Art. He's collapsed. Patricia is with him along with some of the hospital staff. An ambulance is on its way. We think it's his heart."

"Oh my goodness," said Charlie, handing her glass to Jake ready to accompany Susannah. "He's overdone it. I saw him eating a pile of food at the buffet."

"I don't think it was the food. It was the shock."

"Shock?"

"Yes, Pat checked their lottery numbers on her mobile. I think they won the jackpot."

Charlie squinted at the computer screen. "You look sun-tanned and I think you've lost weight," she said.

Art beamed back at her. "I've never felt better. Coming to Italy was the best move we've made."

"He's so much healthier since we started him on a proper Mediterranean diet. The tomatoes here are enormous," Patricia piped up. "As long as he stays off the pasta, he'll be fine. I think the climate and the slower pace of life help too."

"How's the bed and breakfast going?"

"We're fully booked for next summer already. We're going to convert the old barn into a gallery workshop for my classes over the next few months, so it should be ready for the new season. I hope you'll both come over, with Toby, of course next year and see the place."

"Definitely," said Jake, leaning over Charlie's shoulder. "Try and stop us."

"We've spent all the lottery winnings now on renovating the old house. We also bought Art an ultra-modern bicycle, so he can keep up his exercise routine. I don't want him having another health scare," Patricia continued.

"Good thing we only had five numbers and the bonus ball and didn't win the jackpot. I'm sure knowing we had eight million pounds to spend would have killed me," interrupted Art.

"I read in the paper that a syndicate won the money. They've only recently claimed it, too. They've not gone public about it," Charlie said.

"I don't blame them. Imagine all the begging letters. We were more than happy with fifty-five thousand pounds. We don't need any more than that. We have everything we need and each other," said Patricia.

"That's the most important thing," Charlie replied.

"We have to go. Our Italian neighbours have invited us around for dinner. Lovely to talk to you both. Speak again soon."

They signed off, blowing kisses.

"Don't they look well?" said Charlie after they had shut down the computer.

"Yes," Jake agreed. "They needed time to relax and enjoy themselves more. I think the move to Italy was right for them. Now Senorita, let's go out to celebrate our new venture."

Mercedes and Ryan were at the Art café. Mercedes was showing off her latest doggie creation—a Christmas hoody. "They've been selling so well. I love doing this and I can continue with it once the baby's born. It's so enjoyable. I can spend hours crafting new articles."

"You look much more content these days," commented Charlie, wiping paint off the end of her thumb.

"I have every reason to. The baby is due in a few months. I have a wonderful husband and a new career to keep me occupied. I feel completely fulfilled."

"Sounds like a few of us are starting afresh. Thanks to Art and Patricia, we now have this place to keep us happy. It's transformed our lives," said Jake, climbing down from a ladder.

"I thought yours was transformed the day you met Charlie," Mercedes replied.

"Ah, you're right about that."

"Funny how we're all moving on. I spoke to Susannah on Facebook last week. She and Dave have just bought a holiday villa near Agadir in Morocco. They met Maurice and his boyfriend over there and they've all been seeing all the sights together. Susannah has a profile picture of her sitting on a camel on her Facebook page. Marcia's returned to Australia with that hunk of hers and is running her own belly-dancing classes. As for Art and Patricia, well, we spoke to them on Skype yesterday and they love Tuscany. Patricia says there's so much to inspire her there and the light is perfect for painting."

"I see you've taken down the old Art Café sign. You changing the name of the café?"

"Yes, they were happy for us to take over completely and change the name and style of the place. It'll still be a café and Jake can't wait to start cooking up his recipes. I'm going to do deserts and cakes and we're taking on a couple of serving staff. Tina is joining us."

"Tina from the hospital coffee shop?"

"Yes, she's going to be a part-time manageress so we don't become slaves to the business. The new sign was delivered this morning.

We're putting it up later this week. Come and see the new room. It's finished."

Charlie led them to the back room, which was no longer the craft shop, but a stylish bistro eating area, in shades of light green, blue, and cream. A tropical island scene had been painted on the far wall. In it, two parrots cavorted on branches of a palm tree overlooking a perfect white-sand beach. One bird looked suspiciously like Bert. A third flew high above the azure blue sea.

"Patricia painted it for me before she left. I told her what I wanted."

"It's beautiful," said Mercedes. "It makes you feel so happy. It's like there are no cares in the world. You can come and sit here and be transported to a happy island."

"That's exactly what I wanted it to do," replied Charlie with a contented sigh.

Charlie pointed out the sign leaning against the wall in the hall. She pulled at a dustcover revealing the new sign for the café.

"Three Little Birds," read Ryan. "Like the three little birds in the Bob Marley song?"

"That's right. I want people to enjoy themselves here. It'll be a place for them to come and chill out when they're having a bad day, or come to for a nice meal. Life doesn't always have to be hard. We shouldn't spend it all worrying. It can be a difficult journey, but, as we all know, in the end, every little thing is alright."

Jake took Ryan off to show him the new kitchen. Mercedes remained behind with Charlie.

"I guess it's time to hand you back your Carpe Diem list. There's one challenge I can't do. Thought you should take it on, if you can. You'd better take a look at that last scrawled line."

Charlie squinted. "Oh dear, this writing is terrible." She read the words, smiled at her friend, and then folded the paper.

"What do you reckon? Think you can handle it?"

"I reckon that's perfectly achievable," Charlie replied, folding the paper and winking at her friend.

Jake yawned and stretched out in the chair.

"Tired?"

"Not really. I think it's more appropriate to say, weary but contented," he replied.

"It's been a crazy few weeks. First, there was the whole Harrison incident, then the birthday celebration, Art declaring he was going to sell the café, and us deciding to buy it, and now Toby is going to be staying with us at weekends and some holidays. I'm so pleased Fiona agreed to let him do weekly boarding."

"Yeah, me too. Thank goodness Tina is going to look after the café at weekends. It means we can have time for him. I'd hate him to feel left out while we served cakes and teas."

"Funny, it was Toby's suggestion that made me think about buying the café. That night I came around for dinner, he told me I should open a cake shop. I guess he's to thank for the idea. Tina's over the moon. She wanted to cut down her hours at the hospital coffee shop and the café is less far to travel. She'll be ideal."

"I'd have never thought about buying it either if you hadn't suggested it. It's perfect for us. I've suddenly developed a new lust for life."

"Just a lust for life?"

Jake chuckled. "You know very well that I have an even stronger lust for you." He grabbed at her, pulled her onto his lap, and kissed her.

"I hope you're not going to do that when we're serving food together," she joked.

"Why not? I'd happily snog you anywhere. You're my woman and I'll kiss you whenever and wherever I want," he grunted, beating his chest like an orang-utan.

"I'm *your* woman, am I?"

"Yes, you *my* wo-man," he continued in a silly voice.

"Good. I'm glad we've clarified that. Because, Jake Meredith, there is one outstanding challenge on my Carpe Diem list and I need you to help me complete it. Come on." Charlie dragged him up from his chair and led him to the kitchen.

"I want you to try my latest cake. It's a recipe I've not baked before."

"It's not made from chocolate locusts, is it?" he asked, horrified.

"No, it's a strawberry and champagne sponge."

"Sounds delicious. Come on then, bring it on."

Jake plopped down on one of the kitchen stools and waited while Charlie produced the cake and placed it on the table in front of Jake. It was a large sponge cake covered in icing. Piped on the top, in red icing, were four words: 'Will you marry me?'

Jake gave an enigmatic smile, pulled her into his arms, and murmured, "Of course, I will."

"Thank goodness for that," she said when they finished kissing. "I was afraid you'd refuse."

"Never. Who could refuse such a good cake maker? Actually," he continued, rummaging about in his trouser pocket, "you beat me to it. I guess great minds think alike."

He raised a small box triumphantly, dropped to one knee, and said, "Charlie, I would be honoured if you'd accept this ring and be my wife. It would make me the happiest man in the world." He opened the box to reveal a diamond ring.

Charlie gasped. "You intended proposing tonight, too?"

Jake nodded, a large smile spread across his face.

"Oh Jake, I'd love to accept your ring and your proposal."

"There's a catch with mine. Not so much a catch as a challenge," he said. "I hope you're up for it."

"I'm up for anything," Charlie replied.

Jake rose. "Goody," he murmured and pulled her into his arms, kissing her with tenderness that soon turned to passion.

"So, was that what you wrote on your list?" he asked as they sat back in the kitchen. Charlie was photographing the cake for posterity.

"I had trouble reading my own writing but I'd scrawled, 'Find the perfect man to fill your empty heart and prove you love him.' It was vague. I must have been completely drunk by then. I always get all romantic and giddy when I'm very drunk. I thought the way to a man's heart was through his stomach, hence the cake."

"No, the way to a man's heart is through his heart. And you, Charlie Blundell, soon to be Mrs. Charlie Meredith, have captured mine."

"Next up is a song especially for Peggy, Gordon, Bert, and Sunny who are celebrating Christmas with their family who've come to see them all the way from Canada. I understand this is the first time the grandchildren have been over to the UK. Hope Bert's been a good boy this year and Santa brings him some nice toys and maybe some new plastic balls. So, for you and everyone here, here's Noddy Holder and the boys."

Sam sang along to *Merry Christmas* by Slade. He was in his element. With his wife currently at the shops buying up half of Sainsbury's food and most of John Lewis's stock, he was happy to be at the studio. He was also glad to take on a few extra slots that had been offered when Charlie reduced her hours. Sean was doing a couple of shows and seemed to have decided that a career in radio was just up his street. He had signed up for a university course in journalism and was hoping to land himself a prime job in broadcasting when he completed it.

"They're on!" Sean said, pointing at the television screen now in the studio thanks to Art and Patricia. Vivienne, Vernon, and Tina were clustered in the studio with him. Sam turned up the volume. On the television, sitting opposite presenters Alex Jones and Matt Evans, were Charlie and Jake holding hands.

"Most couples get married in a church or a registry office. Some might marry in a special venue, but our guests tonight are doing it in unconventionally. Jake Meredith and Charlie Blundell are going to get married in a most unusual way. Jake, how on earth did you come up with the idea of getting married while skydiving and how did Charlie react?" asked Matt.

"Before I answer that, I must explain that I met Charlie when she was doing a list of challenges to help raise money for City Hospital Radio where she presents. Having watched her go zip-lining, dive with sharks, and having tumbled down a hill in a zorb with her, it seemed only fitting to give her a wedding that would be memorable."

Charlie beamed at him. Jake squeezed her hand.

"Well," said Alex. "I don't think she'll forget her big day. That's for sure."

"The other reason was to raise money for the radio station. In spite of Charlie's best efforts, the station was still some way off its target. I was thinking about ways to surprise Charlie with a marriage proposal and had one of those Eureka moments. I thought if people sponsored us to do a special sky dive on our wedding day rather than give us wedding gifts, it would help raise funds for the outstanding amount we needed to build a new studio."

"I understand you raised far more than you expected," said Matt.

"Yes, not only did we get sponsorship from several companies including a well-known legal company based in Birmingham and London, but money poured in once the press got hold of the story. It seemed to capture the public's imagination. We're donating the excess to a couple of worthy charities. That's the children's charity Rainbow Trust which provides emotional and practical support to families who have a child with a life-threatening or terminal illness and the Back-Up Trust which is a national charity dedicated to providing opportunities for spinally-injured and able-bodied individuals to experience the buzz of outdoor activities together and so increase self-belief, independence, and motivation."

"Excellent stuff. So, Charlie, how do you feel about this wedding? It's not every bride's dream wedding. No walk down the aisle, no confetti, no point in doing your hair or makeup. It'll be quite an event. What are you worried about most? Your dress billowing up to reveal your underwear, or your veil coming off?"

Charlie laughed. "I'll be too busy clinging onto Jake to worry about my dress, my hair, or anything else. It's going to be a tandem dive. We're doing two practice sky dives before the big day, so we'll know what to expect. I'm very proud of Jake, because this is completely out of his comfort zone. It's out of mine too, but I'm sure we'll enjoy it when it happens. It'll be a question of making sure I wear decent underwear for the wedding video. I have a feeling it's going to be on show quite a bit. The video is being taken by a skydiver who'll jump out ahead of us and film."

"The vicar won't be diving with you, will he?"

"No, he'll do the ceremony in the plane, then we'll leap out and skydive down towards our guests who should be waiting on terra firma with the champagne. We need to make sure we land at the right point and not in a field a few miles away."

"I'm sure it'll be a very special day for all. Jake, Charlie, we are so impressed and good luck for the big day. Hope you raise loads more money and thank you for being on the show." Matt beamed at them.

"So," he said, turning to face camera one, if any of you out there would like to help raise money for City Hospital Radio and associated charities, please send all donations to City Hospital Radio, details on the screen below and can be found on their website www. cityhospitalradio.org. Thank you both."

The camera panned away from Charlie and Jake and the presenters moved onto the next topic. Sam cancelled the volume and grinned at the people who'd assembled in the studio with him. There were smiles all around.

"Hats off to them. I for one shall be cheering like mad when they land," said Vernon.

Vivienne wiped away a tear.

"You okay, Viv?" asked Sean.

"Yes, just a bit emotional. They're perfect together, aren't they?"

There was general consent and then Sam shooed them away so he could carry on with his show.

"It's been huge excitement in the studio. We've just been watching Charlie and her fiancé, Jake, on *The One Show*. They're an inspiration to us all. I remember when Charlie was a quaking mess here in front of me, worried about going on a roller coaster ride and now look at her. Goes to prove that with determination, we can accomplish a lot. My next track is especially for her and Jake, our favourite soon-to-be-weds. It's Van Halen and *Jump*."

Sam smiled to himself. The future was looking much brighter for the radio station. They would be able to bring music and company to many more patients for years to come. Sam hummed. He decided he would buy a Harley Davidson with some of his pension money, then take some time off and go travelling on it. He had seen a television programme about motor biking in France. He fancied that idea. Charlie had taught him an important lesson: life was for living. He was going to live his while he still had time.

Charlie clutched Jake's hand. They stood together in St. Peter's churchyard. The wind blew and lifted the few dry leaves in the churchyard and rustled them. Charlie dropped to her knees by her daughter's headstone.

"Daddy's coming to visit you next week when he comes up to stay with us. Baby Mark, your half-brother, is recovering from measles, so he's not up to travelling at the moment. This is Jake. I've spoken a lot about him to you these last few weeks. He wanted to come and visit you today. You'd love him. He's kind, thoughtful and makes me happy.

We finished renovating the café. We're going to open it next week. There's still a room for children to play in and one for people to read. Jake's had a book published, so we're going to put some copies of it in the reading room. The best room is the new dining room. It's especially for you. It's your room. I think about you every time I walk in there. It's as if part of you is still with us. You see, there are three happy parrots on one wall, like those you saw when we all went to Tenerife, to the Loro Parque. They're exactly like the ones from the song. They're flying about together in the trees, swooping over the never-ending sea, playing and whistling. They make people happy. They help them when they're sad. They remind them that things can get better even when it seems that they won't."

She stopped to clear the lump in her throat. "I miss you, sweetheart, but I know that you're in a peaceful place, a beautiful place, and you're surrounded by pretty little birds and they're all playing with you and singing to you. Here are another three to watch over you. Sleep well, my little angel."

She unwrapped the pottery sculpture of the three parrots and placed it on the grave, stood up, and smiled bravely at Jake. He took her hand once more.

They stood again in silence, and then, as the wind picked up, Jake squeezed her hand and led her out of the churchyard. A few dead leaves swirled about their feet in small clusters. As they left, the wind suddenly dropped and a small heart-shaped deep-red leaf tumbled onto the grave of Amy Louise Blundell. Above it, a robin burst into song.

A Word From The Author

Many years ago, I had to spend a long time in hospital stuck flat on my back on traction, with little to occupy me. Hospital radio helped see me through that time. Even today, I can remember the comfort it brought me and others on my ward. Nowadays, with the advances in technology and iPods and the like, there are fewer radio stations in hospitals and those that are run by volunteers often require funding and are reliant on communities for support.

Hospital radio still provides a service for those who need company during their time in hospital and I hope this book brings them and the wonderful service they offer to the attention of the public.

Although Charlie Blundell is a fictitious character, she was created not only from my own past experience in radio broadcasting but from a wonderful author and part-time volunteer radio presenter on Brighton Coastway Hospital, Charlie Plunkett. There, the resemblance ends presents a Saturday evening show chat during which she plays lots of feel good music and talks about the joyful moments in life including her favourite topics: weddings and babies, both of which she has written about in her books *The True Diary of a Bride-to-be* and *The True Diary of a Mum-to-be*.

Mercedes Thomson is an incredible character, but is certainly not unique. I had the good fortune to meet, in a virtual sense, Priscilla Hartman Hedlin from Austin, Texas. She is an astonishing woman who writes a blog called The Wheelchair Mommy[1] and is an inspiration to all. I learned a great deal about being a paraplegic from her and modelled Mercedes' positive attitude on hers. You can learn more about her by visiting her site. Of course, she is not alone and there are a huge number of men and women who live life to the maximum and have fulfilled dreams and goals that the rest of us can only dream of.

There have been very few reported incidents of shark attacks off the English coast. I took Charlie's childhood experience from one of the rare occasions when a shark has been seen. In July 2008, off the coast of Sussex, two sixteen year old boys, Luke Jones and James Sequin, had a surprise visitor to the inflatable dinghy they were

---

[1]   http://www.wheelchairmommy.com/

rowing at the time, when a three-foot-long starry smooth-hound shark leapt into their boat. Luckily, neither boy was injured. I have dived many times and never spotted a shark. Thank goodness!

And last but no means least, I am indebted to both author Lizzie Lamb for allowing me to borrow her delightful parrot's name (The real Jasper does not lives in the UK and is a red-shouldered macaw from South America) and to Katie Phillips for allowing me to model Bert on her wonderful parrot called, not surprisingly, Bert. Katie's Bert frequently appears on her Facebook page and gets up to all sorts of mischief including phoning people at random and taking selfies. She kindly sent me photographs and videos of him along with regular updates of what he got up to. He does indeed own a small shopping trolley, can hurl plastic balls with accuracy, and says, "mmm mmm". He's a bright little soul who captured my heart with his antics. To my knowledge, he has not sung *Like A Virgin,* but there are many examples on YouTube of parrots who can perform incredible tricks and can sing far better than me.

If you ever need a laugh, buy a kazoo and attempt to play it. It's ridiculously addictive. You can watch me on YouTube attacking mine with gusto. Try playing *Three Little Birds* or *Always Look on The Bright Side of Life.* You'll soon feel ready to face the world again.

Have you started a Carpe Diem list? You're never too young to make one. I started mine when I was forty and have completed many of the challenges on it. Here are some ideas for you to think about. Remember, life is for living. Have a go. They don't have to be wild ideas. They are personal goals and desires for you.

One Hundred Ideas for a Carpe Diem List

- Aerobatics lesson in a stunt plane
- Flying lesson in a small aeroplane
- Fly a helicopter
- Hang-glider lesson
- Heli-skiing
- Microlighting
- Wing-walk
- Sky dive
- Indoor skydiving
- Wacky racing (drive a bed, office desk, or sofa)
- Test drive a sports car
- Drive a fast car around a circuit
- Race in a Segway rally
- Drive a tank or military vehicle
- Go on a desert Jeep safari
- Do the human slingshot
- Surfing
- Hover crafting
- Sail
- Windsurf
- Kayaking
- Bungee jumping
- Abseil
- Take up cycling and follow the Tour de France
- Paintballing
- Go-karting
- Skiing
- Coasteering
- Rock climbing
- Ice climbing
- Caving or potholing
- Snowboarding
- Jet skiing
- Try a skidoo
- Have a husky sled ride

- Spend the night in an ice hotel
- Go for a reindeer sleigh ride
- Zorbing (sphering) down a hill
- Aqua-zorbing or hydra-zorbing
- Go on a zero gravity flight (and experience weightlessness)
- Ride in a dune buggy through a desert
- Quad bike in the desert or up a mountain
- Zip lining or extreme zip lining in Costa Rica through the rain forest tree canopy
- Hover craft racing
- White water rafting
- Zap cat racing— an extremely fast speedboat that bounces along on the water.
- Hold a snake
- Or a monkey
- Or even a tarantula
- Run a half marathon
- Run a marathon
- Swim a mile
- Hike up a mountain
- Fly an airline-style jet simulator
- Fly in a sea plane
- Take a trip in a submarine
- Go out on a hobby cat boat or a catamaran
- Fly in a hot air balloon
- Book a cruise
- Skinny dipping
- Ice fishing
- Go to Disney World
- Swim with a dolphin
- Scuba diving
- Swim with sharks/crocodiles
- Snorkelling
- Safari in Africa
- Swim or shower under a giant waterfall
- Ride on an elephant
- Or on a camel
- Canter along a deserted beach on a horse
- Serve Christmas dinner to homeless people

- Self-defence lessons
- Fire walking
- Pole-dancing class
- Bollywood class
- Belly-dancing
- Hot Yoga or Bikram Yoga
- Learn a new language
- Learn sign language
- Go on a luxurious spa weekend
- Fly on a trapeze
- Take up juggling
- Try your hand at stand-up comedy
- Write a book and publish it
- Break a Guinness Book record
- Play an instrument
- Say 'hello' in fifty different languages
- Go to the carnival in Venice
- Walk the Great Wall of China
- Visit Machu Pichu
- Climb the Eiffel Tower
- Go on the London Eye
- Visit each of the seven continents
- See every capital city in Europe
- Watch the Northern Lights
- Take part in a television show/quiz
- Ride in a limousine
- Learn to cook with a famous chef
- Hire a 1970's VW campervan and go off exploring

About the Author

A graduate of the University of Keele in Staffordshire, Carol E Wyer is a former teacher, linguist, and physical trainer.

She spent her early working life in Casablanca, Morocco, where she translated for companies and taught English as a foreign language. She then returned to work in education back in the UK and set up her own language company in the late eighties.

In her forties, Carol retrained to become a personal trainer to assist people, who, like herself, had undergone major surgery.

Having spent the last decade trying out all sorts of new challenges such as kickboxing, diving, and flying helicopters, she is now ensuring her fifties are "fab not drab". She has put her time to good use by learning to paint, attempting to teach herself Russian, and writing a series of novels and articles which take a humorous look at getting older.

Carol lives in rural Staffordshire with her own retired Grumpy. It is little wonder that she is a regular blogger and social networking addict.

Award-winning novels by Carol E Wyer

Surfing in Stilettos

Amanda Wilson is all geared up for an exciting gap-year, travelling across Europe. She soon finds her plans thwarted when she is abandoned in France with only a cellarful of Chateau Plonk, a large, orange Space Hopper, and Old Ted, the dog, for company.

Fate has intervened to turn Amanda's life on its head. First, Bertie, the camper van, breaks down. Then her dopey son, Tom, who is staying in their house in the UK, is wrecking it, one piece at a time. Next, the jaw-dropping video Skype calls that her irrepressible mother insists on making are, by contrast, making Amanda's humdrum trip even less palatable.

Finally, she discovers that her new-found, French friend, Bibi Chevalier, had engineered a plan to ensure that her philandering husband would never stray again; unfortunately, Amanda is unwittingly drawn into the scheme, becoming a target.

Meanwhile, on a beach in Sydney, a lonely Todd Bradshaw realises that his first true love, Amanda Wilson, is definitely the only woman for him. Can he get back into her good books and hopefully back into her arms with his latest plan? Or will fate intervene yet again and turn everyone's lives upside down?

Just Add Spice

Dawn Ellis needs to escape from her painfully dull existence. Her unemployed husband spends all day complaining about life, moping around, or fixing lawnmowers on her kitchen table. The local writing class proves to be an adequate distraction with its eccentric collection of wannabe authors and, of course, the enigmatic Jason, who soon shows a romantic interest in her.

Dawn pours her inner frustrations into her first novel about the extraordinary exploits of Cinnamon Knight, an avenging angel -- a woman who doesn't believe in following the rules. Cinnamon is ruthless and wanton, inflicting suffering on any man who warrants it. Little does Dawn realise that soon the line between reality and fiction will blur. Her own life will be transformed, and those close to her will pay the price.

Miniskirts and Laughter Lines

Amanda Wilson can't decide between murder, insanity, or another glass of red wine. Facing fifty and all that it entails is problematic enough. What's the point in minking your eyes when your husband would rather watch *Russia Today* than admire you strutting in front of the television in only thigh boots and a thong?

Her son has managed to perform yet another magical disappearing act. Could he actually be buried under the mountain of festering washing strewn on his bedroom floor? He'll certainly be buried somewhere when she next gets her hands on him.

At least her mother knows how to enjoy herself. She's partying her twilight years away in Cyprus. Queen of the Twister mat, she now has a toy boy in tow.

Amanda knows she shouldn't have pressed that *Send* button. The past always catches up with you sooner or later. Still, her colourful past is a welcome relief to her monochrome present—especially when it comes in the shape of provocative Todd Bradshaw, her first true love.

Amanda has a difficult decision to make – one that will require more than a few glasses of Chianti.

Lightning Source UK Ltd.
Milton Keynes UK
UKOW03f1450190814

237168UK00005B/563/P